Australian
Literature

Australian Literature

An Anthology of Writing from the Land Down Under

EDITED BY
Phyllis Fahrie Edelson

BALLANTINE BOOKS · NEW YORK

Compilation, introduction and notes copyright © 1993 by Phyllis Fahrie Edelson

Map copyright © 1993 by Random House, Inc.

Owing to limitations of space, permissions acknowledgments appear at the back of this book.

Library of Congress Catalog Card Number: 91-92153

ISBN: 0-345-36800-2

Text design by Debby Jay
Map by Patrick O'Brien
Cover design by Kristine Mills
Cover painting: "A Hot Day" by David Davies. National Gallery of Victoria, Melbourne, Victoria, Australia

Manufactured in the United States of America

First Edition: April 1993

10 9 8 7 6 5 4 3 2

Terrors would come. But wonders, too, as in the past.
Terrors and wonders, as always.

—Randolph Stow
Tourmaline (1963)

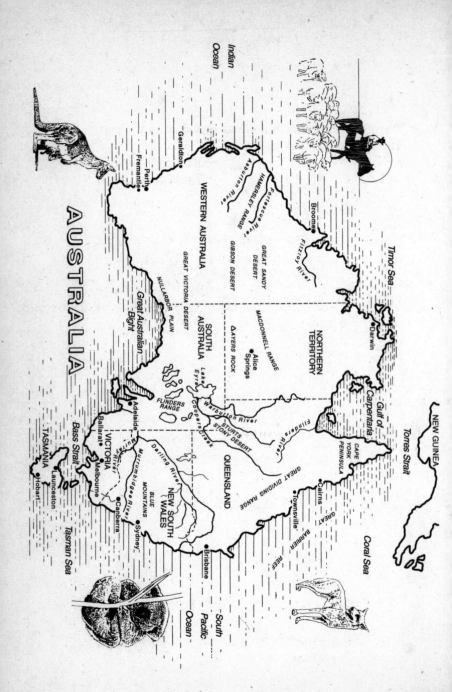

AUSTRALIA

Indian
Ocean

Geraldton
Perth
Fremantle

WESTERN AUSTRALIA

HAMERSLEY RANGE
Fortescue River
Ashburton River

GREAT SANDY DESERT

GIBSON DESERT

GREAT VICTORIA DESERT

NULLARBOR PLAIN

Great Australian Bight

Fitzroy River
Broome

Timor Sea

Darwin

NORTHERN TERRITORY

MACDONNELL RANGE
△AYERS ROCK
Alice Springs

SOUTH AUSTRALIA

Lake Eyre
Warburton River
STURTS STONY DESERT
Coopers Creek
Flinders River
FLINDERS RANGE

Gulf of Carpentaria

NEW GUINEA

Torres Strait

CAPE YORK PENINSULA

Cairns
GREAT BARRIER REEF
Townsville

QUEENSLAND

Brisbane

Coral Sea

GREAT DIVIDING RANGE

Adelaide
Ballarat
VICTORIA
Melbourne

Murray River
Murrumbidgee River
Darling River
BLUE MOUNTAINS

NEW SOUTH WALES

Canberra
Sydney

TASMANIA
Launceston
Hobart

Bass Strait

Tasman Sea

South Pacific Ocean

CONTENTS

ACKNOWLEDGMENTS

——

Thanks to my husband, Stuart Roy Edelson, for his devoted interest in this book from start to finish. Thanks to Pace University for scholarly research funds, and to Bob Loomis and the reference staffs of the Pace Mortola and Hayes libraries for their expertise and assistance. Thanks also to Dr. Robert Ross of the Harry Ransom Humanities Research Center, University of Texas at Austin, for suggesting that Peter Carey's "American Dreams" be included.

INTRODUCTION

I am a "White convert." This phrase is used by teachers and scholars in the field of Australian literature to identify enthusiasts who find their way to Australian fiction through the works of the novelist Patrick White.

It was during the late 1960s in a Boston hotel room that, by chance, I found a copy of White's novel *Voss*. I was there for a teachers' conference, but, as things turned out, that night I was the student. Turning the pages of White's masterpiece, I was exhilarated and read until dawn. I learned that a great voice, a major writer in English, was alive and well and living in Australia. All I remember about that conference now is my reaction to Patrick White, contemplating what I read, wondering what else was out there. As soon as I got home, I looked for his work, but not much was then readily available. From London I got his other books, which confirmed my first impression. I had encountered a literary giant.

Most of his fiction is set at the other end of the world, Australia, a place to which I, like many Americans at the time, had not given much thought. White's novels led me to investigate the literature further, and I found that there is, in fact, a storehouse of strong and delightful fiction, a treasury, written by Australians. Much of this fiction is in one way or another actually about Australia, at once both faintly familiar and strange.

Australia seemed to me to be the distant home of distant family.

I felt both the strangeness of the writing and the tug of a common bond. That I, or any American, should experience a lingering sense of knowing is not surprising. The United States and Australia are, after all, parts of the new world built of immigrant dreams and colonial economics. History records that in the British Empire both were colonies, seen as children, all bound to the founding mother, England, by ties of sentiment as well as trade.

Nineteenth-century observers tell us just how closely the United States and Australia were linked in the colonial mind. In 1885, for example, a Melbourne statesman envisioned Australia as becoming "a second United States in the Southern Hemisphere."[1] And a Victorian writer impressed with the good manners of Australians described them as having an "American smartness" tempered by an "Australian softness," of which he greatly approved.[2] There were and are resemblances, serious and substantial parallels, between the United States and Australia, including our common language, our pioneer experience, our historical encounter with native peoples, and, of course, our tradition of democratic political values.

My recognition of national kinship, the sense that I knew these people from somewhere way back, made Australian novels and short fiction accessible and comfortable for me. However, the more I read, the more I took note of significant differences between American and Australian national experiences. Probing deeply into their country's history and culture, Australian writers tell a distinctive story. Their fiction reveals, underneath the surface similarities, a unique heritage.

It can be a real surprise for an American to discover, for example, just how different the land of Australia is from North America, how harsh and forbidding it was to early colonists. Unlike fertile, well-watered North America, Australia's river systems are scanty, its rainfall modest. As the first Australian literature—diaries, journals, and official reports—suggests, the continent was not a place that early settlers could easily call home. They took possession of a flat land, a large part of it desert, that seemed immense.

Everything about it was strange to European eyes. There were trees whose bark fell off in sheets, birds that could not fly, and egg-laying mammals. In the very center of the land early settlers found a "dead heart." The sand and stone of the Outback penetrated deeply into the Australian psyche, even though most Australians settled in the forest and woodland coastal basins. Early Europeans were struck by the vast silence. We find in their writing such phrases as "the trackless immeasurable desert," the "awful silence,"[3] the "indescribable solitude [of] untenanted wastes."[4] This reaction to the land persists, finding its way into contemporary literature.

In fact, a number of central themes in Australian literature have their roots in the Australian national experience. Knowing something of Australia's history enriches the reader's pleasure in its fiction.

A Brief History of Australia and Its Literature

Early Australian literature can be traced back in time to well before the British arrived on the continent. For there was in Europe a literature about Australia, a number of legends that whispered of gold in a southern continent inhabited by a savage race. It was legend that spurred the exploration of the great land mass that stretched out between Africa and America, called on old maps *terra australis*. Although the Portuguese and the Dutch visited the continent with their ships, looking for gold or other marketable resources, the English came to stay. They did not come, however, for typical colonial reasons.

To look at colonial origins, it is necessary to go back to the English explorer Captain James Cook, who visited the east coast of Australia in the ship *Endeavour* in 1770 and found a good harbor just south of present-day Sydney. The expedition's passengers busily collected specimens of strange plants, suggesting the name for the spot — Botany Bay. Cook annexed the eastern coast of Australia for England and called it New South Wales. The captain is justly celebrated in Australian poetry, but the settlers who followed him are of much greater literary concern. Most of them arrived in chains.

Following the war of independence with its American colonies,

England was forced to find a new place to dump its overflow of convicts. That place was Australia. Eleven vessels arrived in Australia in January 1788: two armed ships, three cargo boats, and six transports loaded with convict passengers. These new settlers, already exiled from their own society thanks to their prison terms, were exiled once again, this time dispatched across an ocean to an unknown world.

Australia was a strange settlement and certainly didn't fit the notion of "colony" that Americans associate with their own historical beginnings. Convicts and their guards, a special corps of military police, made up the community. Survival was a question and near-starvation a reality for a few years, but gradually the new place took shape. Convicts worked on government farms or officers' lands.[5] The guards accumulated large property holdings, backed by supplies, seed, and free convict labor, courtesy of the English Crown. While they policed the convicts, many of them also prospered in business, particularly the rum trade, buying from incoming ships and selling at a profit.[6]

The ladder of social class was firmly constructed right from the beginning. Convicts serving time were at the bottom. Convicts who, for various reasons, were allowed to work on their own were known as ticket-of-leave workers and were a step above. In time, some convicts were pardoned or their sentences expired; they were called emancipists and stood a rung higher, but of course below those who came to the colony as free settlers. Civil officers sent by the Crown were near the top of the social ladder, while the military officer corps was the "aristocracy" of the prison settlement, at least insofar as power was concerned.[7]

The governors sent from England to take charge of the colony had no lack of work. Economic troubles; difficulty in controlling the unbridled military, which wanted to run things its own way; conflict with Aborigines who resisted the loss of their land; the threat from rebellious Irish convicts, many of whom were political prisoners—all of these were recurrent problems.[8]

Given such a start, it is not surprising that the very first Australian novel was a convict narrative. *Quintus Servinton, a Tale Founded upon Incidents of Real Occurrence* (1830), written by a convicted forger and debtor, Henry Savery, is autobiographical. The central character is an English businessman who is imprisoned and transported. Another convict-theme colonial work, *Ralph Rashleigh* by James Tucker, was written in the late 1840s. The very Australian experiences of the central character, a London thief, include his convict days, his life with a gang of outlaws, and his encounters with Aborigines.

Many Australian novels and short stories make central use of the convict or prison theme. However, the centerpiece of this tradition is Marcus Clarke's classic *His Natural Life* (1870–1872), unfortunately little known outside Australia. (A portion of this novel is included in the present volume.) To tell the story of Rufus Dawes, an innocent man unjustly dispossessed, exiled, and brutalized, Clarke did on-site research into the prison system and shaped a narrative based in good part on history. The experience of Rufus Dawes has haunted me ever since I read this novel. Going far beyond merely a literary re-creation of the convict era, *His Natural Life* describes life itself as a prison and suffering as human destiny.

In a different style, another convict tale, this time by the contemporary Thomas Keneally, adopts the point of view of an unwilling soldier conscripted by force into the low ranks of the military police. *Bring Larks and Heroes* (1967) narrates the miseries of life for a thoughtful and sensitive man in Australia's first prison colony. Patrick White also makes excellent use of a convict character and a setting of whips and leg irons in the Tasmanian prison colony. His vivid novel *A Fringe of Leaves* (1967) combines adventure and early Australian history to trace the contours of the human spirit when it is challenged to the extreme.

Australia's prison heritage has left a deep cultural impression. It was no small enterprise. More than 160,000 men, women, and children, sentenced for crimes ranging from attendance at a politically suspect meeting to murder, were sent to Australia before the last penal colony was closed in 1877. The idea of the prison has been used metaphorically as well as literally. For example, John Ireland in an experimental novel, *The Unknown Industrial Prisoner* (1971), portrays contemporary industrial Australia as one huge prison. The modern worker is captive to international business that is mindless, rudderless, and heartless. The contemporary worker is like the convict, a slave to a dehumanizing system.

The reader of Australian literature begins to think about the consequences of a prison origin for a nation's self-image and sense of identity. What a contrast Australia's origins pose, for example, to Americans whose nation grew out of the search for religious freedom. What does it mean for a nation to know that it began as a society of convicts and guards?

Australian scholars and writers, of course, have pondered this question. Various analysts have discovered traits or characteristics in the Australian psyche that they believe are effects of this traumatic early history. Some see, for example, the well-known Australian tendency toward informality and egalitarian values as coming down from the convicts' sense that they were all at rock bottom together. Out of their common bankruptcy, it is said, came a feeling of togetherness or loyalty in their dispossessed state. The very Australian ethos of mateship, a bonding and loyalty between friends, or "mates," is connected to the convicts' perspective. The other side of this is the possible effect on many early successful settlers of having free convict labor at their disposal. Could this experience, scholars wonder, have contributed to a certain arrogance with which wealthy Australians have treated the lower classes?[9]

There is much speculation about Australia's origins, but no one can deny that it has lived through an extraordinary beginning. Although the nation as a whole has felt the weight of the convict legacy and England's policy of transportation, the convict population actually varied in the different colonies. The colony of Victoria, established in 1851, saw itself as superior to the convict-tainted first colony of New South Wales, as a settlers' rather than a convicts' homeland.[10] Its residents considered themselves the "true sons of Britain."[11] Queensland, the second largest colony, developed around the city of Brisbane, which had its start as a penal camp—the Moreton Bay settlement.

South Australia, on the other hand, had a high percentage of small landowners and was the only Australian colony with no connection to convicts. Born independently of New South Wales, it was never a penal colony. It was organized as a settlers' colony following the theories of one Gibbon Wakefield, who developed his ideas about colonization while he himself was in prison in London.

Western Australia, the largest colony, was removed from the eastern settlements by Australia's great distances. Impoverished, it requested convicts as an answer to its economic struggles. The convicts built roads, bridges, docks, and lighthouses, and labored for the landholders.[12] Tasmania, the island state to the south of the mainland, was also associated with prison life since it was home to Macquarie Harbour and Port Arthur, two of the infamous prisons where incorrigibles or uncooperative prisoners were sent from other locations.

The Australian tendency to resent authority figures and to identify with the underdog has been connected to this convict period.[13] An interest in the figure of the outlaw is particularly apparent in the popularity of the folk hero Ned Kelly. In Australian terms, he was a bushranger. This word, originally used for an escaped convict, came to mean any armed robber. Bushranger Kelly died on the gallows in 1880, hated by the police whom he had outwitted many a time. His life story prompted the familiar Australian expression of praise, "game as Ned Kelly," and inspired biographies, plays, films, paintings, and a TV series.

A classic Australian novel is built on the bushranger theme. In *Robbery Under Arms* (1888), by Rolf Boldrewood, the bushrangers are finally caught and punished, but not until readers have been thoroughly captivated, as I was, by the charms of the dashing Captain Starlight and his gang. Before the novel ends, provocative questions have been raised as well. Issues of justice, social and economic, are stirred in this delightful novel that strikes a reader as somewhat like an American western.

Some Australian literature certainly calls up the image of John Wayne. But our American idea of the "West" is not synonymous with the Australian image of the bush. The word "bush" as used by Australians refers to uncultivated wilderness, unsettled and un-cleared. It means land unprofitable and difficult to settle. Geographically, it can refer to desert, semi-desert, grassland, and jungle. Australian usage of the word even extends to what Americans would call "the country."[14]

For a significant period of time, the bush became an image of Australia, a locus of national identity. The bushman was seen as the repository of truly Australian values and a distinctly Australian way of life. This cultural image may seem somewhat surprising in an area that is, in fact, highly urbanized, but nevertheless it has had an enormous influence on the country's literature.[15] It is a version of Australia that magnifies the landscape. This notion of the bush has played a more complex role in the Australian national psyche than the American landscape has in our own national profile. Something of the brooding, mysterious quality of their physical surroundings captured the Australian imagination, and bush life was canonized in the literary mind.

It was in the 1890s and early 1900s, the golden age of Australian literature, that the bush came to the fore as the predominant image. (This is also the time when the separate Australian colonies were federated into one nation.) In ballads, poems, short stories, and novels, the bush profile became the national profile despite the fact that few Australian writers spent their lives in the bush. It is true that there was already some novelistic interest in bush life as far back as *Settlers and Convicts or Recollections of Sixteen Years' Labour in the Australian Backwoods* (1847) by Alexander Harris. This novel describes Australia in the 1830s from the point of view of a free laborer and farmer. English interest in Australian life and the opportunities open to settlers ran high, so Harris had an eager readership for both this book and another novel, *The Emigrant Family or the Story of an Australian Settler* (1849), really a guide-book for those considering emigration.

In addition to bush life, early Australian novels portrayed sheep raising. *Geoffry Hamlyn* (1859), a novel by English author Henry Kingsley, captured sheep-raising life in the 1830s and 1840s. As this novel suggests, Australians had already developed an economy in which sheep played a major role. Beginning in 1795, John Macarthur, an ambitious officer of the New South Wales military police, had started collaborating with several local farmers on the breeding of sheep. Australia's successful wool industry grew out of these beginnings. Free settlers arrived eager to raise sheep. As Australia's absorption with the great sheep-grazing enterprise grew, the demand for convicts as pastoral laborers also increased. When the convict era passed, however, itinerant rural workers provided labor. They came and went according to the rhythm of work at the sheep stations—arriving to shear sheep, clear land, or fix fences, and leaving when their temporary work was done. While they worked, they slept in makeshift cabins and ate food supplied by the squatters (large ranch owners), who often gained fortunes.

Originally, land was considered the property of the Crown, but sheep needed many thousands of acres for grazing. Settlers, the first squatters, simply took the land they needed or got title through a license or lease. The term "squatter" came to mean the owner of a large-scale grazing operation. Squatters were members of a high socioeconomic class.

In the literary flowering of the 1890s, shepherds, shearers, swagmen (transient workers who carried their belongings in a blanket roll on their backs or across their shoulders), and drovers (drivers who moved herds over great distances) emerged in great numbers on the pages of Australian poetry and fiction. Classics were born in that era. Many significant authors emerged. Henry Lawson, the father of the Australian short story and a symbol of the bush, wrote popular poetry and fiction, like the short story that opens this collection, "The Drover's Wife." Barbara Baynton, another of the writers featured in this anthology, wrote gripping bush tales that speak with women's voices at a time of powerful male values. Joseph Furphy wrote a unique rural novel, *Such Is Life* (1903), that has an intriguing vein of philosophic speculation and sophisticated narrative technique. And Miles Franklin described bush life from the point of view of an ambitious and nonconforming young girl.

The life these authors describe, although often favorable to large herds of sheep, was not so kind to the family farmer. Unlike the American West, which offered climatic and soil conditions that made prosperity possible for the small farmer or modest cattle owner, family farming on Australian soil was often unprofitable. However, the British wanted Australia to be a nation of small farmers and some efforts were made in this direction. In the 1860s, for example, free land for farming—land that was not being used for grazing—was distributed. This selection movement was an effort at land reform, a way to balance out the thousands of acres squatters had taken for large-scale wool production. But the land left for distribution was not particularly good, and many selectors gave up or led marginal existences. Henry Lawson writes about these people, as does Patrick White, who managed to reinvent to modern taste and metaphoric depth many old Australian literary traditions. *The Tree of Man*, White's pioneering story, traces successive generations, portraying their struggle to make a living and to build Australia.

Mastering the land was not the only obstacle. On the question of national ownership, there was a complication, going back to the European settlement of Australia. For an American, this complication is uncomfortably familiar. It has to do with the displacement and exploitation of an indigenous people, a displacement upon which modern Australia was built. The lot of the Aboriginals in Australia as evoked in the literature of the country suggests at times the plight of Native Americans, at other times the experience of American blacks. It is, of course, identical to neither situation. Rather, as Australian literature tells the story, it is a sad and singular tale of its own, the subject of sensitive, moving, sometimes searing fiction. To see this theme in its historical context, it is necessary to go back to the beginnings, before English settlement.

The first Australians were Aboriginals. They had migrated thousands of years ago from Asia, when the Australian mainland was connected by land to New Guinea, not separated by water as it is today. Similarly, the Australian mainland on the south was then connected to what is now Tasmania. When a geological shift occurred and both Tasmania and New Guinea broke away from the mainland, the various Aboriginal peoples were isolated. Without contacts with other Asians, Australian Aboriginals continued to live in a Stone Age culture. Neighboring and trading peoples came near but did not find their way to them. They remained undisturbed until the British arrived.[16]

The British discoverer Captain Cook and his companions saw Australian Aborigines when they landed in the Great South Land in 1770, but they did not perceive them as an obstacle to settlement. Estimates of the Aboriginal population at this time vary from 250,000 to 750,000 people of various tribes and languages. Since these nomads roamed from place to place, the British did not consider them owners of the land. Accordingly, they did not bother to negotiate a treaty as they had done elsewhere. Instead, England merely used the legal phrase *terra nullius*, vacant land, to describe its new possession.

This omission was and is significant to the Aboriginal peoples of Australia. At the least, a treaty would have been a sign that the Aborigines existed and had some rights to the continent. The British failure to sign a treaty meant a loss of dignity, a loss of identity, and a cancellation, as some see it, of Aboriginal existence. Without a treaty, the British were saying, no one lived in Australia prior to the landing of the first fleet.[17]

Contrary to early British belief, however, Aboriginal communities were highly developed. Communal life was grounded in a rich tribal mythology tied intimately to their land. Aboriginals traveled in search of food, periodically revisiting sacred spots vital to their traditions and rituals. Losing their land was the equivalent of losing their culture.

Unfortunately, the British were not concerned with Aboriginal culture. In fact, they soon developed a distinctly negative view. They could not understand why the Aborigines did not erect buildings and cultivate crops. They resented the natives' lack of interest in regular work. Indeed, Aboriginal life seemed the antithesis of their own vigorous, ambitious white society, struggling to tame the land and build, at this great distance, a replica of England. Many settlers believed that only the strongest races were programmed to survive. They decided that the Aborigines were an inferior race and, therefore, doomed. It seemed impractical, fruitless to be concerned about them.[18]

The colonists' growing hunger for land pushed the Aborigines farther and farther back as white settlement expanded. When the Aborigines resisted, even in small ways, large-scale revenge often followed. Group massacres and poisonings and officially sanctioned expeditions to punish troublesome Aboriginals were not unusual. European diseases and alcoholism also took a heavy toll. It is no wonder that by 1900 the Aboriginal population was drastically reduced. In fact, full-blooded Aborigines of Tasmania no longer existed.

For some time, the problem of how to get rid of the remaining Aboriginals was a major concern.[19] Officials tried two tacks:

segregation-masked-as-protection and forced assimilation. Missions lured natives with food. Experiments in schooling and farming were also tried. Mostly, they failed. Aboriginal ways and cultural values did not jibe with white expectations.

Between 1929 and 1945 Aborigines lived largely in poverty, subject to gross discrimination. Missions that cared for them were poorly financed, and wages for Aboriginal workers on sheep stations were abysmally low. In the thirties, many were forced on to reserves and mixed-blood children were taken from their families and placed in institutions or foster homes among whites.[20]

One place, however, where Aboriginals found sensitivity to their history and recognition of the injustices done to them was in Australian fiction. White writers wrote with feeling, as well as with social and psychological insight. One novel that holds a special place in this tradition is Susannah Katherine Prichard's *Coonardoo: The Well in the Shadow*. Mindful of the history of sexual exploitation of Aboriginal women by European men, especially in Queensland and the Northern Territory, Prichard broke new ground. Her novel was radical for 1929. It was not socially acceptable at the time for a white man to marry or officially live with an Aboriginal woman. White men who did so, scorning social pressures, were derisively called "combos."[21] Ignoring traditional taboos, Prichard's novel delves into black/white relations in Australia and focuses on interracial love.

Similar ideas are taken up in *Capricornia* (1937), a novel by Xavier Herbert. Set in Darwin at the start of the twentieth century, portraying the violence and turbulent growth of that place and time, *Capricornia* is a work of magnificent, at times, overwhelming force. The central figure in this novel of race relations is Norman Shillingsworth, a half-caste boy and heir to a profitable sheep ranch, who has been reared to think of himself as white. In telling Norman's story, Herbert indicts a nation for its color mania and its indifference to human suffering. The power of this work is remarkable.

Many contemporary novels also focus on white/Aboriginal relationships. *The Chant of Jimmie Blacksmith* (1972) by Thomas Keneally is a particularly good example. Like most of Keneally's work this novel is based on historical fact. Keneally traces the conversion of a law-abiding half-Aboriginal man into a revengeful murderer. The protagonist's yearning to "live white" and be accepted turns to rage when all his efforts are rejected and he is humiliated.

Although Australian literature pointed the way to better understanding, actual change for Aborigines was slow to come. As late as the 1920s there were still reprisal massacres of native peoples, a legacy from colonial days. During World War II, however, Aborigines in the military enjoyed a status close to that of whites. They received decent wages and met black American soldiers who stretched their aspirations.[22]

Emboldened by their wartime venture into wanting a better quality of life, they were disheartened when the postwar economic boom left them back at the bottom. Aboriginals who had moved south seeking work found themselves unemployed again after the war and living in poverty with their kin on the fringes of cities. The 1960s were a turning point, however. Inspired by American activism, freedom rides and marches in Australia called attention to years of neglect and suffering. Political advances were made, although they represented only a beginning.

The 1960s proved to be a turning point in the literary fortunes of Aboriginal Australia. The Aboriginals' story was told again, but this time Aboriginals were telling it. Kath Walker (Aboriginal name: Oodgeroo) wrote poetry that asserted the needs of Aborigines and criticized their treatment by the majority culture. But her poetry was just the start. Aboriginal dramatists, short story writers, novelists, and poets are today reclaiming the place that is theirs by birthright and talent. Colin Johnson (Mudrooroo Narogin), Archie Weller, and Sally Morgan are just a few of the many writers at work re-creating Aboriginal culture, reintegrating it into the larger frame of Australian literature.

Australian writers have also probed another aspect of the nation's profile—that of Australia's political and cultural independence. This issue can be somewhat puzzling for Americans. Long secure in a distinctive culture, self-confident and prone to take leadership for granted, we may wonder about Australia's long bondage to a "cultural cringe."[23] For many years, Australia was perceived by England and by itself as an outpost of the empire.

London was headquarters. To be recognized, to be an important author, it was necessary to win garlands in London. To be at the intellectual center was to be in London, not in Sydney or Melbourne. This attitude, a consequence of colonial status, led Henry Lawson in 1894 to bitterly advise any talented young Australian to go to London (or the United States or Timbuktu) rather than stay in Australia. If such a trip were not possible, Lawson advised suicide.[24]

Lawson's assessment of Australia's cultural dependence remained applicable for a long time. It was quite in line with Australia's extended period of political dependence on England, and very much the opposite of the American experience. Unlike the United States, Australia never fought a revolutionary war against Great Britain. It never made the break through a war of independence. Australia's separation from England evolved by a slow process affected by world events.[25]

From the beginning, there were those Australians comfortable with the status conferred by the word "colony," comfortable with an image of Australia inseparable from the idea of colonialism. They felt tied to England and found the notion of separation from it unthinkable. Other Australians were anti-imperialist, separatist, nationalist to the extreme. These reactions suggest the opposing pulls of mother country, on the one hand, and promise of the new land, on the other. The settler attracted to the culture, natural beauty, and heritage of the old world, but planted in the soil of the new, is a familiar figure in Australian literature. Themes of journey, departure, and return recur.

The best-known novel on this motif is Henry Handel Richardson's *The Fortunes of Richard Mahony* (1917–1929). Its hero travels back and forth between Australia and England, finding a permanent and satisfying home in neither. A firm identity eludes him. This engrossing novel records, among much else, the colonial dilemma.

The image of Australia as colony, though, did give way eventually to an image separate from England. Although federation took place in 1901, historians generally cite World War I as the pivotal event in the development of a strong Australian national identity.

World War I was the young nation's first large-scale military experience. It was deeply traumatic for a country that had been protected from foreign entanglement and the horrors of warfare by colonial status. Australia's war effort revealed both its loyalty to England and its desire to prove its nationhood. The number of volunteers who went to war was very high, and so were the losses. Many of Australia's troops, called diggers, died at Gallipoli, a battle planned by England to gain Allied access to the Black Sea, to help defeat Turkey, and to aid Russia.[26]

Gallipoli was a costly failure and shocking to Australians, as the selection from A. B. Facey in this collection makes clear. Strategically placed Turkish forces were able to mow down tenacious and courageous ANZAC (Australian and New Zealand Army Corps) soldiers. When the Australian troops were sent back to Egypt after Gallipoli, they left behind 7,600 dead.[27] Through their sacrifice, the nation recognized its ability to defend itself. At the same time, that sacrifice shook Australian confidence in the wisdom and dependability of London. British planning had, after all, caused a heavy loss of Australian blood. Historians point to Gallipoli, the subject of fiction and film,[28] as the moment when the idea of the valiant Australian soldier coalesced with earlier images of the brave bushman. The sense of Australian nationhood deepened.[29]

If World War I was one turning point in Australia's movement away from England, World War II was another. Australia worried about invasion from the north. Prime Minister Robert Menzies said: "What Great Britain calls the Far East is to us the near north."[30] Furthermore, Australia believed that Singapore was the key to its security. Great Britain gave assurances that warships would be there to protect it. But when Singapore fell to the Japanese, Australians knew they could no longer count on the British Empire for protection.[31]

The United States and Australia joined forces during World War II and were victorious against the Japanese, but both countries suffered considerably. More than 30,000 Australians alone were taken as prisoners of war. Subject to terrible deprivation and captive for long periods of time, many came home seriously traumatized. As a result, the prisoner of war memoir is an important Australian literary genre from this period.[32] I've included a selection from what might be seen as one of these—The Merry-Go-Round in the Sea (1965) by Randolph Stow.

After World War II it was clear that Britain was withdrawing as Australia's protective "mother," but some Australians worried about the surrogate who seemed to be moving in. Postwar U.S. capital investments in Australia increased, and so did the influence of American culture. As the United States became chief protector, it nudged England aside through advertising, movies, popular music, and, most important, television. Australian observers, for instance, have pointed out the changes in Australian sports as wealthy owners took over sports and sporting events, packaging them American style. Traditional Australian sports—auto races, football games, and homegrown recreation—gave way to "canned sport."[33] More recently, American sports such as baseball and basketball have appeared on an Australian scene that has been traditionally dominated by cricket, rugby, and netball.[34]

In the 1950s American TV programming came close to overtaking Australian airtime. In self-defense, a quota system was introduced that required a certain percentage of programs to be Australian.[35] More recently, conservative political forces in Australia seem to have become increasingly "American" in their thinking about economics and business. As a result, Australia worries about inundation from the United States. Many in Australia still see themselves threatened both politically and culturally. They do not wish to see their national identity, so newly emerged from that of Britain, lost in a rapidly growing American imprint. They do not wish to see the feathers of the black swan (native to Australia) turn red, white, and blue.

Although a strong American presence continues in Australian life, there are some new trends as well. First, Australian foreign policy is increasingly focused on Asia. Second, Australia is fast becoming a multicultural nation. The previously homogeneous population has expanded to include new groups. As a result, the literature now includes Italian-Australian, Greek-Australian, Asian-Australian, and Jewish-Australian fiction.

This movement toward widening the mainstream has also been happening with women. Australian feminist scholars see a strong misogynist tradition in Australian society. The most popular Australian folk song "Waltzing Matilda" illustrates the point. Matilda is a bundle or blanket roll that carries the few worldly goods of the swagman, or itinerant worker. He "waltzes" Matilda, that is, carries his bag as he walks the roads looking for work.[36] Thus, the female is equated with the swagman's lowly swag or bundle. Feminists also believe that this misogyny is still exerting a powerful influence on art and literature.

Why is this so? Feminists point to Australia's early years as a prison colony. Since many more men than women were transported, the country began with a decidedly masculine cast. Exploitation of convict women by both the male guards and convicts set a tone in which denigration of the female was the norm.[37]

Bush life also contributed to this cultural misogyny. For years there were very few women who lived in the deserted countryside. The bush tradition valued the idea of a "battler," a term familiar in Australian writing. The battler was a fighter against the odds, someone who struggled courageously for a livelihood.[38] This image fit in well with the idea of "man in the bush" depending on his physical strength, his outdoor acumen, his self-reliance. These qualities, however, were not the ones traditionally associated with women. Thus, the bush, a central Australian image, left out women.[39] Along this line, consider Crocodile Dundee, the film macho man who delighted American moviegoers a few years back. How does his bush image make room for women? Only as conquests.

Many works by women writing in Australia today are reactions to the roles and position of women. Such writers as Thea Astley, Helen Garner, Beverley Farmer, and Jessica Anderson are exploring women's lives and roles in our contemporary world. These writers and many others have a sturdy tradition of Australian women's writing on which to build. In the beginning, there were letters home that described the new world for those left behind. During the colonial period, novels with a domestic focus explored social issues and prevailing values in the manner of England's women novelists of the 1800s.[40] Some strong female heroines ahead of their time made appearances. One example from this period is *Clara Morison: A Tale of South Australia During the Gold Fever* (1854) by Catherine Spence. An entertaining anatomy of manners, it contrasts the lives and opportunities of intelligent middle-class women in socially restrictive England with the servantless domesticity or life-in-service that was often their lot in tougher but freer Australia.

Starting in the 1920s and continuing through the 1950s, there is extraordinary fiction by women. These works open up Australia. They re-create past eras, investigate specific locales, and define particular kinds of work and ways of life. They take readers straight into the history of the land. Even wonderful books of history cannot equal the "living it" experience of the migratory unemployed that is chronicled, for example, by Kylie Tennant in *The Battlers* (1941). Nor can any history equal the tour Eve Langley offers in *The Pea Pickers* (1942), a country journey to Gippsland with two young girls disguised as boys, picking crops with Italian migrants and falling in love, most passionately with the countryside itself.

For a longer journey in time, there is that priceless invitation to early Australia, *The Timeless Land* (1941) by Eleanor Dark. Dark respects the historical record but allows the reader to observe the first colony of New South Wales through the eyes of a British official, a convict, an Aborigine, a servant girl, a schoolteacher, and a vibrant, refreshing heroine.

Authors like Miles Franklin and Henry Handel Richardson are important names in any general history of Australia's major writers. One name, however, stands out and that is Christina Stead. Among her novels, novellas, and short stories, there is top-drawer modern fiction. At the very center of her oeuvre is her masterpiece, *The Man Who Loved Children* (1940). This portrayal of family life was a particular favorite of the American poet Randall Jarrell, who wrote a justly celebrated introduction in 1965 that brought the novel to prominence after twenty-five years of obscurity. Recent criticism has recognized in this novel a major twentieth-century work to be read and reread.

With the advent of Patrick White and the unleashing of Australian talent that followed him, fiction has exploded in Australia. Both novelists and short-story writers are being published outside Australia as never before. Contemporary Australian fiction is among the best works being written in English today. It is fiction about a contemporary world we recognize, seen from a different perspective.

About this Book

I began my work on this anthology with a wish list of many titles of Australian fiction. It was long, too long, and needed to be pruned. The rich literary harvest from Australia could never fit between the covers of any one book. So this book is a sampling designed to tempt readers' appetites to deeper and wider indulgence. It is not a comprehensive collection. My purpose, rather, is to share my pleasure with readers new to Australian fiction and to extend the acquaintance of readers who have already encountered some.

The greatest writers from Australia appear here: Henry Lawson, Henry Handel Richardson, Christina Stead, Patrick White, and Randolph Stow. Also present are a number (certainly not all) who have special places of significance: Marcus Clarke, Katharine Susannah Prichard, and Barbara Baynton. The range of the anthology is from 1870 to 1989. Approximately half the collection is written by contemporaries. Some are internationally known—Peter Carey, Elizabeth Jolley, and David Malouf. Others, well known in Australia, do not yet have the international reputation they should enjoy. Both short stories and excerpts from longer works are included. Patrick White and Henry Lawson each appear twice, appropriate to their literary power and place in Australian letters.

I chose these selections because they are good reading, but I organized them to call attention to significant motifs. Approaching this literature through themes is, I believe, very useful. Preoccupations of Australian culture provide focal points for the reader.

Part I is concerned with the well-known Australian literary preoccupation—the bush. The writing that follows in Part II focuses on equally significant Australian images—the role of the Aborigine in Australian life, the legacy of the convict past, and Australia's quest for political and cultural independence. The final section includes fiction by both men and women that explores a range of contemporary relationships between the sexes.

I.

The Idea of the Bush

The selections in this section all look toward the bush. They focus on the land, on making a home or community in the wilds. But the fictional bush as a sign or symbol of Australian experience has elasticity. The authors here bring different perspectives; they re-create a variety of landscapes.

Henry Lawson in "The Drover's Wife" describes a challenging bush where danger is constant and isolation unrelieved. His heroine, however, emerges triumphant. The land cannot destroy her, although her victory is not without cost.

In Barbara Baynton's "The Chosen Vessel" the bush is a place of menace, a totally hostile environment that the heroine finds alien. Baynton sees terror where Lawson sees heroism. Writing in the same time period about the same place, they read the bush landscape differently.

Lawson's "The Loaded Dog" offers another dimension, a comic vision, typical of the local humor from which a rural community's legends can grow.[41] Male camaraderie and animals are at the center of this bush tale; women play no role.

In both Lawson's and Baynton's work, however, there is the evocation of struggle and sacrifice. This is also present in the excerpt from Patrick White. In chapters 3 and 4 from *The Tree of Man,* White transforms the constricted lives of ordinary farmers involved in the pioneer struggle. From an uncommon angle of vision White sees poetry. In a monotonous landscape he points out mystery. He probes the yearnings and dreams of his characters, uneducated people who cannot easily articulate their feelings.

Steele Rudd's sketch of a dirt-poor rural family trying to eke out a living taps again the comic vein. Yet the comedy does not mask, perhaps makes all the more poignant, the poverty and hardship that accompanied the settling of the land. With Elizabeth Jolley's contemporary story we turn to modern land-fever. She portrays with wry humor the ingenuity such hunger can still inspire.

The Drover's Wife (1892)

—

HENRY LAWSON

Henry Lawson is the central mythmaker of the bush legend, and "The Drover's Wife" is its central story. "The Drover's Wife" appears regularly in Australian anthologies and has inspired paintings and several modern versions. Lawson was only twenty-five when it was published.

The two-roomed house is built of round timber, slabs, and stringy bark, and floored with split slabs. A big bark kitchen standing at one end is larger than the house itself, verandah included.

Bush all round—bush with no horizon, for the country is flat. No ranges in the distance. The bush consists of stunted, rotten native apple trees. No undergrowth. Nothing to relieve the eye save the darker green of a few sheoaks which are sighing above the narrow, almost waterless creek. Nineteen miles to the nearest sign of civilisation—a shanty on the main road.

The drover, an ex-squatter, is away with sheep. His wife and children are left here alone.

Four ragged, dried-up-looking children are playing about the house. Suddenly one of them yells: 'Snake! Mother, here's a snake!'

The gaunt, sun-browned bushwoman dashes from the kitchen, snatches her baby from the ground, holds it on her left hip, and reaches for a stick.

'Where is it?'

'Here! gone into the wood-heap!' yells the eldest boy—a sharp-faced, excited urchin of eleven. 'Stop there, mother! I'll have him. Stand back! I'll have the beggar!'

3

'Tommy, come here, or you'll be bit. Come here at once when I tell you, you little wretch!'

The youngster comes reluctantly, carrying a stick bigger than himself. Then he yells, triumphantly:

'There it goes—under the house!' and darts away with club uplifted. At the same time the big, black, yellow-eyed dog-of-all-breeds, who has shown the wildest interest in the proceedings, breaks his chain and rushes after that snake. He is a moment late, however, and his nose reaches the crack in the slabs just as the end of its tail disappears. Almost at the same moment the boy's club comes down and skins the aforesaid nose. Alligator takes small notice of this, and proceeds to undermine the building; but he is subdued after a struggle and chained up. They cannot afford to lose him.

The drover's wife makes the children stand together near the doghouse while she watches for the snake. She gets two small dishes of milk and sets them down near the wall to tempt it to come out; but an hour goes by and it does not show itself.

It is near sunset, and a thunderstorm is coming. The children must be brought inside. She will not take them into the house, for she knows the snake is there, and may at any moment come up through the cracks in the rough slab floor; so she carries several armfuls of firewood into the kitchen, and then takes the children there. The kitchen has no floor—or, rather, an earthen one—called a 'ground floor' in this part of the bush. There is a large, roughly made table in the centre of the place. She brings the children in, and makes them get on this table. They are two boys and two girls—mere babies. She gives them some supper, and then, before it gets dark, she goes into the house, and snatches up some pillows and bedclothes—expecting to see or lay her hand on the snake any minute. She makes a bed on the kitchen table for the children, and sits down beside it to watch all night.

She has an eye on the corner, and a green sapling club laid in readiness on the dresser by her side, together with her sewing basket and a copy of the *Young Ladies' Journal*. She has brought the dog into the room.

Tommy turns in, under protest, but says he'll lie awake all night and smash that blinded snake.

His mother asks him how many times she has told him not to swear.

He has his club with him under the bedclothes, and Jacky protests:

'Mummy! Tommy's skinnin' me alive wif his club. Make him take it out.'

Tommy: 'Shet up, you little—! D'yer want to be bit with the snake?'

Jacky shuts up.

'If yer bit,' says Tommy, after a pause, 'you'll swell up, an' smell, an' turn red an' green an' blue all over till yer bust. Won't he, mother?'

'Now then, don't frighten the child. Go to sleep,' she says.

The two younger children go to sleep, and now and then Jacky complains of being 'skeezed.' More room is made for him. Presently Tommy says: 'Mother! listen to them (adjective) little 'possums. I'd like to screw their blanky necks.'

And Jacky protests drowsily:

'But they don't hurt us, the little blanks!'

Mother: 'There, I told you you'd teach Jacky to swear.' But the remark makes her smile. Jacky goes to sleep.

Presently Tommy asks:

'Mother! Do you think they'll ever extricate the (adjective) kangaroo?'

'Lord! How am I to know, child? Go to sleep.'

'Will you wake me if the snake comes out?'

'Yes. Go to sleep.'

Near midnight. The children are all asleep and she sits there still, sewing and reading by turns. From time to time she glances round the floor and wall-plate, and whenever she hears a noise she reaches for the stick. The thunderstorm comes on, and the wind, rushing through the cracks in the slab wall, threatens to blow out her candle. She places it on a sheltered part of the dresser and fixes up a newspaper to protect it. At every flash of lightning, the cracks between the slabs gleam like polished silver. The thunder rolls, and the rain comes down in torrents.

Alligator lies at full length on the floor, with his eyes turned towards the partition. She knows by this that the snake is there.

There are large cracks in that wall opening under the floor of the dwelling-house.

She is not a coward, but recent events have shaken her nerves. A little son of her brother-in-law was lately bitten by a snake, and died. Besides, she has not heard from her husband for six months, and is anxious about him.

He was a drover, and started squatting here when they were married. The drought of 18—ruined him. He had to sacrifice the remnant of his flock and go droving again. He intends to move his family into the nearest town when he comes back, and, in the meantime, his brother, who keeps a shanty on the main road, comes over about once a month with provisions. The wife has still a couple of cows, one horse, and a few sheep. The brother-in-law kills one of the sheep occasionally, gives her what she needs of it, and takes the rest in return for other provisions.

She is used to being left alone. She once lived like this for eighteen months. As a girl she built the usual castles in the air; but all her girlish hopes and aspirations have long been dead. She finds all the excitement and recreation she needs in the *Young Ladies' Journal*, and, Heaven help her! takes a pleasure in the fashion-plates.

Her husband is an Australian, and so is she. He is careless, but a good enough husband. If he had the means he would take her to the city and keep her there like a princess. They are used to being apart, or at least she is. 'No use fretting,' she says. He may forget sometimes that he is married; but if he has a good cheque when he comes back he will give most of it to her. When he had money he took her to the city several times—hired a railway sleeping compartment, and put up at the best hotels. He also bought her a buggy, but they had to sacrifice that along with the rest.

The last two children were born in the bush—one while her husband was bringing a drunken doctor, by force, to attend to her. She was alone on this occasion, and very weak. She had been ill with a fever. She prayed to God to send her assistance. God sent Black Mary—the 'whitest' gin in all the land. Or, at least, God sent 'King Jimmy' first, and he sent Black Mary. He put his black face round the door-post, took in the situation at a glance, and said cheerfully: 'All right, Missis—I bring my old woman, she down alonga creek.'

One of her children died while she was here alone. She rode nineteen miles for assistance, carrying the dead child.

It must be near one or two o'clock. The fire is burning low. Alligator lies with his head resting on his paws, and watches the wall. He is not a very beautiful dog to look at, and the light shows numerous old wounds where the hair will not grow. He is afraid of nothing on the face of the earth or under it. He will tackle a bullock as readily as he will tackle a flea. He hates all other dogs—except kangaroo-dogs—and has a marked dislike to friends or relations of the family. They seldom call, however. He sometimes makes friends with strangers. He hates snakes and has killed many, but he will be bitten some day and die; most snake-dogs end that way.

Now and then the bushwoman lays down her work and watches, and listens, and thinks. She thinks of things in her own life, for there is little else to think about.

The rain will make the grass grow, and this reminds her how she fought a bush fire once while her husband was away. The grass was long, and very dry, and the fire threatened to burn her out. She put on an old pair of her husband's trousers and beat out the flames with a green bough, till great drops of sooty perspiration stood out on her forehead and ran in streaks down her blackened arms. The sight of his mother in trousers greatly amused Tommy, who worked like a little hero by her side, but the terrified baby howled lustily for his 'mummy'. The fire would have mastered her but for four excited bushmen who arrived in the nick of time. It was a mixed-up affair all round; when she went to take up the baby he screamed and struggled convulsively, thinking it was a 'black man'; and Alligator, trusting more to the child's sense than his own instinct, charged furiously, and (being old and slightly deaf) did not in his excitement at first recognise his mistress's voice, but continued to hang on to the moleskins until choked off by Tommy with a saddle-strap. The dog's sorrow for his blunder, and his anxiety to let it be known that it was all a mistake, was as evident as his ragged tail and a twelve-inch grin could make it. It was a glorious time for the boys; a day to look back to, and talk about, and laugh over for many years.

She thinks how she fought a flood during her husband's absence. She stood for hours in the drenching downpour, and dug an over-flow gutter to save the dam across the creek. But she could not save it. There are things that a bushwoman cannot do. Next morning the dam was broken, and her heart was nearly broken too, for she thought how her husband would feel when he came home and saw the result of years of labour swept away. She cried then.

She also fought the *pleuro-pneumonia*—dosed and bled the few remaining cattle, and wept again when her two best cows died.

Again, she fought a mad bullock that besieged the house for a day. She made bullets and fired at him through cracks in the slabs with an old shotgun. He was dead in the morning. She skinned him and got seventeen-and-six for the hide.

She also fights the crows and eagles that have designs on her chickens. Her plan of campaign is very original. The children cry 'Crows, mother!' and she rushes out and aims a broomstick at the birds as though it were a gun, and says, 'Bung!' The crows leave in a hurry; they are cunning, but a woman's cunning is greater.

Occasionally a bushman in the horrors, or a villainous-looking sundowner, comes and nearly scares the life out of her. She gener-ally tells the suspicious-looking stranger that her husband and two sons are at work below the dam, or over at the yard, for he always cunningly enquires for the boss.

Only last week a gallows-faced swagman—having satisfied him-self that there were no men on the place—threw his swag down on the verandah, and demanded tucker. She gave him something to eat; then he expressed his intention of staying for the night. It was sundown then. She got a batten from the sofa, loosened the dog, and confronted the stranger, holding the batten in one hand and the dog's collar with the other. 'Now you go!' she said. He looked at her and at the dog, said 'All right, mum,' in a cringing tone, and left. She was a determined-looking woman, and Alligator's yellow eyes glared unpleasantly—besides, the dog's chawing-up apparatus greatly resembled that of the reptile he was named after.

She has few pleasures to think of as she sits here alone by the fire, on guard against a snake. All days are much the same to her, but on Sunday afternoon she dresses herself, tidies the children, smartens up baby, and goes for a lonely walk along the bush-track, pushing an old perambulator in front of her. She does this every Sunday. She takes as much care to make herself and the children look smart as she would if she were going to do the block in the city. There is nothing to see, however, and not a soul to meet. You might walk for twenty miles along this track without being able to fix a point in your mind, unless you are a bushman. This is because of the everlasting, maddening sameness of the stunted trees—that monotony which makes a man long to break away and travel as far as trains can go, and sail as far as ships can sail—and further.

But this bushwoman is used to the loneliness of it. As a girl-wife she hated it, but now she would feel strange away from it.

She is glad when her husband returns, but she does not gush or make a fuss about it. She gets him something good to eat, and tidies up the children.

She seems contented with her lot. She loves her children, but has no time to show it. She seems harsh to them. Her surroundings are not favourable to the development of the 'womanly' or senti-mental side of nature.

It must be near morning now; but the clock is in the dwelling-house. Her candle is nearly done; she forgot that she was out of candles. Some more wood must be got to keep the fire up, and so she shuts the dog inside and hurries round to the wood-heap. The rain has cleared off. She seizes a stick, pulls it out, and—crash! the whole pile collapses.

Yesterday she bargained with a stray blackfellow to bring her some wood, and while he was at work she went in search of a missing cow. She was absent an hour or so, and the native black made good use of his time. On her return she was so astonished to see a good heap of wood by the chimney, that she gave him an extra fig of tobacco, and praised him for not being lazy. He thanked her, and left with head erect and chest well out. He was the last of his tribe and a King; but he had built that wood-heap hollow.

She is hurt now, and tears spring to her eyes as she sits down again by the table. She takes up a handkerchief to wipe the tears away, but pokes her eyes with her bare fingers instead. The handkerchief is full of holes, and she finds that she has put her thumb through one, and her forefinger through another.

This makes her laugh, to the surprise of the dog. She has a keen, very keen, sense of the ridiculous; and some time or other she will amuse bushmen with the story.

She has been amused before like that. One day she sat down 'to have a good cry,' as she said—and the old cat rubbed against her dress and 'cried too.' Then she had to laugh.

It must be near daylight. The room is very close and hot because of the fire. Alligator still watches the wall from time to time. Suddenly he becomes greatly interested; he draws himself a few inches nearer the partition, and a thrill runs through his body. The hair on the back of his neck begins to bristle, and the battle-light is in his yellow eyes. She knows what this means, and lays her hand on the stick. The lower end of one of the partition slabs has a large crack on both sides. An evil pair of small, bright, bead-like eyes glisten at one of these holes. The snake—a black one—comes slowly out, about a foot, and moves its head up and down. The dog lies still, and the woman sits as one fascinated. The snake comes out a foot further. She lifts her stick, and the reptile, as though suddenly aware of danger, sticks his head in through the crack on the other side of the slab, and hurries to get his tail round after him. Alligator springs, and his jaws come together with a snap. He misses, for his nose is large and the snake's body close down in the angle formed by the slabs and the floor. He snaps again as the tail comes round. He has the snake now, and tugs it out eighteen inches. Thud, thud comes the woman's club on the ground. Alligator pulls again. Thud, thud. Alligator gives another pull and he has the snake out—a black brute, five feet long. The head rises to dart about, but the dog has the enemy close to the neck. He is a big, heavy dog, but quick as a terrier. He shakes the snake as though he felt the original curse in common with mankind. The eldest boy wakes up, seizes his stick, and tries to get out of bed, but his mother forces him back with a grip of iron. Thud, thud—the snake's back is broken in several places. Thud, thud—its head is crushed, and Alligator's nose skinned again.

She lifts the mangled reptile on the point of her stick, carries it to the fire, and throws it in; then piles on the wood, and watches the snake burn. The boy and dog watch, too. She lays her hand on the dog's head, and all the fierce, angry light dies out of his yellow eyes. The younger children are quieted, and presently go to sleep. The dirty-legged boy stands for a moment in his shirt, watching the fire. Presently he looks up at her, sees the tears in her eyes, and throwing his arms round her neck, exclaims:

'Mother, I won't never go drovin'; blast me if I do!'

And she hugs him to her worn-out breast and kisses him; and they sit thus together while the sickly daylight breaks over the bush.

The Chosen Vessel (1902)

BARBARA BAYNTON

This is one of the stories in Baynton's volume Bush Studies. *All of them emphasize the experience of women. Baynton lived in the bush herself, with her first husband and young children.*

She laid the stick and her baby on the grass while she untied the rope that tethered the calf. The length of the rope separated them. The cow was near the calf, and both were lying down. Feed along the creek was plentiful, and every day she found a fresh place to tether it, since tether it she must, for if she did not, it would stray with the cow out on the plain. She had plenty of time to go after it, but then there was her baby; and if the cow turned on her out on the plain, and she with her baby,—she had been a town girl and was afraid of the cow, but she did not want the cow to know it. She used to run at first when it bellowed its protest against the penning up of its calf. This satisfied the cow, also the calf, but the woman's husband was angry, and called her—the noun was cur. It was he who forced her to run and meet the advancing cow, brandishing a stick, and uttering threatening words till the enemy turned and ran. "That's the way!" the man said, laughing at her white face. In many things he was worse than the cow, and she wondered if the same rule would apply to the man, but she was not one to provoke skirmishes even with the cow.

It was early for the calf to go to "bed"—nearly an hour earlier than usual; but she had felt so restless all day. Partly because it was Monday, and the end of the week that would bring her and the

13

baby the companionship of his father, was so far off. He was a shearer, and had gone to his shed before daylight that morning. Fifteen miles as the crow flies separated them.

There was a track in front of the house, for it had once been a wine shanty, and a few travellers passed along at intervals. She was not afraid of horsemen; but swagmen, going to, or worse coming from, the dismal, drunken little township, a day's journey beyond, terrified her. One had called at the house to-day, and asked for tucker.

That was why she had penned up the calf so early. She feared more from the look of his eyes, and the gleam of his teeth, as he watched her newly awakened baby beat its impatient fists upon her covered breasts, than from the knife that was sheathed in the belt at his waist.

She had given him bread and meat. Her husband she told him was sick. She always said that when she was alone and a swagman came; and she had gone in from the kitchen to the bedroom, and asked questions and replied to them in the best man's voice she could assume. Then he had asked to go into the kitchen to boil his billy, but instead she gave him tea, and he drank it on the wood heap. He had walked round and round the house, and there were cracks in some places, and after the last time he had asked for tobacco. She had none to give him, and he had grinned, because there was a broken clay pipe near the wood heap where he stood, and if there were a man inside, there ought to have been tobacco. Then he asked for money, but women in the bush never have money.

At last he had gone, and she, watching through the cracks, saw him when about a quarter of a mile away, turn and look back at the house. He had stood so for some moments with a pretence of fixing his swag, and then, apparently satisfied, moved to the left towards the creek. The creek made a bow round the house, and when he came to the bend she lost sight of him. Hours after, watching intently for signs of smoke, she saw the man's dog chasing some sheep that had gone to the creek for water, and saw it slink back suddenly, as if it had been called by some one.

More than once she thought of taking her baby and going to her husband. But in the past, when she had dared to speak of the dangers to which her loneliness exposed her, he had taunted and sneered at her. "Needn't flatter yerself," he had told her, "nobody 'ud want ter run away with yew."

Long before nightfall she placed food on the kitchen table, and beside it laid the big brooch that had been her mother's. It was the only thing of value that she had. And she left the kitchen door wide open.

The doors inside she securely fastened. Beside the bolt in the back one she drove in the steel and scissors; against it she piled the table and the stools. Underneath the lock of the front door she forced the handle of the spade, and the blade between the cracks in the flooring boards. Then the prop-stick, cut into lengths, held the top, as the spade held the middle. The windows were little more than portholes; she had nothing to fear through them.

She ate a few mouthfuls of food and drank a cup of milk. But she lighted no fire, and when night came, no candle, but crept with her baby to bed.

What woke her? The wonder was that she had slept—she had not meant to. But she was young, very young. Perhaps the shrinking of the galvanized roof—hardly though, since that was so usual. Yet something had set her heart beating wildly; but she lay quite still, only she put her arm over her baby. Then she had both round it, and she prayed, "Little baby, little baby, don't wake!"

The moon's rays shone on the front of the house, and she saw one of the open cracks, quite close to where she lay, darken with a shadow. Then a protesting growl reached her; and she could fancy she heard the man turn hastily. She plainly heard the thud of something striking the dog's ribs, and the long flying strides of the animal as it howled and ran. Still watching, she saw the shadow darken every crack along the wall. She knew by the sounds that the man was trying every standpoint that might help him to see in; but how much he saw she could not tell. She thought of many things she might do to deceive him into the idea that she was not alone. But the sound of her voice would wake baby, and she dreaded that as though it were the only danger that threatened her. So she prayed, "Little baby, don't wake, don't cry!"

Stealthily the man crept about. She knew he had his boots off, because of the vibration that his feet caused as he walked along the verandah to gauge the width of the little window in her room, and the resistance of the front door.

Then he went to the other end, and the uncertainty of what he was doing became unendurable. She had felt safer, far safer, while he was close, and she could watch and listen. She felt she must watch, but the great fear of wakening her baby again assailed her. She suddenly recalled that one of the slabs on that side of the house had shrunk in length as well as in width, and had once fallen out. It was held in position only by a wedge of wood underneath. What if he should discover that? The uncertainty increased her terror. She prayed as she gently raised herself with her little one in her arms, held tightly to her breast.

She thought of the knife, and shielded its body with her hands and arms. Even the little feet she covered with its white gown, and the baby never murmured—it liked to be held so. Noiselessly she crossed to the other side, and stood where she could see and hear, but not be seen. He was trying every slab, and was very near to that with the wedge under it. Then she saw him find it; and heard the sound of the knife as bit by bit he began to cut away the wooden support.

She waited motionless, with her baby pressed tightly to her, though she knew that in another few minutes this man with the cruel eyes, lascivious mouth, and gleaming knife, would enter. One side of the slab tilted; he had only to cut away the remaining little end, when the slab, unless he held it, would fall outside.

She heard his jerked breathing as it kept time with the cuts of the knife, and the brush of his clothes as he rubbed the wall in his movements, for she was so still and quiet, that she did not even tremble. She knew when he ceased, and wondered why, being so well concealed; for he could not see her, and would not fear if he did, yet she heard him move cautiously away. Perhaps he expected the slab to fall—his motive puzzled her, and she moved even closer, and bent her body the better to listen. Ah! what sound was that? "Listen! Listen!" she bade her heart—her heart that had kept so still, but now bounded with tumultuous throbs that dulled her ears. Nearer and nearer came the sounds, till the welcome thud of a horse's hoof rang out clearly.

"O God! O God! O God!" she panted, for they were very close

before she could make sure. She rushed to the door, and with her baby in her arms tore frantically at its bolts and bars.

Out she darted at last, and running madly along, saw the horseman beyond her in the distance. She called to him in Christ's Name, in her babe's name, still flying like the wind with the speed that deadly peril gives. But the distance grew greater and greater between them, and when she reached the creek her prayers turned to wild shrieks, for there crouched the man she feared, with outstretched arms that caught her as she fell. She knew he was offering terms if she ceased to struggle and cry for help, though louder and louder did she cry for it, but it was only when the man's hand gripped her throat, that the cry of "Murder" came from her lips. And when she ceased, the startled curlews took up the awful sound, and flew wailing "Murder! Murder!" over the horseman's head.

"By God!" said the boundary rider, "it's been a dingo right enough! Eight killed up here, and there's more down in the creek—a ewe and a lamb, I'll bet; and the lamb's alive!" He shut out the sky with his hand, and watched the crows that were circling round and round, nearing the earth one moment, and the next shooting skywards. By that he knew the lamb must be alive; even a dingo will spare a lamb sometimes.

Yes, the lamb was alive, and after the manner of lambs of its kind did not know its mother when the light came. It had sucked the still warm breasts, and laid its little head on her bosom, and slept till the morn. Then, when it looked at the swollen disfigured face, it wept and would have crept away, but for the hand that still clutched its little gown. Sleep was nodding its golden head and swaying its small body, and the crows were close, so close, to the mother's wide-open eyes, when the boundary rider galloped down.

"Jesus Christ!" he said, covering his eyes. He told afterwards how the little child held out its arms to him, and how he was forced to cut its gown that the dead hand held.

It was election time, and as usual the priest had selected a candidate. His choice was so obviously in the interests of the squatter, that Peter Hennessey's reason, for once in his life, had over-ridden superstition, and he had dared promise his vote to another. Yet he was uneasy, and every time he woke in the night (and it was often), he heard the murmur of his mother's voice. It came through the partition, or under the door. If through the partition, he knew she was praying in her bed; but when the sounds came under the door, she was on her knees before the little Altar in the corner that enshrined the statue of the Blessed Virgin and Child.

"Mary, Mother of Christ! save my son! Save him!" prayed she in the dairy as she strained and set the evening's milking. "Sweet Mary! for the love of Christ, save him!" The grief in her old face made the morning meal so bitter, that to avoid her he came late to his dinner. It made him so cowardly, that he could not say good-bye to her, and when night fell on the eve of the election day, he rode off secretly.

He had thirty miles to ride to the township to record his vote. He cantered briskly along the great stretch of plain that had nothing but stunted cotton bush to play shadow to the full moon, which glorified a sky of earliest spring. The bruised incense of the flowering clover rose up to him, and the glory of the night appealed vaguely to his imagination, but he was preoccupied with his present act of revolt.

Vividly he saw his mother's agony when she would find him gone. Even at that moment, he felt sure, she was praying.

"Mary! Mother of Christ!" He repeated the invocation, half unconsciously, when suddenly to him, out of the stillness, came Christ's Name—called loudly in despairing accents.

"For Christ's sake! Christ's sake! Christ's sake!" called the voice. Good Catholic that he had been, he crossed himself before he dared to look back. Gliding across a ghostly patch of pipe-clay, he saw a white-robed figure with a babe clasped to her bosom.

All the superstitious awe of his race and religion swayed his brain. The moonlight on the gleaming clay was a "heavenly light" to him, and he knew the white figure not for flesh and blood, but for the Virgin and Child of his mother's prayers. Then, good Catholic that once more he was, he put spurs to his horse's sides and galloped madly away.

His mother's prayers were answered, for Hennessey was the first to record his vote—for the priest's candidate. Then he sought the priest at home, but found that he was out rallying the voters. Still, under the influence of his blessed vision, Hennessey would not go near the public-houses, but wandered about the outskirts of the town for hours, keeping apart from the towns-people, and fasting as penance. He was subdued and mildly ecstatic, feeling as a repentant chastened child, who awaits only the kiss of peace.

And at last, as he stood in the graveyard crossing himself with reverent awe, he heard in the gathering twilight the roar of many voices crying the name of the victor at the election. It was well with the priest.

Again Hennessey sought him. He was at home, the housekeeper said, and led him into the dimly lighted study. His seat was immediately opposite a large picture, and as the housekeeper turned up the lamp, once more the face of the Madonna and Child looked down on him, but this time silently, peacefully. The half-parted lips of the Virgin were smiling with compassionate tenderness; her eyes seemed to beam with the forgiveness of an earthly mother for her erring but beloved child.

He fell on his knees in adoration. Transfixed, the wondering priest stood, for mingled with the adoration, "My Lord and my God!" was the exaltation, "And hast Thou chosen me?"

"What is it, Peter?" said the priest.

"Father," he answered reverently; and with loosened tongue he poured forth the story of his vision.

"Great God!" shouted the priest, "and you did not stop to save her! Do you not know? Have you not heard?"

Many miles further down the creek a man kept throwing an old cap into a water-hole. The dog would bring it out and lay it on the opposite side to where the man stood, but would not allow the man to catch him, though it was only to wash the blood of the sheep from his mouth and throat, for the sight of blood made the man tremble. But the dog also was guilty.

The Loaded Dog (1901)

—

HENRY LAWSON

"The Loaded Dog" is an excellent example of bush humor. It was first published in Lawson's volume of short stories, Joe Wilson and His Mates.

Dave Regan, Jim Bently, and Andy Page were sinking a shaft at Stony Creek in search of a rich gold quartz reef which was supposed to exist in the vicinity. There is always a rich reef supposed to exist in the vicinity; the only questions are whether it is ten feet or hundreds beneath the surface, and in which direction. They had struck some pretty solid rock, also water which kept them bailing. They used the old-fashioned blasting-powder and time-fuse. They'd make a sausage or cartridge of blasting-powder in a skin of strong-calico or canvas, the mouth sewn and bound round the end of the fuse; they'd dip the cartridge in melted tallow to make it watertight, get the drill-hole as dry as possible, drop in the cartridge with some dry dust, and wad and ram with stiff clay and broken brick. Then they'd light the fuse and get out of the hole and wait. The result was usually an ugly pot-hole in the bottom of the shaft and half a barrow-load of broken rock.

There was plenty of fish in the creek, fresh-water bream, cod, cat-fish, and tailers. The party were fond of fish, and Andy and Dave of fishing. Andy would fish for three hours at a stretch if encouraged by a 'nibble' or a 'bite' now and then—say once in twenty minutes. The butcher was always willing to give meat in exchange for fish when they caught more than they could eat; but now it was winter, and these fish wouldn't bite. However, the creek was low, just a chain of muddy waterholes, from the hole with a few bucketfuls in it to the sizable pool with an average depth of six or seven feet, and they could get fish by bailing out the smaller holes or muddying up the water in the larger ones till the fish rose to the surface. There was the cat-fish, with spikes growing out of the sides of its head, and if you got pricked you'd know it, as Dave said. Andy took off his boots, tucked up his trousers, and went into a hole one day to stir up the mud with his feet, and he knew it. Dave scooped one out with his hand and got pricked, and he knew it too; his arm swelled, and the pain throbbed up into his shoulder, and down into his stomach, too, he said, like a toothache he had once, and kept him awake for two nights—only the toothache pain had a 'burred edge,' Dave said.

Dave got an idea.

'Why not blow the fish up in the big waterhole with a cartridge?' he said. 'I'll try it.'

He thought the thing out and Andy Page worked it out. Andy usually put Dave's theories into practice if they were practicable, or bore the blame for the failure and the chaffing of his mates if they weren't.

He made a cartridge about three times the size of those they used in the rock. Jim Bently said it was big enough to blow the bottom out of the river. The inner skin was of stout calico; Andy stuck the end of a six-foot piece of fuse well down in the powder and bound the mouth of the bag firmly to it with whipcord. The idea was to sink the cartridge in the water with the open end of the fuse attached to a float on the surface, ready for lighting. Andy dipped the cartridge in melted bees-wax to make it watertight. 'We'll have to leave it some time before we light it,' said Dave, 'to give the fish time to get over their scare when we put it in, and come nosing round again; so we'll want it well watertight.'

Round the cartridge Andy, at Dave's suggestion, bound a strip of sail canvas—that they used for making water-bags—to increase the force of the explosion, and round that he pasted layers of stiff brown paper—on the plan of the sort of fireworks we called 'gun-crackers.' He let the paper dry in the sun, then he sewed a covering of two thicknesses of canvas over it, and bound the thing from end to end with stout fishing-line. Dave's schemes were elaborate, and he often worked his inventions out to nothing. The cartridge was rigid and solid enough now — a formidable bomb; but Andy and Dave wanted to be sure. Andy sewed on another layer of canvas, dipped the cartridge in melted tallow, twisted a length of fencing-wire round it as an afterthought, dipped it in tallow again, and stood it carefully against a tent-peg, where he'd know where to find it, and wound the fuse loosely round it. Then he went to the camp-fire to try some potatoes which were boiling in their jackets in a billy, and to see about frying some chops for dinner. Dave and Jim were at work in the claim that morning.

They had a big black young retriever dog — or rather an over-grown pup, a big, foolish, four-footed mate, who was always slobbering round them and lashing their legs with his heavy tail that swung round like a stock-whip. Most of his head was usually a red, idiotic slobbering grin of appreciation of his own silliness. He seemed to take life, the world, his two-legged mates, and his own instinct as a huge joke. He'd retrieve anything; he carted back most of the camp rubbish that Andy threw away. They had a cat that died in hot weather, and Andy threw it a good distance away in the scrub; and early one morning the dog found the cat, after it had been dead a week or so, and carried it back to camp, and laid it just inside the tent-flaps, where it could best make its presence known when the mates should rise and begin to sniff suspiciously in the sickly smothering atmosphere of the summer sunrise. He used to retrieve them when they went in swimming; he'd jump in after them, and take their hands in his mouth, and try to swim out with them, and scratch their naked bodies with his paws. They loved him for his goodheartedness and his foolishness, but when they wished to enjoy a swim they had to tie him up in camp.

He watched Andy with great interest all the morning making the cartridge, and hindred him considerably, trying to help; but about noon he went off to the claim to see how Dave and Jim were getting on, and to come home to dinner with them. Andy saw them coming, and put a panful of mutton-chops on the fire. Andy was cook to-day; Dave and Jim stood with their backs to the fire, as Bushmen do in all weathers, waiting till dinner should be ready. The retriever went nosing round after something he seemed to have missed.

Andy's brain still worked on the cartridge; his eye was caught by the glare of an empty kerosene-tin lying in the bushes, and it struck him that it wouldn't be a bad idea to sink the cartridge packed with clay sand, or stones in the tin, to increase the force of the explosion. He may have been all out, from a scientific point of view, but the notion looked all right to him. Jim Bently, by the way, wasn't interested in their 'damned silliness.' Andy noticed an empty treacle-tin—the sort with the little tin neck or spout soldered on to the top for the convenience of pouring out the treacle—and it struck him that this would have made the best kind of cartridge-case: he would only have had to pour in the powder, stick the fuse in through the neck, and cork and seal it with bees-wax. He was turning to suggest this to Dave, when Dave glanced over his shoulder to see how the chops were doing—and bolted. He explained afterwards that he thought he heard the pan spluttering extra, and looked to see if the chops were burning. Jim Bently looked behind and bolted after Dave. Andy stood stock-still, staring after them.

'Run, Andy! Run!' they shouted back at him. 'Run! Look behind you, you fool!' Andy turned slowly and looked, and there, close behind him, was the retriever with the cartridge in his mouth—wedged into his broadest and silliest grin. And that wasn't all. The dog had come round the fire to Andy, and the loose end of the fuse had trailed and waggled over the burning sticks into the blaze; Andy had slit and nicked the firing end of the fuse well, and now it was hissing and spitting properly.

Andy's legs started with a jolt; his legs started before his brain did, and he made after Dave and Jim. And the dog followed Andy.

Dave and Jim were good runners—Jim the best—for a short distance; Andy was slow and heavy, but he had the strength and the wind and could last. The dog capered round him, delighted as a dog could be to find his mates, as he thought, on for a frolic. Dave and Jim kept shouting back, 'Don't foller us! Don't foller us, you col-oured fool!' But Andy kept on, no matter how they dodged. They could never explain, any more than the dog, why they followed each other, but so they ran, Dave keeping in Jim's track in all its turnings, Andy after Dave, and the dog circling round Andy—the live fuse swishing in all directions and hissing and spluttering and stinking. Jim yelling to Dave not to follow him, Dave shouting to

Andy to go in another direction—to 'spread out,' and Andy roaring
at the dog to go home. Then Andy's brain began to work, stimulated by the crisis: he tried to get a running kick at the dog, but the
dog dodged; he snatched up sticks and stones and threw them at
the dog and ran on again. The retriever saw that he'd made a
mistake about Andy, and left him and bounded after Dave. Dave,
who had the presence of mind to think that the fuse's time wasn't
up yet, made a dive and a grab for the dog, caught him by the tail,
and as he swung round snatched the cartridge out of his mouth and
flung it as far as he could; the dog immediately bounded after it and
retrieved it. Dave roared and cursed at the dog, who, seeing that
Dave was offended, left him and went after Jim, who was well
ahead. Jim swung to a sapling and went up it like a native bear; it
was a young sapling, and Jim couldn't safely get more than ten or
twelve feet from the ground. The dog laid the cartridge, as carefully
as if it was a kitten, at the foot of the sapling, and capered and
leaped and whooped joyously round under Jim. The big pup reck-
oned that this was part of the lark—he was all right now—it was
Jim who was out for a spree. The fuse sounded as if it were going
a mile a minute. Jim tried to climb higher and the sapling bent and
cracked. Jim fell on his feet and ran. The dog swooped on the
cartridge and followed. It all took but a very few moments. Jim ran
to a digger's hole, about ten feet deep, and dropped down into it
—landing on soft mud—and was safe. The dog grinned sardoni-
cally down on him, over the edge, for a moment, as if he thought
it would be a good lark to drop the cartridge down on Jim.

'Go away, Tommy,' said Jim feebly, 'go away.'

The dog bounded off after Dave, who was the only one in sight
now; Andy had dropped behind a log, where he lay flat on his face,
having suddenly remembered a picture of the Russo-Turkish war
with a circle of Turks lying flat on their faces (as if they were
ashamed) round a newly-arrived shell.

There was a small hotel or shanty on the creek, on the main
road, not far from the claim. Dave was desperate, the time flew
much faster in his stimulated imagination than it did in reality, so
he made for the shanty. There were several casual Bushmen on the
veranda and in the bar; Dave rushed into the bar, banging the door
to behind him. 'My dog!' he gasped, in reply to the astonished stare

of the publican, 'the blanky retriever—he's got a live cartridge in his mouth—'

The retriever, finding the front door shut against him, had bounded round and in by the back way, and now stood smiling in the doorway leading from the passage, the cartridge still in his mouth and the fuse spluttering. They burst out of that bar. Tommy bounded first after one and then after another, for, being a young dog, he tried to make friends with everybody.

The Bushmen ran round corners, and some shut themselves in the stable. There was a new weather-board and corrugated-iron kitchen and wash-house on piles in the backyard, with some women washing clothes inside. Dave and the publican bundled in there and shut the door—the publican cursing Dave and calling him a crimson fool, in hurried tones, and wanting to know what the hell he came here for.

The retriever went in under the kitchen, amongst the piles, but, luckily for those inside, there was a vicious yellow mongrel cattle-dog sulking and nursing his nastiness under there—a sneaking, fighting, thieving canine, whom neighbours had tried for years to shoot or poison. Tommy saw his danger—he'd had experience from this dog—and started out and across the yard, still sticking to the cartridge. Halfway across the yard the yellow dog caught him and nipped him. Tommy dropped the cartridge, gave one terrified yell, and took to the Bush. The yellow dog followed him to the fence and then ran back to see what he had dropped. Nearly a dozen other dogs came from round all the corners and under the buildings—spidery, thievish, cold-blooded kangaroo dogs, mongrel sheep- and cattle-dogs, vicious black and yellow dogs—that slip after you in the dark, nip your heels, and vanish without explaining —and yapping, yelping small fry. They kept at a respectable dis-tance round the nasty yellow dog, for it was dangerous to go near him when he thought he had found something which might be good for a dog to eat. He sniffed at the cartridge twice, and was just taking a third cautious sniff when—

It was very good blasting-powder—a new brand that Dave had recently got up from Sydney; and the cartridge had been excellently well made. Andy was very patient and painstaking in all he did, and nearly as handy as the average sailor with needles, twine, canvas and rope.

Bushmen say that that kitchen jumped off its piles and on again. When the smoke and dust cleared away, the remains of the nasty yellow dog were lying against the paling fence of the yard looking as if he had been kicked into a fire by a horse and afterwards rolled in the dust under a barrow, and finally thrown against the fence from a distance. Several saddle-horses, which had been 'hanging-up' round the veranda, were galloping wildly down the road in clouds of dust, with broken bridle-reins flying; and from a circle round the outskirts, from every point of the compass in the scrub, came the yelping of dogs. Two of them went home, to the place where they were born, thirty miles away, and reached it the same night and stayed there; it was not till towards evening that the rest came back cautiously to make inquiries. One was trying to walk on two legs, and most of 'em looked more or less singed; and a little, singed, stumpy-tailed dog, who had been in the habit of hopping the back half of him along on one leg, had reason to be glad that he'd saved up the other leg all those years, for he needed it now. There was one old one-eyed cattle-dog round that shanty for years afterwards, who couldn't stand the smell of a gun being cleaned. He it was who had taken an interest, only second to that of the yellow dog, in the cartridge. Bushmen said that it was amusing to slip up on his blind side and stick a dirty ramrod under his nose: he wouldn't wait to bring his solitary eye to bear—he'd take to the Bush and stay out all night.

For half an hour or so after the explosion there were several Bushmen round behind the stable who crouched, doubled up, against the wall, or rolled gently on the dust, trying to laugh without shrieking. There were two white women in hysterics at the house, and a half-caste rushing aimlessly round with a dipper of cold water. The publican was holding his wife tight and begging her between her squawks, to 'hold up for my sake, Mary, or I'll lam the life out of ye.'

Dave decided to apologise later on, 'when things had settled a bit,' and went back to camp. And the dog that had done it all, Tommy, the great, idiotic mongrel retriever, came slobbering round

Dave and lashing his legs with his tail, and trotted home after him, smiling his broadest, longest, and reddest smile of amiability, and apparently satisfied for one afternoon with the fun he'd had.

Andy chained the dog up securely, and cooked some more chops, while Dave went to help Jim out of the hole.

And most of this is why, for years afterwards, lanky, easygoing Bushmen, riding lazily past Dave's camp, would cry, in a lazy drawl and with just a hint of the nasal twang:

'El-lo, Da-a-ve! How's the fishin' getting on, Da-a-ve?'

FROM
The Tree of Man (1955)

—

PATRICK WHITE

In this excerpt from his novel Patrick White chronicles the early days of Amy and Stan Parker's long marriage. Before the novel ends they will experience fire, flood, wartime, and loss. They will also know fulfillment and pleasure. For Stan, there will be those precious moments of insight into the nature of life itself that White celebrates in all of his novels.

Stan Parker did not decide to marry the Fibbens girl, if decision implies pros and cons; he simply knew that he would do it, and as there was no reason why the marriage ceremony should be delayed, it was very soon performed, in the little church at Yuruga, which looks a bit cockeyed, because built by hands less skilled than willing, on a piece of bumpy ground.

Clarrie Bott came to the church, because, as he explained to his reluctant lady and disgusted girls, the boy's mother was his dead, or rather his defunct, cousin. Uncle Fibbens was there too, in boots, with a handful of family, but not Aunt, whose seventh was at breast. Only Mrs. Erbey benefited emotionally by the ceremony. The parson's wife was happy at a wedding, especially if she knew the girl. She gave Amy Fibbens a Bible, a blouse as good as new (it was only slightly singed near the waist), and a little silver nutmeg grater that someone had given her at her own wedding and with which she had never known what to do.

Amy Parker, fingering the silver nutmeg grater, found it a similar problem but the loveliest thing she had ever seen, and she thanked Mrs. Erbey gratefully.

The day was fine, if cold, on the steps of the blunt church, when Amy Parker prepared to stow herself and her goods in her husband's cart and leave Yuruga. Her nutmeg grater in her pocket, her singed blouse concealed beneath her jacket, she carried in her hands the Bible and a pair of cotton gloves.

"Good-bye, Ame," mouthed Uncle Fibbens.

The wind had made him water, and the rims of his eyes were very red.

The cousins clawed.

"Good-bye, Uncle," said Amy calmly. "Good-bye, youse!" As she smacked a random bottom.

She was quite calm.

Meanwhile the draper, who had given several yards of calico, was telling the bridegroom to make the best of life, and the young man, because his attention had been bought, was screwing up his eyes and nodding his head in a way altogether unlike him. His face too had grown thinner since morning.

"After all, it is respect," said the draper in some torment of moustaches, "it is respect that counts."

The young man stood nodding like a boy as the draper struggled to soar on wings of wisdom.

Finally, when the kids had thrown a handful of rice, and Mrs. Erbey was standing on tiptoe to wave, and dab, and smile, and pull the ends of hair from out of her mouth, and wave again, and the cart was beginning to pull away from the stumpy church, under the needles of dark twisted trees that tore at hats, the Parkers, which was what they now were, knew that it was over, or that it had begun.

The cart drove away, over the ruts in that part of the town. The gay horse tossed his forelock. Thin clouds flew.

"Well, there we are," laughed the man's warm voice. "It's a long ride. You mustn't mind."

"Wouldn't help if I did." The girl lazily smiled at the landscape, holding her hat.

Their different bodies jolted with the cart. For they were changed, since what had been agony, for a split second of confessed agreement in the church. Now they were distinct, and one, they could look without effort into each other's eyes.

Only, as the town of Yuruga jerked past and away from them, Amy Parker's eyes were at present for the landscape. What she had just done, whether momentous or usual, did not concern other people. She did not belong to anyone in that town. Her fat aunt had not cried, nor had she expected it. She herself had never cried for any specific person. But now she began to feel a sadness as she struggled against the possessive motion of the cart. As if the cart, with its aspiring roll, and the retrospective landscape, were fighting for a declaration of her love. To force from her an admission of tenderness that, until now, she had carefully sat on.

The cart rocked. The road pulled at her heart. And Amy Parker, now in the full anguish of departure, was torn slowly from the scene in which her feeling life had been lived. She saw the bones of the dead cow, of which she could even remember the maggots, of Venables' Biddy with the short tits, that had died of the milk fever. Ah, she did feel now. It came swimming at her, that valley, from which the nap had been rubbed in parts, by winter, and by rabbits. Its patchiness had never coruscated more, not beneath the dews of childhood even. But what had been, and what was still a shining scene, with painted houses under the blowing trees, with the carts full of polished cans in which the farmers put the milk, with staring children and with dabbling ducks, with blue smoke from morning fires, and enamelled magpies, and the farmers' wives, spanking into town in sulkies, wheezing inside their stays and the red foxes at their necks, all would fade forever at the bend in the road.

For this last look Amy Parker turned, holding her hat in the wind. There was a sheet of iron on the ground, that had come off Fibbens' roof in a gale once, and that they had always talked about putting back. Ah dear, then she could not hold it. She was all blubbery at the mouth.

He had begun to make the clucking noises at the horse, and stroking with the whip the hairy rump.

"You are sorry then," he said, moving his hand farther along the board, so that it touched.

"I've nothing to lose at Yuruga," she said. "Had me ears boxed, and roused on all this time."

But she blew her nose. She remembered a bull's-eye she had

eaten under a bridge, and the wheels ground over the planks of the bridge, and there in the hollow afternoon swallows flew, the scythes of their wings mowing the light. She could not escape her childhood. Out of her handkerchief its slow, sad scent of peppermint.

So he stayed quiet beside her. There are the sadnesses of other people that it is not possible to share. But he knew that, in spite of her racked body, which he could feel fighting against the motion of the cart, she was not regretful. It was something, just, that must be fought out. So he was content.

It was a long ride. It was soon the sandy kind of bush road that there is no consuming. But they crunched and lurched. And the horse gave strong, leathery snorts, flicking the health defiantly out of his pink nostrils. The man would have liked to tell his wife, We are coming to This or That, or we are so many miles from So-and-so. But he could not. The distance was quite adamant.

Well, she could sit a lifetime if necessary, she said, once the crying was done.

The girl sat with her eyes on the road. She was not concerned, as, at odd moments, her husband was afraid she might be. Because in her complete ignorance of life, as it is lived, and the complete poverty of the life she had lived, she was not sure but that she might have to submit thus, interminably bolt upright in a cart. Life was perhaps a distance of stones and sun and wind, sand-coloured and monotonous. Dressed too much, as she was, for her wedding, and in an unfamiliar, undistinguished place, she could have believed anything.

But once they passed a tin nailed on top of a stump, and in the tin were a stone and a dead lizard.

And once their wheels thrashed through brown water, and the coolness of fresh, splashed water drank at her hot skin.

That, he said, was Furlong Creek.

She would remember, she felt, gravely, this that her husband was telling her.

The cart was livelier after that. Wind flung the sweat from the horse's shoulders back into their faces. There was a reckless smell of wet leather, and broken leaves that the wind had been dashing from the trees in that part of the bush. All and all were flung together, twig and leaf, man and woman, horse's hair and ribbony reins, in the progress that the landscape made. But it was principally a progress of wind. The wind took back what it gave.

"Does it always blow in these parts?" She laughed.

He made a motion with his mouth. It was not one of the things to answer. Besides, he recognized and accepted the omnipotence of distance.

But this was something she did not, and perhaps never would. She had begun to hate the wind, and the distance, and the road, because her importance tended to dwindle.

Just then, too, the wind took the elbow of a bough and broke it off, and tossed it, dry and black and writhing, so that its bark harrowed the girl's cheek, slapped terror for a moment into the horse, and crumbled, used and negative, in what was already their travelled road.

Achhh, cried the girl's hot breath, her hands touching the livid moment of fright that was more than wound, while the man's body was knotted against the horse's strength.

When they were settled into a recovered breathing the man looked at the cut in his wife's cheek. It was the cheek of the thin girl whose face had become familiar to him the night of the ball, and whom apparently he had married. And he was thankful.

Oh dear, she gasped thankfully, feeling the hardness of his body.

Their skins were grateful. And unaccustomedly tender.

They had not kissed much.

He looked at the bones in her cheek, and in her neck, exposed willingly to him.

She looked into his mouth, of which the lips were rather full and parted, roughened by the wind, and on his white teeth the blood from the small wound in her cheek.

They looked at each other, exchanging the first moment their souls had lived appreciably together. Then, quietly, they rearranged their positions and drove on.

No other event disturbed the monotony of emotion, the continuity of road, the relentlessness of scrub that first day, until, about evening, just as their faces were beginning to grow grey, they came to the clearing the man had made to live in.

Now his modest achievement was fully exposed. The voice of

a dog, half-aggressive, half-hopeless, leaped into the cool silence.

"This is the place," the man said, as if it must be got over quietly and quickly.

"Ah," she smiled, withdrawn, "this is the house you have built."

It is not much better, oh dear, than Fibbens' shed, she said, and you can cut the silence.

"Yes," he grunted, jumping down, "it's not all violets, as you can see."

As she could see, but she must also speak, she knew.

"Once I saw a house," she said, in the even dreamlike voice of inspiration, "that had a white rosebush growing beside it, and I always said that if I had a house I would plant a white rose. It was a tobacco rose, the lady said."

"Well," he said, laughing up at her, "you have the house."

"Yes," she said, getting down.

It did not help much, so she touched his hand. And there was a dog smelling at the hem of her skirt, that she looked down dubiously to see. The dog's ribs were shivering.

"What is his name?" she asked.

He said that the dog had no particular name.

"But he should have one," she said.

The moment a conviction had animated her bones she began to take the things from their cart, and to arrange their belongings in the house, as if it were the natural thing to do. Carefully she went here and there. She gave the impression she was not sticking her nose into what was already there. In fact, most of the time she was so careful to look straight ahead in her husband's house that there was a great deal she did not see at all.

But she knew it was there. And would look later on.

"There is water," he said, coming and standing a bucket inside the doorway.

The level of the water lapped quietly and settled down.

She went to and fro in what was becoming her house. She heard the sound of his axe. She thrust her shoulders through the window, outside which it was determined she should plant the white rose, and where the slope of the land was still restless from the jagged stumps of felled trees.

"Where is the flour?" she called. "And I cannot see the salt."

"I shall come," he said, rummaging after the sticks of wood.

It was that hour of evening when the sky is bled white as scattered woodchips. The clearing was wide open. The two people and their important activities could not have been more exposed. About that importance there was no doubt, for the one had become two. The one was enriched. Their paths crossed, and diverged, and met, and knotted. Their voices spoke to each other across gulfs. Their mystery of purpose had found the solution to the mystery of silence.

"I shall like it here." She smiled, over the crumbs on the table, when they had eaten the damper she had slapped together, and some rancid remnants of salt beef.

He looked at her. It had never really occurred to him, in the deep centre of conviction, that she might not like his place. It would never occur to him that what must be, might not. The rose that they would plant was already taking root outside the window of the plain house, its full flowers falling to the floor, scenting the room with its scent of crushed tobacco.

Already, as a boy, his face had been a convinced face. Some said stony. If he was not exactly closed, certainly he opened with difficulty. There were veins in him of wisdom and poetry, but deep, much of which would never be dug. He would stir in his sleep, the dream troubling his face, but he would never express what he had seen.

So instead of telling her smooth things, that were not his anyway, he took her hand over the remnants of their sorry meal. The bones of his hand were his, and could better express the poem that was locked inside him and that would never otherwise be released. His hand knew stone and iron, and was familiar with the least shudder of wood. It trembled a little, however, learning the language of flesh.

The whole night had become a poem of moonlight. The moon, just so far from full as to be itself a bit crude, cut crooked from its paper, made the crude house look ageless. Its shape was impregnable under the paper moon, the moon itself unperturbed.

So that the thin girl, when she had taken off her dress, and put her shoes together, and rolled into a ball the gloves she had held but had not used, took courage from the example of the moon. The furniture, huge in the moonlight, was worn by and accustomed to the habits of people. So she only had a moment of fright, and chafed that easily off.

Flesh is heroic by moonlight.

The man took the body of the woman and taught it fearlessness. The woman's mouth on the eyelids of the man spoke to him from her consoling depths. The man impressed upon the woman's body his sometimes frightening power and egotism. The woman devoured the man's defencelessness. She could feel the doubts shudder in his thighs, just as she had experienced his love and strength. And out of her she could not wring the love that she was capable of giving, at last, enough, complete as sleep or death.

Later, when it had begun to be cold, and the paper moon had sunk a bit tattered in the trees, the woman got beneath the blanket, against the body of the sleeping man who was her husband. She locked her hand into the iron pattern of the bedstead above her head and slept.

Life continued in that clearing in which the Parkers had begun to live. The clearing encroached more and more on the trees, and the stumps of the felled trees had begun to disappear, in ash and smoke, or rotted away like old teeth. But there remained a log or two, big knotted hulks for which there seemed no solution, and on these the woman sometimes sat in the sun, shelling a dish of peas or drying her slithery hair.

Sometimes the red dog sat and looked at the woman, but not closely as he did at the man. If she called to him, his eyes became shallow and unseeing. He was the man's dog. So for this reason she had never given him the name she had promised. He remained Your Dog. Walking stiffly past the stumps and the tussocks of grass, stiffly lifting his leg. In time he killed a little fuchsia that she had planted in the shadow of the house, and in her exasperation she threw a woody carrot at him. But she did not hit the dog. He continued to ignore her, even in his laughing moments, when his tongue lolled and increased with the laughter in his mouth. But it was not laughter for the woman. He did not see her. He licked his private parts or looked along his nose at the air.

Never far from the dog the man would be at work. With axe, or scythe, or hammer. Or he would be on his knees, pressing into the earth the young plants he had raised under wet bags. All along the morning stood the ears of young cabbages. Those that the rabbits did not nibble off. In the clear morning of those early years the cabbages stood out for the woman more distinctly than other things, when they were not melting, in a tenderness of light.

The young cabbages, that were soon a prospect of veined leaves, melted in the mornings of thawing frost. Their blue and purple flesh ran together with the silver of water, the jewels of light, in the smell of warming earth. But always tensing. Already in the hard, later light the young cabbages were resistant balls of music, until in time they were the big, placid cabbages, all heart and limp panniers, and in the middle of the day there was the glandular stench of cabbages.

If the woman came and stood by the man, when the sun had risen, after frost, when the resentful blood had settled in the veins, he would show her how he was chipping the earth in the rows between the cabbages.

"Not this way," he said, "because you cover up the weeds. But this way."

Not that she had to be shown. Or listened. Not that he did not know this, but had her by him. The earth was soft and exhausted after frost. After the awful numbing and clawing and screeching of the fingernails, it was gently perfect to be beside each other. Not particularly listening or speaking. He could feel her warmth. She wore a big old straw hat with frayed spokes where the binding had come unsewn, and the hat made her face look too small and white. But her body had thickened a little. She no longer jerked when she turned, or threatened to break at the hips. Her flesh was growing conscious and suave.

"Not this way. But this way," he said.

Teaching her not this, but the movements of her own body as she walked between the rows of cabbages. She walked narrowly, on account of the hummocks of earth that he had hilled up to serve as beds, but her movement pervaded the orbit of his vision. He did not often raise his eyes, chipping the thawed earth, but he carried against him the shape of her body.

So that he too was taught. She was imprinted on him.

Sometimes she would look up from her plate and speak, after tearing a mouthful of bread, speak with her mouth too full, the voice torn. He would hear and remember this voice again when he was alone. Her too greedy voice. Because she *was* rather greedy, for bread, and, once discovered, for his love.

Her skin devoured the food of love, and resented those conspiracies of life that took it from her before she was filled. She would look from the window into the darkness, hearing the swing of metal and the thwack of leather, seeing the dark distortion of a cart with its mountain of cabbages against the stars.

"I have filled the water-bag," she would call.

As the man tore at stiff buckles, and cold leather resisted his hands. As he moved round and round the horse and cart, preparing for the journey of cabbages.

"And there's a slice of pie beneath the sandwiches," she said.

To say.

Because it was cold on her shoulders in the morning, and in the bed when he had gone, and the hoofs of the horse were striking their last notes from the stones, and the cart had creaked its final music. She could not warm back his body in the forsaken bed.

Sometimes he would be gone a whole day and night after the market, if there was business to transact or things to buy.

Then the forsaken woman was again the thin girl. The important furniture of her marriage were matchsticks in the hollow house. Her thin, child's life was a pitiful affair in the clearing in the bush. As she walked here and there, tracing maps in scattered sugar or in the receded undergrowth, close to the ground, staring eye to eye with the ant.

Sometimes she mumbled the words she had been taught to say to God.

She would beg the sad, pale Christ for some sign of recognition. On the scratched mahogany table which the man had bought at auction, she had put the Bible from the parson's wife. She turned the pages respectfully. She said or read the words. And she waited for the warmth, the completeness, the safety of religion. But to achieve this there was something perhaps that she had to do, something that she had not been taught, and in its absence she would get up, in a desperation of activity, as if she might acquire the secret in performing a ritual of household acts, or merely by walking about. Suspecting she might find grace in her hands, suddenly, like a plaster dove.

But she did not receive the grace of God, of which it had been spoken under coloured glass. When she was alone, she was alone. Or else there was lightning in the sky that warned her of her transitoriness. The sad Christ was an old man with a beard, who spat death from full cheeks. But the mercy of God was the sound of wheels at the end of market day. And the love of God was a kiss full in the mouth. She was filled with the love of God, and would take it for granted, until in its absence she would remember again. She was so frail.

The woman Amy Fibbens was absorbed in the man Stan Parker, whom she had married. And the man, the man consumed the woman. That was the difference.

The Night We Watched for Wallabies (1899)

STEELE RUDD

Steele Rudd, whose real name was Arthur Hoey Davis, wrote comic tales about life on a small farm, or selection. His first stories were collected in the volume On Our Selection, *in 1899. These and later narratives concern principally Dad, Mum, and Dave, their son, who live on the Darling Downs in Queensland. Widely popular, Rudd's stories have been adapted for film and radio.*

The wallaby refers to a variety of smaller marsupials common in Australian hill and scrub country. Small kangaroos are also known as wallabies.

It had been a bleak July day, and as night came on a bitter westerly howled through the trees. Cold! wasn't it cold! The pigs in the sty, hungry and half-fed (we wanted for ourselves the few pumpkins that had survived the drought) fought savagely with each other for shelter, and squealed all the time like—well, like pigs. The cows and calves left the place to seek shelter away in the mountains; while the draught horses, their hair standing up like barbed-wire, leaned sadly over the fence and gazed at the green lucerne. Joe went about shivering in an old coat of Dad's with only one sleeve to it—a calf had fancied the other one day that Dad hung it on a post as a mark to go by while ploughing.

"My! it'll be a stinger tonight," Dad remarked to Mrs. Brown— who sat, cold-looking, on the sofa—as he staggered inside with an immense log for the fire. A log! Nearer a whole tree! But wood was nothing in Dad's eyes.

Mrs. Brown had been at our place five or six days. Old Brown called occasionally to see her, so we knew they couldn't have quarrelled. Sometimes she did a little housework, but more often she didn't. We talked it over together, but couldn't make it out. Joe asked Mother, but she had no idea—so she said. We were full up, as Dave put it, of Mrs. Brown, and wished her out of the place. She had taken to ordering us about, as though she had something to do with us.

After supper we sat round the fire—as near to it as we could without burning ourselves—Mrs. Brown and all, and listened to the wind whistling outside. Ah, it was pleasant beside the fire listening to the wind! When Dad had warmed himself back and front he turned to us and said:

"Now, boys, we must go directly and light some fires and keep those wallabies back."

That was a shock to us, and we looked at him to see if he were really in earnest. He was, and as serious as a judge.

"Tonight!" Dave answered, surprisedly—"why tonight any more than last night or the night before? Thought you had decided to let them rip?"

"Yes, but we might as well keep them off a bit longer."

"But there's no wheat there for them to get now. So what's the good of watching them? There's no sense in *that*."

Dad was immovable.

"Anyway"—whined Joe—"*I'm* not going—not a night like this —not when I ain't got boots."

That vexed Dad. "Hold your tongue, sir!" he said—"you'll do as you're told."

But Dave hadn't finished. "I've been following that harrow since sunrise this morning," he said, "and now you want me to go chasing wallabies about in the dark, a night like this, and for nothing else but to keep them from eating the ground. It's always the way here, the more one does the more he's wanted to do," and he commenced to cry. Mrs. Brown had something to say. *She* agreed with Dad and thought we ought to go, as the wheat might spring up again.

"Pshah!" Dave blurted out between his sobs, while we thought of telling her to shut her mouth.

. . .

Slowly and reluctantly we left that roaring fireside to accompany
Dad that bitter night. It *was* a night!—dark as pitch, silent, forlorn
and forbidding, and colder than the busiest morgue. And just to
keep wallabies from eating nothing! They *had* eaten all the wheat
—every blade of it—and the grass as well. What they would start
on next—ourselves or the cart-harness—wasn't quite clear.

We stumbled along in the dark one behind the other, with our
hands stuffed into our trousers. Dad was in the lead, and poor Joe,
bare-shinned and bootless, in the rear. Now and again he tramped
on a Bathurst-burr, and, in sitting down to extract the prickle,
would receive a cluster of them elsewhere. When he escaped the
burr it was only to knock his shin against a log or leave a toe-nail
or two clinging to a stone. Joe howled, but the wind howled louder,
and blew and blew.

Dave, in pausing to wait on Joe, would mutter:

"To *hell* with everything! Whatever he wants bringing us out a
night like this, I'm *damned* if *I* know!"

Dad couldn't see very well in the dark, and on this night couldn't
see at all, so he walked up against one of the old draught horses that
had fallen asleep gazing at the lucerne. And what a fright they both
got! The old horse took it worse than Dad—who only tumbled
down—for he plunged as though the devil had grabbed him, and
fell over the fence, twisting every leg he had in the wires. How the
brute struggled! We stood and listened to him. After kicking panels
of the fence down and smashing every wire in it, he got loose and
made off, taking most of it with him.

"That's one wallaby on the wheat, anyway," Dave muttered, and
we giggled. *We* understood Dave; but Dad didn't open his mouth.

We lost no time lighting the fires. Then we walked through the
"wheat" and wallabies! May Satan reprove me if I exaggerate their
number by one solitary pair of ears—from the row and scatter they
made there was a *million*.

Dad told Joe, at last, he could go to sleep if he liked, at the fire. Joe
went to sleep—*how*, I don't know. Then Dad sat beside him, and
for long intervals would stare silently into the darkness. Sometimes
a string of the vermin would hop past close to the fire, and another

time a curlew would come near and screech its ghostly wail, but he never noticed them. Yet he seemed to be listening.

We mooched around from fire to fire, hour after hour, and when we wearied of heaving fire-sticks at the enemy we sat on our heels and cursed the wind, and the winter, and the night-birds alternately. It was a lonely, wretched occupation.

Now and again Dad would leave his fire to ask us if we could hear a noise. We couldn't, except that of wallabies and mopokes. Then he would go back and listen again. He was restless, and, somehow, his heart wasn't in the wallabies at all. Dave couldn't make him out.

The night wore on. By-and-by there was a sharp rattle of wires, then a rustling noise, and Sal appeared in the glare of the fire. "*Dad!*" she said. That was all. Without a word, Dad bounced up and went back to the house along with her.

"Something's up!" Dave said, and, half-anxious, half-afraid, we gazed into the fire and thought and thought. Then we stared, nervously, into the night, and listened for Dad's return, but heard only the wind and the mopoke.

At dawn he appeared again, with a broad smile on his face, and told us that Mother had got another baby—a fine little chap. *Then* we knew why Mrs. Brown had been staying at our place.

A Gentleman's Agreement (1984)

ELIZABETH JOLLEY

—

This is a different kind of bush story, a contemporary version. The characters described here and their preoccupations reappear in several stories from Jolley's collection, The Five Acre Virgin.

In the home science lesson I had to unpick my darts as Mrs Kay said they were all wrong and then I scorched the collar of my dress because I had the iron too hot. And then the sewing machine needle broke and there wasn't a spare and Mrs Kay got really wild and Peril Page cut all the notches off her pattern by mistake and that finished everything.

'I'm not ever going back to that school,' I said to Mother in the evening. 'I'm finished with that place!' So that was my brother and me both leaving school before we should have and my brother kept leaving jobs too, one job after another, sometimes not even staying long enough in one place to wait for his pay.

But Mother was worrying about what to get for my brother's tea.

'What about a bit of lamb's fry and bacon,' I said. She brightened up then and, as she was leaving to go up the terrace for her shopping, she said, 'You can come with me tomorrow then and we'll get through the work quicker.' She didn't seem to mind at all that I had left school.

Mother cleaned in a large block of luxury apartments. She had keys to the flats and she came and went as she pleased and as her work demanded. It was while she was working there that she had the idea of letting the people from down our street taste the pleasures rich people took for granted in their way of living. While these people were away to their offices or on business trips she let our poor neighbours in. We had wedding receptions and parties in the penthouse and the old folk came in to soak their feet and wash their clothes while Mother was doing the cleaning. As she said, she gave a lot of pleasure to people without doing anybody any harm, though it was often a terrible rush for her. She could never refuse anybody anything and, because of this, always had more work than she could manage and more people to be kind to than her time really allowed.

Sometimes at the weekends I went with Mother to look at Grandpa's valley. It was quite a long bus ride. We had to get off at the twenty-nine-mile peg, cross the Medulla brook and walk up a country road with scrub on either side till we came to some cleared acres of pasture which was the beginning of her father's land. She struggled through the wire fence hating the mud. She wept out loud because the old man hung on to his land and all his money was buried, as she put it, in the sodden meadows of cape weed and stuck fast in the outcrops of granite higher up where all the topsoil had washed away. She couldn't sell the land because Grandpa was still alive in a Home for the Aged, and he wanted to keep the farm though he couldn't do anything with it. Even sheep died there. They either starved or got drowned depending on the time of the year. It was either drought there or flood. The weatherboard house was so neglected it was falling apart, the tenants were feckless, and if a calf was born there it couldn't get up, that was the kind of place it was. When we went to see Grandpa he wanted to know about the farm and Mother tried to think of things to please him. She didn't say the fence posts were crumbling away and that the castor oil plants had taken over the yard so you couldn't get through to the barn.

There was an old apricot tree in the middle of the meadow, it was as big as a house and a terrible burden to us to get the fruit at just the right time. Mother liked to take some to the hospital so that Grandpa could keep up his pride and self-respect a bit.

In the full heat of the day I had to pick with an apron tied round me, it had deep pockets for the fruit. I grabbed at the green fruit when I thought Mother wasn't looking and pulled off whole branches so it wouldn't be there to be picked later.

'Don't take that branch!' Mother screamed from the ground. 'Them's not ready yet. We'll have to come back tomorrow for them.'

I lost my temper and pulled off the apron full of fruit and hurled it down but it stuck on a branch and hung there quite out of reach either from up the tree where I was or from the ground.

'Wait! Just you wait till I get a holt of you!' Mother pranced round the tree and I didn't come down till we had missed our bus and it was getting dark and all the dogs in the little township barked as if they were insane, the way dogs do in the country, as we walked through trying to get a lift home.

One Sunday in the winter it was very cold but Mother thought we should go all the same. We passed some sheep huddled in a natural fold of furze and withered grass all frost sparkling in the morning.

'Quick!' Mother said. 'We'll grab a sheep and take a bit of wool back to Grandpa.'

'But they're not our sheep,' I said.

'Never mind!' And she was in among the sheep before I could stop her. The noise was terrible but she managed to grab a bit of wool.

'It's terrible dirty and shabby,' she complained, pulling at the shreds with her cold fingers. 'I don't think I've ever seen such miserable wool.'

All that evening she was busy with the wool, she did make me laugh.

'How will modom have her hair done?' She put the wool on the kitchen table and kept walking all round it talking to it. She tried to wash it and comb it but it still looked awful so she put it round one of my curlers for the night.

'I'm really ashamed of the wool,' Mother said next morning.

'But it isn't ours,' I said.

'I know but I'm ashamed all the same,' she said. So when we were in the penthouse at South Heights she cut a tiny piece off the bathroom mat. It was so soft and silky. And later we went to visit

Grandpa. He was sitting with his poor paralysed legs under his tartan rug.

'Here's a bit of the wool clip Dad,' Mother said, bending over to kiss him. His whole face lit up.

'That's nice of you to bring it, really nice.' His old fingers stroked the little piece of nylon carpet.

'It's very good, deep and soft.' He smiled at Mother.

'They do wonderful things with sheep these days Dad,' she said.

'They do indeed,' he said, and all the time he was feeling the bit of carpet.

'Are you pleased Dad?' Mother asked him anxiously. 'You are pleased aren't you?'

'Oh yes I am,' he assured her.

I thought I saw a moment of disappointment in his eyes, but the eyes of old people often look full of tears.

On the way home I tripped on the steps.

'Ugh! I felt your bones!' Really Mother was so thin it hurt to fall against her.

'Well what d'you expect me to be, a boneless wonder?'

Really Mother had such a hard life and we lived in such a cramped and squalid place. She longed for better things and she needed a good rest. I wished more than anything the old man would agree to selling his land. Because he wouldn't sell I found myself wishing he would die and whoever really wants to wish someone to die! It was only that it would sort things out a bit for us.

In the supermarket Mother thought and thought what she could get for my brother for his tea. In the end all she could come up with was fish fingers and a packet of jelly beans.

'You know I never eat fish! And I haven't eaten sweets in years.' My brother looked so tall in the kitchen. He lit a cigarette and slammed out and Mother was too tired and too upset to eat her own tea.

Grandpa was an old man and though his death was expected it was unexpected really and it was a shock to Mother to find she suddenly had eighty-seven acres to sell. And there was the house too. She had a terrible lot to do as she decided to sell the property herself and, at the same time, she did not want to let down the people at South Heights. There was a man interested to buy the land, Mother had kept him up her sleeve for years, ever since he had stopped once by the bottom paddock to ask if it was for sale. At the time Mother would have given her right arm to be able to sell it and she promised he should have first refusal if it ever came on the market.

We all three, Mother and myself and my brother, went out at the weekend to tidy things up. We lost my brother and then we suddenly saw him running and running and shouting, his voice lifting up in the wind as he raced up the slope of the valley.

'I do believe he's laughing! He's happy!' Mother just stared at him and she looked so happy too.

I don't think I ever saw the country look so lovely before.

The tenant was standing by the shed. The big tractor had crawled to the doorway like a sick animal and had stopped there, but in no time my brother had it going.

It seemed there was nothing my brother couldn't do. Suddenly after doing nothing in his life he was driving the tractor and making fire breaks, he started to paint the sheds and he told Mother what fencing posts and wire to order. All these things had to be done before the sale could go through. We all had a wonderful time in the country. I kept wishing we could live in the house, all at once it seemed lovely there at the top of the sunlit meadow. But I knew that however many acres you have, they aren't any use unless you have money too. I think we were all thinking this but no one said anything though Mother kept looking at my brother and the change in him.

There was no problem about the price of the land, this man, he was a doctor, really wanted it and Mother really needed the money.

'You might as well come with me,' Mother said to me on the day of the sale. 'You can learn how business is done.' So we sat in this lawyer's comfortable room and he read out from various papers and the doctor signed things and Mother signed. Suddenly she said to them, 'You know my father really loved his farm but he only managed to have it late in life and then he was never able to live there because of his illness.' The two men looked at her.

'I'm sure you will understand,' she said to the doctor, 'with your own great love of the land, my father's love for his valley. I feel if I could live there just to plant one crop and stay while it matures, my father would rest easier in his grave.'

'Well I don't see why not.' The doctor was really a kind man. The lawyer began to protest, he seemed quite angry.

'It's not in the agreement,' he began to say. But the doctor silenced him, he got up and came round to Mother's side of the table.

'I think you should live there and plant your one crop and stay while it matures,' he said to her. 'It's a gentleman's agreement,' he said.

'That's the best sort.' Mother smiled up at him and they shook hands.

'I wish your crop well,' the doctor said, still shaking her hand.

The doctor made the lawyer write out a special clause which they all signed. And then we left, everyone satisfied. Mother had never had so much money and the doctor had the valley at last but it was the gentleman's agreement which was the best part.

My brother was impatient to get on with improvements.

'There's no rush,' Mother said.

'Well one crop isn't very long,' he said.

'It's long enough,' she said.

So we moved out to the valley and the little weatherboard cottage seemed to come to life very quickly with the pretty things we chose for the rooms.

'It's nice whichever way you look out from these little windows,' Mother was saying and just then her crop arrived. The carter set down the boxes along the edge of the verandah and, when he had gone, my brother began to unfasten the hessian coverings. Inside were hundreds of seedlings in little plastic containers.

'What are they?' he asked.

'Our crop,' Mother said.

'Yes I know, but what is the crop? What are these?'

'Them,' said Mother, she seemed unconcerned, 'oh they're a jarrah forest,' she said.

'But that will take years and years to mature,' he said.

'I know,' Mother said. 'We'll start planting tomorrow. We'll pick the best places and clear and plant as we go along.'

'But what about the doctor?' I said, somehow I could picture him pale and patient by his car out on the lonely road which went through his valley. I seemed to see him looking with longing at his paddocks and his meadows and at his slopes of scrub and bush.

'Well he can come on his land whenever he wants to and have a look at us,' Mother said. 'There's nothing in the gentleman's agreement to say he can't.'

II.

Images of Australia

The Aborigine, the convict, and the soldier are focal images in the selections in Part II.

Reaching back more than two hundred years to the time when England annexed native people's lands, the writers in this section explore the Aboriginal experience. First seen by the British as an oddity, then perceived as an irritant, the Aborigines were almost destroyed. For a long time they were pushed to the back of Australian public consciousness. Through stories collected here, the reader can trace the tenacity of prejudice, the conflict in the heart of an Aboriginal woman doing a man's work, the colonial invasion of Australia, and the frustration of being an alien in one's own land. Three of the narratives are written by contemporary Aborigines. This is important. Writing from their own perspective, Aboriginal authors are reclaiming their identity. A people given up for dead is now being revived by their descendants. Readers have the chance to participate in a cultural rebirth.

Writers in this section also portray another figure from Australia's past—the convict. The convict image is one of powerlessness, and of loss of hope and identity. In both Marcus Clarke's and Price Warung's fiction, the prisoner is the captive of a dehumanizing system. The penal colony is a bureaucracy that promotes the worst elements of human nature and invites the abuse of power.

Images that grow out of Australia's modern history—portraits of war and its effects—are found in the final selections. World Wars I and II were landmark events in the life of this nation and its citizens. This section includes autobiographical fiction and prose that re-creates some of the traumas of those years. The battle of Gallipoli during World War I and the Japanese invasion during World War II are remembered here.

The final story, "American Dreams" by Peter Carey, considers a different kind of invasion, peaceful but dangerous. Carey describes the upheaval in a community when American tastes threaten to overtake an Australian town.

THE ABORIGINAL EXPERIENCE

Northern Belle (1979)

—

THEA ASTLEY

A witty writer known for her skill in portraying the realities of small-town life, Thea Astley is adept at exploring moral values and/or their absence. In this story from her collection Hunting the Wild Pineapple, *she creates an Australian northern belle reminiscent of some Southern belles in American fiction.*

The night Willy Fourcorners sat with me, awkward in his Christian clothing, he told me, between the clubbing blocks of rain, what it was like sometimes to be black in these parts. He's sat with me other nights as well and what he told me of this one or that, this place or that, was like taking a view from the wrong side of the fence. Wrong's not the word. Photographing in shadow, the object that is? No. I'm still hunting the wild simile. It was . . . it was like inspecting the negative, framing and hanging its reversals, standing back to admire, then crying in despair, 'But it's all different!'

People I knew, he knew, but he knew them some other—how —as if he saw Lawyer Galipo and Father Rassini from the lee side of the banks of heaven. I asked him once why he'd ever left his little house on the outskirts of Tobaccotown, and he was silent a long time. I coddled his silence and at last he told me. I put his story onto their stories and still I get one story.

This is Willy's story, my words.

She was born in one of those exhausted, fleetingly timbered places that sprang up round the tin mines of the north. Not in the poverty of a digger's shack, let it be understood, but in the more impressive veranda'd sprawl of one of those cedar houses that loiter in heavy country gardens. How capture the flavour of those years? Horse-rumps, sweat, hard liquor, crippled shanties, all forgotten in the spacious hours after lunch and before tea when baking fragrance settled as gently as the shadows across and into the passion-vined trellis.

A porky child with a fine cap of almost white dead-straight hair, her body gave no indication of the handsome bones that were to emerge in late adolescence. Skip some years. Now we have her at fourteen bounding confidently across the town hard-court, shimmering with sweat, her hair longer now, darkening now, still fine and unmanageable; but it's still no pointer to the strong-minded Clarice of nineteen who, despite a profile of pleasing symmetry, still boyishly racquet-scooped balls, served low and hard, and later dispensed lemon squash in the tin side-line shed where other acceptables of the town gathered each Saturday afternoon.

She had early the confidence of her class. Her father was a mine manager and owner. 'AG' they called him, and he knew to a nicety what line of familiarity to draw with the blacks who still hung about the perimeters of town, even instigating a curfew for them, but was less certain when it came to men of his own colour. Which was either bright red or mottled white. In snapshots from the period he, heavily moustached and mutton-chopped beside his wife, dominated rows of sawney after-picnic guests. She always appeared formidably silked and hatted and her bust was frightening. 'Breasts' is somehow too pretty, too delicate a word to describe that shelf of righteousness on which many a local upstart had foundered. Along with the bust was a condescending familiarity with the town's priest, two ministers of other religions, and four members of parliament whom she had seen come and helped go. Clarice was an only child, not as much of a son as the father had hoped for and something less of a daughter; but with the years her looks fined and softened; and if she was not in fact a beauty privilege made her just as desirable in a country where a fine bank account is as good for launching a thousand ships as a face: it's even better.

Her mother was determined Clarice would marry well, but no one was ever quite well enough.

Motor-cars and Clarice's teens created small tensions. There were various young men; but the town had little to offer beyond bank- and railway-clerks, or the sons of Italian tobacco farmers whose morals the mother suspected to be doubtful. Should too long a time elapse between the drawing-up of a young man's car and Clarice's flushed entry to the house, her mother would tighten her mouth, draw up that juridical bust, and struggle to find words that were at once proper and admonitory. She was rarely able to draw that nice balance and one afternoon, as she worked with her daughter in the kitchen crumbing butter and flour for scones, she said without preamble and quite formally:

'I was once attacked by a sexually maddened blackfellow.'

Clarice was startled.

'That is why.' Her mother shut her lips tightly and a little line was ruled.

'Why what?'

'Why you must keep men—all men—at a distance.'

'All men?' inquired Clarice. 'Or just sexually maddened blackfel-lows?'

'You are too young, Clarice,' her mother said sharply, 'to use such words. Girls of sixteen should not even know such words.'

'But I don't understand,' Clarice persisted. 'Were you—?' she hesitated. 'Harmed' seemed not an exact enough word. 'Were you carnally known?'

Her mother fainted.

'I do not know where,' she later gabbled to Clarice's father, 'where this—this child—could pick up such . . . I have done all . . . appalling knowledge . . . how the good nuns . . . wherever . . . she must be protected from. . . .'

She spoke at length to her daughter on the necessity of virtue, the rigours of beauty, of chastity, the clean mind, and the need to expunge lust. She went so far as to summon Father Rassini to give spiritual advice. She read her daughter an improving poem. Clarice listened to all this with an expression on her face as if she were trying to remember a knitting pattern. Young men were discouraged from calling. Her current bank-clerk went away in the army and Clarice, after dreadful scenes in which she finally proved herself her father's daughter, took the little branch train to the coast, caught the main line south, and burrowed into essential war industry.

The city was only partly strange to her, for she had been educated at a southern convent where her only achievements had been to stagger the nuns by the ferocity with which she played badminton and Mendelssohn's *Rondo Capriccioso*. She revealed no other talents. They taught her a little refined typing and book-keeping, insufficient to addle or misdirect any feminine drives; enough French to cope with a wine list in the better restaurants; and some basic techniques in water-colours. She had a full and vigorous voice that dominated, off-key, the contralto section of the school choir for three years, but even this mellowed into suitable nuances before the onslaught of the mistress in charge of boarders.

'My dear Clarice,' she would reprove icily, 'you are not a man.'

'*Non, ma mère,*' Clarice would reply dutifully, giving the little curtsey this particular order required.

'And further, you seem to forget that men do not . . . oh, never mind!' Mother Sulpice rolled her fine brown eyes upwards, a kind of ecstatic St Teresa, and swished off with her beads rattling.

The boarders pondered Mother Sulpice.

'You can see she was quite beautiful,' Clarice's best friend, a thumping girl, commented doubtfully. 'Quite Renaissance.'

'Do you think she was jilted in love?' The students spent much time in these speculations.

'Oh, I heard. I heard.'

'What? What did you hear?'

'I shouldn't say.'

'Oh, come on! What?'

'My mother told me something.'

'Told you what?'

'I shouldn't really say.'

'Oh, yes you should,' Clarice insisted. She kicked quite savagely at the iron railing of the terrace that looked out over Brisbane hills. 'By not telling me you are creating an occasion of sin.'

Thumper went pink. 'I'm not. How could I be?'

'Who knows what I shall think,' Clarice said cunningly. 'I could think almost anything. In fact, I do think almost anything.'

She looked slyly at her friend and observed the moral contortion with interest.

'You've got to promise,' Thumper said, 'that you won't tell.'

'Well?'

'Do you promise?'

'Of course.'

'Well,' Thumper said with a pretty play of hesitancy, 'well, she was engaged. Before she entered.'

'And what then?'

'He died. He was killed in France. It wasn't,' she said, lowering her voice in horror, 'a true vocation.'

'Oh, stuff that,' Clarice said. 'How did it happen?'

'Mummy said it was quite tragic.' Clarice saw her friend's eyes grow moist and noticed she was getting a new pimple. 'He was running to regain the trenches and he ran the wrong way. He was dreadfully short-sighted.'

Clarice wanted to laugh. Instead, she looked at her friend hard and asked, 'Do you think they'd had sexual intercourse?'

'Now you *will* have to go to confession!' her friend said.

'Poor Mother Sulpice!' Clarice sighed.

But it was for her, perhaps for the wrong reasons, transfiguration.

She studied the nun's graceful walk, imitated the Isadora-like arabesques of her hands, modulated her voice, and began training her hair into expressive curves across her ears.

'How Clarice has changed!' the nuns observed with relief. 'She's growing up at last.'

In class, her mind closed to the finer points of the redundant *ne*, she sought for and thought she discovered the delicate prints of tragedy on Mother Sulpice's completely calm face.

'That will be the way I will bear it,' she said to herself.

After she left home the first job she obtained was as an office assistant in a factory supplying camouflage tents to the troops. She left the day the senior accountant, who was married, suggested they take in dinner and a show. When she leapt offendedly onto a tram, an American serviceman asked could he help her with her bag. She had no bag but was so confused by the nature of his offer that before she had gone three blocks she found herself in conversation with him. He told her many lies, but those she most vividly remembered were about a cotton plantation in Georgia, an interrupted semester at Yale, and no engagement of the heart, legal or otherwise. As she dressed in her YWCA cubicle for her third outing with him, she kept telling herself it was Mother Sulpice all over again, and she dropped her firm tanned neck, glanced back into the speckly mirror, and lowered her eyes in unconscious but perfect parody.

On the sixth outing seven days after they had met, he attempted to take her to bed, but she resisted with much charm. On the seventh he told her he had been drafted to the Pacific and they then exchanged deeply emotional letters that she read again and again, all the time thanking God for the good training which had prevented 'that' from happening. 'That' was happening all about her. Thumper was pregnant to a marine who had crossed the horizon without leaving any other memento of his visit. Men were all like that, Thumper assured Clarice between her sobs. Clarice thought it a pity her nose got so red when she cried.

Clarice managed to repress her feelings of righteousness and exultation that she was the one spared, and after she had seen her friend take a sad train back to her stunned parents up country she slid into Thumper's job in an army canteen. She was totally unprepared for a letter some months later from Roy telling her he had married a nurse in Guam because he had to. 'Honey,' he wrote, 'you will always be very special to me. You will always be my one true love, the purest I have ever known.' He was lying again, but she was spared the knowledge of this.

She was not built for pathos. The troubles of others found in her a grotesque response of incomprehension. She kept meeting more and more men, but they all failed to please, were not rich enough or wise enough or poor enough if wise, or were too worldly or unworldly. And through all of this, growing steadily older and handsomer, she bore her singleness like an outrageous pledge of success.

At parties when other girls more nervous than she spilt claret cup or trifle on the hostess's carpet at those endless bring-a-plate kitchen teas she seemed always to be attending, she would say offhandedly, 'Don't worry. It's not *her* trifle,' and go on flirting tangentially and unconsummatedly with this or that. She was moving up the ranks and knew a lot of colonels now.

When the war was over she settled more or less permanently into a cashier's desk at a large hotel where for half a dozen years she was still courted by desperate interstate commercial travellers who, seeing her framed between the stiff geometry of gladioli, found a *quattrocento* (it was the hairstyle) mystique which they did not recognise as such but longed to explore. She accepted their pre-dinner sherries with every symptom of well-bred pleasure, went to films, dog-races, and car-trials with them, but always bade them firm good-nights outside her own apartment.

Then her hair began to show its first grey.

Her father died suddenly shouting at a foreman; and after Clarice had gone home to help out her mother held onto her for quite a while, determined to see her daughter settled. Rallying from grief, she arranged picnics, dances, barbecues, musical evenings, card suppers; yet even she gave up when Clarice returned home far too early from a picnic race-meeting with a *fin de siècle* languor about the eyes.

'Where's that nice Dick Shepworth?' her mother demanded from a veranda spy-post.

'At the races, I suppose.'

'You left him there?'

'Yes. He is suffering from encroaching youth.'

'But, my God!' cried her mother. 'He's the manager of two cane mills with an interest in a third.'

'He holds his knife badly,' Clarice said, picking up a malformed piece of knitting.

'You must be mad,' her mother said.

'And he chews with his mouth open.'

'Oh, my God!'

She was dead by the end of the party season. Clarice got Father Rassini to bury her alongside AG, sub-divided the property, sold at a profit and, having invested with comfortable wisdom in an American mining corporation, retired into her parents' house and spent her days in steady gardening. It became a show place. It was as if all her restrained fertility poured out into the welter of trees and shrubs; and if the rare and heady perfumes of some of them made occasional sensual onslaughts she refused to acknowledge them.

The day she turned forty she bought herself a dog.

He was a fine labrador who established his rights at once, learnt smartly to keep away from the seedling beds and to share her baked dinner. They ate together on the long veranda which stared down at the mined-out hills beyond the garden, and the tender antithesis of this transferred the deepest of green shadows into her mind, so that she found herself more and more frequently talking to Bixer as if he had just made some comment that deserved her reply. Her dependence on him became engrafted in her days: he killed several snakes for her, barked at the right people, and slept, twitching sympathetically with her insomnia, by the side of her bed. She only had to reach down to pat Roy, a colonel, a traveller, or even Dick Shepworth, and they would respond with a wag of the tail.

Although so many years had passed since her parents' deaths, Clarice still believed she had a position in the town and consequently gave a couple of duty dinner parties each year—but not willingly—to which she invited old school friends, townsfolk who still remembered her father, and occasionally Father Rassini. He dreaded the summons, for she was a bad cook; but attended, always hopeful of some generous donation. Aware of this, she would keep him sweating on her Christmas contribution till it was almost Easter; and when she finally handed him the envelope they both remembered her stoniness as he had talked to her, thirty years ago now, about the sins of the flesh. He'd been young, too; and whenever he sat down to an especially lavish meal at some wealthy parishioner's home he recalled her cool look as she had asked, 'Are you ever tempted, Father?'

As her muscles shrank the garden acre flexed its own, strengthened and grew more robust than a lover. There were rheumatic twinges that worried her. One day when she went to rise from where she had been weeding a splendid planting of dwarf poinsettia, the pain in her back was so violent she lay on the grass panting. Bixer nosed around, worried and whimpering, and she told him it was nothing at all; but she thought it was time she got a little help.

She was fifty when she took in Willy Fourcorners as gardener. He was an elderly Aborigine, very quiet, very gentle, who had been for a long time a lay preacher with one of the churches. Clarice didn't know which one, but she felt this made him respectable. Willy wore a dark suit on Sundays, even in summer, and a tie. He would trudge back from the station sometimes, lugging a battered suitcase and, passing Clarice's house and seeing her wrenching at an overgrowth of acalypha, would raise his stained grey hat and smile. The gesture convinced Clarice that though he was a lesser species he was worthy, and she would permit herself to smile back, but briefly.

'Willy,' she said one day, emerging from the croton hedge, 'Willy, I wonder could I ask your help?'

Willy set down his bag in the dust and rubbed his yellow-palmed hands together.

'Yeah, Miss Geary. What's the trouble then?'

She came straight to the point.

'I need help with the garden, Willy.' She was still used to command and the words came out as less of a request than she intended. She was devastated by the ochreous quality of his skin so close to hers and a kindliness in the old eyes she refused to admit, for she could not believe in a Christian blackskin, preacher or not. 'It's all getting too much for me.'

Willy's face remained polite, concerned but doubtful. He was getting on himself and still worked as a handyman at the hardware store. On week-ends he preached.

'Only got Saturdays,' he said.

'Well, what's wrong with Saturday?'

'I like to keep it for m'self.'

Clarice struggled with outrage.

'But wouldn't you like a little extra money, Willy?'

'Not that little, Miss Geary,' Willy said.

Clarice's irritation riveted at once upon the simple smiling face, and unexpectedly, contrarily, she was delighted with his show of strength.

'I'm a fair woman,' she said. 'You'd get regular wages. What I'd give anyone.'

Willy nodded. He still smiled through the sweat that was running down his face, down his old brown neck and into the elderly serge of his only suit.

'Please,' Clarice heard herself pleading. 'Just occasionally. It would be such a help, Willy. You see, I can't handle the mowing these days.' And she produced for him what she had managed to conceal from almost everyone, a right hand swollen and knobbed with arthritis, the fingers craned painfully away from the thumb into the beginnings of a claw.

Willy looked at her hand steadily and then put out one finger very gently as if he were going to touch it. She tried not to wince.

'That hurts bad, eh?' he said. 'Real bad. I'll pray for you, Miss Geary.'

'Don't pray for me, Willy,' Clarice said impatiently. 'Just mow.'

He grinned at that and looked past her at the thick mat of grass that was starting a choking drive about the base of the trees.

'Saturday,' he said. 'Okay.'

He came every few weeks after that and she paid him well; and after a year, as her right hand became worse and the left developed symptoms, he began to take over other jobs — pruning, weeding, planting out, slapping a coat of paint, fixing a rotted veranda board. She grew to look forward to the clear Saturday mornings when with Bixer, ancient, dilapidated, sniffing behind her, she directed him down side paths as he trimmed and lopped the flashy outbursts of the shrubs. Although at first she tended to treat him and pay him off as she would imagine AG to have done, gradually she became, through her own solitariness, aware of him as a human; so that after a time, instead of returning to the veranda for her cup of tea after taking him his, she got into the habit of joining him at the small table in the side garden.

'Where is it you get to, Willy,' she asked one Saturday morning as they drank their tea, 'when you take the train down to the coast?'

'Don't go to the coast, Miss Geary.'

'Where do you go then?'

'Jus' down as far as Mango.'

'Mango?' Clarice exclaimed. 'Why would you want to go to Mango?'

'Visit m'folks there,' he said. 'Got a sister there. Visit her kids. She got seven.'

'Seven,' Clarice murmured. 'Seven.' She thought of Thumper. 'That's a large number, I must say.'

'They're good kids,' Willy said. 'My sister, see, she'd like me to go an' live down there now they're gettin' on a bit.'

'She's younger than you, then, Willy?'

'Yeah. Fair bit younger.'

'And have you any, Willy? Any children, I mean?' She knew he lived alone, had done since she had come back to live.

'Two,' he said. 'Two boys. Wife died of the second one. But they been gone a long time now. Real long time.'

'Where to?'

'South,' he said. 'Down south.'

'And what do they do? Do they write?'

'Yeah. Come home sometimes an' stay with m'sister. One's a driver for some big factory place. Drives a truck, see? Other feller, he's in the church. He's trainin' to go teachin' one of them mission places.'

'Well, he's certainly done well,' Clarice said. 'You must be very proud of him.'

'Pretty proud,' old Willy said. 'Teachin' up the mission when he's through. Up Bamaga way he'll be. Might get to see him then, eh?'

'Do you get lonely, Willy?' she asked. But he didn't answer.

Bixer developed a growth. When Clarice noticed the swelling in his belly she summoned the vet from Finecut who took one look and said, 'I'll give him a shot if you like.'

'Get out!' Clarice said.

She cared for him as far as she was able, but he could only shamble from bedroom to veranda where he'd lie listless most of the day in the hot northern sun, not even bothering to snap at the flies. He lost control of his bladder and whimpered the first time he disgraced himself on the bedroom floor. Clarice whimpered herself as she mopped up.

Willy found her crying over the dog one Saturday morning. Bixer could hardly move now, but his eyes looked their recognition as Willy bent over him.

'Best you get him put away, Miss Geary,' Willy advised, touching the dog with his gentle fingers. 'Pretty old feller now.'

'Help me, Willy,' she said. 'I can't do that.'

He brought along an old tin of ointment he'd used for eczema on a dog of his own, and though he knew it wouldn't help he rubbed it in carefully, if only to help her.

'There y'are, Miss Geary,' he said looking up from where he knelt by the panting dog. 'That might do the trick.'

She was still tearful but she managed a smile at him.

'Thank you, Willy. You're a good man.'

It didn't do the trick; and when finally on one of the endless bland mornings of that week she found he had dragged away to die under the back garden bushes she could hardly bear it. She sat for a little on the veranda, which became populous with the ghosts of the endless summer parties of her youth. The smack of tennis balls came from a hard-court. The blurred voices of bank-clerks and railway-clerks and service men and travellers, and even the sound of Dick Shepworth eating, hummed and babbled along the empty spaces where her mother still sat in her righteous silks.

She put on her sun-hat and walked down town to the hardware store, where she found Willy sweeping out the yard.

'You've got to come, Willy,' she said. 'He's dead.'

'Strewth, Miss Geary. I'm real sorry. Real sorry.'

'You'll have to help me bury him, Willy. I can't dig the hole.'

'Strewth, Miss Geary,' Willy said. 'Don't know whether I kin leave.'

He propped himself on his broom handle and regarded her awkwardly. She was trying hard not to cry. He felt all his age, too, leaning there in the hot sun thinking about death.

'I'll fix that,' she said. She was still AG's daughter.

After it was over she made some tea and took it out to the garden. Willy looked hopelessly at her with his older wisdom.

'Don't you worry none, Miss Geary,' he kept saying. 'I'll get you a new little pup. A new one. Me sister, she got plenty. Jus' don' worry, eh?'

But she was sobbing aloud now, frightful gulping sounds coming from her as she laid her head on her arms along the table.

'Please, Miss Geary,' Willy said. 'Please.'

He touched her hand with his worn one, just a flicker, but she did not notice, did not look up, and he rubbed his hand helplessly across his forehead.

'Look,' he said, 'I got to be goin' soon. But true, me sister she's got these two dogs an' they jus' had pups. I'll get you one of theirs, eh? You'd like that. There's this little brown feller, see, with a white patch. He's a great little dog. You'd like that, eh?'

Slowly she lifted her head, her face ruined with weeping, and saw the old black man and the concern scribbled all over his face.

'Oh, Willy,' she said, 'that's so kind of you. It really is. But it won't make any difference.'

'But it will,' Willy argued, human to human. 'Nex' time I come to mow I'll bring him back. You see. You'll love him.'

He pushed his chair back, came round the table and stood beside her, wanting to cry himself a bit, she looked that old an' lost. She looked up at him, messy with grief, and Willy put his old arm round her shoulders and gave her a consoling pat.

'There,' he said. 'Don' you mind none.'

He'd never seen a face distort so.

She began to scream and scream.

The Cooboo (1932)

—

KATHARINE SUSANNAH PRICHARD

The works of Katharine Susannah Prichard, a prolific writer, are consistently sympathetic toward the less fortunate and particularly sensitive to racial and sexual issues. Here she re-creates life on the large ranches or stations where Aboriginal men and women worked, mostly underpaid, as herders. It is muster time, a roundup, when cattle are gathered for branding and counting.

They had been mustering all day on the wide plains of Murndoo station. Over the red earth, black with ironstone pebbles, through mulga and curari bush, across the ridges which make a blue wall along the horizon. The rosy, garish light of sunset was on plains, hills, moving cattle, men and horses.

Through red dust the bullocks mooched, restless and scary still, a wild mob from the hills: John Gray, in the rear with Arra, the boy who was his shadow: Wongana, on the right with his gin, Rose: Frank, the half-caste, on the left with Minni.

A steer breaking from the mob before Rose, she wheeled and went after him. Faint and wailing, a cry followed her, as though her horse had stepped on and crushed some small creature. But the steer was getting away. Arra went after him, stretched along his horse's neck, rounded the beast and rode him back to the mob, sulky and blethering. The mob swayed. It had broken three times that day.

John Gray called: "You damn fool, Rosey. Finish!"

71

The gin, on her slight, rough-haired horse, pulled up scowling.

"Tell Meetchie, Thirty Mile, tomorrow," John Gray said. "Miah, new moon."

Rose slewed her horse away from the mob of men and cattle. That wailing, thin and hard as hair-string, moved with her.

"Minni!"

John Gray jerked his head towards Rose. Minni's bare heels struck her horse's belly. With a turn of the wrist she swung her horse off from the mob, turned, leaned forward, rising in her stirrups, and came up with Rose. But the glitter and tumult of Rose's eyes, Minni looked away from them.

Thin, dark figures on their wiry station-bred horses, the gins rode into the haze of sunset towards the hills. The dull, dirty blue of the trousers wrapped round their legs was torn; their short, fairish hair tousled by the wind.

At a little distance, when men and cattle were a moving cloud of red dust, Rose's anger gushed after them.

"Koo!"

Fierce as the cry of a hawk flew her last note of derision and defiance.

A far-away rattle of the men's laughter drifted back across country.

Alone the gins would have been afraid, as darkness coming up behind was hovering near them, secreting itself among the low, writhen trees and bushes: afraid of the evil spirits who wander over the plains and stony ridges when the light of day is withdrawn. But together they were not so afraid. Twenty miles away over there, below that dent in the hills where Nyedee Creek made a sandy bed for itself among white-bodied gums, was Murndoo homestead and the uloo of their people.

There was no track; and in the first darkness, thick as wool after the glow of sunset faded, only their instinct would keep them moving in the direction of the homestead and their own low, round huts of bagging, rusty tin and dead boughs.

Both were Wongana's women: Rose, tall, gaunt and masterful; Minni, younger, fat and jolly. Rose had been a good stockman in her day: one of the best. Minni did not ride or track nearly as well as Rose.

And yet, as they rode along, Minni pattered complacently of how well she had worked that day: of how she had flashed, this way and that, heading-off breakaways, dashing after them, turning them back to the mob so smartly that John had said: "Good man, Minni!" There was the white bullock—he had rushed near the yards. Had Rose seen the chestnut mare stumble in a crab-hole and send Arra flying? Minni had chased the white bullock, chased him for a couple of miles, and brought him back to the yards. No doubt there would be nammery for her and a new gina-gina when the men came in from the muster.

She pulled a pipe from her belt, shook the ashes out, and with reins looped over one arm stuffed the bowl with tobacco from a tin tied to her belt. Stooping down, she struck a match on her stirrup-iron, guarded the flame to the pipe between her short, white teeth, and smoked contentedly.

The scowl on Rose's face deepened, darkened. That thin, fretted wailing came from her breast.

She unslung from her neck the rag rope by which the baby had been held against her body, and gave him a sagging breast to suck. Holding him with one arm, she rode slowly, her horse picking his way over the rough, stony earth.

It had been a hard day. The gins were mustering with the men at sunrise. Camped at Nyedee Well the night before, in order to get a good start, they had been riding through the timbered ridges all the morning, rounding up wild cows, calves and young bullocks, and driving them down to the yards at Nyedee, where John Gray cut out the fats, left old Jimmy and a couple of boys to brand calves, turn the cows and calves back to the ridge again while he took on the mob for trucking at Meekatharra. The bullocks were as wild as birds: needed watching all day. And all the time that small, whimpering bundle against her breast had hampered Rose's movements.

There was nothing the gins liked better than a muster, riding after cattle. They were quicker in their movements, more alert than the men, sharper at picking up tracks, but they did not go mustering very often nowadays.

Since John Gray had married, and there was a woman on Murndoo, she found plenty of washing, scrubbing and sweeping for the gins to do: would not spare them often to go after cattle. But John was short-handed. He had said he must have Rose and Minni to muster Nyedee. And all day her baby's crying had irritated Rose. The cooboo had wailed and wailed as she rode with him tied to her body.

The cooboo was responsible for the wrong things she had done all day. Stupid things. Rose was furious. The men had yelled at her. Wongana, her man, blackguarding her before everybody, had called her "a hen who did not know where she laid her eggs". And John Gray, with his "You damn fool, Rosey. Finish!" had sent her home like a naughty child.

Now there was Minni jabbering of the tobacco she would get and the new gina-gina. How pleased Wongana would be with her! And the cooboo, wailing, wailing. He wailed as he chewed Rose's empty breast, squirming against her: wailed and gnawed.

She cried out with hurt and impatience. Rage, irritated to madness, rushed like waters coming down the dry creek-beds after heavy rain. Rose wrenched the cooboo from her breast and flung him from her to the ground. There was a crack as of twigs breaking.

Minni glanced aside. "Wiah!" she gasped, with widening eyes. But Rose rode on, gazing ahead over the rosy, garish plains and wall of the hills, darkening from blue to purple and indigo.

When the women came into the station kitchen, earth, hills and trees were dark: the sky heavy with stars. Minni gave John's wife his message: that he would be home with the new moon, in about a fortnight.

Meetchie, as the blacks called Mrs John Gray, could not make out why the gins were so stiff and quiet: why Rose stalked, scowling and sulky-fellow, sombre eyes just meeting hers, and moving away again. Meetchie wanted to ask about the muster: what sort of condition the bullocks had been in; how many were on the road; if many calves had been branded at Nyedee. But she knew the women too well to ask questions when they looked like that.

Only when she had given them bread and a tin of jam, cut off hunks of corned beef for them, filled their billies with strong black tea, put sugar in their empty tins, and the gins were going off to the uloo, she realised that Rose was not carrying her baby as usual.

"Why, Rose," she exclaimed, "where's the cooboo?"

Rose stalked off into the night. Minni glanced back with scared eyes and followed Rose.

In the dawn, when a cry, remote and anguished flew through the clear air, Meetchie wondered who was dead in the camp by the creek. She remembered how Rose had looked the night before, when she asked about the cooboo.

Now, she knew the cooboo had died; Rose was wailing for him in the dawn, cutting herself with stones until her body bled, and screaming in the fury of her grief.

FROM
Dr. Wooreddy's Prescription for Enduring the Ending of the World (1983)

COLIN JOHNSON

The setting for this novel is colonial Tasmania in the years when Tas-
manian Aborigines were being destroyed. Johnson's hero, Dr. Wooreddy,
is a wise and learned man of the Bruny Island Aborigines. It is his fate
to witness the destruction of his people as they come under the so-called
protection of George Augustus Robinson, a true historical figure, ap-
pointed Protector of the Aborigines and Commandant of the Flinders
Island Aboriginal Establishment. Johnson portrays this genocide through
Wooreddy's at first uncomprehending, but soon discerning, eyes. We feel
Wooreddy's loss and his puzzlement over the irrational behavior of the
invaders.

The excerpt included here concerns Wooreddy's return to his home-
land, Bruny Island. Having left his home seven years before to escape the
intruding ghosts, or num (white men), Wooreddy has married, become a
father, and participated in an Aboriginal spear attack on a white settler's
hut. By returning, he wishes to see for himself whether it is possible to live
with white men.

Wooreddy stood on the shore staring across the narrow stretch of water. He saw the familiar dips and swells of his island and recognised the few thin lines of smoke as those belonging to his people—but at one point thick foggy masses of *num* smoke hung in the air like a bad omen. As he watched, fog streaked in from the sea to unite with the thick masses of smoke from the fires used to render down whale-blubber into oil. Things had indeed changed since the good doctor had been away. The island vanished from his view, and muttering a spell of protection, Wooreddy set about building a catamaran large enough to transport himself and his children.

Using the sharp *num* hatchet which had been his share of the loot from the hut, he hacked away at the bottom of reeds. He cut and collected a large pile. After laying them out and separating them into three bundles, he bound them together with the thin grass-cord his wife was twisting together. He went to the trees above the beach and using his hatchet cut out long squares of bark which he trimmed to the length of the reed rolls. These he bound around the bundles. If the voyage had been longer, grease would have been smeared over the outer surface of the bark to make them watertight. Wooreddy placed the long three-metre roll in the middle of the two shorter ones, then tightened them together with the net his wife had roughly woven. Now the catamaran had a canoe-shape with the bow and stern higher than the middle. Wooreddy hesitated to push it into the water. He trusted his work, but he did not trust the sea with all its lurking demons or demon, depending on the viewpoint held. He evaded any urge to ponder on the mystery and set about the ritual to keep it or them at bay. After patting mud into a square-shaped fireplace on the high stern of the catamaran, he lit a small fire there while singing the appropriate spell. The earth and the square shape of the fireplace and of the netting held the magic and not the fire. Wooreddy carefully finished the ritual and spell. Everything had been just right. A mistake, even a tiny one, might cause disaster. Gingerly, he pushed the craft into the surf until it floated. After putting the two boys aboard, he scrambled on. The catamaran settled a little, but still rode high fore and aft. His wife, Lunna, protected by her femaleness from the sea, pushed the craft into deeper water, then clinging onto the stern propelled it forward with kicks from her powerful legs.

Wooreddy's eyes clung to the shape of his approaching island. This kept his mind from the encircling water; it gave him solace, and then the earth, which had formed his body and given the hardness to his bones, did have the power to draw him back. This, in a sense, was what was happening now. He had not determined to return home, but forces had determined that he return home. One such force was that of the earth of his home. He dreaded what he would find there. Then he noticed that the catamaran, for apparently no reason, was making a wide detour around an open patch of water. His nervous eyes had glanced down for a second. Now they stayed on the water. Alarm thudded his heart. If he had been able he would have returned to the mainland at once. But then, what if he had returned to the mainland? Only the west coast remained free, and for how long? In the long run, to survive meant accepting that the ghosts were here to stay and learning to live amongst them, or at least next to them until—until the ending of the world! This was the only reason why Wooreddy wanted to live on—and in a friendless world! It was one of the reasons why he had left the relative peace and security of his wife's village.

He let the sight in the water enter into his mind. A bloody patch slowly spreading in circles of pinkish foam as a drizzle of rain fell from the grey sky. He shivered, feeling the presence of *Ria Warrawah*. The patch of blood turned a dull red, the colour of the ochre smeared in his hair. Just below the surface of the water, the dark body of a man drifted hazily like some evil sea creature. It quivered and turned dead eyes on him as Lunna's powerful kick sent the catamaran past and scooting towards what might be the safety of the shore.

At last they grounded. Wooreddy leapt out and raced to the shelter of the undergrowth. Behind him pelted his wife and children. Safely hidden, they stared back towards the beach. The waves marched in assault lines against the land. Wooreddy saw the smoke rising from the stern of the catamaran and remembered his vow always to protect fire. But he hesitated and caused its death. The waves had driven the catamaran broadside to the surf. Now they capsized it. *Ria Warrawah* killed the fire. Then he found that he had left his spear behind. It floated in the surf. He left it there. He still had his club, and a spear, these days, was too much like a broken arm. Calling to his wife and children, he walked along the remembered track leading off this side of the bay. They followed it up over a rise, through thick undergrowth, then around the edge of a small cove. There another sight struck them a blow. The island,

Wooreddy's own earth, had been taken over by ghosts. His wife and children huddled in terror at his side, but the good Doctor Wooreddy donned his cloak of numbness and observed the scene with all the detachment of a scientist.

On the soft, wet beach-sand a naked brown-skinned woman was being assaulted by four ghosts. One held both of her arms over her head causing her breasts to jut into the low-lying clouds; two more each clung to a powerful leg, and the fourth thudded away in the vee. Wooreddy could see only the cropped head of the woman and not her face. The ghost stopped his thudding between her legs and fell limply on her body for a minute, then jerked away, knelt and got to his feet. The doctor noted with interest the whiteness of the ghost's penis. He had accepted the fact of their having a penis—after all they were known to attack women—but he had never thought it would be white. He filed this probably useless piece of information in his mind and watched on. The ghost hid his unnatural organ in his pants, then reached for the arms of the woman. The one holding them, possibly eager for his turn, released his grip and she had her arms free. She did nothing. Experimentally, the other two loosened their hold on her legs. She remained still. The three stood up and watched as the fourth jerked out his pale, bloodless penis, knelt, and lunged forward.

'Hey, Paddy, leave a bit for us,' one yelled. The sound drifted up to Wooreddy. He wondered about the grammatical structure and idiosyncrasies of their language as the rape continued.

'Arrh, Jack, got her all loosened up. Now she's just lying there enjoying every minute of it,' Paddy finally grunted up, spacing the words to the rhythm of his body.

Wooreddy wondered if the ghosts had honorifics and specific forms of address. Perhaps it was not even a real language?—but then each and every species of animal had a language, and so it must be! The kangaroos, possums and even snakes—and though it was not universally accepted, the trees and plants—all had a language. Even the clouds and wind conversed together. Some gifted men and women could listen and understand what they were talking about. It was even debated that such men and women could make them carry them to see a distant friend and after return them to their starting point. It could be true, for he knew that the whole earth murmured with the conversations of the myriad species of things and to understand what they were saying would be to understand all creation.

Paddy finished with a grunt and got off and up. Another took his place while Wooreddy wondered about the necessity of covering the body with skins rather than grease. It was the way of these *num* and could be compared with the strange custom of the North West Nation where women did not crop their hair. He thought about how different peoples held and shaped spears. Variations based on the series of actions of holding and sharpening which were individual to each person, and as they were individual to each person so were they to each nation and even community. Another *num* came and went—to be replaced by another.

The circle circled while the day flowed towards the evening. Wooreddy knew that he and his family had to leave soon if they were to make the camping place by nightfall. He was beginning to find the rape a little tedious. What was the use of knowing that the *num* were overgreedy for women just as they were overgreedy for everything? He could have deduced this from the record of their previous actions and they did appear fixed and immutable in their ways. At long last the rape ground to an end. The *num* without a final glance at the sprawling woman walked off to a boat Wooreddy had not noticed drawn up on the beach. They got in and began rowing across the bay like a spider walking on water.

A few minutes after they had left, the woman got to her feet. The doctor parted the mists of seven years to recognise the youngest daughter of Mangana grown into a woman of seventeen years. She looked a good strong female with the firm, squat body of a provider. Unsteadily she managed a few steps, then stood swaying on her feet. Slowly her face lifted and her dull eyes brightened as she saw Wooreddy standing in the undergrowth. She glared into his eyes, spat in his direction, then turned and dragged her hips down to the waves subsiding in the long rays of the sun setting in a swirl of clearing cloud. He watched as she squatted in the water and began cleaning herself. Then he turned to his wife, told her to follow him, and waddled away with Trugernanna's glare, that dull then bright gaze filled with spite and contempt, in his mind. It upset him and dispelled his numbness which, fortunately for

Wooreddy (though he often didn't realise it) was not the impervious shield of his theorising, and could be easily penetrated. Why had she looked at him in such a way? After all it had been the *num* who had raped her. He would never do such a thing! He thought on as he waddled along in that peculiar gait which had earned him the name, Wooreddy — '*duck*' — and finally concluded that it was a waste of time to try to divine anything about females. What was important about Trugernanna, he recalled, was that she was a survivor. This was what made her important to him — though she did have the body of a good provider!

The track ended in a clearing at the side of a long sweeping bay. Here he found Mangana much the same as seven years ago. He sat alone, smiling into his fire. Wooreddy waited until the older man glanced up and beckoned to him to sit. He sat and waited. Mangana looked across and smiled, not a smile of greeting, but one of resignation. To the old man's despondency over the loss of his first wife had been added that caused by the loss of a second. Now he filled Wooreddy in with the details, using the rich language of an elder. It was part gesture, part expression, part pure feeling allied to a richness of words moulded together in a grammatic structure complex with the experience of the life lived. It was a new and full experience for Wooreddy. The white cloud sails bulged, fluttered like the wings of birds and collapsed in a torrent of rain; a baby boat crawled from the strangeness of its mother ship-island; tottered across the waves on unsteady legs; dragged its tiny body up onto the shore — and reached out insect arms to Mangana's mate. Charmed, she enticed herself to it; charmed, she wanted the insect arms around her and her own arms around the soft body; charmed, she let herself be enticed by the infant-boat to the terrible mothership. Many legs walked the child to it and Mangana's wife was taken along to where the sails fluttered like seagulls, and flew out to sea. The loss of the mate was conveyed by a terrible feeling of emptiness, of the lack felt by the absence of a good provider not filled by the presence of a single young daughter, fickle and strange with the times and often not to be found and not to be managed. Mangana took up the subject of his daughter. With a finger he painted in the soft ashes at the edge of the fire her symbol and her actions.

She spent too much time watching the *num* and being with the *num*. From them she received ghost food, two whites and a black: flour, sugar and tea. He himself had acquired a taste for these strange foods since he rarely hunted and relied on his daughter for provisions. He projected the death of a son at Wooreddy. They lived through it right to the final ashes. Mangana left mental pain to wander in physical pain. He relived the time he had been washed out to sea. His water-logged catamaran sagged beneath his weight and every wave washed over him. All around him the surge of the sea, the breathing of *Ria Warrawah*. A *num* boat came sailing along. Ghosts pulled him from the clutches of *Ria Warrawah*. This affected him even more than the other events as it involved a contradiction: why had the *num*, who allegedly came from *it*, saved him from *its* domain? Unable to formulate a theory to explain this, he now felt that he belonged, or at the least owed his very life, to the ghosts and thus existed only on their whim. They had claimed his soul and sooner rather than later would take it if he could not create a nexus to prevent them from doing so.

Mangana declared with more determination than he had so far shown: 'The *num* think they have me—but an initiated man is never had. He knows how to walk the coloured path to the sparkling path which leads to where the fires flicker in Great Ancestor's camp. There they are forbidden to come, and even now I am building up my fire there.'

Wooreddy nodded. He knew that the older a man grew the more he received and found. Sometimes the old ones had so much knowledge that they could make the very earth tremble. It was even rumoured that they could fly to the sky-land while still alive. Respectfully he kept his eyes lowered. Here was one of the last elders of the Bruny Island people famed for their spiritual knowledge.

'My daughter, she is yours when I go,' the old man said suddenly to him, smiling with a humour which showed that he knew a little too much about Trugernanna—and about Wooreddy!

Wooreddy lifted his head in surprise and lowered it in confusion. He tried to mask his thoughts from the old man. Thankfully Lunna returned with her basket filled with abalone and four crayfish which occupied all of Mangana's attention. His daughter might have the body of a good provider, but she failed to live up to it.

Mangana slavered for the succulent crayfish. His eyes flickered from them to Wooreddy's motions in heaping up the coals of the fire. His eyes lingered on the dark-greenish body of a giant cray as Wooreddy gently and lovingly (at least so it seemed to Mangana) placed it on the coals. He watched as the dark shell began to turn a lightish ochre-red. He openly sighed as Wooreddy with two forked sticks lifted it off the fire, placed it on a piece of bark and put it in front of him. It was delicious, and the first bite freed his attention. He smiled as Wooreddy gave the next one to his wife, and the third to be divided between his children. The younger man felt the eyes on him and would have blushed if he could. On Bruny Island the custom was that first (or, in this case, secondly) the husband took what he wanted and left the remainder for his wife and children. He, without thinking, had done what he had done from the time he had been married and then a father. Ayah! Indeed he had been caught like the crayfish he was eating and put in the basket of this foreign woman without even realising it. He consoled himself with the thought that it must be the times.

Bruny Island had become a cemetery. When Wooreddy had left he had known that his community was dying. Now he found it all but gone. Only Mangana, he and a few females remained alive. The ownership of the island would pass to him, but this was meaningless. Bruny Island belonged to the ghosts. The land rang with their axes, marking it anew just as Great Ancestor had done in the distant past. He heard the crash of falling trees as he watched *num* boats towing to the shore one of the huge animals cursed by *Ria Warrawah*. Like all good animals, they had never got over their capture and often tried to return to the land. *Ria Warrawah* to prevent their escape had slashed off their legs, but this did not stop them from flinging themselves onto the beach. Huge and legless, they would lie helpless on the land, baking under the sun or wheezing under the clouds. They suffered, but never did they try to return to the hated ocean. These large animals, because they belonged to the land, could be eaten along with crayfish, penguins, seals and shellfish. The blubber provided the best oil for smearing the body and catamarans. After one came ashore and was eaten, the giant cradle of bones was flung back into the sea, not as an offering, but in contempt and defiance—to show *Ria Warrawah* that land animals would never belong to him.

Although Wooreddy went to the whaling station to get some of the flesh which the ghosts flung away, he took care that his woman did not go with him. Trugernanna and the other island women went there for both food and excitement. They often spent days at the station and when they finally came back to the camp, they carried with them ghost food. Mangana liked this food and had even begun to smoke the strange herb, tobacco, which his daughter had shown him how to use. He wore over his body a large soft skin which had been given to Trugernanna. He wore this as a sign of surrender and urged Wooreddy to do the same. The *num* were provoked by a naked body so much so that they often killed it. *Num* skins protected a person and if one continued to go naked one courted death. With such a choice before him, Wooreddy took to wearing a blanket.

The ghosts had twisted and upturned everything, Wooreddy thought one day as he went a step further and accepted a *num* skin from a ghost he found with his wife. This did not upset him much as the woman had so increased her demands on him that he had found himself a typical Bruny Islander saddled with a foreign wife. He still consoled himself with the thought that it was the times, and the *num* skin did hide his manhood scars. Not so very long ago, Wooreddy had prided himself on showing the serried rows of arc-shaped scars which showed the degrees of initiation he had passed. Now they had lost all meaning, just as all else had lost meaning. Such alienation brought lassitude and the sudden panic fear that his soul was under attack. To counter this, he pushed his way into the depths of a thicket and made a circular clearing while muttering powerful protection spells. Then he built a small fire in the centre of the circle, heated a piece of shell in the smoke and opened a number of his scars with it. Blood drops fell towards the flames. Anxiously he watched each drop hiss into steam before touching any of the burning brands. This was good: his spells potent and protection assured. Lighting a firestick in order to preserve the strong life of this fire, he took it back and thrust it into the main campfire. His wife was still absent at the whaling station.

Lunna finally returned from the embraces of the *num*. She

carried a bag in which twists of cloth held flour, tea and sugar. Already she had learnt to boil the dark leaves in a shell-like container which did not catch fire and to make 'damper' by mixing the white powder with water and spreading it on hot coals. Wooreddy found that he liked the tea especially when some of the white sand-like grains were added, but the damper stuck in his throat. He preferred seafood, when he could get it, for sometimes when he ordered his wife to go and get some she appeared not to hear. Her large dark eyes would cling to whatever she was doing and she would ignore him. Once when he asked her she continued eating a piece of damper and he took up his spear and felt the tip. It was blunt. He went to the shelter for a sharp piece of stone, then remembered the hatchet and got that instead.

After sharpening his spear, he waddled off to the hunt without a word to his wife. She watched his bottom wobbling off into the bush and smiled. It was one of the things that had attracted her to him. It added a touch of humour which helped to soften his stiff formality of manner. They had had a good relationship, but not as deep as it could have been. Perhaps it was because he belonged to a nation noted for their stiffness. She sighed and began thinking of the *num*.

Wooreddy, not thinking of his wife or his problems, began prowling towards a clearing which had been maintained for a long time and was still not overgrown. With his senses straining for the slightest movement or sound, he achieved a state of blissful concentration which smothered all disagreeable thought. In the clearing three large grey kangaroos hunched, nibbling at the tufts of grass. He crouched behind the trunk of a tree, thanking Great Ancestor that the wind blew in his face, though as a good hunter he had allowed for this. Wooreddy inched forward. One of the animals lifted a delicate face to peer his way. He stopped and after a few moments the animal bent its back to eat the grass. The stalking continued until Wooreddy judged himself close enough to risk a spear throw. Slowly he lifted his leg to take the shaft from between his big toe. Ever so slowly his arm rose as his leg descended at an angle to support his throw. With a lightning-fast stroke, which contrasted with his previous slowness, his spear flashed towards the prey. The force of the blow sent it sprawling onto its side. It leapt up and tried to bound away. It managed only a stagger. The long spear aborted its bound. The kangaroo recovered enough to hop away. Wooreddy trotted after the animal.

In the sudden joy at his success, he had forgotten his club, but no matter. He ran on in his curious duck-like gait which appeared clumsy but was effective. He quickly came upon the animal. It turned to face its pursuer with its back protected by the trunk of a thick tree. Wooreddy picked up a piece of wood as he circled the animal. At bay, it was dangerous. One sudden upward rip of a hind leg could disembowel him. If only he had a companion such as Mangana! Alone, he devised a tactic and ran straight at the kangaroo. At the very last moment he bounded to the left. Animals were like human beings and usually favoured the right side—but not always. He breathed a sigh of relief as the animal brought up its right leg. A fatal move: before the animal could recover he had bashed the thick stick down upon its nose, then belted it on one side of the neck. Wooreddy flung the carcass across his shoulder and took it back to camp. He would feed his sons real food, and not that white junk their mother too often served up.

Going Home (1986)

ARCHIE WELLER

"Going Home" was originally published in Weller's volume of short stories by the same name, the first collection by an Aboriginal author. The difficulties of being half-Aboriginal are important in this narrative, as is another significant theme—the problem of returning home when one is denied the right to be there.

> I want to go home.
> I want to go home.
> Oh, Lord, I want to go home.

Charlie Pride moans from a cassette, and his voice slips out of the crack the window makes. Out into the world of magpies' soothing carols, and parrots' cheeky whistles, of descending darkness and spirits.

The man doesn't know that world. His is the world of the sleek new Kingswood that speeds down the never-ending highway.

At last he can walk this earth with pride, as his ancestors did many years before him. He had his first exhibition of paintings a month ago. They sold well, and with the proceeds he bought the car.

The slender black hands swing the shiny black wheel around a corner. Blackness forms a unison of power.

For five years he has worked hard and saved and sacrificed. Now, on his twenty-first birthday, he is going home.

New car, new clothes, new life.

He plucks a cigarette from the packet beside him, and lights up.

His movements are elegant and delicate. His hair is well-groomed, and his clothes are clean.

Billy Woodward is coming home in all his might, in his shining armour.

Sixteen years old. Last year at school.

His little brother Carlton and his cousin Rennie Davis, down beside the river, on that last night before he went to the college in Perth, when all three had had a goodbye drink, with their girls beside them.

Frogs croaking into the silent hot air and some animal blundering in the bullrushes on the other side of the gentle river. Moonlight on the ruffled water. Nasal voices whispering and giggling. The clink of beer bottles.

That year at college, with all its schoolwork, and learning, and discipline, and uniformity, he stood out alone in the football carnival.

Black hands grab the ball. Black feet kick the ball. Black hopes go soaring with the ball to the pasty white sky.

No one can stop him now. He forgets about the river of his Dreaming and the people of his blood and the girl in his heart.

The year when he was eighteen, he was picked by a top city team as a rover. This was the year that he played for the state, where he was voted best and fairest on the field.

That was a year to remember.

He never went out to the park at Guildford, so he never saw his people: his dark, silent staring people, his rowdy, brawling, drunk people.

He was white now.

Once, in the middle of the night, one of his uncles had crept around to the house he rented and fallen asleep on the verandah. A dirty pitiful carcass, encased in a black greatcoat that had smelt of stale drink and lonely, violent places. A withered black hand had clutched an almost-empty metho bottle.

In the morning, Billy had shouted at the old man and pushed him down the steps, where he stumbled and fell without pride.

The old man had limped out of the creaking gate, not understanding.

The white neighbours, wakened by the noise, had peered out of their windows at the staggering old man stumbling down the street and the glowering youth muttering on the verandah. They had smirked in self-righteous knowledge.

Billy had moved on the next day.

William Jacob Woodward passed fifth year with flying colours. All the teachers were proud of him. He went to the West Australian Institute of Technology to further improve his painting, to gain fame that way as well.

He bought clean, bright clothes and cut off his long hair that all the camp girls had loved.

Billy Woodward was a handsome youth, with the features of his white grandfather and the quietness of his Aboriginal forebears. He stood tall and proud, with the sensitive lips of a dreamer and a faraway look in his serene amber eyes.

He went to the nightclubs regularly and lost his soul in the throbbing, writhing electrical music as the white tribe danced their corroboree to the good life.

He would sit alone at a darkened corner table, or with a painted-up white girl—but mostly alone. He would drink wine and look around the room at all the happy or desperate people.

He was walking home one night from a nightclub when a middle-aged Aboriginal woman stumbled out of a lane.

She grinned up at him like the Gorgon and her hands clutched at his body, like the lights from the nightclub.

'Billy! Ya Billy Woodward, unna?'

'Yes. What of it?' he snapped.

'Ya dunno me? I'm ya Auntie Rose, from down Koodup.'

She cackled then. Ugly, oh, so ugly. Yellow and red eyes and broken teeth and a long, crooked, white scar across her temple. Dirty grey hair all awry.

His people.

His eyes clouded over in revulsion. He shoved her away and walked off quickly.

He remembered her face for many days afterwards whenever he tried to paint a picture. He felt ashamed to be related to a thing like that. He was bitter that she was of his blood.

That was his life: painting pictures and playing football and pretending. But his people knew. They always knew.

In his latest game of football he had a young part-Aboriginal opponent who stared at him the whole game with large, scornful black eyes seeing right through him.

After the game, the boy's family picked him up in an old battered station wagon.

Billy, surrounded by all his white friends, saw them from afar off. He saw the children kicking an old football about with yells and shouts of laughter and two lanky boys slumping against the door yarning to their hero, and a buxom girl leaning out the window and an old couple in the back. The three boys, glancing up, spotted debonair Billy. Their smiles faded for an instant and they speared him with their proud black eyes.

So Billy was going home, because he had been reminded of home (with all its carefree joys) at that last match. It is raining now. The shafts slant down from the sky, in the glare of the headlights. Night-time, when woodarchis come out to kill, leaving no tracks: as though they are cloud shadows passing over the sun.

Grotesque trees twist in the half-light. Black tortured figures, with shaggy heads and pleading arms. Ancestors crying for remembrance. Voices shriek or whisper in tired chants: tired from the countless warnings that have not been heeded.

They twirl around the man, like the lights of the city he knows. But he cannot understand these trees. They drag him onwards, even when he thinks of turning back and not going on to where he vowed he would never go again.

A shape, immovable and impassive as the tree it is under, steps into the road on the Koodup turnoff.

An Aboriginal man.

Billy slews to a halt, or he will run the man over.

Door opens.

Wind and rain and coloured man get in.

'Ta, mate. It's bloody cold 'ere,' the coloured man grates, then stares quizzically at Billy, with sharp black eyes. 'Nyoongah, are ya, mate?'

'Yes.'

The man sniffs noisily, and rubs a sleeve across his nose.

'Well, I'm Darcy Goodrich, any rate, bud.'

He holds out a calloused hand. Yellow-brown, blunt scarred fingers, dirty nails. A lifetime of sorrow is held between the fingers.

Billy takes it limply.

'I'm William Woodward.'

'Yeah?' Fathomless eyes scrutinise him again from behind the scraggly black hair that falls over his face.

'Ya goin' anywheres near Koodup, William?'

'Yes.'

'Goodoh. This is a nice car ya got 'ere. Ya must 'ave plen'y of boya, unna?'

Silence from Billy.

He would rather not have this cold, wet man beside him, reminding him. He keeps his amber eyes on the lines of the road as they flash under his wheels.

White . . . white . . . white . . .

'Ya got a smoke, William?'

'Certainly. Help yourself.'

Black blunt fingers flick open his expensive cigarette case.

'Ya want one too, koordah?'

'Thanks.'

'Ya wouldn't be Teddy Woodward's boy, would ya, William?'

'Yes, that's right. How are Mum and Dad—and everyone?'

Suddenly he has to know all about his family and become lost in their sea of brownness.

Darcy's craggy face flickers at him in surprise, then turns, impassive again, to the rain-streaked window. He puffs on his cigarette quietly.

'What, ya don't know?' he says softly. 'Ya Dad was drinkin' metho. 'E was blind drunk, an' in the 'orrors, ya know? Well, this truck came out of nowhere when 'e was crossin' the road on a night like this. Never seen 'im. Never stopped or nothin'. Ya brother Carl found 'im next day an' there was nothin' no one could do then. That was a couple of years back now.'

Billy would have been nineteen then, at the peak of his football triumph. On one of those bright white nights, when he had celebrated his victories with wine and white women, Billy's father had been wiped off the face of his country—all alone.

He can remember his father as a small gentle man who was the best card cheat in the camp. He could make boats out of duck feathers and he and Carlton and Billy had had races by the muddy side of the waterhole, from where his people had come long ago, in the time of the beginning.

The lights of Koodup grin at him as he swings around a bend. Pinpricks of eyes, like a pack of foxes waiting for the blundering black rabbit.

'Tell ya what, buddy. Stop off at the hotel an' buy a carton of stubbies.'

'All right, Darcy.' Billy smiles and looks closely at the man for the first time. He desperately feels that he needs a friend as he goes back into the open mouth of his previous life. Darcy gives a gap-toothed grin.

'Bet ya can't wait to see ya people again.'

His people: ugly Auntie Rose, the metho-drinking Uncle, his dead forgotten father, his wild brother and cousin. Even this silent man. They are all his people.

He can never escape.

The car creeps in beside the red brick hotel.

The two Nyoongahs scurry through the rain and shadows and into the glare of the small hotel bar.

The barman is a long time coming, although the bar is almost empty. Just a few old cockies and young larrikins, right down the other end. Arrogant grey eyes stare at Billy. No feeling there at all.

'A carton of stubbies, please.'

'Only if you bastards drink it down at the camp. Constable told me you mob are drinking in town and just causing trouble.'

'We'll drink where we bloody like, thanks, mate.'

'Will you, you cheeky bastard?' The barman looks at Billy, in surprise. 'Well then, you're not gettin' nothin' from me. You can piss off, too, before I call the cops. They'll cool you down, you smart black bastard.'

Something hits Billy deep inside with such force that it makes him want to clutch hold of the bar and spew up all his pride.

He is black and the barman is white, and nothing can ever change that.

All the time he had gulped in the wine and joy of the nightclubs and worn neat fashionable clothes and had white women admiring him, played the white man's game with more skill than most of the wadgulas and painted his country in white man colours to be gabbled over by the wadgulas: all this time he has ignored his mumbling, stumbling tribe and thought he was someone better.

Yet when it comes down to it all, he is just a black man.

Darcy sidles up to the fuming barman.

' 'Scuse me, Mr 'Owett, but William 'ere just come 'ome, see,' he whines like a beaten dog. 'We *will* be drinkin' in the camp, ya know.'

'Just come home, eh? What was he inside for?'

Billy bites his reply back so it stays in his stomach, hard and hurtful as a gallstone.

'Well all right, Darcy. I'll forget about it this time. Just keep your friend out of my hair.'

Good dog, Darcy. Have a bone, Darcy. Or will a carton of stubbies do?

Out into the rain again.

They drive away and turn down a track about a kilometre out of town.

Darcy tears off a bottle top, handing the bottle to Billy. He grins.

'Act stupid, buddy, an' ya go a lo—ong way in this town.'

Billy takes a long draught of the bitter golden liquid. It pours down his throat and into his mind like a shaft of amber sunlight after a gale. He lets his anger subside.

'What ya reckon, Darcy? I'm twenty-one today.'

Darcy thrusts out a hand, beaming.

'Tw'n'y-bloody-one, eh? 'Ow's it feel?'

'No different from yesterday.'

Billy clasps the offered hand firmly.

They laugh and clink bottles together in a toast, just as they reach the camp.

Dark and wet, with a howling wind. Rain beating upon the shapeless humpies. Trees thrash around the circle of the clearing in a violent rhythm of sorrow and anger, like great monsters dancing around a carcass.

Darcy indicates a hut clinging to the edge of the clearing.

'That's where ya mum lives.'

A rickety shape of nailed-down tin and sheets of iron. Two oatbags, sewn together, form a door. Floundering in a sea of tins and rags and parts of toys or cars. Mud everywhere.

Billy pulls up as close to the door as he can get. He had forgotten what his house really looked like.

'Come on, koordah. Come an' see ya ole mum. Ya might be lucky, too, an' catch ya brother.'

Billy can't say anything. He gets slowly out of the car while the dereliction looms up around him.

The rain pricks at him, feeling him over.

He is one of the brotherhood.

A mouth organ's reedy notes slip in and out between the rain. It is at once a profoundly sorrowful yet carefree tune that goes on and on.

Billy's fanfare home.

He follows Darcy, ducking under the bag door. He feels unsure and out of place and terribly alone.

There are six people: two old women, an ancient man, two youths and a young, shy, pregnant woman.

The youth nearest the door glances up with a blank yellowish face, suspicion embedded deep in his black eyes. His long black hair that falls over his shoulders in gentle curls is kept from his face by a red calico headband. Red for the desert sands whence his ancestors came, red for the blood spilt by his ancestors when the white tribe came. Red, the only bright thing in these drab surroundings.

The youth gives a faint smile at Darcy and the beer.

'G'day, Darcy. Siddown 'ere. 'Oo ya mate is?'

' 'Oo'd ya think, Carl, ya dopy prick? 'E's ya brother come 'ome.'

Carlton stares at Billy incredulously, then his smile widens a little and he stands up, extending a slim hand.

They shake hands and stare deep into each other's faces, smiling. Brown-black and brown-yellow. They let their happiness soak silently into each other.

Then his cousin Rennie, also tall and slender like a young boomer, with bushy red-tinged hair and eager grey eyes, shakes hands. He introduces Billy to his young woman, Phyllis, and reminds him who old China Groves and Florrie Waters (his mother's parents) are.

His mother sits silently at the scarred kitchen table. Her wrinkled brown face has been battered around, and one of her eyes is sightless. The other stares at her son with a bleak pride of her own.

From that womb I came, Billy thinks, like a flower from the ground or a fledgling from the nest. From out of the reserve I flew.

Where is beauty now?

He remembers his mother as a laughing brown woman, with long black hair in plaits, singing soft songs as she cleaned the house or cooked food. Now she is old and stupid in the mourning of her man.

'So ya come back after all. Ya couldn't come back for ya Dad's funeral, but—unna? Ya too good for us mob, I 'pose,' she whispers in a thin voice like the mouth organ before he even says hello, then turns her eyes back into her pain.

'It's my birthday, Mum. I wanted to see everybody. No one told me Dad was dead.'

Carlton looks up at Billy.

'I make out ya twenty-one, Billy.'

'Yes.'

'Well, shit, we just gotta 'ave a party.' Carlton half-smiles. 'We gotta get more drink, but,' he adds.

Carlton and Rennie drive off to town in Billy's car. When they leave, Billy feels unsure and alone. His mother just stares at him. Phyllis keeps her eyes glued on the mound of her womb and the grandparents crow to Darcy, camp talk he cannot understand.

The cousins burst through the door with a carton that Carlton drops on the table, then he turns to his brother. His smooth face holds the look of a small child who is about to show his father something he has achieved. His dark lips twitch as they try to keep from smiling.

' 'Appy birthday, Billy, ya ole cunt,' Carlton says, and produces a shining gold watch from the ragged pocket of his black jeans.

'It even works, Billy,' grins Rennie from beside his woman, so Darcy and China laugh.

The laughter swirls around the room like dead leaves from a tree.

They drink. They talk. Darcy goes home and the old people go to bed. His mother has not talked to Billy all night. In the morning he will buy her some pretty curtains for the windows and make a proper door and buy her the best dress in the shop.

They chew on the sweet cud of their past. The memories seep through Billy's skin so he isn't William Woodward the talented football player and artist, but Billy the wild, half-naked boy, with his shock of hair and carefree grin and a covey of girls fluttering around his honey body.

Here they are—all three together again, except now young Rennie is almost a father and Carlton has just come from three months' jail. And Billy? He is nowhere.

At last, Carlton yawns and stretches.

'I reckon I'll 'it that bed.' Punches his strong brother gently on the shoulder. 'See ya t'morrow, Billy, ole kid.' He smiles.

Billy camps beside the dying fire. He rolls himself into a bundle of ragged blankets on the floor and stares into the fire. In his mind he can hear his father droning away, telling legends that he half-remembered, and his mother softly singing hymns. Voices and memories and woodsmoke drift around him. He sleeps.

He wakes to the sound of magpies carolling in the still trees. Rolls up off the floor and rubs the sleep from his eyes. Gets up and stacks the blankets in a corner, then creeps out to the door.

Carlton's eyes peep out from the blankets on his bed.

'Where ya goin'?' he whispers.

'Just for a walk.'

'Catch ya up, Billy,' he smiles sleepily. With his headband off, his long hair falls every way.

Billy gives a salutation and ducks outside.

A watery sun struggles up over the hills and reflects in the orange puddles that dot the camp. Broken glass winks white, like the bones of dead animals. Several children play with a drum, rolling it at each other and trying to balance on it. Several young men stand around looking at Billy's car. He nods at them and they nod back. Billy stumbles over to the ablution block: three bent and rusty showers and a toilet each for men and women. Names and slogans are scribbled on every available space. After washing away the staleness of the beer he heads for the waterhole, where memories of his father linger. He wants — a lot — to remember his father.

He squats there, watching the ripples the light rain makes on the serene green surface. The bird calls from the jumble of green-brown-black bush are sharp and clear, like the echoes of spirits calling to him.

He gets up and wanders back to the humpy. Smoke from fires wisps up into the grey sky.

Just as he slouches to the edge of the clearing, a police van noses its way through the mud and water and rubbish. A pale, hard, supercilious face peers out at him. The van stops.

'Hey, you! Come here!'

The people at the fires watch, from the corner of their eyes, as he idles over.

'That your car?'

Billy nods, staring at the heavy, blue-clothed sergeant. The driver growls, 'What's your name, and where'd you get the car?'

'I just told you it's my car. My name's William Jacob Woodward, if it's any business of yours,' Billy flares.

The sergeant's door opens with an ominous crack as he slowly gets out. He glances down at black Billy, who suddenly feels small and naked.

'You any relation to Carlton?'

'If you want to know —'

'I want to know, you black prick. I want to know everything about you.'

'Yeah, like where you were last night when the store was broken into, as soon as you come home causing trouble in the pub,' the driver snarls.

'I wasn't causing trouble, and I wasn't in any robbery. I like the way you come straight down here when there's trouble —'

'If you weren't in the robbery, what's this watch?' the sergeant rumbles triumphantly, and he grabs hold of Billy's hand that has marked so many beautiful marks and painted so many beautiful pictures for the wadgula people. He twists it up behind Billy's back and slams him against the blank blue side of the van. The golden watch dangles between the pink fingers, mocking the stunned man.

'Listen. I was here. You can ask my grandparents or Darcy Goodrich, even,' he moans. But inside he knows it is no good.

'Don't give me that, Woodward. You bastards stick together like flies on a dummy wall,' the driver sneers.

Nothing matters any more. Not the trees, flinging their scraggly arms wide in freedom. Not the people around their warm fires. Not the drizzle that drips down the back of his shirt onto his skin. Just this thickset, glowering man and the sleek oiled machine with POLICE stencilled on the sides neatly and indestructibly.

'You mongrel black bastard, I'm going to make you—and your fucking brother—jump. You could have killed old Peters last night,' the huge man hisses dangerously. Then the driver is beside him, glaring from behind his sunglasses.

'You Woodwards are all the same, thieving boongs. If you think you're such a fighter, beating up old men, you can have a go at the sarge here when we get back to the station.'

'Let's get the other one now, Morgan. Mrs Riley said there were two of them.'

He is shoved into the back, with a few jabs to hurry him on his way. Hunches miserably in the jolting iron belly as the van revs over to the humpy. Catches a glimpse of his new Kingswood standing in the filth. Darcy, a frightened Rennie and several others lean against it, watching with lifeless eyes. Billy returns their gaze with the look of a cornered dingo who does not understand how he was trapped yet who knows he is about to die. Catches a glimpse of his brother being pulled from the humpy, sad yet sullen, eyes downcast staring into the mud of his life—mud that no one can ever escape.

He is thrown into the back of the van.

The van starts up with a satisfied roar.

Carlton gives Billy a tired look as though he isn't even there, then gives his strange, faint smile.

'Welcome 'ome, brother,' he mutters.

FROM
Wanamurraganya: The Story of Jack McPhee (1989)

———

SALLY MORGAN AND JACK MCPHEE

Jack McPhee, whose Aboriginal name was Wanamurraganya, narrated his life story to Sally Morgan, an Aboriginal author and artist, who transcribed it for him. Jack tells the modern history of his people as he recounts incidents in his own life. Approximately eighty-four years old, he offers his perspective on black/white relationships. The excerpt printed here is the epilogue of his biography.

I've had a think, and before I say anything, I want to say this. The way I see things is based on the way I've had to live, please remember that.

I want to talk about stations. They were built on black labour. On sour bread, damper, roo meat and whippings. The squatter had it hard too, because life in those days was hard, but they made money out of it. Two generations on their families are all right, ours aren't. Many of them are now wealthy men with land and businesses and respect, we have nothing.

I can only explain it like this. Two friends of mine were working on a station. The manager, who was an okay fella, went away and put a new bloke in charge. There was a good garden there, my friend looked after it while his wife worked in the house. Now the new boss loved watermelon and my friend had some in the garden. He was told he wasn't allowed to have any of those melons, even though my friend had grown them himself. Instead, when the boss had eaten the good part, he would throw him the leftovers. For years the whiteman's been getting the sweet part of the melon and the blackman, if he's lucky, has had to be content with leftovers.

I can honestly say that I have tried very hard in my life to live quietly and to better myself and my family. When I was just a native I was told that if I wanted to get on in the world I had to become a whiteman, but when I tried to do that people would look at me and say, 'Oh you're just a native!'

Some people think all Aborigines are the same, yet we have different tribal groups, different languages, different customs. Our colour isn't even the same, some of us are black, some are brown, some are only light. Some of us can speak language and some know only English; some can read and write and some can't. Some of us are no-hopers and alcoholics, and others are working men who know right from wrong. People see a few rotten apples and write us off. I've known whitemen who were bastards and I've known whitemen who were the best mates a man could have. I'm sick of people thinking we all look and think the same. A man should be judged on his own and not as part of a group.

Now, about Mulba things. I think it's very sad that some of our people feel ashamed of the old culture, especially our languages and dancing. I can speak five Aboriginal languages and I can sing in seven. I know many Mulbas who can speak their language but won't. Sometimes when I'm sitting in the South Hedland shopping centre, I wait until I see some of my countrymen coming and then I call out to them in language. They get very embarrassed. I tell them I'm not ashamed of my language and they shouldn't be either. I'll speak my language anywhere.

You see, their idea is this. They think if they talk language the white people might think they're running them down. Over the years I've seen the same thing happen at corroboree time. White people are very interested in corroborees, but my people get worried about singing in language in case someone says, 'Oh speak bloody English will ya?!'

For many years there was ill feeling in the North between black and white. No one wanted us to go up in the world, we were classed next to a dog. I'm happy to say that's changing. However, I don't agree with some of the black people who won't speak to white people. They're getting silly themselves now. They blame the white people for everything, especially the past, but I think there are some things happening now that they're responsible for. Young people drinking and stealing, old people gambling everything, mothers and fathers not wanting to work or look after their kids. We had none of that in my day.

It's hard because Mulbas see things differently. We'd rather lend twenty dollars to someone than pay the rent. If people owe us money and won't pay we just walk away. We've got to be in a group all the time, we won't spread out and make an independent living for ourselves. The grandmothers won't say no to anything. They keep taking in all the children the young people don't want instead of making them care for those kids themselves.

Also, if things are all right now like people say, then why are all these boys dying in gaol? I just can't understand that and it really worries me. I am very worried about the young Aboriginal boys and girls and what's going to become of them if they keep on the way they are. I know there are some good ones who try their best, that's why I'm going to make a scholarship, to help the ones that are trying to help themselves. I want to do that, and I want to be remembered as someone who made mistakes like everyone else, but who came through in the end and did something good for his people.

I'm roughly eighty-four now and I've been through a lot in my life. I have to tell you that it's only as you get to the end of your life that you start to realise what things are really important to you. I've been through the Exemption Certificate and Citizenship and I've struggled to live up to the whiteman's standard, but here I am, old, and good for nothing, and what keeps coming back to me? Dances, singing, stories the old people used to tell. Every night I lie in bed and sing myself to sleep with all my old corroboree songs. I go over and over them and I remember that part of my life. They're the things I love, they're the things I miss.

My friend Peter Coppin, I think of him as a young bloke, but he must be in his sixties by now, you should hear him talk about me.

He points to me in front of real young fellas and says, 'You see that fella there, he looks like a whiteman now, but I remember him all dressed up in cockatoo feathers, paint and pearlshell, singing and dancing, doing all the things blackfellas do. He's the only old one left who remembers how it used to be, he's the only one who's number one fella to me.'

THE CONVICT

FROM *His Natural Life* (1870):
Breaking a Man's Spirit

MARCUS CLARKE

This excerpt is from a nineteenth-century convict classic. The hero, Rufus Dawes, has been transported to the prison colony of Van Diemen's Land for a crime he did not commit. A proud man, unwilling to adopt a pose of servility or to jettison his principles, he has, by the time of this excerpt, been through hell. Flogged so many times that his back is "hard and seamed," he survives through sheer grit and fierce will. Mr. Troke, a warden who hates Dawes because he cannot make the convict grovel, has been waiting to trap him.

Rufus Dawes, on being removed to the cells, knew what he had to expect.

The insubordination of which he had been guilty was, in this instance, tolerably insignificant. It was the custom of the newly-fledged constables of Captain Frere to enter the wards at night, armed with cutlasses, tramping about, and making a great noise. Mindful of the report of Pounce, they pulled the men roughly from their hammocks, examined their persons for concealed tobacco, and compelled them to open their mouths to see if any was inside. The men in Dawes's gang—to which Mr Troke had an especial objection—were often searched more than once in a night, searched going to work, searched at meals, searched going to prayers, searched coming out, and this in the roughest manner. Their sleep broken, and what little self-respect they might yet presume to retain harried out of them, the objects of this incessant persecution were ready to turn upon and kill their tormentors.

The great aim of Troke was to catch Dawes tripping, but the leader of the 'Ring' was too wary. In vain had Troke, eager to sustain his reputation for sharpness, burst in upon the convict at all times and seasons. He had found nothing. In vain had he laid traps for him; in vain had he 'planted' figs of tobacco, and attaching long threads to them, waited in a bush hard by until the pluck at the end of his line should give token that the fish had bitten. The experienced 'old hand' was too acute for him. Filled with disgust and ambition, he determined upon an ingenious little trick. He was certain that Dawes possessed tobacco; the thing was to find it upon him.

Now, Rufus Dawes, holding aloof, as was his custom, from the majority of his companions, had made one friend — if so mindless and battered an old wreck could be called a friend — Blind Mooney. Perhaps this oddly-assorted friendship was brought about by two causes — one that Mooney was the only man on the island who knew more of the horrors of convictism than the leader of the Ring; the other, that Mooney was blind, and, to a moody, sullen man, subject to violent fits of passion, and a constant suspicion of all his fellow-creatures, a blind companion was more congenial than a sharp-eyed one.

Mooney was one of the 'First Fleeters.' He had arrived in Sydney fifty-seven years before, in the year 1789, and when he was transported he was fourteen years old. He had been through the whole round of servitude, had worked as a bondsman, had married, had been 'up country,' and had been again sentenced, and was a sort of dismal patriarch of Norfolk Island, having been there at its former settlement. He had no friends. His wife was long since dead, and he stated, without contradiction, that his master, having taken a fancy to her, had despatched the uncomplaisant husband to imprisonment. Such cases were not uncommon.

Mooney was accustomed to relate strange stories of his early life.

'When I first arrived,' said he to Dawes, 'there were but eight houses in the colony. I and eighteen others lay in a hollow tree for seventeen weeks, and cooked out of a kettle with a wooden bottom. We used to stick it in a hole in the ground and make a fire round it. For seventeen weeks we only had five ounces of flour a day. We never got a full ration except when the ship was in harbour. I have taken grass and pounded it, and made soup from a native dog. Any man would have committed murder for a week's provisions. I was chained seven weeks on my back for being out getting greens and wild herbs. I knew a man hung then and there for stealing a few biscuits, and another for stealing a duck frock. A man was condemned—no time—take him to the tree and hang him.

'The motto used to be, "Kill 'em or work 'em, their provisions is in store." I've been yoked like a bullock, with twenty or thirty others, to drag along timber. We used to be taken in large parties to raise a tree; when the body of the tree was raised, the overseer would call some of the men away; then more; the men were bent double; they could not bear it; they fell; the tree on one or two, killed on the spot. "Take him away, put him in the ground." There was no more about it. I've seen a man flogged for pulling six turnips instead o' five. Those were the days! I've seen seventy men flogged at night—twenty-five lashes each. One man came ashore in the *Pitt*; his name was Dixon. He was a guardsman. He was put to the drag; it soon did for him. He began on a Thursday and died on the Saturday, as he was carrying a load down Constitution-hill. How they used to die! There was a great hole for the dead; once a day, men were sent down to collect the corpses of prisoners, and throw them in without ceremony or service. The native dogs used to come down at night, and fight and howl, in packs, gnawing the poor dead bodies. Eight hundred died in six months, at Constitution-hill—or Toongabbie as it was called. I knew a man, so weak that he was thrown into the grave, when he said, "Don't cover me up, I'm not dead; for God's sake don't cover me up!" The overseer answered, "Damn your eyes, you'll die to-night, and we shall have the trouble to come back again." '

Such dismal recollections as these were Mooney's consolation in his blindness. One would have thought that, having passed through such an ordeal, doomed for life to such a punishment, he would at seventy-one have been glad to slip into his grave; but it was not so. The old blind man believed that he must soon be released on account of his great age. 'What's the good of a blind old fool like me?' he would ask; and he looked forward to his release with the greatest eagerness, for he believed himself master of millions. 'I've found a gold mine,' he used to say, to the amusement of his comrades. Dawes, however, with some dim remembrance of those chemical and metallurgical studies in which he had once delighted, listened to the old man with patience. It was just wildly possible that Australia was auriferous, and that Mooney's story of the gold dust in the bed of the creek was a true one. The old shepherd himself believed it, and would draw to his comrade wonderful pictures of what he meant to do when he got out. 'Mooney's gold mine' was a standing joke in the prison, and the old man, pressed in rough sarcasm to reveal its whereabouts, was incited to paroxysms of rage. Dawes sometimes allowed himself to speculate upon the probable consequences of a similar discovery being made by himself. With money one could do anything.

One of the many ways in which Rufus Dawes had secured the affection of the old blind man was the gift of such fragments of tobacco as he from time to time secured. Troke knew this; and on the evening in question hit upon an excellent plan. Admitting himself noiselessly into the boatshed, where the gang slept, he crept close to the sleeping Dawes, and counterfeiting Mooney's mumbling utterance, asked for 'some tobacco.' Rufus Dawes was but half awake, and on repeating his request, Troke felt something put into his hand. He grasped Dawes's arm and struck a light. He had got his man this time. Dawes had conveyed to his (fancied) friend a piece of tobacco almost as big as the top joint of his little finger.

One can understand the feelings of a man entrapped by such base means. Rufus Dawes no sooner saw the hated face of Warder Troke peering over his hammock, than he sprang out, and exerting to the utmost his powerful muscles, slung out his left hand from his hip with such tremendous violence that Mr Troke was knocked fairly off his legs into the arms of the incoming constables. A desperate struggle took place, at the end of which, the convict, overpowered by numbers, was borne senseless to the cells, gagged, and chained to the ring-bolt on the bare flags. While in this condition he was dreadfully beaten by five or six constables.

To this maimed and manacled rebel was the Commandant ushered by Troke the next morning.

'Ha! ha! my man,' says the Commandant. 'Here you are again, you see. How do you like this sort of thing?'

Dawes, glaring, makes no answer.

'You shall have fifty lashes, my man,' says Frere. 'We'll see how you'll feel then!'

The fifty were duly administered, and the Commandant called the next day. The rebel was still mute.

'Give him fifty more, Mr Troke. We'll see what he's made of.'

Fifty more lashes were inflicted in the course of the morning, but still the sullen convict refused to speak. He was then treated to fourteen days' solitary confinement in one of the new cells. On being brought out and confronted with his tormentor, he merely laughed. For this he was sent back for another fourteen days; and still remaining obdurate, was flogged again, and got fourteen days more. Had the chaplain then visited him, he would have found him open to consolation, but the chaplain—so it was stated—was sick. When brought out at the conclusion of his third confinement, he was found to be in so exhausted a condition, that the doctor ordered him to the hospital. As soon as he was sufficiently recovered, Frere visited him, and finding his 'spirit' not yet 'broken,' ordered that he should be put to grind maize. Dawes declined the work. So they chained his hand to one arm of the grindstone, and placed another prisoner at the other arm. As the second prisoner turned, the hand of Dawes of course revolved.

'You're not such a pebble as folks seem to think,' grinned Frere, pointing to the turning wheel.

Upon which the indomitable poor devil straightened his sorely-tried muscles, and prevented the wheel from turning at all.

Frere gave him fifty more lashes, and sent him the next day to grind cayenne pepper.

This was a punishment more dreaded by the convicts than any other. The pungent dust filled their eyes and lungs, causing them the most excruciating torments. For a man with a raw back the work was one continued agony. In four days, Rufus Dawes, emaciated, blistered, blinded, broke down.

'For God's sake, Captain Frere, kill me at once!' he said.

'No fear,' said the other, rejoiced at this proof of his power. 'You've given in; that's all I wanted. Troke, take him to the hospital.'

Absalom Day's Promotion (1892)

PRICE WARUNG

Price Warung is the pen name of William Astley, a writer best known for
Tales of the Convict System. *"Absalom Day's Promotion" is an excerpt
from* Tales. *Warung was a socialist who harbored strong anti-English,
anti-imperialist feelings. He wrote this story using prison data; mass
hangings like the one described here were a fact of Australian prison
history.*

I

The sound of a bell came floating on the pellucid atmosphere
to the ears of the dense, waiting crowd.

"That ain't the 'Tench clapper yet, surely?" exclaimed a bleary-
eyed old ticket-of-leave man who stood in the front rank, so close
to the files of the military guard that his noisome breath dulled the
pipe-clayed polish on the nearest private's shoulder-belt.

"Yer ought'r know, ol' chap," sneered an "F.S." (free-by-
servitude) man. "Yer slep' of'n 'nuff in the ol' lumber-yard dorm'-
tories."

"Wot stoopids ye must be as not to know as that's the bell of the
Beagle as is striking eight bells!" broke in a third person whose
assumption of superiority, evidenced in many airs of dress and
manner, was based on the circumstance that he was still "free"—
a state or condition which, if his physiognomy possessed any value
as an index, rather reflected on the vigilance of the authorities. And
then he proceeded to inform his precious companions that the

113

Beagle was a King's ship, "as was a-goin' round the world a-takin' soundin's an' a-collectin' of shells."

"Well," said the T.L. man, "th' curi*ows*est thing as they'll see aboard of her will be this 'ere exe*cus*hun." Which remark, though somewhat ungrammatical, was certainly not far from the truth.

"Eight bells, was it?" continued the passholder; "then th' 'Tench will give tongue soon."

His bristly lips had not ceased to vibrate before the sound they were waiting for was borne on the aromatic mountain breeze.

"One—"

The deep solemn tone of Trinity Church-bell—the St. Sepulchre's of Hobart Town—swayed the chattering, jostling, jesting crowd into silence and stillness for a moment only. Before the second toll of the passing bell reached the throng the chattering became excited and furious talk, the jests more biting and brutal, the jostling an angry struggle for a foremost place. The soldiers guarding the vacant space in front of the monstrous scaffold which ran almost the full length of the gaol-facade, were ordered to face about and press back the surging mass with their extended firelocks. The tolling of the bell had communicated a passion like the madness of fever to the veins of the people. The madness of fever, say we? Better, the delirium of blood-thirst. The people of Hobart Town were about to enjoy a rare treat, and their lips were dry for it.

"Execution Mondays" were common enough in the Van Diemen's Land calendar, and it was an exceptional day of the series when only one doomed wretch swung off the platform and into the Mystery which men in their ignorance label Eternity. But it was still more exceptional to have a round dozen of hangings on one day, at the one hour, and in the one place. In fact, there was nothing but a vague tradition to encourage the notion that the event which had occasioned the assembling of the crowd was not absolutely unprecedented in Vandemonian history. The circumstance was, anyhow, quite exceptional in the experience of the existing authorities, and they had been in some doubt as to whether they ought not to divide the twelve criminals left for execution by the last Court of Oyer and Terminer and General Gaol Delivery into two batches of six each. The desire, however, to afford to the criminal element of the population a peculiarly "impressive warning" prevailed, and, accordingly, the simultaneous execution of the twelve was decided upon.

Furthermore, it had been resolved by the Executive Council— present, the Governor, the Chief Justice, the Attorney-General, the Colonial Secretary, and the Archdeacon—that the event should be surrounded with ceremonial details of a unique and peculiarly impressive kind. As the Clerk of the Council was entering upon the minutes the programme for the day as approved by that august body, he paused in his work to nod acquiescence in the opinion expressed by the sonorous accents of the Very Reverend the Archdeacon. "The terrible exemplification," said the dignitary, "which Your Excellency, with the advice of your Council, has prepared, of the majesty of the Law and the heinousness of wrong-doing *must* beneficially impress the evil-disposed among the people." Vandemonia could not boast of a Bishop in those days, or else this very proper sentiment would have fallen from episcopal lips. It was just the sort of sentiment that the superior ecclesiastical functionary of the colony would be impelled to utter by the obligations of his office as representative of Christ. The Crown, ever mindful of the moral and spiritual welfare of its subjects, always desired the approval of the Church. And, as the Crown paid the Church its stipend and allowances, the approval was never witheld.

"Ten—Eleven—"

The noise caused by the crowd did not prevent the little group of civil and military officials which had gathered round the entrance-gate of the gaol and just underneath the extremity of the gallows to which the ladder was attached, from counting the pulsings of the minute-bell so far. A resonant shout drowned the twelfth stroke.

"They are coming!" cried the crowd. "Look, look!"

Into Murray Street from Campbell Street turned a grim and grisly procession. Up the hill it came slowly—so slowly. A regimental officer marched at the head and gave the measured pace. He recalled to himself as he walked that once before he had done the same thing; but then it was for a cortège of honour; now it was for one of dishonour; and his brow compressed and his lips set hard as he cursed the fate which had made him, an English gentleman, the marshal of a massacre, the leader of a felon funeral. Behind him his guard, four deep, with bayonets fixed and ball-cartridge rammed well home. Behind the soldiers one, two, three carts in succession; close beside each walking, first a file of javelin-men, and at a distance of "intervals" as many warders with loaded muskets at the "ready." Behind the carts again, more soldiers and javelin-men, and, last of all, the Sheriff, the Under-Sheriff, and the Gaoler.

And the carts—what of them? Each was drawn by a horse with rusty harness and dilapidated gear, a wisp of yarn being substituted in more than one place for a missing strap or part of a trace. Each was driven by a grey-clad figure on whose clothing stood the prong symbol which proclaimed to all men that the creature within it was a Thing—a Chattel—a Number—anything, rather than a man. Four other figures were also in the cart—no, let us be precise— we should say five. And yet, perhaps, we would not be wrong in saying that there were four only. The fifth other man in each other vehicle was a functionary, and such importance as he had was the reflection of the glory encompassing his four companions. The crowd which lined the streets and which blackened the hill by the Public Offices scarcely gave a thought to him. It was upon the four upon whom it gazed—and gloated. The four were principals in the ensuing drama. The fifth man in each cart was simply an accessory, indispensable, it is true—for he was either the chief or an assistant-executioner—but still an accessory.

The four in each cart were the cynosure of every eye. They had the seats of distinction, for each sat on his own coffin.

One—again to be precise—sat on the fragments of his. Two prisoners in the House of Correction workshops were constantly engaged in making coffins, and, to save trouble and inconvenience in emergencies, the shells were made to average sizes and uniform patterns. Consequently, it happened very frequently that a condemned man found his coffin a trifle too small for him. The law of averages was, however, respected, and the official accounts were balanced by some other wretch finding *his* a trifle too large. On this exceptional occasion, the particular shell assigned to John Bond, No. 440, per *Asia* (1) was not only apparently too small for him, but was not strong enough to grant him the poor consolation of a comfortable seat to the spot where he was to be hanged by the neck till dead. As he cast his huge carcase upon its lid on entering the cart, his great weight burst one flimsy side from its fastenings, and, the lid slipping, John Bond was deposited prematurely in his shell, or, rather, on its planks. "Why, Jack, you *are* in a hurry to get in!" laughed James Travis, No. 2320, per *Norfolk*. Travis was always ready-witted. He had begged for the first pick of the coffins that morning. "He wished to get one," he said, "which would just suit him. He liked to be comfortable;" and he had found an opportunity to lie jocosely at full length in his narrow bed, "so as to be sure he fitted it." Finding the measure satisfactory, he hilariously flung his feet into the air. "Taste and try before you buy," said he. "That's been my rule of life, and see how successful it has made me!"

Up the hill came the procession. Most of the condemned laughed at and waved their hands to the crowd. Only one of the twelve sat glum and silent on his sombre perch. This was the youngest of the lot—Absalom Day, who had taken advantage of the comparative liberty he enjoyed as a Sheriff's javelin-man to break into a dwelling-house, and, failing in his endeavour to throw the blame on another convict, had been capitally sentenced.

This was only Day's third conviction, and, consequently, he was not absolutely disgusted with life. It was a shame, he considered, to be "top'd off" so young; other men were allowed to live when they had, perhaps, 39 or 40 convictions, including two or three "life" sentences recorded against them. He had expressed his dissatisfaction with his impending fate to Jim Travis. "You're blest 'appy, my son," rejoined that effervescent sinner, "if you only knew it. Them as the gods love dies young." But Day's soul declined to be comforted.

Up the hill it came. The passing-bell tolled in the ear of the Condemned. That was rather unpleasant, certainly. But, then, the bright morning sunshine glanced upon them genially, and the breeze from Mount Wellington puffed piney perfume into their nostrils, and the crowd cheered them, and the atmosphere of distinction was about them. All these things were pleasant; and, pleasantest of all, was not Freedom waiting for them on top of the timber platform yonder? Why should they grieve? Was not the balance in their favour? The door to which yon dangling ropes, when looped, would prove the key-holes, could not open upon a chamber of greater horror than that from which they had emerged in the glorious sunlight of *their* Execution Monday. Thus, thought the Condemned: all, except Absalom Day.

Two members of the little group of officials beforementioned, mounted the steps of the scaffold in order to gain a better view of the procession's progress.

"Very impressive," said Captain Grove, of His Majesty's—the Fusiliers, to Chaplain Ford. "Very impressive, indeed!"

"Yes," replied the Chaplain, "it was a happy thought of the Council to order the men to spend their last night at the Barracks instead of in the gaol here. It enabled the Sheriff to organise a very impressive—ah—ceremonial, indeed. Such a spectacle must have the best possible effect upon the convict class." He took from his fob a silver snuff-box, and, having titillated his own organ, tendered the box to the officer. "Have a pinch, Captain? I need a little stimulant on these occasions. My duty is so trying!"

"Just so—thanks!" sympathetically answered Captain Grove. "It must be, I'm sure. I don't like hanging myself. I prefer a platoon at twenty paces, you know."

"Ah, that would be too good for some of our men," smiled the parson. "But I think it's time I put on my surplice." He turned to descend when a thought struck him. He looked up.

"By the way, Captain, do you think that beam is strong enough? The weight will be rather much today. I'd not like any scandal; it would be most unedifying."

To assure themselves, the Chaplain and the Captain walked along the platform and inspected the beam.

"I think it will do," said Chaplain Ford, taking a second pinch. "Have another?"

"I think so. Ah—thanks!" The Captain injected some more of the pungent snuff into his nostrils. "Very good snuff, this of yours, sir."

"Yes, Tandy's best, I import it myself. And, you know," he whispered roguishly, "it doesn't pay duty!"

The Captain laughed, and they descended.

Chaplain Ford put on his surplice which his prisoner clerk—a former mayor of an English city—had brought him from the vestry of the 'Tench Chapel ("Trinity" was so called), and went to the corner of the square, where the soldiers were already forcing the people to clear a passage for the entrance of the procession.

II

"I am the resurrection and the life, saith the Lord," began Chaplain Ford, as he led the way to the gallows. "He that believeth on Me, though he were dead, yet shall he live."

The rear-guard of the soldiers closed up round the carts. One by one the Condemned got down. Two by two they followed Parson Ford. They left their coffins behind them; they would not require them again for an hour or so. By their side walked the javelin-men. Behind them, the Sheriff and Under-Sheriff—and the executioner and his assistants.

At the foot of the steps, Chaplain Ford moved aside and mumbled some more portions of the burial-service. "Halt!" called the Sheriff. The Condemned paused. The Sheriff beckoned to the executioner and his assistants to make ready. The chief hangman went into the gaol, came out a moment later with a bundle in his hands, and ran lightly up the steps. He passed along the platform, forming twelve little heaps of calico and cordage as he traversed it. The bundle was composed of the white caps and the pinioning-cords. The Condemned looked on and smiled—all except Absalom Day. He shivered.

"The Condemned will take their stations as their names are called out," said the Sheriff.

"*Absalom Day,*" said Under-Sheriff Ropewell.

Day shuffled up the steps, trembling. Assistant-Executioner Sharp assisted him to mount the last, and guided him to the farther side of the drop, where Chief-Executioner Johnson received him into his grasp.

The others mounted as their names were called from the dread roll—some bravely, the others with mere bravado; all without assistance. They were ranged in order of age—the youngest, Day, on the extreme right of the platform as the crowd faced it.

A word from Johnson to his subordinates, and the task of pinioning was commenced. The tension of the crowd freed itself by a sigh; the actual drama had begun; the tedious prologue was ended.

Johnson, being an expert, had taken Nos. 6 to 12 of the Condemned to pinion. Assistants Sharp and Muggins, being only pupils in the school of the Law's Finishing Schoolmaster, were allotted but three each. As it was, they bungled their proportion of the work. Johnson pinioned his six in half the time taken by each of the others for his three. The crowd did not complain, however. Once the drama had begun, the longer its performance the more prolonged their pleasure.

Johnson stopped in front of the Condemned to "cap" them. The assistants fell back to hand the shapeless calico hoods to him as he wanted them.

By a singular chance, the whole of the Condemned were Protestants. Hence, Chaplain Ford alone was in requisition as the moment of doom drew nigh. He was about to mount to say a few final words —he had seen each man in his cell early in the morning—when the Sheriff stopped him.

"Not yet, Mr. Ford, the death-warrants have not been read. The Under-Sheriff will now please read the warrants."

Under-Sheriff Ropewell stepped up and Chaplain Ford stepped down petulantly. How could he, the experienced prison Chaplain, so familiarised with the proper routine by frequent attendance on similar occasions, have made such a blunder? Chaplain Ford was vexed with himself.

Under-Sheriff Ropewell opened the roll of parchment sheets which he had carried under his arm. He glibly recited the preambles as though he knew them by heart—as was, indeed, probable. By the time a man has read a form aloud a couple of hundred times he should be able to repeat it by rote.

For each of the warrants the preamble was the same. The "orders," of course, varied in their terms.

Beginning, on the left hand, with the oldest criminal, the Under-Sheriff went down the line.

To John Bond, No. 440, per *Asia* (1), he read the order of the Governor for his execution. His crime was murder. And to John M'Kenzie, No. 8764, *Elphinstone*, crime ...; to Charles Argyle, No. 687. *Arab* (2) ...; to Edward M'Gavin, No. 12,351, *Royal Sover-*

eign, murder; to Robert Smith, free, attempt to murder; to James Travis, No. 2320, *Norfolk*, rendering into tallow a sheep suspected to be stolen (he had sold the tallow for 7s. 6d., and the skin for 1s.); to Richard Bennett, No. 9244, *Lord Lynedoch*, robbery under arms; to Michael Green, free, robbery under arms; to Philip Grafton, No. 12,755, *Pyramus*, forgery and murder of arresting constable; to Joseph Madden, *Tory*, No. 14,009, murder; to Peter Fyfe, No. 16,150, *George III* (boys' cargo), sheep-stealing; and to Absalom Day, native, burglary with violence. To all these he read the documents of doom.

As the last clause—

These are therefore in His Majesty's name strictly to charge and command you the Sheriff of this Colony and Dependency of Van Diemen's Land that you see the said sentence against the said ABSALOM DAY duly put into execution according to the tenor hereof. And for so doing this shall be your sufficient warrant—

was read, the crowd heaved another and deeper sigh. The drama was approaching the climax.

Under-Sheriff Ropewell finished, Chaplain Ford took up his reverend duty.

"Now, my men," he said loudly, "remember what I told you this morning. God will forgive you all your sins if you really believe in Christ. Even for such sinners as you, there is hope. Grafton, you are not listening, sir." Over the crowd, solitary in the blue vault, hung a fleck of snow-white cloud. Grafton had been gazing on it. His fancy had traced in the fleecy outlines the profile of his dead mother's face. He turned at the parson's words.

"My dear sir," he replied—Grafton's "educational" rank in the penal records was "C"—"I have heard your remarks so often that I am tired of them—and of you. But pardon me this time—I will not offend again." He laughed, and the others of the condemned joined in the chorus of derision—all except Absalom Day.

"Silence!" cried the Sheriff. The Chaplain descended.

Once more the Sheriff spoke. "Men," he asked, "have you anything to say? Now is your last opportunity. You, Bond?"

A thrill penetrated the crowd as Bond flung himself on his knees, and in so doing nearly precipitated himself from the gallows, as, his hands and legs being pinioned, he had no power to balance himself. Assistant Muggins pulled him on his knees with a jerk.

Bond looked up to the smiling heavens. "I wish to say this," he shouted, "that I thank God my time has come at last. I killed Morrison because I wanted to die."

"So do I, thank God!" exclaimed the next man. A dreadful "Hear, hear!" broke from the lips of almost every man forming the doomed row.

When it came to Travis's turn to speak, he said:

"I'm—glad I'm going to be hanged, I am. But I don't thank God, for I don't believe there is any God. A God would have given me a chance, and a chance I never had—no, never. Or if He did give me one, the police and the beaks, and the Com'troller took it from me. That's all I've got to say. Good-bye all." He had spoken with a clarion-like fulness of voice that reached the outskirts of the now silent mass. As he uttered his farewell he made a bow of mock-dignity. From the centre of the throng came a loud cheer, and a timid "God have mercy on you!"

The scandal of these proceedings determined the Sheriff to prevent the remainder of the Condemned from speaking.

He motioned the executioner to begin "capping." In a second the pallid visage of Absalom Day was shrouded. The crowd, irritated at losing "a last dying speech," yelled in disappointment.

Johnson took the second cap from an assistant's hand, and was placing it on Fyfe's head when the boy—he was only twenty—spoke to him.

"It's a long time, Dick, since we met, isn't it? An' so you've started in the wholesale butcherin' line, have yer? Well, as you are an ol' pal, I don't min' a-paternising yer!"

Johnson threw down the cap with an oath. "You're right, Pete —it is wholesale butcherin'. I don't min' one or two, but a dozen! I'm d——d if I hang so many—so there, Mr. Sheriff!"

And, defiantly, and never giving a thought to the lashes which he must have known awaited him, he walked off the gallows.

III

Not so the Sheriff. To say that he was surprised would be to use an absurdly-mild phrase. He was stupefied by the executioner's declaration. The revolt of a hangman was absolutely unprecedented.

"Do you mean it, Johnson?" he gasped, at last. Johnson did, and said so. "I'll give you two hundred!" said the Sheriff. The Sheriff didn't mean shillings, or sovereigns. He meant lashes.

There was a minute's conference between the Sheriff and the other civil officials, and then the former ordered the assistant-executioner to proceed with the awful business.

"Please, sir, I can't," said Muggins, "I never assisted before."

"Nor I," said Sharp.

But these replies were not occasioned by any delicate doubt entertained by the Pupils as to their own ability to carry the proceedings through to the rope's end. Messrs. Muggins and Sharp were simply desirous of adding to the Sheriff's embarrassment.

The Sheriff was dangerously near his wits' extremity.

"I'll 'sist, sir, if yer can get some 'un else to knot th' ropes, an' yer'll make my ticket a pardon," spoke a voice from the crowd. It was the old ticket-of-leave man who proffered his services.

The words suggested to the Sheriff that he should ask for volunteers from the throng. He did so. None were forthcoming except the T.L. man.

The Sheriff grew pale with alarm. The Governor had left town on Saturday evening on a hunting-excursion to Richmond, and he knew that there was, therefore, no possibility of obtaining a formal respital of the men till a fresh executioner could be obtained. To postpone the execution on less authority than his Excellency's he dare not. It would invalidate the sentences. Neither dare he contemplate the fearful but legally imperative alternative of hanging the men himself. To hang a dozen men by proxy was one thing; to adjust nooses and pull levers with his own shapely hands was another. And then a thought flashed into his mind which he told his "lady" at dinner that evening he regarded as a Providential inspiration. Acting upon it he addressed Bond.

"Bond," he said, "I promise you life and a free pardon if you will hang the rest."

A terrible second, and Bond's answer came clear and decisive. "No!"

The crowd was tremulous to its margin with delight. This was something not in the bill.

"Will you, M'Kenzie?"

"No!"

"Argyle?"

"No!"

"You, McGavin?"

"I'll see you in hell first!" said M'Gavin.

"Smith?"

"No!"

"Travis, you?"

"Life on such terms? No, sir; I ain't a sneak!"

"Bennett, you? Remember, life and freedom!"

"Bah!"

"Green?"

"What would my old father say if he 'eard such a thing o' me?"

As Mr. Green's father had some years before undergone a suspensory operation in front of Horsemonger Gaol, London, Mr. Green was putting an insoluble conundrum to the Sheriff, which, to say the least, was not respectful of Mr. Green, considering the perturbed state of the Sheriff's feelings.

"Grafton? think what you refuse!" cried the great law-officer.

Grafton thought for fully a minute. He gazed at the sky. The fleck of cloud had vanished. Then he said:—

"Will you throw the permanent billet of executioner in, sir?"

There was a note of general relief in the Sheriff's voice as he replied: "Yes, certainly." He thought his troubles were ended.

"What is the screw, sir."

"Thirty pounds a year, rations, and the usual fee for each—ah —execution."

"Not good enough," sneered the reprobate, delighted at the way in which he had excited the Sheriff's hopes.

Away down the Cove the sentry on the quarter-deck of H.M.S. *Beagle* was roused from semi-slumber by the mighty roar of laughter which broke from the crowd at Grafton's reply.

"Madden—you?"

"Mr. Madden's compliments to the Sheriff, and he respectfully declines the honour."

Another roar from the multitude.

The tenth man had now refused life and freedom on the Sheriff's terms. Before Fyfe, the eleventh, could be asked Absalom Day, the only one who had been finally "capped," was observed to struggle violently, as though he were already in the convulsions of death. In his contortions he nearly threw himself over the scaffold. As it would be an act of inhumanity to allow Day to suffocate, even though it was intended to break his neck in a few moments' time by due course of law, and as the System distinctly repudiated, by countless Regulations, inhumane conduct of all kinds, the Sheriff ordered the cap to be taken off. Muggins obeyed, and Absalom Day looked once more upon the world.

Barely had his ghastly face been freed before he gasped out: "I'll do it, Mr. Sheriff; I'll hang 'em, sir, if you'll grant me my life. I don't want freedom, sir—only life, sir, only life!"

"It's *my* chance, first, Sheriff," said Fyfe.

Day shrieked.

"Will you do it, Fyfe?" asked the Sheriff.

"Oh, sir, I'udn't like to take th'billet from poor Day; he hankers so arter it!" laughed the wretch. "Let him do it."

IV

Eleven dangling forms, a few minutes afterwards, testified to the fact that Absalom Day had "done it," and had performed his share of the bargain.

That the Sheriff performed his may be inferred from the following extracts from the *Hobart Town Gazette* of the week following the execution:—

PARDON (*Conditional*).—Absalom Day, native, for meritorious services rendered to the Crown.

PROMOTION.—Absalom Day, native, from Javelin-man, to executioner, *vice* Johnson, dismissed.

DISMISSAL.—Richard Johnson, No. 4563, per *Rodney*, from his post of executioner, for disobedience of orders. Transferred to the chain-gang at the settlement to serve the remainder of his sentence.

The details of flogging were not gazetted, otherwise we would be also able to read in the files of the official paper this:—

By order of the Comptroller-General, Richard Johnson, No. 4563, per *Rodney*, 200 lashes, for gross disobedience of orders. Scourger, Muggins.

We may here observe that owing to the expeditious manner in which the law acted, there was no necessity to proclaim Absalom Day's dismissal from his post of javelin-man. Found guilty and sentenced to death on Saturday morning, he had won promotion on the Monday; and as no *Gazette* intervened between the one date and the other, all legal requirements were met by simply notifying his pardon and his elevation from the inferior post to the superior one.

The first of the Civil officials to leave the scene of the massacre was Chaplain Ford. In his progress towards St. David's, where he was to hold a christening service, he was stopped by an acquaintance who wished to introduce to him a young naturalist who was voyaging on board the *Beagle*.

"Proud to know you, sir," said Parson Ford, effusively. "I hope we shall be able to show you a thing or two in this colony before you leave."

"I don't doubt it," said Charles Darwin—for *he* was the young naturalist—who had witnessed the execution; "I have already got some new light on a subject on which I am theorising—the kinship of man with the lower orders of animal life."

"Indeed," said the Chaplain; "how very interesting, to be sure!"

V

As demonstrating the effective manner in which the criminal classes were impressed by the edifying ceremony of the morning, it may be mentioned that, the same night, an atrocious murder was perpetrated within half-a-mile of Hobart Town Gaol. The murderer was the ticket-of-leave man who had volunteered "to'sist." He had spent the afternoon in company with an old "Norfolker," and had quarrelled as to the interpretation of a certain ship-signal floating from Mount Nelson. The Norfolker had contended that the flags denoted a vessel from India. The old T.L. man asserted they formed the "Ship with female convicts from England" symbol. As it happened, he was right; and, determined that his friend should not forget the lesson, killed him. The System taught by the agency of Death; so did the "ticket" holder.

THE SEARCH FOR
A NATIONAL IDENTITY

FROM *A Fortunate Life* (1981):
The First Days

——

A. B. FACEY

A. B. Facey's biography, A Fortunate Life, *was a great success in Australia when it was originally published. Readers responded to what they recognized as their own or their families' experiences. In the two excerpts included here, Facey describes the fighting at Gallipoli, a peninsula in the European part of Turkey, during World War I. The Turks were installed at a height above the entering Australian and New Zealand soldiers and their counteroffensive, while not finally successful, was very damaging.*

When daylight came we were all very confused. There was no set plan to follow so we formed ourselves into a kind of defensive line, keeping as much as possible under cover from shell-fire. The shelling was very severe and machine-gun fire was coming from all directions. Snipers were active too and were picking us off.

By midday we had moved a distance forward by crawling along, and at times, running from covered positions to new shelters. We were moving forward in small groups, sending scouts ahead to find new positions, and then charging them or getting there as best we could. Often it was the men in the ranks with the Corporals and Sergeants making the plans. Many of the officers were dead—the snipers seemed to be picking them off in preference to the lower ranks.

We met a lot of resistance that first day but I found out later that we had missed most of the Turkish counter-attack. The full blast of it was to the south of my group and the casualties there were even more shocking.

By nightfall our small group had moved into a gully which later became known as Shrapnel Gully. This was one of the hottest spots that we had to face. On each side were very high hills and on the hills were the Turks, including many snipers. They had the advantage because they had a clear view of the whole valley. We used our trenching tools to dig mounds of earth to protect us from stray bullets during the night. We kept guard in turns all through the night. Nobody slept much—if at all.

By this time we were short of ammunition and water. (We had strict orders not to drink any water we might find unless it had been tested for poison.) In the morning a group was sent back to the beach to get supplies and to report our progress and position. It seemed to me that we were only about a quarter of a mile from where Headquarters had been set up on the beach.

When the men returned they had plenty of supplies and brought with them more troops and a lieutenant and sergeant. They reported that the Engineers were building a jetty so that small boats could come alongside with supplies, reinforcements and so on. The officer told us that our troops had moved inland for some distance and were to the left and right of the main landing spot so that our holding was a sort of half circle in from the beach. We were to try and make contact with troops on both sides of our group and hold that contact. If we were hard pressed we were to dig in and hold our position at all cost.

We were a mixed group of troops from different states—Victorians, South Australians, New South Welshmen, Tasmanians and Western Australians. Most of us were young and in battle for the first time.

Our casualties were heavy. We lost many of our chaps to snipers and found that some of these had been shot from behind. This was puzzling so several of us went back to investigate, and what we found put us wise to one of the Turks' tricks. They were sitting and standing in bushes dressed all in green—their hands, faces, boots, rifles and bayonets were all the same colour as the bushes and scrub. You could walk close to them and not know. We had to find a way to flush these snipers out. What we did was fire several shots into every clump of bush that was big enough to hold a man. Many times after we did this Turks jumped out and surrendered or fell out dead.

All the second day we advanced slowly along the valley. We were joined by other troops and late in the afternoon plans were made to get snipers off the hills. As well as the ones hiding in bushes, we were being continually sniped at from above. These snipers were in fairly secure positions. They were concealed in shallow trenches and would take cover in these whenever the shelling was bad. When the shelling eased off they would bob up and start sniping us again.

What we did to tackle this problem was form into three groups of about ten men. One group's job was to observe the Turks' positions and find out exactly where the shots were coming from by looking for the puffs of smoke that a rifle makes when discharged. To draw the fire they had four dummies made from tunics stuffed with scrub and with Australian hats on the top. They moved these around to make them look like the real thing. When the snipers' fire was fixed the other two groups would move in from the sides and attack the Turks with bayonets. The first group would keep steady fire up at the snipers' position to distract their attention while the other two groups were approaching. This was a very successful method of attack and we managed to clear a lot of snipers off the hills on both sides of Shrapnel Gully. Those Turks we didn't kill or capture soon got out because they didn't like the bayonet.

It is a terrible thing, a bayonet charge. I was in several in the first few days, and about eleven altogether. You would have to be in a charge to know how bad it is. You are expecting all the time to get hit and then there is the hand-to-hand fighting. The awful look on a man's face after he has been bayoneted will, I am sure, haunt me for the rest of my life; I will never forget that dreadful look. I killed men too with rifle-fire—I was on a machine-gun at one time and must have killed hundreds—but that was nothing like the bayonet.

People often ask me what it is like to be in war, especially hand-to-hand fighting. Well, I can tell you, I was scared stiff. You never knew when a bullet or worse was going to whack into you.

A bullet is red hot when it hits you and burns like mad.

Fear can do terrible things to a man. There were a lot of nerve cases that came from Gallipoli, and sometimes a man would pack up under fire. A frightened man is a strange thing—you could grab him and pull him up and say, 'Come on, you're all right. Come on, you can shoot, go on, shoot,' and he would turn right around and be all right (if he didn't run like hell). I was so frightened myself one day I didn't know I was injured. Several of us had been sneaking along one of the Turks' narrow trenches to get into a position to charge a bunch of snipers. A machine-gun opened fire but seemed to be firing at random because we were not exposed—there was scrub on both sides of the trench. Suddenly the Corporal yelled, 'Look out! Get down!' They were cutting the scrub off with machine-gun fire. We all ducked down quickly into a crouching position and shuffled along on our haunches to safer ground. When I stood up one of my mates said, 'Hey, what's that!' At that moment I could feel what was wrong. I always carried a knife and fork pushed down into my puttees and when I had squatted down the prongs of the fork had pierced my flesh to the depth of an inch or more. I had been moving along with a fork sticking out of my bottom and hadn't known. I don't think you can be more scared than that.

Despite the fear the men mostly took everything that was thrown at them. I saw some very brave things at Gallipoli. One thing that made a big impression on us was the actions of a man we called 'The Man with a Donkey.' He was a stretcher-bearer, or so we were told, and he used to carry the wounded men down to the clearing station on the beach. (They were then put onto motor boats and taken out to a hospital ship anchored a good way off shore.) This man, Simpson his name was, was exposed to enemy fire constantly all the days I was there, and when I left Shrapnel Gully he was still going strong. I considered, and so did my mates, that he should be given the Victoria Cross.

By nightfall on the third day, we had established a temporary firing-line linking up from the sea and circling half a mile or more inland. Our bridge-head covered about a mile of seashore. For this piece of land the casualties had been shocking.

We now had more officers and non-commissioned officers and

our actions became more orderly. The first two days had been a shambles. It seemed that many small groups had gone off after the enemy and been cut off. Those that returned had lost more than half their troops.

We continued moving up to the head of Shrapnel Gully and kept after the Turks on the hills. The Turks kept shelling us all day long. We had wonderful assistance from the British Navy which kept up a continual shelling, mostly shrapnel, mostly forward of our position. They read our signals well—on only a few occasions did we get shelled by our own.

On the fifth day we dug ourselves in, making a temporary firing-line at the southern end of the Gully, where the ground rose sharply forming into a ridge. We were getting sniped at from this ridge and during the day we got continuous shelling. (That is one of the things I remember most clearly about the campaign—all the shelling. It seemed as if you could always hear it and weren't far from it even if your own section wasn't at that time under fire.) We built a sand-bag protection for extra cover.

The graves at Shrapnel Gully mounted. We buried most of our dead in this valley near the sea, and as things became more organised, a wooden cross was placed at the head of each grave and on each cross was printed the soldier's name and regimental number.

Eventually word came along to the effect that each brigade had been allotted a section of the main firing-line. The Third Brigade's section was from a point at the head of a gully (near a place later to be known and remembered as Lone Pine) curving back towards the sea at what was called Brighton Beach. The other brigades were to take up positions in turn to the side of us, making a more or less continuous front. All personnel were to make their way to their designated areas.

At these positions over the next few days, we managed to get what was left of us into our units and build a proper trenchline. From this time on the fighting changed. It was now trench warfare. We were told that we had to hold our present line at all costs.

IN THE TRENCHES

Digging a trench with a pick and shovel was hard work. The main trench had to be from seven to eight feet deep and made in a way that it would protect us from shrapnel and rifle-fire. Every few yards a parapet was constructed so that we could get into a high position for keeping an eye on the enemy. Sand-bags were arranged to protect us while we were in the parapets on look-out duty. These bags were built up at least eighteen inches higher than a man standing, and had spaces left between, about five inches wide and six inches high. These holes were used for observation and for sniping through.

The Turks established a trench firing-line in front of ours—in some places they wouldn't have been more than twenty or so yards from our line. We had been told to always be ready for a counter-attack. During the first weeks of May, the Turks made no move in force to drive us out but subjected us to terrific shell-fire.

An invasion that did occur at about this time was body-lice—millions of them—and didn't they give us hell. Some of them were as big as a grain of wheat and they seemed to just come up out of the ground. The nuisance was made worse because we were compelled to wear cholera bands covering our kidneys and the lower parts of our body. These bands were made of a flannel material and had a strong smelling medicinal treatment in them to help combat the cholera disease. The lice didn't mind the smell at all, and used to get under the bands and give us hell until we could get off duty from the firing line. Then we would strip everything off and crack all the lice and eggs between our nails to give ourselves some relief.

The food that we were given wasn't very good. All we had to eat was tinned meat and dry hard biscuits. The meat was very salty and the biscuits were so hard that we had to soak them for a few hours to be able to scrape the outside off. We would eat this and then soak them again. These biscuits were about five inches square with holes through them about an inch apart. Oh, what we would have done for a good meal.

Enemy submarines were operating against our ships in the Mediterranean Sea and the Aegean with some success, so supplies were hard to get through to us. This may have had something to do with the kind of food we were getting.

The isolation in the trenches, and being confined to one area, was hard to take. It wasn't so bad when there was action, but living day in and day out almost underground and being lousy all the time got us down.

Our daily duty was two hours on in the frontline trenches, then two hours in the first line reserves, two hours in a dugout and then back to trench duty again. That was our routine—the only break we got was when it was our turn to go to the beach Headquarters and guard a donkey train of supplies up to our unit. Each company had to send its own guards for its supplies. (The donkey trains were worked by Indians who had been sent to Gallipoli with their donkeys especially for this purpose.)

It was while I was doing guard duty on one of these trips that our section was treated to a change of menu. I managed to secure a fourteen pound tin of butter and a kind of cheese. The cheese was round like a grindstone, and about eighteen inches across and four to five inches thick. Both the cheese and the butter looked very appetizing to me. I hunted around and found a bag to put them in, then slung the bag over one of the donkeys, telling the boss Indian that it was for me.

The supply trains travelled only in darkness because of shelling during the day, so it was next morning before my section divided the food. The butter was beautiful. We were now getting a few loaves of bread—one a week—so we had something to spread on it. After dividing the butter we set about cutting the cheese into fourteen pieces, a piece for each man. When I drove my bayonet through the middle of it, the stink that came out of that cheese would have to be smelled to be believed. I was advised by my mates to throw the cheese into No-Man's Land as they felt sure it would stink the Turks out of their trenches. So, although we were starving for a change of food, we weren't able to touch that cheese.

I dug a hole and buried it about three feet underground.

Water was another problem for us in the trenches. We had to carry all our water up from the beach near Headquarters and each section had to carry its own. Each day four men were detailed for water-carrying duty—we all took turns at this. Each man would carry two two-gallon cans which meant that we had no hands for our rifles. It was a common thing for us to be walking along with a can of water in each hand and our rifles slung over our shoulders, and have one can or both punctured by shrapnel. That meant a return trip to the beach to start all over again. That is, if we were lucky enough not to have been hit ourselves. None of us liked water-carrying; it was a very dangerous job.

On about the seventeenth of May we noticed the Turks becoming very active at night. We could hear their carts rattling down the roads, travelling towards the British positions to our right. There also seemed to be Turkish troops massing in and along our front, and during the daytime we could see, by looking through field-glasses and telescopes, quite large numbers of troops moving about. After this we received a message to the effect that a mass attack was expected at any time and every man was required to stand by.

On the evening of the eighteenth of May, the Turks bombarded us heavily for a time. Then in the early hours of the morning, before daylight, the attack came, and every available man was in position. The Turks had to come over a small rise and our trenches were just below this so that when the enemy appeared they showed out clearly to us. They were running but we were able to shoot them down as fast as they appeared. When daylight came there were hundreds of dead and wounded lying in No-Man's Land, some only a few yards in front of our firing-line. The Turks hit our line in places for what seemed like a couple of hours. My section was rushed a couple of times but we stopped them before they reached us—not one Turk got in our trench. Finally the Turks called it a day and word came through to the effect that we had defeated them all along the line.

No-Man's Land was now littered with bodies. Attempts were made to remove these for burial but enemy fire made this impossible. Many of our men were hit trying to bring in the bodies. The weather was very hot during the day and before long the corpses began to rot. The smell from this became almost unbearable, particularly when there was no breeze blowing.

At this time we had a distinguished visitor—a high-ranking British officer. He came along our main frontline trench with several of our Staff Officers and Commanding Officers. He got a whiff of the smell coming from No-Man's Land and asked the Australian officers, 'Why don't you bury the bodies?' Our Commanding Officer explained that the Turks opened fire every time this was attempted and that we had lost men trying. The officer's reply to this shocked all of us who heard him. He said, 'What is a few men?' He was standing only about ten feet from me when he said this and I was disgusted to think that life seemed to mean nothing to this man. We referred to him as 'Lord Kitchener' from then on.

Later the Turks sent an officer in under a white flag—he was blindfolded and on horseback. He was taken back from our lines to Headquarters to see our Command. Later, we received word that an armistice had been arranged for the twenty-fourth of May to enable both sides to bury the dead.

I will never forget the armistice—it was a day of hard, smelly, nauseating work. Those of us assigned to pick up the bodies had to pair up and bring the bodies in on stretchers to where the graves were being dug. First we had to cut the cord of the identification disks and record the details on a sheet of paper we were provided with. Some of the bodies were rotted so much that there were only bones and part of the uniform left. The bodies of men killed on the nineteenth (it had now been five days) were awful. Most of us had to work in short spells as we felt very ill. We found a few of our men who had been killed in the first days of the landing.

This whole operation was a strange experience—here we were, mixing with our enemies, exchanging smiles and cigarettes, when the day before we had been tearing each other to pieces. Apart from the noise of the grave-diggers and the padres reading the burial services, it was mostly silent. There was no shelling, no rifle-fire. Everything seemed so quiet and strange. Away to our left there were high table-topped hills and on these were what looked like thousands of people. Turkish civilians had taken advantage of the cease-fire to come out and watch the burial. Although they were several miles from us they could be clearly seen.

The burial job was over by mid-afternoon and we retired back to our trenches. Then, sometime between four and five o'clock, rifle-fire started again and then the shelling. We were at it once more.

On May twenty-fifth something happened that shocked all who saw it. Quite a few of us were sitting on the edge of our dugouts watching the navy ships shelling the Turkish positions away beyond our frontline. One large ship, the *Triumph*, was sending shells over our position from what seemed about two miles off shore. Suddenly there was a terrible explosion and for a few seconds we wondered what had happened. Then we realised that the *Triumph* had been hit by a torpedo. She started to list to the side and within fifteen minutes was completely upside down with her two propellers out of the water. In another half an hour she had disappeared completely. After the torpedo struck, the guns, both fore and aft, were firing as fast as they could and those gunners must have gone down with their ship. We considered this one of the most gallant acts of bravery that we had seen and we had seen many by this time. Most of the crew jumped overboard, and destroyers and small boats went to their rescue. We were told that about four hundred had lost their lives.

A few days after the armistice we received some trench comfort parcels from home. Everything was very quiet this day, and a sergeant-major and several men with bags of parcels came along our line and threw each of us a parcel. I got a pair of socks in my parcel. Having big feet—I take a ten in boots—I called out to my mates saying that I had a pair of socks that I would be glad to swap for a bigger pair as I didn't think they would fit. Strange as it seems, I was the only person in my section to get socks; the others got all kinds of things such as scarves, balaclavas, vests, notepaper, pencils, envelopes and handkerchiefs. I found a note rolled up in my socks and it read: 'We wish the soldier that gets this parcel the best of luck and health and a safe return home to his loved ones when the war is over.' It was signed, 'Evelyn Gibson, Hon. Secretary, Girl Guides, Bunbury, W.A.' A lot of my mates came from Bunbury so I asked if any of them knew an Evelyn Gibson. They all knew her and said that she was a good-looker and very smart, and that she came from a well-liked and respected family. I told them that she was mine and we all had an argument, in fun, about this girl and we all claimed her.

The socks, when I tried them on, fitted perfectly and they were hand-knitted with wool. That was the only parcel I received while at Gallipoli.

FROM
The Merry-Go-Round in the Sea (1965)

RANDOLPH STOW

Randolph Stow drew on his own Australian childhood to write his novel about the life of Rob Coram. In this excerpt, the hero, who is six years old, feels World War II creep into his life in 1940's Geraldton, Western Australia. "The people in Japan were suddenly wicked," he thinks. His beloved cousin Rick will fight in the war and return very much damaged, a victim of a Japanese prisoner-of-war camp. War becomes Rob's enemy. It takes Rick away from him and destroys the security of his childhood in the large Maplestead clan.

The merry-go-round had a centre post of cast iron, reddened a little by the salt air, and of a certain ornateness: not striking enough to attract a casual eye, but still, to an eye concentrated upon it (to the eye, say, of a lover of the merry-go-round, a child) intriguing in its transitions. The post began as a square pillar, formed rings, continued as a fluted column, suddenly bulged like a diseased tree with an excrescence of iron leaves, narrowed to a peak like the top of a pepperpot, and at last ended, very high in the sky, with an iron ball. In the bulge where the leaves were, was an iron collar. From this collar eight iron stays hung down, supporting the narrow wooden octagonal seat of the merry-go-round, which circled the knees of the centre post rather after the style of a crinoline. The planks were polished by the bottoms of children, and on every one of the stays was a small unrusted section where the hands of adults had grasped and pulled to send the merry-go-round spinning.

143

When the merry-go-round was moving it grated under its collar. But now it was still, there were no children playing about it, only the one small boy who had climbed out of the car by the curb and stood studying the merry-go-round from a distance, his hands jammed down inside the waistband of his shorts.

Under his sandals, leaves and nuts fallen from the Moreton Bay figtrees crunched and popped. Beyond the merry-go-round was the sea. The colour of the sea should have astounded, but the boy was seldom astounded. It was simply the sea, dark and glowing blue, bisected by seagull-gray timbers of the rotting jetty, which dwindled away in the distance until it seemed to come to an end in the flat-topped hills to the north. He did not think about the sea, or about the purple bougainvillaea that glowed against it, propped on a sagging shed. These existed only as the familiar backdrop of the merry-go-round. Nevertheless, the colours had entered into him, printing a brilliant memory.

He went, scuffing leaves, to the merry-go-round, and hanging his body over the narrow seat he began to run with it, lifting his legs from the ground as it gained momentum. But he could not achieve more than half a revolution by this means, and presently he stopped, feeling vaguely hard-used.

His mother was in the Library, getting books. He could see her now, coming out on to the veranda. The Library was a big place with an upstairs. It used to be the railway station in the Old Days, which made it very old indeed. In fact, everything about the merry-go-round was old, though he did not know it. Across the street the convict-built courthouse crumbled away, sunflowers sprouting from the cracked steps. The great stone barn at the next corner was Wainwright's store, where the early ships had landed supplies. That, too, was crumbling, like the jetty and the courthouse and the bougainvillaea-torn shed, like the upturned boat on the foreshore with sunflowers blossoming through its ribs.

The boy was not aware of living in a young country. He knew that he lived in a very old town, full of empty shops with dirty windows and houses with falling fences. He knew that he lived in an old, haunted land, where big stone flour mills and small stone farmhouses stood windowless and staring among twisted trees. The land had been young once, like the Sleeping Beauty, but it had been stricken, like the Sleeping Beauty, with a curse, called sometimes the Depression and sometimes the Duration, which would never end, which he would never wish to end, because what was was what should be, and safe.

He stood by the merry-go-round, watching his mother. She went to the car and opened the door, putting her books in. Then she looked up, anxious.

"Here I am," he called.

"You're a naughty boy," she said. "I told you to stay in the car."

"I want a ride," he said, "on the merry-go-round."

"We haven't time," said his mother. "We're going to Grandma's to pick up Nan and then we're going to the beach."

"I want a ride," he said, setting his jaw.

She came towards him, giving in, but not meekly. "Don't *scowl* at me, Rob," she said. She had curly brown hair, and her eyes were almost as blue as the sea.

He stopped scowling, and looked blank. He had blue eyes like hers, and blond hair which was darkening as he grew older, but was now bleached with summer. Summer had also freckled his nose and taken some of the skin off it. When he squinted he could see shreds of skin on his nose where it was peeling.

"Lift me up," he said.

His mother stooped and lifted him to the seat of the merry-go-round. "Oof," she said. "You are getting heavy."

"Aunt Kay lets me ride on her back," he said, "and she's old."

"Aunt Kay is very naughty. You mustn't let her give you piggybacks."

"You're not as strong as Aunt Kay," he said.

"Do you *want* a ride?" asked his mother, dangerously.

"Yes," he said. "Push me."

So she heaved on the iron stay that she was holding, and the merry-go-round started to turn. It moved slowly. She hauled on the other stays as they passed, but still it moved slowly.

"Faster," he shouted.

"Oh, Rob," she said, "it's too hot."

"Why don't you run round with it," he called, "like Mavis does."

"It's too hot," said his mother, with dampness on her forehead. The merry-go-round revolved. The world turned about him.

The Library, the car, the old store, the courthouse. Sunflowers, Moreton Bay figtrees, the jetty, the sea. Purple bougainvillaea against the sea.

"That's enough," his mother said. "We must go now." The merry-go-round slowed, and then she stopped it. He was sullen as she lifted him down.

"Mavis made it go fast," he said. "She ran with it."

"Mavis is a young girl," said his mother.

"Why did Mavis go away?"

"To get married."

"Why don't we have another maid?"

"People don't have maids now," said his mother.

"Why don't people have maids?"

"Because of the war. People don't have maids in wartime."

He was silent, thinking of that. The war was a curse, a mystery, an enchantment. Because of the war there were no more paper flowers. That was how he first knew that the curse had fallen. Once there had been little paper seeds that he had dropped into a bowl of water, and slowly they had opened out and become flowers floating in the water. The flowers had come from Japan. Now there was a war, and there would never be paper flowers again. The people in Japan were suddenly wicked, far wickeder than the Germans, though once they had only been funny, like Chinamen. For days and days he had heard the name Pearl Harbour, which was the name of a place where the people in Japan had done something very wicked. It must be a place like Geraldton. The sea he was looking at was called the Harbour. At a place like Geraldton the people in Japan had done something very wicked, and nothing would ever be the same again.

His mother had almost reached the car. She turned and looked back. "Come along," she called, "quick sticks."

He followed, crunching the big dry leaves. He was thinking of time and change, of how, one morning when he must have been quite small, he had discovered time, lying in the grass with his eyes closed against the sun. He was counting to himself. He counted up to sixty, and thought: That is a minute. Then he thought: It will never be that minute again. It will never be today again. Never.

He would not, in all his life, make another discovery so shattering.

He thought now: I am six years and two weeks old. I will never be that old again.

He climbed into the car beside his mother. The car jerked and moved, turning down the street between the courthouse and the store. The street was sandy, barren. The houses looked old and poor. Only the vacant blocks offered splashes of color, bright heads of sunflowers, the town's brilliant weed.

He thought, often, of himself, of who he was, and why. He would repeat to himself his name, Rob Coram, until the syllables meant nothing, and all names seemed absurd. He would think: I am Australian, and wonder why. Why was he not Japanese? There were millions of Japanese, and too few Australians. How had he come to be Rob Coram, living in this town?

The town was shabby, barren, built on shifting sandhills jutting out into the sea. To the north and south of the town the white dunes were never still, but were forever moving in the southerly, finding new outlines, windrippled, dazzling. If ever people were to leave the town the sand would come back to bury it. It would be at first like a town under snow. And then no town at all, only the woolwhite hills of Costa Branca.

To the north and south the dunes moved in the wind. Each winter the sea gnawed a little from the peninsula. Time was irredeemable. And far to the north was war.

Mrs. Maplestead's house was an old station homestead sitting in a town. This was because to Mrs. Maplestead, and to Miss Mackay MacRae, her sister, and to the late Charles Maplestead, her husband, a house meant a homestead and nothing less. The house was really two houses. At the front, there was a house for living in, a stone house of the convict era with massive walls and dark small rooms. At the back there was a wooden house composed of storerooms, some of which had highly specialized functions, among them an apple room, where big yellow-green Granny Smith apples lay about on tables, smelling sweetly. Joining the two houses was a covered cemented place, darkened by the rainwater tanks. And hung from the beams over the cement was a swing, which dated from the days when Rob had been the only grandchild.

As the years passed, Mrs. Maplestead's homestead had become more townified. The underground tank was unroofed and filled now, and Miss MacRae grew chrysanthemums inside its round wall. The cowshed sometimes stabled a horse, but no longer a cow, since the last Maplestead cow had got drunk on bad grapes, and walked round and round the paddock in circles, and died. But the contents of the house had never changed. Anywhere in Mrs. Maplestead's store-rooms one was likely to come across an odd stirrup, a bit, part of a shearing-piece, a lump of gold-bearing quartz. The late Charles Maplestead had thrown nothing away, and some of his leavings were inexplicable. No one could explain the two copper objects Rob had found in the wash-house, but everyone was agreed that there was only one thing they could be. They were false teeth for a horse.

He was satisfied with that. Sometimes when he asked what something was they would say: "It's a triantiwontigong. It's a wig-wam for a goose's bridle." That made him furious.

Mrs. Maplestead's house had a garden. At some time in the past load upon load of rich loam had come from one of Charles Maple-stead's farms, pockets of red soil had been imbedded in the sand, and things grew. But the best thing in the garden had been there always. It was the giant Moreton Bay figtree that arched over the stone house, carpeting the ground with its crackling leaves and dropping its dried fruits, clatter clatter, on the iron roof.

Mrs. Maplestead hated the tree. It choked up the gutters and buried the lawns. It pushed up the footpath in the street with its roots and tangled electric light wires in its branches. But the boy and his Aunt Kay loved it. At dawn and sunset the butcher-birds came, they warbled under the great dome of the tree, and their voices echoed as if they were singing in a huge empty rainwater tank, which was something that the boy himself liked to do.

Now the southerly had come in, the tough leaves of the tree were making a faint clapping. The boy followed his mother through the side gate in the plumbago hedge. The flowers of the white oleander beside the gate were withered and browned by the hot easterly that blew in the mornings, and in the heat the bigger flowers of the red oleander smelled overwhelmingly, sickeningly sweet. They walked the path beside the veranda, under swaying date-palms that were softly scraping the veranda roof. The dates were green, on stalks that were bright yellow. He reached out and pulled one off the tree and bit into it, and instantly his tongue dried up and shrivelled in his mouth and he stopped in the path and spat, and kept on spitting, spitting among the fallen jacaranda flowers, which were a colour he had no name for, neither blue nor purple, but more beautiful than any colour in the world.

"You silly boy," his mother said. "They might be poisonous."

He knew and she knew that they were not. But that was the sort of thing she always said, and he accepted.

Now they came upon a strange sight. Behind a clump of plumbago tangled with red tecoma was a lady with no face, only hair. She was bending over a basin, which stood on a small table, which stood on the lawn. Her hair was as white as the white basin. She was wearing an old flowered wrapper over her dress, and held a towel to the place where her face should have been.

"Grandma and Aunt Kay are always washing their hair," said the boy.

"Is that you, Rob?" his grandmother asked, still bending, covering her weeping hair with the towel. "Is Mummy there?"

"Yes," he said, watching her hands rubbing with the towel. There were dark marks on the skin of her hands, because she was old.

She straightened, drying her face, and said: "Oh, hullo." When she was not wearing her hair in a bun it was very long, it reached almost to her waist, and it was pure white. Once when she was in the garden moving a sprinkler a willie-wagtail swooped on her and pulled her hair, trying to get some to make a nest with, because it was whiter than wool. That was one of the funniest things that had ever happened. He teased his grandmother, who was frightened of birds, she said, since that day.

"Are you going to the beach, then?" Grandma said to his mother. She had sat down on a kitchen chair and reached for her hairbrush, sweeping the brush down the long white hair as it dried in the sun.

She had a nice face, and nice hair. She was looking at her face in her mirror. The back of the mirror, of beaten silver with patterns of flowers and cherubs, flashed in the sun.

"I suppose so," said his mother, long-sufferingly. "I'd love a cup of tea."

"Well, there's time," said Mrs. Maplestead.

The water in the basin was sharp in his nose. He knew what the smell was. It was ammonia. He could not think why Grandma would want that smell in her hair.

He moved away from it, into another smell, a sweetness. Stephanotis grew all over Mrs. Maplestead's rustic lavatory, and a penetrating fragrance spread out from the waxy flowers.

"Grandma," he said, "where's Aunt Kay?"

"She's in the playroom," his grandmother said, "she's with Nan."

"Oh," he said. He had not much time for Nan.

"Can you whistle yet, Rob?" asked his grandmother.

"No," said the boy, keeping his mouth almost closed. He was being teased, because he had no front teeth.

"Say: 'Six thick thistle sticks.' "

"No," he said. "That's silly." But it made him think of Aunt Kay again. In winter Aunt Kay was always picking thistles in the paddock and taking them out to the street to give to the baker's horse or the milkman's horse or any other horse she could find. Aunt Kay was mad about horses. On the corner near his house there was a horse-trough with a plate on it saying that it was a present to the horses from George and Annis Wills. Nobody knew who George and Annis Wills were, but Aunt Kay said they must be very good people, and he supposed that if Aunt Kay were rich there would be horse troughs all over the town with plates on them saying that they were a present to the horses from Miss MacKay MacRae.

He decided that he would go and talk to Aunt Kay after all, and went away, walking across the covered cement and into the second, the wooden house. The first room was the pantry, hung with big black preserving pans, its highest shelf a regular folk museum of Colonial household gear. There were silver lamps there that he would have liked to get down, because they looked like Aladdin's; but even standing on a box he could not reach them. The pantry smelled. It smelled of spice, and onions, and stifling heat.

His sister Nan was sitting in the doorway between the pantry and the play-room, her dark head bent over an album of ancient postcards. He stepped over her. Nan was four, and beneath contempt.

The window of the play-room was propped open with a board, letting in a little coolness, though the southerly could hardly penetrate the jungle of date palms outside. Half swallowed in the palm thicket, a figtree shot out from its rough leaves sudden volleys of greeneyes that were tearing at the ripe fruit.

Aunt Kay was sitting at the sewing machine, but she was not using it. She was darning men's socks. Aunt Kay was always darning men's socks, because she loved men. She went about the Maplestead clan soliciting men's socks to darn, and when she was not darning socks she was knitting socks, or picking grass seeds out of socks, or asking for news of the sock situation in outlying parts of the family.

At the moment she was darning a khaki sock. He stood looking at her. She was a little deaf, and had not heard him come in. She was wearing a grey-blue dress and a gold-and-opal brooch on her left breast. Aunt Kay had different-coloured dresses and different-shaped brooches, but the dress was always the same dress and the brooch was always in the same place; and on her left hand, hidden now in the sock, she always wore a big man's ring with a bloodstone in it. She wore her hair in a bun, like his grandmother's, but it was grey, and she had showed him once that it was still dark at the roots, although she was much older than Grandma, nearly seventy.

He stood looking at Aunt Kay. She was very thin, and strong. She still carried him on her back across the paddock to his own house, and when she needed firewood she put on a big pink frilly sunbonnet that almost covered her face and went out and chopped wood like a man. She carried buckets of water and killed snakes. He somehow knew, and knew that other people knew, that Aunt Kay was not like anybody else in the world.

"Aunt Kay," he said.

She jumped, though he had tried not to startle her. "Oh, Jeff," she said. "I mean, Gordon. I mean — *Rob*."

Aunt Kay was always getting his name wrong, and always referring to his grandmother as "your mother." She lived a good deal in the past, and her past was full of little boys. The names she called him by were the names of little brothers and little nephews, little boys to whom she had been governess, brothers-in-law and nieces' husbands, or simply male Maplesteads, Charles Maplestead's kin. Often she could go on for a long time getting his name wrong, fumbling her way through three generations. Usually she called him Jack, after her youngest brother, who was forever nine years old, and forever sneaking into bed fully clothed and with his boots on, so that he could go off shooting at first light.

He liked hearing her talk about Jack. He could not think of Jack as his great-uncle. Jack was a boy a little older than himself. He was called Little Jack, or Iain Vicky, to distinguish him from his cousin Big Jack, or Iain Mor. The names, Iain Vicky and Iain Mor, astonished him. They were words in a foreign language, called Gaelic, which was Aunt Kay's father's language. Aunt Kay and Grandma and Jack and all their brothers and sisters were Australians, like himself, but their father had had to go to school to learn English. This meant that in them and in himself there was something foreign and enchanted, something that connected them with the barely credible places where there was snow. He kept the names in his memory as a sort of password to the fatherland, his blood's speech.

Aunt Kay had even been to Scotland. Aunt Kay and his Uncle Paul were the only people who had ever been so far away. Nobody else had ever been farther than Singapore, except Gordon, who was at the war. Aunt Kay talked about snow and skating, and a lot about Bonnie Prince Charlie. His grandmother said that Aunt Kay was "fearfully Scotch."

"Scots," Aunt Kay would murmur. She considered that people ought not to say "Scotch," and she thought that Grandma at least should know better.

Aunt Kay's left hand, with the bloodstone ring, was hidden in a sock, a khaki sock. "That's one of Daddy's Garrison socks," he said.

"No," said Aunt Kay, "it's one of Rick's."

"Oh," said the boy, pleased, "is that Rick's?"

Rick Maplestead was his second cousin, whom he and Aunt Kay worshiped from afar.

"We're going to Sandalwood tomorrow," he said, "we'll see Rick."

"That will be nice," said Aunt Kay. "I hope he'll come and say goodbye to us before he goes."

"He'll have to come, to get his socks," said the boy.

He was poking around in Aunt Kay's sewing basket. It had funny things in it: bits of chalk, a candle-end, a pair of scissors shaped like a stork. And Aunt Kay had no less than ten thimbles. He fitted one on each finger, then leaned down and drummed a tune on the top of Nan's head.

Nan screamed.

"Rob," said Aunt Kay.

He took the thimbles off and dropped them in the basket. No matter what he did, he felt assured that Aunt Kay would not be cross with him, because he was a boy.

The door was open from the play-room into the big dark wash-house where the galvanized tubs sat in a row on the pinewood bench. Aunt Kay and Grandma had no taps in their wash-house or in their kitchen. They carried water in buckets and jugs from the rainwater tanks, and they were mean with water, because they came from a sheep station in western Victoria. Sometimes they filled the tubs days before they used them. They had done that this week. He knelt on the broad bench and looked at his face in the water. He brought his face down towards his other face, and merged his two faces, plunging his head in the water. Then he went back to the play-room, and stood over Nan, and dripped on her.

Nan screamed.

"Rob," said Aunt Kay.

He meant Nan no harm, but suddenly she bit him in the leg, so he had to kick her.

"I'm going now," he said. But he had hardly reached the pantry door before Nan streaked past him, off to lay a complaint.

On the lawn his mother and his grandmother turned and looked at him. Nan pointed and howled.

"Rob," his mother called, "did you kick Nan?"

"She bit me."

"What did you do to make her bite you?"

"I dripped water on her," he said, "that's all. That didn't hurt her. She's coming for a swim, isn't she?"

"How did you get wet?"

"I put my head in the washing water."

"You're *not* to do that," his mother said, "you'll fall in and drown."

The boy stopped feeling guilty and felt merely bored. His mother knew of an infinite number of ways to die. Once, one hot day at Sandalwood, he and his cousin Didi had got into the big Coolgardie safe on the back veranda and closed the door. It was very cool in there, water seeping continually down the clinker-packed walls. They shared the safe with half a sheep, and amused themselves by swinging the meat back and forth on its hook like a punching bag.

Suddenly the door swung open, and there stood Rob's mother.

"Come out," she said, "this *instant*, before you both get consumption."

After that the boy had stopped listening to his mother's warnings of doom. But because no catastrophe was possible which she would not have foreseen, he felt secure with her, he felt that she could thwart any danger, except the one danger he really feared, which was made up of time and change and fragmentary talk of war.

"Well," he said, "if we go to the beach now, and you teach me to swim, then I *can't* drown, can I?"

"Pig of a boy," Margaret Coram remarked to her mother. "I think he's going to be a lawyer like his father."

He could never beat her. She might give in, but not meekly.

The beach where the small children swam was called the West End. The water was shallow there, and the sand white and hard, so that cars could drive right to the edge. On hot nights there used always to be lines of cars there, before the war; and fish jumped out of the sea and shone in the headlights. The boy, in those days, would try to get his father to leave the headlights on; but his father, who liked to be invisible, never would.

It was on the beach that the boy liked his father most. He would cling to his father's freckled back and his father would swim away, out into the deep water, where it was dark blue instead of pale green. He would slip off his father's back sometimes, and swallow a lot of water, and choke with excitement. He was in love with the sea, and more than anything wanted to swim.

Or to go in a boat. Once Uncle Paul had taken him in a dinghy right to the end of the breakwater, and he had looked back and seen the town transformed, another town completely, rising out of deep green sea, below high sandhills which became flat-topped rock hills to the north. There had been a big ship at the wharf, and a fishing-boat had passed them, bound for the Abrolhos. The ends of the two grey jetties had seemed a short dog-paddle away. Because the whole world had been changed he had thought that then, at last, he might go to the merry-go-round. But on that day too there had been something to prevent it, and so they had come back again to the everyday shore.

Now Uncle Paul was away in the Air Force, and his father was in camp for the weekend, and he paddled listlessly in the warm shallows. He had been playing by himself in a circle of sandbags among the beach-olives, which had something to do with the war. His legs were caked with white sand. He bent to wash them.

The sun was going down behind the breakwater, gold and orange. Now more than ever the black merry-go-round was real.

His mother sat by the water, on a red towel, in blue bathers. He went and sat beside her, hugging his knees, staring at the merry-go-round. Sand kept falling on the towel as Nan dug canals with her spade.

"Mummy," he said.

"Yes, Rob?"

"Can't I go to the merry-go-round? Just once?"

"You've had one ride on the merry-go-round today."

"Not that one," he said, impatiently. "The other merry-go-round. The merry-go-round in the sea."

"Oh, Rob," she said, laughing, "won't you ever believe me? It's not a merry-go-round."

"It *looks* like a merry-go-round. It *must* be a merry-go-round, Mummy."

"It's a big boat," Margaret Coram said. "It's a big sort of barge that was carting rocks to build the breakwater. And one night there was a storm, and it sank. What you can see is the mast and the iron things that hold the mast up. It just happens to look like a merry-go-round."

He stared at it. It was very far away, but he could see the bulge where the iron leaves would be, and the collar from which the iron stays descended to support the seat. It could be nothing else but a merry-go-round in the sea.

"Have you been there?" he asked her, sullenly.

"Yes," she said, "I've seen it."

"Well, can't I go then? Can't I go there with you?"

"No, we can't, Rob. We can't go there."

"Why? Why can't we go there?"

"Oh—because of the war," his mother said.

Somehow he had foreseen that answer. He would never reach it, because of the war.

"Darling," his mother said, "you know that that end of the beach is where Daddy's camp is, and no one can go there now except the Garrison. There are barbed wire fences there to keep people out. So we just can't go to the merry-go-round—I mean the wreck—not till after the war. But you'll go there someday, if you really want to see it. The war won't last forever."

He listened to her with deep cynicism. The war always had been and always would be. The barbed wire would never come down.

"When I'm big," he said, slowly, getting up, "I'll *swim* there."

It was a threat.

He went back to the ring of sandbags, he lay in the sand. He thought how he would swim far out into the deep water, past all the fences, so far that looking back he would see the world transformed, as it had been from the dinghy. He would swim miles and miles, until at last the merry-go-round would tower above him, black, glistening, perfect, rooted in the sea. The merry-go-round would turn by itself, just a little above the green water. The world would revolve around him, and nothing would ever change. He would bring Rick to the merry-go-round, and Aunt Kay, and they would stay there always, spinning and diving and dangling their feet in the water, and it would be today forever.

The Kyogle Line (1985)

DAVID MALOUF

David Malouf, partly of Lebanese ancestry, is a poet, short story writer, novelist, and essayist. "The Kyogle Line" is taken from his volume of personal essays, 12 Edmondstone Street. Malouf re-creates in this essay his own childhood experience during World War II. He is on a train trip between Brisbane and Sydney when he glimpses three Japanese prisoners of war.

In July 1944, when train travel was still romantic, and hourly flights had not yet telescoped the distance between Brisbane and Sydney to a fifty-five minute interval of air-conditioned vistas across a tumble of slow-motion foam, we set out, my parents, my sister and I, on the first trip of my life—that is how I thought of it—that would take me over a border. We left from Kyogle Station, just a hundred yards from where we lived, on a line that was foreign from the moment you embarked on it, since it ran only south out of the state and had a gauge of four-foot-eight. Our own Queensland lines were three-foot-six and started from Roma Street Station on the other side of the river.

I was familiar with all this business of gauges and lines from school, where our complicated railway system, and its origins in the jealously guarded sovereignty of our separate states, was part of our lessons and of local lore, but also because, for all the years of my later childhood, I had seen transports pass our house ferrying troops across the city from one station to the other, on their way to Townsville and the far north. We lived in a strip of no-man's-land between lines; or, so far as the thousands of Allied troops were concerned, between safe, cosmopolitan Sydney and the beginning, at Roma Street, of their passage to the war.

Our own journey was for a two weeks' stay at the Balfour Hotel at the corner of King and Elizabeth Streets, Sydney. The owner was an old mate of my father's, which is why, in wartime, with all hotel rooms occupied, we had this rare chance of accommodation. Train bookings too were hard to come by. We would sit up for sixteen hours straight—maybe more, since the line was used for troop movements. I was delighted. It meant I could stay up all night. Staying awake past midnight was also, in its way, a border to be crossed.

I had been many times to see people off on the 'First Division,' and loved the old-fashioned railway compartments with their foliated iron racks for luggage, their polished woodwork, the spotty black-and-white pictures of Nambucca Heads or the Warrumbungles, and the heavy brocade that covered the seats and was hooked in swags at the windows. When we arrived to claim our seats, people were already crammed into the corridor, some of them preparing to stand all the way. There were soldiers in winter uniform going on leave with long khaki packs, pairs of gum-chewing girls with bangles and pompadours, women with small kids already snotty or smelly with wet pants, serious men in felt hats and double-breasted suits. The afternoon as we left was dry and windy, but hot in the compartment. It was still officially winter. When the sun went down it would be cold.

My mother would spend the journey knitting. She was, at that time, engaged in making dressing-gowns, always of the same pattern and in the same mulberry-coloured nine-ply, for almost everyone she knew. There was rationing, but no coupons were needed for wool. I had been taught to knit at school and my mother let me do the belts—I had already made nine or ten of them—but was waiting because I didn't want to miss the border and the view.

What I was hungry for was some proof that the world was as varied as I wanted it to be; that somewhere, on the far side of what I knew, difference began, and that the point could be clearly recognised.

The view did change, and frequently, but not suddenly or

sharply enough. It was a matter of geological forms I couldn't read, new variants of eucalypt and pine. The journey from this point of view was a failure, though I wouldn't admit it. I stayed excited and let my own vivid expectations colour the scene. Besides, it wasn't a fair test. We had barely passed the border when it was dark. It did get perceptibly colder. But was that a crossing into a new climate zone or just the ordinary change from day to night? The train rocked and sped, then jolted and stopped for interminable periods in a ring-barked nowhere; then jerked and clashed and started up again. We saw lights away in the darkness, isolated farmhouses or settlements suggesting that some of the space we were passing through was inhabited. We got grimy with smuts.

My mother knitted, even after the lights were lowered and other people had curled up under blankets. I too kept wide awake. I was afraid, as always, of missing something—the one thing that might happen or appear, that was the thing I was intended not to miss. If I did, a whole area of my life would be closed to me for ever.

So I was still awake, not long after midnight, when we pulled into Coff's Harbour and the train stopped to let people get off and walk for a bit, or buy tea at the refreshment room.

'Can *we*?' I pleaded. 'Wouldn't you like a nice cup of tea, Mummy? I could get it.'

My mother looked doubtful.

'It wouldn't do any harm,' my father said, 'to have a bit of a stretch.'

'I need to go to the lav,' I threw in, just to clinch the thing. It had been difficult to make your way through standing bodies and over sleeping ones to the cubicles at either end of the carriage. The last time we went we had had to step over a couple, one of them a soldier, who were doing something under a blanket. My father, who was modest, had been shocked.

'Come on then.' We climbed down.

It was a clear cold night and felt excitingly different, fresher than I had ever known, with a clean smell of dark bushland sweeping away under stars to the escarpments of the Great Divide. People, some of them in dressing-gowns and carrying thermos flasks, were bustling along the platform. The train hissed and clanged. It was noisy; but the noise rose straight up into the starry night as if the air here were thinner, offered no resistance. It felt sharp in your lungs.

We passed a smoky waiting-room where soldiers were sprawled in their greatcoats, some on benches, others on the floor, their rifles in stacks against the wall; then the refreshment room with its crowded bar. It was a long walk to the Men's, all the length of the platform. I had never been out after midnight, and I expected it to be stranger. It *was* strange but not strange enough. In some ways the most different thing of all was to be taking a walk like this with my father.

We were shy of one another. He had always worked long hours, and like most children in those days I spent my time on the edge of my mother's world, always half-excluded but half-involved as well. My father's world was foreign to me. He disappeared into it at six o'clock, before my sister and I were up, and came back again at tea-time, not long before we were packed off to bed. If we went down under-the-house on Saturdays to watch him work, with a stub of indelible pencil behind his ear, as some men wear cigarettes, it was to enter a world of silence there that belonged to his deep communication with measurements, and tools, and dove-tail joints that cast us back on our own capacity for invention.

He was not much of a talker, our father. He seldom told us things unless we asked. Then he would answer our questions too carefully, as if he feared, with his own lack of schooling, that he might lead us wrong. And he never told stories, as our mother did, of his family and youth. His family were there to be seen, and however strange they might be in fact, did not lend themselves to fairytale. My father had gone out to work at twelve. If he never spoke of his youth it was, perhaps, because he had never had one, or because its joys and sorrows were of a kind we could not be expected to understand. There was no grand house to remember, as my mother remembered New Cross; no favourite maids; no vision of parents sweeping into the nursery to say goodnight in all the ballroom finery of leg o'mutton sleeves and pearl combs and shirt-fronts stiff as boards. His people were utterly ordinary. The fact that they were also *not* Australian, that they ate garlic and oil, smelled different, and spoke no English, was less important than that they had always been there and had to be taken as they were.

Our father himself was as Australian as anyone could be—except for the name. He had made himself so. He had played football for the State, and was one of the toughest welterweights of his day, greatly admired for his fairness and skill by an entire generation.

But all this seemed accidental in him. A teetotaller and non-smoker, very quiet in manner, fastidiously modest, he had an inner life that was not declared. He had educated himself in the things that most interested him, but his way of going about them was his own; he had worked the rules out for himself. He suffered from never having been properly schooled, and must, I see now, have hidden deep hurts and humiliations under his studied calm. The best he could do with me was to make me elaborate playthings—box-kites, a three-foot yacht—and, for our backyard, a magnificent set of swings. My extravagance, high-strung fantasies, which my mother tended to encourage, intimidated him. He would have preferred me to become, as he had, a more conventional type. He felt excluded by my attachment to books.

So this walk together was in all ways unusual, not just because we were taking it at midnight in New South Wales.

We walked in silence, but with a strong sense, on my part at least, of our being together and at one. I liked my father. I wished he would talk to me and tell me things. I didn't know him. He puzzled me, as it puzzled me too that my mother, who was so down on our speaking or acting 'Australian,' should be so fond of these things as they appeared, in their gentler form, in him. She had made, in his case, a unique dispensation.

On our way back from the Men's we found ourselves approaching a place where the crowd, which was generally very mobile, had stilled, forming a bunch round one of the goods wagons.

'What is it?' I wanted to know.

'What is it?' my father asked another fellow when we got close. We couldn't see anything.

'Nips,' the man told us. 'Bloody Nips. They got three Jap P.O.W.'s in there.'

I expected my father to move away then, to move me on. If he does, I thought, I'll get lost. I wanted to see them.

But my father stood, and we worked our way into the centre of the crowd; and as people stepped away out of it we were drawn to the front, till we stood staring in through the door of a truck.

It was too big to be thought of as a cage, but was a cage, just the same. I thought of the circus wagons that sometimes came and camped in the little park beside South Brisbane Station, or on the waste ground under Grey Street Bridge.

There was no straw, no animal smell. The three Japs, in a group, if not actually chained then at least huddled, were difficult to make out in the half-dark. But looking in at them was like looking in from our own minds, our own lives, on another species. The vision imposed silence on the crowd. Only when they broke the spell by moving away did they mutter formulas, 'Bloody Japs,' or 'The bastards,' that were meant to express what was inexpressible, the vast gap of darkness they felt existed here—a distance between people that had nothing to do with actual space, or the fact that you were breathing, out here in the still night of Australia, the same air. The experience was an isolating one. The moment you stepped out of the crowd and the shared sense of being part of it, you were alone.

My father felt it. As we walked away he was deeply silent. Our moment together was over. What was it that touched him? Was he thinking of a night, three years before, when the Commonwealth Police had arrested his father as an enemy alien?

My grandfather came to Brisbane from Lebanon in the 1880s; though in those days of course, when Australia was still unfederated, a parcel of rival states, Lebanon had no existence except in the mind of a few patriots. It was part of greater Syria; itself then a province of the great, sick Empire of the Turks. My grandfather had fled his homeland in the wake of a decade of massacres. Like other Lebanese Christians, he had sorrowfully turned his back on the Old Country and started life all over again in the New World.

His choice of Australia was an arbitrary one. No one knows why he made it. He might equally have gone to Boston or to Sao Paolo in Brazil. But the choice, once made, was binding. My father and the rest of us were Australians now. That was that. After Federation, in the purely notional view of these things that was practised by the immigration authorities, greater Syria (as opposed to Egypt and Turkey proper) was declared white—but only the Christian inhabitants of it, a set of official decisions, in the matter of boundary and distinction, that it was better not to question. My father's right to be an Australian, like any Scotsman's for example, was guaranteed by this purely notional view—that is, officially. The rest he had to establish for himself; most often with his fists. But my grandfather, by failing to get himself naturalised, remained an alien. At first a Syrian, later a Lebanese. And when Lebanon, as a dependency of France, declared for Vichy rather than the Free French, he became an enemy as well.

He was too old, at more than eighty, to be much concerned by any of this, and did not understand perhaps how a political decision made on the other side of the world had changed his status, after so long, on this one. He took the bag my aunts packed for him and went. It was my father who was, in his quiet way—what?—shaken, angered, disillusioned?

The authorities—that is, the decent local representatives—soon recognised the absurdity of the thing and my grandfather was released: on personal grounds. My father never told us how he had managed it, or what happened, what he *felt*, when he went to fetch his father home. If it changed anything for him, the colour of his own history for example, he did not reveal it. It was just another of the things he kept to himself and buried. Like the language. He must, I understood later, have grown up speaking Arabic as well as he spoke Australian; his parents spoke little else. But I never heard him utter a word of it or give any indication that he understood. It went on as a whole layer of his experience, of his understanding and feeling for things, of alternative being, that could never be expressed. It too was part of the shyness between us.

We got my mother her nice cup of tea, and five minutes later, in a great bustle of latecomers and shouts and whistles, the train started up again and moved deeper into New South Wales. But I thought of it now as changed. Included in its string of lighted carriages, along with the sleeping soldiers and their packs and slouch-hats with sunbursts on the turn-up, the girls with their smeared lipstick and a wad of gum hardening now under a rim of the carriage-work, the kids blowing snotty bubbles, the men in business suits, was that darker wagon with the Japs.

Their presence imposed silence. That had been the first reaction. But what it provoked immediately after was some sort of inner argument or dialogue that was in a language I couldn't catch. It had the rhythm of the train wheels over those foreign four-foot-eight inch rails—a different sound from the one our own trains made— and it went on even when the train stalled and waited, and long after we had come to Sydney and the end of our trip. It was, to me, as if I had all the time been on a different train from the one I thought. Which would take more than the sixteen hours the time-table announced and bring me at last to a different, unnameable destination.

American Dreams (1974)

PETER CAREY

Peter Carey, a best-selling novelist, has also written two volumes of short stories. His fiction has been called surreal, fantastic, and absurdist. He has been labeled as a member of the Latin American school of magical realism. However, Carey creates his own brand of fictional magic that does not fit comfortably under any label.

No one can, to this day, remember what it was we did to offend him. Dyer the butcher remembers a day when he gave him the wrong meat and another day when he served someone else first by mistake. Often when Dyer gets drunk he recalls this day and curses himself for his foolishness. But no one seriously believes that it was Dyer who offended him.

But one of us did something. We slighted him terribly in some way, this small meek man with the rimless glasses and neat suit who used to smile so nicely at us all. We thought, I suppose, he was a bit of a fool and sometimes he was so quiet and grey that we ignored him, forgetting he was there at all.

When I was a boy I often stole apples from the trees at his house up in Mason's Lane. He often saw me. No, that's not correct. Let me say I often sensed that he saw me. I sensed him peering out from behind the lace curtains of his house. And I was not the only one. Many of us came to take his apples, alone and in groups, and it is possible that he chose to exact payment for all these apples in his own peculiar way.

Yet I am sure it wasn't the apples.

What has happened is that we all, all eight hundred of us, have come to remember small transgressions against Mr. Gleason who once lived amongst us.

My father, who has never borne malice against a single living creature, still believes that Gleason meant to do us well, that he loved the town more than any of us. My father says we have treated the town badly in our minds. We have used it, this little valley, as nothing more than a stopping place. Somewhere on the way to somewhere else. Even those of us who have been here many years have never taken the town seriously. Oh yes, the place is pretty. The hills are green and the woods thick. The stream is full of fish. But it is not where we would rather be.

For years we have watched the films at the Roxy and dreamed, if not of America, then at least of our capital city. For our own town, my father says, we have nothing but contempt. We have treated it badly, like a whore. We have cut down the giant shady trees in the main street to make doors for the school house and seats for the football pavilion. We have left big holes all over the countryside from which we have taken brown coal and given back nothing.

The commercial travellers who buy fish and chips at George the Greek's care for us more than we do, because we all have dreams of the big city, of wealth, of modern houses, of big motor cars: American Dreams, my father has called them.

Although my father ran a petrol station he was also an inventor. He sat in his office all day drawing strange pieces of equipment on the back of delivery dockets. Every spare piece of paper in the house was covered with these little drawings and my mother would always be very careful about throwing away any piece of paper no matter how small. She would look on both sides of any piece of paper very carefully and always preserved any that had so much as a pencil mark.

I think it was because of this that my father felt that he understood Gleason. He never said as much, but he inferred that he understood Gleason because he, too, was concerned with similar problems. My father was working on plans for a giant gravel crusher, but occasionally he would become distracted and become interested in something else.

There was, for instance, the time when Dyer the butcher bought a new bicycle with gears, and for a while my father talked of nothing else but the gears. Often I would see him across the road squatting down beside Dyer's bicycle as if he were talking to it.

We all rode bicycles because we didn't have the money for anything better. My father did have an old Chev truck, but he rarely used it and it occurs to me now that it might have had some mechanical problem that was impossible to solve, or perhaps it was just that he was saving it, not wishing to wear it out all at once. Normally, he went everywhere on his bicycle and, when I was younger, he carried me on the cross bar, both of us dismounting to trudge up the hills that led into and out of the main street. It was a common sight in our town to see people pushing bicycles. They were as much a burden as a means of transport.

Gleason also had his bicycle and every lunchtime he pushed and pedalled it home from the shire offices to his little weatherboard house out at Mason's Lane. It was a three-mile ride and people said that he went home for lunch because he was fussy and wouldn't eat either his wife's sandwiches or the hot meal available at Mrs. Lessing's café.

But while Gleason pedalled and pushed his bicycle to and from the shire offices everything in our town proceeded as normal. It was only when he retired that things began to go wrong.

Because it was then that Mr. Gleason started supervising the building of the wall around the two-acre plot up on Bald Hill. He paid too much for this land. He bought it from Johnny Weeks, who now, I am sure, believes the whole episode was his fault, firstly for cheating Gleason, secondly for selling him the land at all. But Gleason hired some Chinese and set to work to build his wall. It was then that we knew that we'd offended him. My father rode all the way out to Bald Hill and tried to talk Mr. Gleason out of his wall. He said there was no need for us to build walls. That no one wished to spy on Mr. Gleason or whatever he wished to do on Bald Hill. He said no one was in the least bit interested in Mr. Gleason. Mr. Gleason, neat in a new sportscoat, polished his glasses and smiled vaguely at his feet. Bicycling back, my father thought that he had gone too far. Of course we had an interest in Mr. Gleason. He pedalled back and asked him to attend a dance that was to be held on the next Friday, but Mr. Gleason said he didn't dance.

"Oh well," my father said, "any time, just drop over."

Mr. Gleason went back to supervising his family of Chinese labourers on his wall.

Bald Hill towered high above the town and from my father's small filling station you could sit and watch the wall going up. It was an interesting sight. I watched it for two years, while I waited for customers who rarely came. After school and on Saturdays I had all the time in the world to watch the agonizing progress of Mr. Gleason's wall. It was as painful as a clock. Sometimes I could see the Chinese labourers running at a jog-trot carrying bricks on long wooden planks. The hill was bare, and on this bareness Mr. Gleason was, for some reason, building a wall.

In the beginning people thought it peculiar that someone would build such a big wall on Bald Hill. The only thing to recommend Bald Hill was the view of the town, and Mr. Gleason was building a wall that denied that view. The top soil was thin and bare clay showed through in places. Nothing would ever grow there. Everyone assumed that Gleason had simply gone mad and after the initial interest they accepted his madness as they accepted his wall and as they accepted Bald Hill itself.

Occasionally someone would pull in for petrol at my father's filling station and ask about the wall and my father would shrug and I would see, once more, the strangeness of it.

"A house?" the stranger would ask. "Up on that hill?"

"No," my father would say, "chap named Gleason is building a wall."

And the strangers would want to know why, and my father would shrug and look up at Bald Hill once more. "Damned if I know," he'd say.

Gleason still lived in his old house at Mason's Lane. It was a plain weatherboard house with a rose garden at the front, a vegetable garden down the side, and an orchard at the back.

At night we kids would sometimes ride out to Bald Hill on our bicycles. It was an agonizing, muscle-twitching ride, the worst part of which was a steep, unmade road up which we finally pushed our bikes, our lungs rasping in the night air. When we arrived we found nothing but walls. Once we broke down some of the brickwork and another time we threw stones at the tents where the Chinese labourers slept. Thus we expressed our frustration at this inexplicable thing.

The wall must have been finished on the day before my twelfth birthday. I remember going on a picnic birthday party up to Eleven Mile Creek and we lit a fire and cooked chops at a bend in the river from where it was possible to see the walls on Bald Hill. I remember standing with a hot chop in my hand and someone saying, "Look, they're leaving!"

We stood on the creek bed and watched the Chinese labourers walking their bicycles slowly down the hill. Someone said they were going to build a chimney up at the mine at A.1 and certainly there is a large brick chimney there now, so I suppose they built it.

When the word spread that the walls were finished most of the town went up to look. They walked around the four walls which were as interesting as any other brick walls. They stood in front of the big wooden gates and tried to peer through, but all they could see was a small blind wall that had obviously been constructed for this special purpose. The walls themselves were ten feet high and topped with broken glass and barbed wire. When it became obvious that we were not going to discover the contents of the enclosure, we all gave up and went home.

Mr. Gleason had long since stopped coming into town. His wife came instead, wheeling a pram down from Mason's Lane to Main Street and filling it with groceries and meat (they never bought vegetables, they grew their own) and wheeling it back to Mason's Lane. Sometimes you would see her standing with the pram halfway up the Gell Street hill. Just standing there, catching her breath. No one asked her about the wall. They knew she wasn't responsible for the wall and they felt sorry for her, having to bear the burden of the pram and her husband's madness. Even when she began to visit Dixon's hardware and buy plaster of paris and tins of paint and waterproofing compound, no one asked her what these things were for. She had a way of averting her eyes that indicated her terror of questions. Old Dixon carried the plaster of paris and the tins of paint out to her pram for her and watched her push them away. "Poor woman," he said, "poor bloody woman."

From the filling station where I sat dreaming in the sun, or from the enclosed office where I gazed mournfully at the rain, I would see, occasionally, Gleason entering or leaving his walled compound, a tiny figure way up on Bald Hill. And I'd think "Gleason," but not much more.

Occasionally strangers drove up there to see what was going on, often egged on by locals who told them it was a Chinese temple or some other silly thing. Once a group of Italians had a picnic outside the walls and took photographs of each other standing in front of the closed door. God knows what they thought it was.

But for five years between my twelfth and seventeenth birthdays there was nothing to interest me in Gleason's walls. Those years seem lost to me now and I can remember very little of them. I developed a crush on Susy Markin and followed her back from the swimming pool on my bicycle. I sat behind her in the pictures and wandered past her house. Then her parents moved to another town and I sat in the sun and waited for them to come back.

We became very keen on modernization. When coloured paints became available the whole town went berserk and brightly coloured houses blossomed overnight. But the paints were not of good quality and quickly faded and peeled, so that the town looked like a garden of dead flowers. Thinking of those years, the only real thing I recall is the soft hiss of bicycle tyres on the main street. When I think of it now it seems very peaceful, but I remember then that the sound induced in me a feeling of melancholy, a feeling somehow mixed with the early afternoons when the sun went down behind Bald Hill and the town felt as sad as an empty dance hall on a Sunday afternoon.

And then, during my seventeenth year, Mr. Gleason died. We found out when we saw Mrs. Gleason's pram parked out in front of Phonsey Joy's Funeral Parlour. It looked very sad, that pram, standing by itself in the windswept street. We came and looked at the pram and felt sad for Mrs. Gleason. She hadn't had much of a life.

Phonsey Joy carried old Mr. Gleason out to the cemetery by the Parwan Railway Station and Mrs. Gleason rode behind in a taxi. People watched the old hearse go by and thought, "Gleason," but not much else.

And then, less than a month after Gleason had been buried out at the lonely cemetery by the Parwan Railway Station, the Chinese labourers came back. We saw them push their bicycles up the hill. I stood with my father and Phonsey Joy and wondered what was going on.

And then I saw Mrs. Gleason trudging up the hill. I nearly didn't recognize her, because she didn't have her pram. She carried a black umbrella and walked slowly up Bald Hill and it wasn't until she stopped for breath and leant forward that I recognized her.

"It's Mrs. Gleason," I said, "with the Chinese."

But it wasn't until the next morning that it became obvious what was happening. People lined the main street in the way they do for a big funeral but, instead of gazing towards the Grant Street corner, they all looked up at Bald Hill.

All that day and all the next people gathered to watch the destruction of the walls. They saw the Chinese labourers darting to and fro, but it wasn't until they knocked down a large section of the wall facing the town that we realized there really was something inside. It was impossible to see what it was, but there was something there. People stood and wondered and pointed out Mrs. Gleason to each other as she went to and fro supervising the work.

And finally, in ones and twos, on bicycles and on foot, the whole town moved up to Bald Hill. Mr. Dyer closed up his butcher shop and my father got out the old Chev truck and we finally arrived up at Bald Hill with twenty people on board. They crowded into the back tray and hung on to the running boards and my father grimly steered his way through the crowds of bicycles and parked just where the dirt track gets really steep. We trudged up this last steep track, never for a moment suspecting what we would find at the top.

It was very quiet up there. The Chinese labourers worked diligently, removing the third and fourth walls and cleaning the bricks which they stacked neatly in big piles. Mrs. Gleason said nothing either. She stood in the only remaining corner of the walls and looked defiantly at the townspeople who stood open-mouthed where another corner had been.

And between us and Mrs. Gleason was the most incredibly beautiful thing I had ever seen in my life. For one moment I didn't recognize it. I stood open-mouthed, and breathed the surprising beauty of it. And then I realized it was our town. The buildings were two feet high and they were a little rough but very correct. I saw Mr. Dyer nudge my father and whisper that Gleason had got the faded "U" in the BUTCHER sign of his shop.

I think at that moment everyone was overcome with a feeling of simple joy. I can't remember ever having felt so uplifted and happy. It was perhaps a childish emotion but I looked up at my father and saw a smile of such warmth spread across his face that I knew he felt just as I did. Later he told me that he thought Gleason had built the model of our town just for this moment, to let us see the beauty of our own town, to make us proud of ourselves and to stop the American Dreams we were so prone to. For the rest, my father said, was not Gleason's plan and he could not have foreseen the things that happened afterwards.

I have come to think that this view of my father's is a little sentimental and also, perhaps, insulting to Gleason. I personally believe that he knew everything that would happen. One day the proof of my theory may be discovered. Certainly there are in existence some personal papers, and I firmly believe that these papers will show that Gleason knew exactly what would happen.

We had been so overcome by the model of the town that we hadn't noticed what was the most remarkable thing of all. Not only had Gleason built the houses and the shops of our town, he had also peopled it. As we tip-toed into the town we suddenly found ourselves. "Look," I said to Mr. Dyer, "there you are."

And there he was, standing in front of his shop in his apron. As I bent down to examine the tiny figure I was staggered by the look on its face. The modelling was crude, the paintwork was sloppy, and the face a little too white, but the expression was absolutely perfect: those pursed, quizzical lips and the eyebrows lifted high. It was Mr. Dyer and no one else on earth.

And there beside Mr. Dyer was my father, squatting on the footpath and gazing lovingly at Mr. Dyer's bicycle's gears, his face marked with grease and hope.

And there was I, back at the filling station, leaning against a petrol pump in an American pose and talking to Brian Sparrow who was amusing me with his clownish antics.

Phonsey Joy standing beside his hearse. Mr. Dixon sitting inside his hardware store. Everyone I knew was there in that tiny town. If they were not in the streets or in their backyards they were inside their houses, and it didn't take very long to discover that you could lift off the roofs and peer inside.

We tip-toed around the streets peeping into each other's windows, lifting off each other's roofs, admiring each other's gardens, and, while we did it, Mrs. Gleason slipped silently away down the hill towards Mason's Lane. She spoke to nobody and nobody spoke to her.

I confess that I was the one who took the roof from Cavanagh's house. So I was the one who found Mrs. Cavanagh in bed with young Craigie Evans.

I stood there for a long time, hardly knowing what I was seeing. I stared at the pair of them for a long, long time. And when I finally knew what I was seeing I felt such an incredible mixture of jealousy and guilt and wonder that I didn't know what to do with the roof.

Eventually it was Phonsey Joy who took the roof from my hands and placed it carefully back on the house, much, I imagine, as he would have placed the lid on a coffin. By then other people had seen what I had seen and the word passed around very quickly.

And then we all stood around in little groups and regarded the model town with what could only have been fear. If Gleason knew about Mrs. Cavanagh and Craigie Evans (and no one else had), what other things might he know? Those who hadn't seen themselves yet in the town began to look a little nervous and were unsure of whether to look for themselves or not. We gazed silently at the roofs and felt mistrustful and guilty.

We all walked down the hill then, very quietly, the way people walk away from a funeral, listening only to the crunch of the gravel under our feet while the women had trouble with their high-heeled shoes.

The next day a special meeting of the shire council passed a motion calling on Mrs. Gleason to destroy the model town on the grounds that it contravened building regulations.

It is unfortunate that this order wasn't carried out before the city newspapers found out. Before another day had gone by the government had stepped in.

The model town and its model occupants were to be preserved. The minister for tourism came in a large black car and made a speech to us in the football pavilion. We sat on the high, tiered seats eating potato chips while he stood against the fence and talked to us. We couldn't hear him very well, but we heard enough. He called the model town a work of art and we stared at him grimly. He said it would be an invaluable tourist attraction. He said tourists would come from everywhere to see the model town. We would be famous. Our businesses would flourish. There would be work for guides and interpreters and caretakers and taxi drivers and people selling soft drinks and ice creams.

The Americans would come, he said. They would visit our town in buses and in cars and on the train. They would take photographs and bring wallets bulging with dollars. American dollars.

We looked at the minister mistrustfully, wondering if he knew about Mrs. Cavanagh, and he must have seen the look because he said that certain controversial items would be removed, had already been removed. We shifted in our seats, like you do when a particularly tense part of a film has come to its climax, and then we relaxed and listened to what the minister had to say. And we all began, once more, to dream our American Dreams.

We saw our big smooth cars cruising through cities with bright lights. We entered expensive night clubs and danced till dawn. We made love to women like Kim Novak and men like Rock Hudson. We drank cocktails. We gazed lazily into refrigerators filled with food and prepared ourselves lavish midnight snacks which we ate while we watched huge television sets on which we would be able to see American movies free of charge and forever.

The minister, like someone from our American Dreams, re-entered his large black car and cruised slowly from our humble sportsground, and the newspaper men arrived and swarmed over the pavilion with their cameras and notebooks. They took photographs of us and photographs of the models up on Bald Hill. And the next day we were all over the newspapers. The photographs of the model people side by side with photographs of the real people. And our names and ages and what we did were all printed there in black and white.

They interviewed Mrs. Gleason but she said nothing of interest.

She said the model town had been her husband's hobby.

We all felt good now. It was very pleasant to have your photograph in the paper. And, once more, we changed our opinion of Gleason. The shire council held another meeting and named the dirt track up Bald Hill, "Gleason Avenue." Then we all went home and waited for the Americans we had been promised.

It didn't take long for them to come, although at the time it seemed an eternity, and we spent six long months doing nothing more with our lives than waiting for the Americans.

Well, they did come. And let me tell you how it has all worked out for us.

The Americans arrive every day in buses and cars and sometimes the younger ones come on the train. There is now a small airstrip out near the Parwan cemetery and they also arrive there, in small aeroplanes. Phonsey Joy drives them to the cemetery where they look at Gleason's grave and then up to Bald Hill and then down to the town. He is doing very well from it all. It is good to see someone doing well from it. Phonsey is becoming a big man in town and is on the shire council.

On Bald Hill there are half a dozen telescopes through which the Americans can spy on the town and reassure themselves that it is the same down there as it is on Bald Hill. Herb Gravney sells them ice creams and soft drinks and extra film for their cameras. He is another one who is doing well. He bought the whole model from Mrs. Gleason and charges five American dollars admission. Herb is on the council now too. He's doing very well for himself. He sells them the film so they can take photographs of the houses and the model people and so they can come down to the town with their special maps and hunt out the real people.

To tell the truth most of us are pretty sick of the game. They come looking for my father and ask him to stare at the gears of Dyer's bicycle. I watch my father cross the street slowly, his head hung low. He doesn't greet the Americans any more. He doesn't ask them questions about colour television or Washington, D.C. He kneels on the footpath in front of Dyer's bike. They stand around him. Often they remember the model incorrectly and try to get my father to pose in the wrong way. Originally he argued with them, but now he argues no more. He does what they ask. They push him this way and that and worry about the expression on his face which is no longer what it was.

Then I know they will come to find me. I am next on the map. I am very popular for some reason. They come in search of me and my petrol pump as they have done for four years now. I do not await them eagerly because I know, before they reach me, that they will be disappointed.

"But this is not the boy."

"Yes," says Phonsey, "this is him alright." And he gets me to show them my certificate.

They examine the certificate suspiciously, feeling the paper as if it might be a clever forgery. "No," they declare. (Americans are so confident.) "No," they shake their heads, "this is not the real boy. The real boy is younger."

"He's older now. He used to be younger." Phonsey looks weary when he tells them. He can afford to look weary.

The Americans peer at my face closely. "It's a different boy."

But finally they get their cameras out. I stand sullenly and try to look amused as I did once. Gleason saw me looking amused but I can no longer remember how it felt. I was looking at Brian Sparrow. But Brian is also tired. He finds it difficult to do his clownish antics and to the Americans his little act isn't funny. They prefer the model. I watch him sadly, sorry that he must perform for such an unsympathetic audience.

The Americans pay one dollar for the right to take our photographs. Having paid the money they are worried about being cheated. They spend their time being disappointed and I spend my time feeling guilty that I have somehow let them down by growing older and sadder.

III.

Relationships

The selections in Part III trace personal relationships and quests for identity that are influenced by sexual politics. This fiction reflects the ongoing process of redefining gender rules. The shaping of national identity is, as Australian fiction suggests, a challenge. Shaping a personal identity is for each of us no less a task. Part of the development of a secure self-image, national or personal, involves having balanced, healthy relationships with others. But these relationships, the bedrock of growth, are not often easily achieved.

The possibilities of close partnership and commitment are evoked in Tim Winton's story about becoming parents. However, suburban marriage falls far short of partnership in Patrick White's satiric scrutiny, while Olga Masters explores obstacles to healthy sexuality in the form of provincial repression. In most of these sensitive and beautifully written stories, there are no easy roads to good relationships and healthy self-development. A satisfying adultery, for example, in Helen Garner's tale, commands its price when it is time to return home. Similarly, maintaining loving gay relationships is a matter of struggle in stories by Henry Handel Richardson and Frank Moorhouse.

For women particularly, close sexual relationships have often meant a loss of individual identity. Men, traditionally more powerful, are presented as victimizers of women in the selections by Christina Stead, Marian Eldridge, and Beverley Farmer. In an episode from a novel, Stead uncovers the miseries of a bright, ambitious young female trapped in a male world. She describes a damaging father–daughter dynamic in the traditional patriarchal household. Powerlessness and victimization of another kind, equally destructive, is represented in Eldridge's young, abandoned welfare mother. Dispossessed on all fronts, she is a casualty of the men who impregnate her and leave, and of her own dreams of male saviors. Farmer's story goes further. Her heroine is robbed of all the characteristics of individual identity. She becomes the object of a twisted male fantasy.

Some of the selections here carry a strong scent of Australia, obvious when the bush becomes an important resource for a central character or when Moorhouse's hero, in his search for male bonding, evokes the Australian mateship tradition. However, the basic concerns of this fiction are insistently universal and timeless, although dressed in contemporary garb. We recognize the demands of sex, love, and maturity that impinge upon our lives, overriding cultural boundaries.

Willy-wagtails by Moonlight (1964)

PATRICK WHITE

This polished tale of deceit comes from The Burnt Ones, *a collection of short fiction by Patrick White. His heroine, Nora, a social failure in the eyes of her world, is not a failure in the eyes of the author or the reader. Quite the contrary, since White endows her with the gift of natural grace, a kind of transcendence that he reserves for those characters in his works who belong to the spiritual elite. These characters are always seekers of something beyond the material. They search for something beyond the small ambitions and received opinions of characters like the Wheelers in this story.*

The Wheelers drove up to the Mackenzies' punctually at six-thirty. It was the hour for which they had been asked. My God, thought Jum Wheeler. It had been raining a little, and the tyres sounded blander on the wet gravel.

In front of the Mackenzies', which was what is known as a Lovely Old Home—colonial style—amongst some carefully natural-looking gums, there stood a taxi.

"Never knew Arch and Nora ask us with anyone else," Eileen Wheeler said.

"Maybe they didn't. Even now. Maybe it's someone they couldn't get rid of."

"Or an urgent prescription from the chemist's."

Eileen Wheeler yawned. She must remember to show sympathy, because Nora Mackenzie was going through a particularly difficult one.

Anyway, they were there, and the door stood open on the lights inside. Even the lives of the people you know, even the lives of Nora and Arch look interesting for a split second, when you drive up and glimpse them through a lit doorway.

"It's that Miss Cullen," Eileen said.

For there was Miss Cullen, doing something with a brief-case in the hall.

"Ugly bitch," Jum said.

"Plain is the word," corrected Eileen.

"Arch couldn't do without her. Practically runs the business."

Certainly that Miss Cullen looked most methodical, shuffling the immaculate papers, and slipping them into a new pigskin brief-case in Arch and Nora's hall.

"Got a figure," Eileen conceded.

"But not a chin."

"Oh, hello, Miss Cullen. It's stopped raining."

It was too bright stepping suddenly into the hall. The Wheelers brightly blinked. They looked newly made.

"Keeping well, Miss Cullen, I hope?"

"I have nothing to complain about, Mr Wheeler," Miss Cullen replied.

She snapped the catch. Small, rather pointed breasts under the rain-coat. But, definitely, no chin.

Eileen Wheeler was fixing her hair in the reproduction Sheraton mirror.

She had been to the hairdresser's recently, and the do was still set too tight.

"Well, good-bye now," Miss Cullen said.

When she smiled there was a hint of gold, but discreet, no more than a bridge. Then she would draw her lips together, and lick them ever so slightly, as if she had been sucking a not unpleasantly acid sweetie.

Miss Cullen went out the door, closing it firmly but quietly behind her.

"That was Miss Cullen," said Nora Mackenzie coming down. "She's Arch's secretary.

"He couldn't do without her," she added, as though they did not know.

Nora was like that. Eileen wondered how she and Nora had tagged along together, ever since Goulburn, all those years.

"God, she's plain!" Jum said.

Nora did not exactly frown, but pleated her forehead the way she did when other people's virtues were assailed. Such attacks seemed to affect her personally, causing her almost physical pain.

"But Mildred is so kind," she insisted.

Nora Mackenzie made a point of calling her husband's employees by first names, trying to make them part of a family which she alone, perhaps, would have liked to exist.

"She brought me some giblet soup, all the way from Balgowlah, that time I had virus flu."

"Was it good, darling?" Eileen asked.

She was going through the routine, rubbing Nora's cheek with her own. Nora was pale. She must remember to be kind.

Nora did not answer, but led the way into the lounge-room.

Nora said: "I don't think I'll turn on the lights for the present. They hurt my eyes, and it's so restful sitting in the dusk."

Nora *was* pale. She had, in fact, just taken a couple of Disprin.

"Out of sorts, dear?" Eileen asked.

Nora did not answer, but offered some dry martinis.

Very watery, Jum knew from experience, but drink of a kind.

"Arch will be down presently," Nora said. "He had to attend to some business, some letters Miss Cullen brought. Then he went in to have a shower."

Nora's hands were trembling as she offered the dry martinis, but Eileen remembered they always had.

The Wheelers sat down. It was all so familiar, they did not have to be asked, which was fortunate, as Nora Mackenzie always experienced difficulty in settling guests into chairs. Now she sat down herself, far more diffidently than her friends. The cushions were standing on their points.

Eileen sighed. Old friendships and the first scent of gin always made her nostalgic.

"It's stopped raining," she said, and sighed.

"Arch well?" Jum asked.

As if he cared. She had let the ice get into the cocktail, turning it almost to pure water.

"He has his trouble," Nora said. "You know, his back."

Daring them to have forgotten.

Nora loved Arch. It made Eileen feel ashamed.

So fortunate for them to have discovered each other. Nora Leadbeatter and Arch Mackenzie. Two such bores. And with bird-watching in common. Though Eileen Wheeler had never believed Nora did not make herself learn to like watching birds.

At Goulburn, in the early days, Nora would come out to Glen Davie sometimes to be with Eileen at week-ends. Mr Leadbeatter had been manager at the Wales for a while. He always saw that his daughter had the cleanest notes. Nora was shy, but better than nothing, and the two girls would sit about on the veranda those summer evenings, buffing their nails, and listening to the sheep cough in the home paddock. Eileen gave Nora lessons in making up. Nora had protested, but was pleased.

"Mother well, darling?" Eileen asked, sipping that sad, watery gin.

"Not exactly *well*," Nora replied, painfully.

Because she had been to Orange, to visit her widowed mother, who suffered from Parkinson's disease.

"You know what I mean, dear," said Eileen.

Jum was dropping his ash on the carpet. It might be better when poor bloody Arch came down.

"I have an idea that woman, that Mrs Galloway, is unkind to her," Nora said.

"Get another," Eileen advised. "It isn't like after the war."

"One can never be sure," Nora debated. "One would hate to hurt the woman's feelings."

Seated in the dusk Nora Mackenzie was of a moth colour. Her face looked as though she had been rubbing it with chalk. Might have, too, in spite of those lessons in make-up. She sat and twisted her hands together.

How very red Nora's hands had been, at Goulburn, at the convent, to which the two girls had gone. Not that they belonged to *those*. It was only convenient. Nora's hands had been red and trembly after practising a tarantella, early, in the frost. So very early all of that. Eileen had learnt about life shortly after puberty. She had tried to tell Nora one or two things, but Nora did not want to hear.

Oh, no, no, *please*, Eileen, Nora cried. As though a boy had been twisting her arm. She had those long, entreating, sensitive hands.

And there they were still. Twisting together, making their excuses. For what they had never done.

Arch came in then. He turned on the lights, which made Nora wince, even those lights which barely existed in all the neutrality of Nora's room. Nora did not comment, but smiled, because it was Arch who had committed the crime.

Arch said: "You two toping hard as usual."

He poured himself the rest of the cocktail.

Eileen laughed her laugh which people found amusing at parties.

Jum said, and bent his leg, if it hadn't been for Arch and the shower, they wouldn't have had the one too many.

"A little alcohol releases the vitality," Nora remarked ever so gently.

She always grew anxious at the point where jokes became personal.

Arch composed his mouth under the handle-bar moustache, and Jum knew what they were in for.

"Miss Cullen came out with one or two letters," Arch was taking pains to explain. "Something she thought should go off tonight. I take a shower most evenings. Summer, at least."

"Such humidity," Nora helped.

Arch looked down into his glass. He might have been composing further remarks, but did not come out with them.

That silly, bloody English-air-force-officer's moustache. It was the only thing Arch had ever dared. War had given him the courage to pinch a detail which did not belong to him.

"That Miss Cullen, useful girl," Jum suggested.

"Runs the office."

"Forty, if a day," Eileen said, whose figure was beginning to slacken off.

Arch said he would not know, and Jum made a joke about Miss Cullen's cul-de-sac.

The little pleats had appeared again in Nora Mackenzie's chalky brow. "Well," she cried, jumping up, quite girlish, "I do hope the dinner will be a success."

And laughed.

Nora was half-way through her second course with that woman at the Chanticleer. Eileen suspected there would be avocados stuffed with prawns, chicken *Mornay*, and *crêpes Suzette*.

Eileen was right.

Arch seemed to gain in authority sitting at the head of his table. "I'd like you to taste this wine," he said. "It's very light."

"Oh, yes?" said Jum.

The wine was corked, but nobody remarked. The second bottle, later on, was somewhat better. The Mackenzies were spreading themselves tonight.

Arch flipped his napkin once or twice, emphasizing a point. He smoothed the handle-bar moustache, which should have concealed a harelip, only there wasn't one. Jum dated from before the moustache, long, long, very long.

Arch said: "There was a story Armitage told me at lunch. There was a man who bought a mower. Who suffered from indigestion. Now, how, exactly, did it . . . go?"

Jum had begun to make those little pellets out of bread. It always fascinated him how grubby the little pellets turned out. And himself not by any means dirty.

Arch failed to remember the point of the story Armitage had told.

It was difficult to understand how Arch had made a success of his business. Perhaps it was that Miss Cullen, breasts and all, under the rain-coat. For a long time Arch had messed around. Travelled in something. Separator parts. Got the agency for some sort of phoney machine for supplying *ozone* to public buildings. The Mackenzies lived at Burwood then. Arch continued to mess around. The war was quite a godsend. Arch was the real Adj type. Did a conscientious job. Careful with his allowances, too.

Then, suddenly, after the war, Arch Mackenzie had launched out, started the import-export business. Funny the way a man will suddenly hit on the idea to which his particular brand of stupidity can respond.

The Mackenzies had moved to the North Shore, to the house which still occasionally embarrassed Nora. She felt as though she ought to apologize for success. But there was the bird-watching.

Most week-ends they went off to the bush, to the Mountains or somewhere. She felt happier in humbler circumstances. In time she got used to the tape recorder which they took along. She made herself look upon it as a necessity rather than ostentation.

Eileen was dying for a cigarette.

"May I smoke, Arch?"

"We're amongst friends, aren't we?"

Eileen did not answer that. And Arch fetched the ash-tray they kept handy for those who needed it.

Nora in the kitchen dropped the beans. Everybody heard, but Arch asked Jum for a few tips on investments, as he always did when Nora happened to be out of the room. Nora had some idea that the Stock Exchange was immoral.

Then Nora brought the dish of little, pale, tinned peas.

"Ah! *Pet—ty pwah!*" said Jum.

He formed his full and rather greasy lips into a funnel through which the little rounded syllables poured most impressively.

Nora forgot her embarrassment. She envied Jum his courage in foreign languages. Although there were her lessons in Italian, she would never have dared utter in public.

"Can you bear *crêpes Suzette?*" Nora had to apologize.

"Lovely, darling." Eileen smiled.

She would have swallowed a tiger. But was, *au fond*, at her gloomiest.

What was the betting Nora would drop the *crêpes Suzette?* It was those long, trembly hands, on which the turquoise ring looked too small and innocent. The Mackenzies were still in the semi-precious bracket in the days when they became engaged.

"How's the old bird-watching?"

Jum had to force himself, but after all he had drunk their wine.

Arch Mackenzie sat deeper in his chair, almost completely at his ease.

"Got some new tapes," he said. "We'll play them later. Went up to Kurrajong on Sunday, and got the bell-birds. I'll play you the lyre-bird, too. That was Mount Wilson."

"Didn't we hear the lyre-bird last time?" Eileen asked.

Arch said: "Yes."

Deliberately.

"But wouldn't you like to hear it again? It's something of a collector's piece."

Nora said they'd be more comfortable drinking their coffee in the lounge.

Where Arch fetched the tape recorder. He set it up on the Queen Anne walnut piecrust. It certainly was an impressive machine.

"I'll play you the lyre-bird."

"The *pièce de résistance*? Don't you think we should keep it?"

"He can never wait for the lyre-bird."

Nora had grown almost complacent. She sat holding her coffee, smiling faintly through the steam. The children she had never had with Arch were about to enter.

"Delicious coffee," Eileen said.

She had finished her filter-tips. She had never felt drearier.

The tape machine had begun to snuffle. There was quite an unusual amount of crackle. Perhaps it was the bush. Yes, that was it. The bush!

"Well, it's really quite remarkable how you people have the patience," Eileen Wheeler had to say.

"Ssh!"

Arch Mackenzie was frowning. He had sat forward in the period chair.

"This is where it comes in."

His face was tragic in the shaded light.

"Get it?" he whispered.

His hand was helping. Or commanding.

"Quite remarkable," Eileen repeated.

Jum was shocked to realize he had only two days left in which to take up the ICI rights for old Thingummy.

Nora sat looking at her empty cup. But lovingly.

Nora could have been beautiful, Eileen saw. And suddenly felt old, she who had stripped once or twice at amusing parties. Nora Mackenzie did not know about that.

Somewhere in the depths of the bush Nora was calling that it had just turned four o'clock, but she had forgotten to pack the thermos.

The machine snuffled.

Arch Mackenzie was listening. He was biting his moustache.

"There's another passage soon." He frowned.

"Darling," Nora whispered, "after the lyre-bird you might slip into the kitchen and change the bulb. It went while I was making the coffee."

Arch Mackenzie's frown deepened. Even Nora was letting him down.

But she did not see. She was so in love.

It might have been funny if it was not also pathetic. People were horribly pathetic, Eileen Wheeler decided, who had her intellectual moments. She was also feeling sick. It was Nora's *crêpes Suzette*, lying like blankets.

"You'll realize there are one or two rough passages," Arch said, coming forward when the tape had ended. "I might cut it."

"It could do with a little trimming," Eileen agreed. "But perhaps it's more natural without."

Am I a what's-this, a masochist, she asked.

"Don't forget the kitchen bulb," Nora prompted.

Very gently. Very dreamy.

Her hair had strayed, in full dowdiness, down along her white cheek.

"I'll give you the bell-birds for while I'm gone."

Jum's throat had begun to rattle. He sat up in time, though, and saved his cup in the same movement.

"I remember the bell-birds," he said.

"Not these ones, you don't These are new. These are the very latest. The best bell-birds."

Arch had started the tape, and stalked out of the room, as if to let the bell-birds themselves prove his point.

"It is one of our loveliest recordings," Nora promised.

They all listened or appeared to.

When Nora said: "Oh, dear"—getting up—"I do believe"—panting almost—"the bell-bird tape"—trembling—"is damaged."

Certainly the crackle was more intense.

"Arch will be so terribly upset."

She had switched off the horrifying machine. With surprising skill for one so helpless. For a moment it seemed to Eileen Wheeler that Nora Mackenzie was going to hide the offending tape some-where in her bosom. But she thought better of it, and put it aside on one of those little superfluous tables.

"Perhaps it's the machine that's broken," suggested Jum.

"Oh, no," said Nora, "it's the tape. I know. We'll have to give you something else."

"I can't understand"—Eileen grinned—"how you ever got around, Nora, to being mechanical."

"If you're determined," Nora said.

Her head was lowered in concentration.

"If you want a thing enough."

She was fixing a fresh tape.

"And we do love our birds. Our Sundays together in the bush."

The machine had begun its snuffling and shuffling again. Nora Mackenzie raised her head, as if launched on an invocation.

Two or three notes of bird-song fell surprisingly pure and clear, out of the crackle, into the beige and string-coloured room.

"This is one," Nora said, "I don't think I've ever heard before."

She smiled, however, and listened to identify.

"Willy-wagtails," Nora said.

Willy-wagtails were suited to tape. The song tumbled and ex-ulted.

"It must be something," Nora said, "that Arch made while I was with Mother. There were a couple of Sundays when he did a little field-work on his own."

Nora might have given way to a gentle melancholy for all she had foregone if circumstances had not heightened the pitch. There was Arch standing in the doorway. Blood streaming.

"Blasted bulb collapsed in my hand!"

"Oh, darling! Oh *dear!*" Nora cried.

The Wheelers were both fascinated. There was the blood drip-ping on the beige wall-to-wall.

How the willy-wagtails chortled.

Nora Mackenzie literally staggered at her husband, to take upon herself, if possible, the whole ghastly business.

"Come along, Arch," she moaned. "We'll fix. In just a minute," Nora panted.

And simply by closing the door, she succeeded in blotting the situation, all but the drops of blood that were left behind on the carpet.

"Poor old Arch! Bleeding like a pig!" Jum Wheeler said, and laughed.

Eileen added:

"We shall suffer the willy-wags alone."

Perhaps it was better like that. You could relax. Eileen began to pull. Her step-ins had eaten into her.

The willy-wagtails were at it again.

"Am I going crackers?" asked Jum. "Listening to those bloody birds!"

When somebody laughed. Out of the tape. The Wheelers sat. Still.

Three-quarters of the bottle! Snuffle crackle. *Arch Mackenzie, you're a fair trimmer!* Again that rather brassy laughter.

"Well, I'll be blowed!" said Jum Wheeler.

"But it's that Miss Cullen," Eileen said.

The Wheeler spirits soared as surely as plummets dragged the notes of the wagtail down.

But it's far too rocky, and far too late. Besides, it's willy-wagtails we're after. How Miss Cullen laughed. *Willy-wagtails by moonlight!* Arch was less intelligible, as if he had listened to too many birds, and caught the habit. Snuffle crackle went the machine. . . . *the buttons are not made to undo* . . . Miss Cullen informed. *Oh, stop it, Arch!* ARCH! *You're* TEARING *me!*

So that the merciless machine took possession of the room. There in the crackle of twigs, the stench of ants, the two Wheelers sat. There was that long, thin Harry Edwards, Eileen remembered, with bony wrists, had got her down behind the barn. She had hated it at first. All mirth had been exorcised from Miss Cullen's recorded laughter. Grinding out. Grinding out. So much of life was recorded by now. Returning late from a country dance, the Wheelers had fallen down amongst the sticks and stones, and made what is called love, and risen in the grey hours, to find themselves numb and bulging.

If only the tape, if you knew the trick with the wretched switch.

Jum Wheeler decided not to look at his wife. Little, guilty pockets were turning themselves out in his mind. That woman at the Locomotive Hotel. Pockets and pockets of putrefying trash. Down along the creek, amongst the tussocks and the sheep pellets, the sun burning his boy's skin, he played his overture to sex. Alone.

This sort of thing's all very well, Miss Cullen decided. *It's time we turned practical. Are you sure we can find our way back to the car?*

Always trundling. Crackling. But there were the blessed wagtails again.

"Wonder if they forgot the machine?"

"Oh, God! hasn't the tape bobbed up in Pymble?"

A single willy-wagtail sprinkled its grace-notes through the stuffy room.

"Everything's all right," Nora announced. "He's calmer now. I persuaded him to take a drop of brandy."

"That should fix him," Jum said.

But Nora was listening to the lone wagtail. She was standing in the bush. Listening. The notes of bird-song falling like mountain water, when they were not chiselled in moonlight.

"There is nothing purer," Nora said, "than the song of the wagtail. Excepting Schubert," she added, "some of Schubert."

She was so shyly glad it had occurred to her.

But the Wheelers just sat.

And again Nora Mackenzie was standing alone amongst the inexorable moonlit gums. She thought perhaps she had always felt alone, even with Arch, while grateful even for her loneliness.

"Ah, there you are!" Nora said.

It was Arch. He stood holding out his bandaged wound. Rather rigid. He could have been up for court martial.

"I've missed the willy-wagtails," Nora said, raising her face to him, exposing her distress, like a girl. "Some day you'll have to play it to me. When you've the time. And we can concentrate."

The Wheelers might not have existed.

As for the tape, it had discovered silence.

Arch mumbled they'd all better have something to drink.

Jum agreed it was a good idea.

"Positively brilliant," Eileen said.

A Good Marriage (1980)

___

OLGA MASTERS

Olga Masters, a part-time journalist and mother of seven, was in her fifties when she became a fiction writer. Most of her stories are about families; her settings are often small towns or poor rural areas. In this story, as in her other works, her sympathy rests with characters who struggle to keep passion, energy, and vitality from fading out of their lives.

My father sat at the kitchen table much longer than he should have talking about Clarice Carmody coming to Berrigo.

My mother got restless because of the cigarettes my father was rolling and smoking. She worked extra fast glancing several times pointedly through the doorway at the waving corn paddock which my father had come from earlier than he need have for morning tea.

He creaked the kitchen chair as he talked especially when he said her name.

"Clarice Carmody! Sounds like one of them Tivoli dancers!"

My mother put another piece of wood in the stove.

"God help Jack Patterson, that's all I can say," my father said. My mother's face wore an expression that said she wished it was.

"A mail order marriage!" my father said putting his tobacco tin in his hip pocket. Suddenly he laughed so loud my mother turned around at the dresser.

"That's a good one!" he said, slapping his tongue on his cigarette paper with his brown eyes shining.

My mother strutted to the stove on her short fat legs to put the big kettle over the heat.

"It might be too," she said.

"Might be what too?" my father said, almost but not quite mocking her.

"A good marriage," my mother said, emptying the teapot into the scrap bucket which seemed another way of saying morning tea time was over.

"They've never set eyes on each other!" my father said. "They wouldn't know each other's faults . . . "

"They'll soon learn them," my mother said dumping the biscuit tin on the dresser top after clamping the lid on.

The next sound was a clamping noise too. My father crossed the floor on the way out almost treading on me sitting on the doorstep.

"Out of the damn way!" he said, quite angry.

My mother sat on a chair for a few moments after he'd gone watching through the doorway with the hint of a smile which vanished when her eyes fell on me.

"You could be out there giving him a hand," she said.

My toe began to smart a little where his big boots grazed it.

I bit at my kneecaps hoping my mother would say no more on the idea.

She didn't. She began to scrape new potatoes splashing them in a bowl of water.

Perhaps she was thinking about Clarice Carmody. I was. I was seeing her dancing on the stage of the old School of Arts. I thought of thistledown lifted off the ground and bowling along when you don't believe there is a wind. In my excitement I wrapped my arms around my knees and licked them.

"Stop that dirty habit," my mother said. "Surely there is something you could be doing."

"Will we visit Clarice Carmody?" I asked.

"She won't be Clarice Carmody," my mother said, vigorously rinsing a potato. "She'll be Clarice Patterson."

She sounded different already.

She came to Berrigo at the start of the September school holidays.

"The spring and I came together!" she said to me when at last I got to see her at home.

She and Jack Patterson moved into the empty place on the

Pattersons' farm where a farm hand and his family lived when the Patterson children were little. When the two boys left school they milked and ploughed and cleared the bush with old Bert Patterson the father. The girl Mary went to the city to work in an office which sounded a wonderful life to me. Cecil Patterson the younger son married Elsie Clark and brought her to the big old Patterson house to live. Young Mrs Patterson had plenty to do as old Mrs Patterson took to her bed when another woman came into the house saying her legs went.

My father was always planning means of tricking old Mrs Patterson into using her legs, like letting a fire get out of control on Berrigo sports' day, or raising the alarm on Berrigo picture night.

For old Mrs Patterson's disability didn't prevent her from going to everything that was on in Berrigo carried from the Pattersons' car by Jack and Cecil. Immediately she was set down, to make up for the time spent in isolation on the farm where Elsie took out her resentment with long sulky silences, she turned her fat, creamy face to left and right looking for people to talk to.

Right off she would say "not a peep out of the silly things" when asked about her legs.

My father who called her a parasite and a sponger would sit in the kitchen after meals and roll and smoke his cigarettes while he worked out plans for making her get up and run.

My mother sweeping his saucer away while his cup was in midair said more than once good luck to Gladdie Patterson, she was the smartest woman in Berrigo, and my father silenced would get up after a while and go back to work.

Jack Patterson went to the city and brought Clarice back. My father said how was anyone to know whether they were married or not and my mother said where was the great disadvantage in not being married? My father's glance fell on the old grey shirt of his she was mending and he got up very soon and clumped off to the corn paddock.

I tried to see now by looking at Clarice whether she was married to Jack Patterson. She wore a gold ring which looked a bit loose on her finger. My father having lost no time in getting a look at Clarice when she first arrived said it was one of Mrs Patterson's old rings or perhaps he said one of old Mrs Patterson's rings. He described

Clarice as resembling "one of them long armed golliwog dolls kids play with." Then he added with one of his short quick laughs that she would be about as much use to Jack Patterson as a doll.

The wedding ring Clarice wore didn't seem to match her narrow hand. I saw it plainly when she dug her finger into the jar of jam I'd brought her.

Her mouth and eyes went round like three O's. She waggled her head and her heavy frizzy hair shook.

"Lovely, darlink," she said. "You must have the cleverest, kindest mother in the whole of the world."

I blushed at this inaccurate description of my mother and hoped the two would not meet up too soon for Clarice to be disappointed.

Sitting there on one of her kitchen chairs, which like all the other furniture were leftovers from the big house, I did not want ever to see Clarice disappointed.

My hopes were short-lived. Jack Patterson came in then and Clarice's face and all her body changed. She did look a little like a golliwog doll although her long arms were mostly gracefully loose. Now she seemed awkward putting her hand on the kettle handle, looking towards Jack as if asking should she be making tea. Both Jack and I looked at the table with several dirty cups and saucers on it. Jack looked over my head out the window. Clarice walked in a stiff-legged way to the table and picked up the jam.

"Look!" she said holding it to the light. "The lovely colour! Jam red!" Jack Patterson had seen plenty of jam so you couldn't expect him to be impressed. He half hung his head and Clarice tried again.

"This is Ellen from across the creek! Oh, goodness me! I shouldn't go round introducing people! Everyone knows everyone in the country!"

Jack Patterson took his yard hat and went out.

"Oh, darlink!" Clarice said in a defeated way putting the jam on the shelf above the stove. I wanted to tell her that wasn't where you kept the jam but didn't dare.

She sat on a chair with her feet forward, the skirt of her dress reaching to her calves. She looked straight at me, smiling and crinkling her eyes.

"I think, darlink," she said, "you and I are going to be really great friends."

People said that in books. Here was Clarice saying it to me. She had mentioned introducing me too, which was something happening to me for the first time in my life. I was happy enough for my heart to burst through my skinny ribs.

But I had to get off the chair and go home. My mother said I was to give her the jam and go.

But she asked me about Clarice and Jack Patterson as if she expected me to observe things while I was there. "What's the place like?" she said.

I remembered the dark little hall and the open bedroom door showing the bed not made and clothes hanging from the brass knobs and the floor mat wrinkled. And Clarice with her halo of frizzy hair and her wide smile drawing me down the hall to her.

"She's got it fixed up pretty good," I lied.

"The work all done?" my mother asked.

I said yes because I felt Clarice had done all the work she intended to do for that day anyway.

I felt unhappy for Clarice because the Berrigo women most looked up to were those who got their housework done early and kept their homes neat all the time.

I next saw Clarice two months later at Berrigo show.

She wore a dress of soft green material with a band of the same stuff holding her wild hair above her forehead.

"Look!" said Merle Adcock, who was eighteen and dressed from Winn's mail order catalogue. "She got her belt tied round her head!"

Clarice had her arm through Jack Patterson's, which also drew scornful looks from Berrigo people. When Jack Patterson talked to other men about the prize cows and bulls Clarice stayed there, and watching them I was pretty sure Jack would have liked to have shaken Clarice's arm off.

My mother worked all day in the food tent at the show but managed to get what Berrigo called "a good gander" at Clarice with Jack.

"A wife hasn't made a difference to Jack Patterson," she said at home that afternoon. "He looks as hang dog as ever."

My father, to my surprise and perhaps to hers too, got up at once and went off to the yard.

The sports day was the week after the show and that was when my father and Clarice met.

Clarice saw me and said "Hello, darlink" and laid a finger on my nose to flatten the turned up end. She laughed when she did it so my feelings wouldn't be hurt.

My father suddenly appeared behind us.

I was about to scuttle off thinking that was why he was there, but he stood in a kind of strutting pose looking at Clarice and putting a hand on the crown of my hat.

"I'm this little one's Dad," he said. "She could introduce us."

I was struck silent by his touch and by his voice with a teasing note in it, so I couldn't have introduced them even if practised at it.

"Everyone is staring at me," Clarice said. "So they know who I am."

"Berrigo always stares," said my father taking out his tobacco tin and cigarette papers and staring at Clarice too.

She lifted her chin and looked at him with all her face in a way she had. "Like the cows," she said and laughed.

Her glance fell on his hands rolling his smoke, so different from my mother's expression. I thought smoking was sinful but started to change my ideas seeing Clarice's lively interested eyes and smiling mouth.

"Your father was talking to Clarice Carmody," my mother said at home after the sports as if it was my fault.

I noticed she said Clarice Carmody, not Clarice Patterson and perhaps she read my thoughts.

"I doubt very much that she's Clarice Patterson," my mother said, hanging up the potholder with a jab.

I felt troubled. First it was my father who seemed opposed to Clarice. Now it was my mother. I wondered how I would get to see her.

My chance came when I least expected it. My mother sent me with the slide normally used to take the cans of cream to the roadside to be picked up by the cream lorry, to load with dry sticks to get the stove and copper fire going.

The shivery grass was blowing and I was imagining it was the sea which I had never seen, and the slide was a ship sailing through it.

Clarice was standing there in the bush as if she had dropped from the sky.

"Darlink!" she called stalking towards me holding her dress away from the tussocks and blackberries sprouting up beside the track which led down to the creek separating Patterson's from our place.

"It's so hot, darlink isn't it?" she said lifting her mop of hair for the air to get through it.

No one else looked at me the way Clarice did with her smiling mouth, wrinkling nose and crinkling eyes. I hoped she didn't find me too awful with straight hair and skin off my sunburned nose and a dress not even fit to wear to school.

She put out a finger and pressed my nose and laughed.

"Why don't we go for a swim, darlink?" she said.

Behind her below the bank of blackberries there was a water-hole. A tree felled years and years ago and bleached white as a bone made a bridge across the creek. The water banked up behind it so it was deep on one side and just a trickle on the other.

I wasn't allowed to swim there. In fact I couldn't swim and neither could any other girls in Berrigo my age. The teacher at school who was a man took the boys swimming in the hole but there was no woman to take the girls so we sat on the school verandah and read what we liked from the school bookshelf supervised by Cissy Adcock the oldest girl in the school.

But how could I tell Clarice I couldn't swim much less take my clothes off? I would certainly be in for what my mother called the father of a belting for such a crime.

"I'll swim and you can cool your tootsies," Clarice said throwing an arm around me.

We walked down the track crushed together, me thinking already of looking back on this wonderful change of events, but worried about my bony frame not responding to her embrace.

She let go of me near the bank and stepping forward a pace or two began to take off her clothes.

One piece after another.

She lifted her dress and petticoat over her head and cast them onto the branch of a sapling gum. Her hands came around behind her unhooking her brassiere which was something I dreamed of wearing one day and threw it after her other things. When she bent and raised one leg to take off her pants I thought she looked like a young tree. Not a tree everyone would say was beautiful but a tree you would look at more than once.

She jumped into the water ducking down till it covered her to the neck which she swung around to look at me.

"Oh, you should come in, darlink!" she said. She lifted both her arms and the water as if reluctant to let go of her flowed off them.

"Watch, darlink," she said and swam, flicking her face from side to side, churning up the water with her white legs. She laughed when she reached the other bank so quickly because the hole was so small.

She sat on a half submerged log and lifting handfuls of mud rubbed it into her thighs.

"Very healthy, darlink," she said without looking at my shocked face.

She rubbed it on her arms and shoulders and it ran in little grey dollops between her breasts.

Then she plunged in and swam across to me. She came up beside me slipping a bit and laughing.

"That was wonderful, darlink," she said a little wistfully though, as if she doubted she would ever do it again.

The bush was quiet, so silent you could hear your own breath until a bird called and Clarice jumped a little.

"That's a whip bird," I said hearing it again a little further away, the sound of a whip lashed in the air.

"Oh darlink, you are so clever," she said and began to get dressed.

No one at home noticed I'd been away too long. My father was dawdling over afternoon tea just before milking and my mother bustling about made a clicking noise with her tongue every time a cow bellowed.

"It's no life for a girl," my father said referring to Clarice and making me jump nervously as if there was a way of detecting what we'd been up to.

"She took it on herself," said my mother, prodding at some corned beef in a saucepan on the stove.

"I'll bet they never let on to her about old lolly legs," said my father slapping away almost savagely with his tongue on his cigarette paper. "Landing a young girl into that! They'll expect her to wait on that old sponger before too long."

He put his tobacco away. "I'll bet Jack Patterson hardly says a word to her from one week's end to the next." He stared at his smoke. "Let alone anything else."

My mother straightened up from the stove. Her sweaty hair was spikey around her red face which wore a pinched and anxious expression, perhaps because of the late start on the milking. She crushed her old yard hat on.

"I'll go and start," she said.

My father smoked on for a minute or two then got up and looked around the kitchen as if seeing it for the first time.

He reached for his yard hat and put it on.

"What do you think of Clarice?" he said.

I laid my face on my knees to hide my guilt.

"She's beautiful," I said.

When he stomped past me sitting on the step he kept quite clear to avoid stepping on me.

I got a chance to go and see Clarice one day in the Christmas holidays when my mother went into Berrigo to buy fruit for the Christmas cake and cordial essence.

Clarice put her arm around me standing at the window watching Elsie Patterson at the clothesline.

Elsie was football shaped under her apron and she carefully unpegged shirts and dresses, turning them around and pegging them again. She took the sides of towels and tea towels between her hands and stretched them even.

"Why does she do that, darlink?" Clarice asked me.

Berrigo women were proud of their wash, but I found this hard to explain to Clarice.

She laughed merrily when we turned away. "People are so funny, aren't they darlink?"

She suggested going for a swim because the day was what my mother called a roaster.

This time she took off all her underwear at home leaving her thin dress showing her shape.

"Oh, darlink!" she said when I looked away.

I followed her round bottom with a couple of lovely little dents in it down to the waterhole.

The bush was not as quiet as before. Someone is about, I thought with a bush child's instinct for such things.

"I'll go and watch in case someone comes," I said, and she threw a handful of water at me for my foolishness.

I ran a little way up the track and when I lifted my head there shielded by some saplings astride his horse was my father.

I stopped so close the flesh of the horse's chest quivered near my eyes.

"Don't go any further," I said. "Clarice is swimming."

My father jumped off the horse and tied the bridle to a tree.

"Go on home," he said. But I didn't move.

"Go on!" he said and I moved off too slowly. He picked up a piece of chunky wood and threw it.

The horse plunged and the wood glanced off my arm as I ran.

At home I beat at the fire in the stove with the poker and put the kettle over the heat relieved when it started to sing.

I went to the kitchen door and my mother was coming down the track from the road. I heard Tingle's bus which went in and out of Berrigo every day go whining along the main road after dropping her off.

She had both arms held away from her body with parcels hanging from them.

I went to meet her not looking at her face but seeing it all the same red under the grey coloured straw hat with the bunch of violets on the brim. She had had the hat a long time.

String from the parcels was wound around her fingers and it was hard to free them.

"Be careful!" she said, hot and angry. "Don't drop that one!"

When she was inside and saw the fire going and the kettle near the boil she spoke more gently.

"It's a shaving mug," she said, hiding the little parcel in the back of the dresser. "For your father for Christmas."

Civilization and Its Discontents (1985)

HELEN GARNER

A precise stylist, the novelist and short story writer Helen Garner captures small moments that contain large experiences. At the center of her work are women, their everyday outer lives and their inner turbulence. Most of her heroines, like the protagonist of this story, are portrayed as they try to cope with a world where love is uncertain and security fleeting.

P hilip came. I went to his hotel: I couldn't get there fast enough. He stepped up to me when I came through the door, and took hold of me.

"Hullo," he said, "my dear."

People here don't talk like that. My hair was still damp.

"Did you drive?" he said.

"No. I came on the bus."

"The *bus?*"

"There's never anywhere to park in the city."

"You've had your hair cut. You look like a boy."

"I know. I do it on purpose. I dress like a boy and I have my hair cut like a boy. I want to *be* a boy. So I can have a homosexual affair with *you.*"

He laughed. "Good girl!" he said. At these words I was so flooded with well-being that I could hardly get my breath. "If you were a boy some of the time and a girl the rest," he said, "I'd be luckier. Because I could have both."

"No," I said. "I'd be luckier. Because I could *be* both."

I scrambled out of my clothes.

"You're so thin," he said.

"I don't eat. I'm sick."

"Sick? Are you?" He put his two hands on my shoulders and looked into my eyes like a doctor.

"Sick with love."

"Your eyes are healthy. Lustrous. Are mine?"

His room was on the top floor. Opposite, past some roofs and a deep street, was the old-fashioned tower of the building in which a dentist I used to go to had his rooms. That dentist was so gentle with the drill that I never needed an injection. I used to breathe slowly, as I had been taught at yoga: the pain was brief. I didn't flinch. But he made his pile and moved to Queensland.

The building had a flagpole. Philip and I stood at the window with no clothes on and looked out. The tinted glass made the cloud masses more detailed, richer, more spectacular than they were.

"Look at those," I said. "Real boilers. Coming in from some-where."

"Just passing through," said Philip. He was looking at the building with the tower. "I love the Australian flag," he said. "Every time I see it I get a shiver."

"I'm like that about the map." Once I worked in a convent school in East London. I used to go to the library at lunchtime, when the nuns were locked away in their dining room being read to, and take down the atlas and gaze at the page with Australia on it: I loved its upper points, its vast inlets, its fat sides, the might of it, the mass from whose south-eastern corner my small life had sprung. I used to crouch between the stacks and rest the heavy book on the edge of the shelf: I could hardly support its weight. I looked at the map and my eyes filled with tears.

"Did I tell you she's talking about coming back to me?" said Philip.

"Do you want her to?"

"Of course I do."

I sat down on the bed.

"We'll have to start behaving like adults," he said. "Any idea how it's done?"

"Well," I said, "it must be a matter of transformation. We have to turn what's happening now into something else."

"You sound experienced."

"I am."

"What can we turn it into?"

"Brother and sister? A lifelong friendship?"

"Oh," he said, "I don't know anything about that. Can't people just go on having a secret affair?"

"I don't like lying."

"You don't have to. I'm the liar."

"What makes you so sure she won't find out? People always know. She'll take one look at you and know. That's what wives are for."

"We'll see."

"How can you stand it?" I said. "It's dishonourable. How can you lie to someone and still love her?"

"Forced to. Forced by love to be a hypocrite."

I thought for a second he was joking.

"We could drop it now," I said.

"What are you *saying*?"

"I don't mean it."

Not yet. The sheets in those hotels are silky, but crisp. How do they get them like that? A lot of starch, and ironing, things no housewife in her right mind could be bothered doing. The bed was wide enough for another two people to have lain in it, and still none of us would have had to touch sides. I don't usually go to bed in the daylight. And as if the daylight were not enough, the room was full of lamps. I started to switch them off, one after another, and thinking of the phrase "full of lamps" I remembered something my husband said to me, long after we split up, about a Shakespeare medley he had seen performed by doddering remnants of a famous British company that was touring Australia. "The stage," he said, "was covered in *thrones*," and his knees bent with laughter. He was the only man I have ever known who would rejoice with you over the petty triumphs of the day. I got under the sheet. I couldn't help laughing to myself, but it was too complicated to explain why.

Philip had a way of holding me, when we lay down: he made small rocking movements, so small that I sometimes wondered if

I were imagining them, if the comfort of being held were translating itself into an imaginary cradling.

"I've never told anyone I loved them, before," said Philip.

"Don't be silly," I said.

"You don't know anything about me."

"At your age?" I said. "A married man? You've never loved anyone before?"

"I've never *said* it before."

"No wonder she went away," I said. "Men are really done over, aren't they. At an early age."

"Why do you want to fuck like a boy, then?"

"Just for play."

"Is it allowed?" he said.

"Who by?" I said. I was trying to be smart; but seriously, who says we can't? Isn't that why women and men make love? To bend the bars a little, just for a little; to let the bars dissolve? Philip pinched me. He took hold of the points of my breasts, between forefingers and thumbs. I could see his teeth. He pinched hard. It hurt. I liked it. And he bit me. He *bit* me. When I got home I looked in the mirror and my shoulders and arms were covered in small round bruises.

I went to his house, in the town where he lived. I told him I would be passing through on my way south, and he invited me, and I went, though I had plenty of friends I could have stayed with in that city.

There was a scandal in the papers as I passed through the airport that evening, about a woman who had made a contract to have a baby for a childless couple. The baby was born, she changed her mind, she would not give it up. Everyone was talking about her story.

I felt terrible at his house, for all I loved him, with his wife's forgotten dressing gown hanging behind the door like a witness. I couldn't fall asleep properly. I "lay broad waking" all night long, and the house was pierced by noises, as if its walls were too flimsy to protect it from the street: a woman's shoes striking the pavement, a gate clicking, a key sliding into a lock, stairs breathing in and out. It never gets truly dark in cities. Once I rolled over and looked at him. His face was sleeping, serene, smiling on the pillow next to mine like a cherub on a cloud.

He woke with a bright face. "I feel unblemished," he said, "when I've been with you." This is why I loved him, of course: because he talked like that, using words and phrases that most people wouldn't think of saying. "When I'm with you," he'd say, "I feel happy and free."

He made the breakfast and we read the papers in the garden.

"She should've stuck to her word," he said.

"Poor thing," I said. "How can anyone give a baby away?"

"But she promised. What about the couple? They must be dying to have a kid."

"Are you?"

"Yes," he said, and looked at me with the defiant expression of someone expecting to be crossed. "Yes. I am."

"I think in an ideal world everyone would have children," I said. "That's how people learn to love. Kids suck love out of your bones."

"I suppose you think that only mothers know how to love."

"No. I don't think that."

"Still," he said. "She signed a contract. She *signed*. She made a promise."

"Philip," I said, "have you ever smelled a baby's head?"

The phone started to ring inside the house, in the room I didn't go into because of the big painting of her that was hanging over the stereo. Thinking that he loved me, though I understood and believed I had accepted the futurelessness of it, I amused myself by secretly calling it The Room in Which the First Wife Raved, or Bluebeard's Bloody Chamber: it repelled me with an invisible force, though I stood at times outside its open door and saw its pleasantness, its calm, its white walls and wooden floor on which lay a bent pattern of sunlight like a child's drawing of a window.

He ran inside to answer the phone. He was away for quite a while. I thought about practising: how it is possible to learn with one person how to love, and then to apply the lesson learnt to somebody else: someone teaches you to sing, and then you wait for a part in the right opera. It was warm in the garden. I dozed in my chair. I had a small dream, one of those shockingly vivid dreams that occur when one sleeps at an unaccustomed time of day, or when one ought to be doing something other than sleeping. I dreamed that I was squatting naked with my vagina close to the ground, in the posture we are told primitive women adopt for childbearing ("They just squat down in the fields, drop the baby, and go on working"). But someone was operating on me, using sharp medical instruments on my cunt. Bloody flesh was issuing from it in clumps and clots. I could watch it, and see it, as if it were somebody else's cunt, while at the same time experiencing it being done to me. It was not painful. It didn't hurt at all.

I woke up as he came down the steps smiling. He crouched down in front of me, between my knees, and spoke right into my face.

"You want me to behave like a married man, and have kids, don't you?"

"*Want* you to?"

"I mean you think I should. You think everyone should, you said."

"Sure—if that's what you want. Why?"

"Well, on the phone just now I went a bit further towards it."

"You mean you *lined* it *up?*"

"Not exactly—but that's the direction I'm going in."

I looked down at him. His forearms were resting across my knees and he was crouching lightly on the balls of his feet. He was smiling at me, smiling right into my eyes. He was waiting for me to say, *Good boy!*

"Say something reassuring," he said. "Say something close, before I go."

I took a breath, but already he was not listening. He was ready to work. Philip loved his work. He took on more than he could comfortably handle. Every evening he came home with his pockets sprouting contracts. He never wasted anything: I'd hear him whistling in the car, a tiny phrase, a little run of notes climbing and falling as we drove across the bridges, and then next morning from the room with the synthesiser in it would issue the same phrase but bigger, fuller, linked with other ideas, becoming a song: and a couple of months after that I'd hear it through the open doors of every cafe, record shop and idling car in town. "Know what I used to dream?" he said to me once. "I used to dream that when I pulled up at the lights I'd look into the cars on either side of me and in front and behind, and everyone would be singing along with the radio, and they'd all be singing the same song. Even if the windows were wound up and we'd read each other's lips, and everyone would laugh, and wave."

I made my own long distance call. "I'll be home tonight, Matty," I said.

His voice was full of sleep. "They rang up from the shop," he said. "I told them you were sick. Have you seen that man yet?"

"Yes. I'm on my way. Get rid of the pizza boxes."

"I need money, Mum."

"When I get there."

Philip took me to the airport. I was afraid someone would see us, someone he knew. For me it didn't matter. Nothing was secret, I had no-one to hide anything from, and I would have been proud to be seen with him. But for him I was worried. I worried enough for both of us. I kept my head down. He laughed. He would not let me go. He tried to make me lift my chin; he gave it soft butts with his forehead. My cheeks were red.

"I'm always getting on planes with tears in my eyes," I said.

"They'll be getting to know you," he said. "Are you too shy to kiss me properly?"

I bolted past the check-in desk. I looked back and he was watching me, still laughing, standing by himself on the shining floor.

On the plane I was careful with myself. I concentrated on the ingenuity of the food tray, its ability to remain undisturbed by the alterations in position of the seatback to which it was attached. I called for a scotch and drank it. My mistake was to look inside a book of poems, the only reading matter I had on me. They were poems so charged with sex and death and longing that it was indecent to read them in public: I was afraid that their power might leak out and scandalise the onlookers. Even as I slammed the book shut I saw *"I want to know, once more, / how it feels / to be peeled and eaten whole, time after time."* I kept the book turned away from two men who were sitting between me and the window. They were drinking German beer and talking in a European language of which I did not recognise a single word. One of them turned his head and caught my eye. I expected him to look away hastily, for

I felt myself to be ugly and stiff with sadness; but his face opened into a dazzling smile.

My son was waiting for the plane. He had come out on the airport bus. He saw how pleased I was, and looked down with an embarrassed smile, but he permitted me to hug him, and patted my shoulder with little rapid pats.

"Your face is different," he said. "All sort of emotional."

"Why do you always pat me when you hug me?" I said.

"Pro'ly 'cause you're nearly always in a state," he said.

He asked me to wait while he had a quick go on the machines. His fingers swarmed on the buttons. *Death by Acne* was the title of a thriller he had invented to make me laugh: but his face in concentration lost its awkwardness and became beautiful. I leaned on the wall of the terminal and watched the people passing.

A tall young man came by. He was carrying a tiny baby in a sling against his chest. The mother walked behind, smooth-faced and long-haired, holding by the hand a fat-nappied toddler. But the man was the one in love with the baby. He walked slowly, with his arms curved round its small bulk. His head was bowed so he could gaze into its face. His whole being was adoring it.

I watched the young family go by in its peaceful procession, each one moving quietly and contentedly in place, and I heard the high-pitched death wails of the space creatures my son was murdering with his fast and delicate tapping of buttons, and suddenly I remembered walking across the street the day after I brought him home from hospital. The birth was long and I lost my rhythm and made too much noise and they drugged me, and when it was over I felt that now I knew what the prayerbook meant when it said *the pains of death gat hold upon me*. But crossing the road that day, still sore from knives and needles, I saw a pregnant woman lumbering towards me, a woman in the final stages of waiting, putting one heavy foot in front of the other. Her face as she passed me was as calm and as full as an animal's: "a face that had not yet received the fist". And I envied her. I was stabbed, pierced with envy, with longing for what was about to happen to her, for what she was ignorantly about to enter. I could have cried out, Oh, let me do it again! Give me another chance! Let me meet the mighty forces again and struggle with them! Let me be rocked again, let me lie helpless in that huge cradle of pain!

"Another twenty cents down the drain," said my son. We set out together towards the automatic doors. He was carrying my bag. I wanted to say to him, to someone, "Listen. Listen. I am *hopelessly in love*." But I hung on. I knew I had brought it on myself, and I hung on until the spasm passed. And then I began to re-create from memory the contents of the fridge.

The Train Will Shortly Arrive (1967)

___

FRANK MOORHOUSE

Well known in Australia as a master of the short story, Moorhouse has written, among other themes, about city life, the counterculture, and sex. His own life is often a barely disguised source for his material. In this story, the hero's suffering is uncovered in casual but, on closer inspection, finely honed dialogues with the past.

Τ*he train will be arriving at Eden in approximately five minutes. Would passengers wishing to alight from the train at Eden please move to car five. The train will stop at Eden for approximately one minute. Thank you.*

In the rocking train toilet he tried to do *something* with his hair. He smoothed it down with water. He sighed. They were just going to have to put up with it. It had been trimmed and shaped. It wasn't as though it was *scruffy*. It was just *long*. He pulled a face at himself and began to move unsteadily along the corridor to his seat. No one would look twice in the city but at Eden . . .

"Your stop next," the bore next to him said, in case he'd forgotten.

The train stopped, and stood making those impatient steaming noises. "All right, I'm getting off, don't rush me," he said. He looked around for his mother or father although his mother had written to say they couldn't meet the train because they had visitors. He went to a cab drowsing at the curb.

He got in. *Rylands Cabs for fast reliable service. Radio controlled. Twenty-four hours a day. Telephone Eden 2343.* He gave the driver the address. The driver knew it.

"You'd be Fred Turner's son—young Bernie—," the driver said, screwing around to look at him.

He nearly denied it for no particular reason.

"Yes. I'm home on a visit."

The cab driver gave him another glance. Glanced at his hair, his sunglasses, his bracelet and then started the cab.

Satisfied?

"You've changed. I remember you as a kid. You wouldn't remember me."

"I do. I remember you but I don't remember your name."

"Jack Ryland. I run a couple of cabs."

Jack Ryland pulled a card from the upholstery trim above the driver's seat and without looking passed it back to him.

"You were a tough little bugger."

What a lie.

"But that'd be going back to when you were about ten. What you be now? Around thirty?"

"That's close enough." How coy.

They drove up the drive of the house. Ryland helped him out with his bag. His parents must have heard the car and they came out to the front porch. His father peering through his reading glasses. Why did he always, but always, wear the wrong pair? His mother was wiping her hands on her apron.

His mother hugged him and they kissed. He shook hands with his father, who said hullo to Ryland.

"Your boy's changed, Fred—I mean he's grown."

Oh, for God's sake get off the *changed* bit. His father looked for bags to carry—anything to distract him.

Inside he was introduced to the visitors who were sitting in the lounge room drinks in hand. They struggled to be interested. He felt the dull private alcoholic humour of a group which had been drinking together for some time. He felt the group stir alcoholically in an effort to fit him in.

"Bernie's been overseas. We haven't had him home for years."

He took off his sunglasses.

"How nice for you," one of the women visitors said, then gave a smothered giggle and said: "I mean that he's home again." The others giggled.

"What'll you have to drink son? We got everything." His father opened the stocked drink cabinet which was lined with mirrors and lit up when the door opened.

"Let Bernie wash his hands dear," his mother said.

"No, have a drink — first things first," his father said, looking to the visitors who laughed accordingly.

The cabinet's range had expanded. Before it had been rum and sherry. The store must be prospering.

"Come on dear," his mother said to him, picking up her sherry. "I've put you in your old room." She guided him out. How much sherry was his mother drinking these days? And how much rum his father? His mother led him off.

"I'll have a gin and dry," he said over his shoulder to his father. He saw his father stare at the cabinet with just the slightest hesitation. "I have some Black and White." For a second he felt like accepting it, to please his father, as a gesture of something, but he didn't. "No, gin and dry would do nicely, thanks Dad."

Out in the hall his self-consciousness slipped away. They were all dull and boozed and he felt clear control. He'd reached a stockade of superiority.

Sherry in hand, his mother led him to his old bedroom.

"You wash and put your things in there while Daddy gets the drinks."

She noticed the bracelet. "What a lovely bracelet, Bernard." He flushed.

"Oh, I bought it . . . for the trip. My blood group's engraved on it," he lied. He twisted it around nervously and moved off to the bathroom.

In the bathroom he was at the mirror again. He rubbed under his eyes and for a cruel second saw age looking at him.

He came into the lounge room to hear his mother say: "He's been working at one of the private schools in Sydney — Grammar . . . " His mother turned to him as he entered.

"Your drink is on the cabinet," his father said. "Hope you like plenty of ginger ale."

He didn't but there wasn't much he could do about it now. "No, that's fine."

"I've been telling everyone about your new position," his mother said.

"Not really new—I've been there six months now."

Someone asked him how he liked it. He said that conditions could be better.

"We teachers are becoming worse than farmers with all our complaining and carrying-on," he swizzled his drink.

"You deserve better dear," his mother said. "Education is so important." And with that the conversation left him. They talked bowls, business, with the women talking across at each other and the men talking across at each other. Now and then it would all link up coming back together on the same subject. Now and then his mother would make a reference to him or seek his opinion or give him an explanation—lacing him back into the group as best she could.

He went to bed after dinner, bored and slightly tense.

In bed he missed Mervyn. He ran his hands down his body, aware of his masculinity. He took his penis and it grew rigid in his hand. He longed for Mervyn. Mervyn was probably lying in his bed doing the same. In their flat. How long would he and Mervyn last? Another few months? They had both been with girls. Pathetic attempts. They got along. But there were the days when he said: "Go *away*, Mervyn. Fuck off. Leave me *alone*." Those days of deep angry depression about God knows what. But didn't all people feel that? And there were the days of glorious fun and loving nights. Of waking to feel Mervyn close and hard. Of the delightful relaxation together in front of television after hectic times. The relaxation and pleasure of showering and then going to Mervyn's bed. Of putting his head on Mervyn's chest. The shouting rows were worth that. The flowers they grew together. He remembered Mervyn teaching him how to garden.

He was careful of the sheets. The climax exploded away some of his tension. Immediately after he had a glimpse of his father— distant and puzzled—and of his mother, so unsurely and clumsily devoted, and then they passed from his mind with the tension.

Cum was messy after lonely masturbation. With someone there

was usually affection and cum was a binding thing and a tangible expression of it. No, that was bullshit. It was sometimes true—but not always true of those drunken promiscuous nights. Sometimes it was then the mess of spent desire. Sometimes it was the mess of guilt. If the guilt anxieties were troublesome then the "tangible affection" baby, became "tangible guilt." Which one wanted to wipe away quickly.

He awoke to the early morning ABC news.

He'd forgotten the early rising Saturday mornings. The big morning at the store.

His father and mother, alcoholically sour, were probably not talking. He knew his mother would bring a cup of tea and shortbread biscuits. He didn't want to get up. All through childhood he had been made to get up, except now and then when his father and mother fought about whether he should be made to work in the store and his mother won. This morning he would not get up.

His mother brought him the tea, and kissed him good morning.

"I'll stay in bed," he said.

"Yes, do that darling. No need for you to get up. Father's in a foul mood."

He drowsed, leaving his tea to grow cold on the bedside table. Later in the morning he arose, ate his breakfast alone, put on his sunglasses and strolled up town.

Saturday morning in the country town. People stood on the sunlit side of the street at the gutter's edge talking about yesterday. Children ran slow messages. Young people swaggered on their bicycles propped against walls. A few early drinkers stood at hotel doorways with their first-of-the-day beers calming the jumping nerves and taking away the bitter taste of last night's sweetness. The adolescents out of schoolclothes flirted with tough aloofness in laminex milk bars. In the Red Rose, the New York, and the Paragon. He'd taken tense girls there after Saturday night movies at the Kings or the Victory for cold milk shakes and later when older, to the coffee shop for sophisticated black coffee and sophisticated raisin toast. He'd liked double dating with Peter best. Mainly because it was reassuring to have male company when one was so unfamiliar and ignorant about girls. But he had liked, or perhaps loved, Peter. He'd not been fully aware, and could not have admitted it, and it could not have been advanced. Only later when they were about twenty and he was beginning to recognise and admit his sexual nature had he recognised what he felt about Peter and it was then too late. Peter was tough and could never have been approached. But there had been a timid, guilty, mutual masturbation at about sixteen. Amazingly spontaneous at its beginning—a sexual urge forcing itself awkwardly, but strongly, through their conventions and inhibitions. It had been at Peter's home. It was left undiscussed. They both feigned sleep immediately after. He must have been staying with Peter that night. Peter's parents were probably away. It had never been repeated and never mentioned. He had dreamed of Peter and thought of him while masturbating in the years since. Had Peter thought of him? He doubted it. Peter had married a Catholic. Of course, Peter hadn't been the first. There had been a younger sexual thing—unselfconscious and pubescent. Of a different nature. Before girls. Girls had been necessary for Peter and him. Necessary for all of them then, for status at school and for curiosity, and so that they could say "I love you" for the first time and feel the first breast since infancy. But oh the tension of it.

He went into the Red Rose and ordered a banana malted. The taste of it made him shiver with memories.

He sat in a stall and watched people as they went by on Saturday business, some he vaguely knew. Some he'd seen fifteen years ago walking by on Saturday mornings as they did now. God how comfortable. Knowing that you'd be doing that on Saturday morning, every Saturday morning. Knowing that there was nothing hostile, hysterical, or dangerous to face in the journey through Saturday. Or perhaps there were horrors in that Saturday journey for some. As they went down the sunlit street some must have feared creditors, had to face forbidden people they desired, face people who held grudges. But weren't his Friday nights and Saturday mornings also ritualistic? But they were frantic—frantic rising late on Saturday morning, frantic hangovers, and hungover shopping with Mervyn at the supermarket with all the other frantic Jews and camps and bedsitter girls. He smiled and wanted to be back in the frantic ritual. It wasn't all *that* depressing and at least one knew one was *alive*. But it didn't have the . . . blandness . . . of the country town Saturday.

A man came into the milk bar. No. A boy came into the milk bar. In his mind the man was a boy. The boy, Harrison Bryant, was about thirty—in his mind he remembered him as a soft boy of eleven. The boy had coarsened into a man. It frightened him a little. He could hardly see a trace of the soft boy. Bryant's hair was cropped up to the crown. He had fattened at the waist. His belt pulled tight was his only attempt at control. His clothes were the characterless light greys and fawns. A singlet formed a vee across the neck of his sports shirt. Harrison Bryant's hands seemed frightfully wrinkled. He looked down at his own in shock. But he could not see them as someone else would see them. They seemed as they had always seemed—young and vivacious—if hands could be vivacious.

Harrison Bryant wore rubber thongs. He abhorred rubber thongs—ugly, common, and probably harmful to the feet. The thirty-year-old Harrison Bryant was buying a packet of cigarettes and with cupped hands had lit one, dragged on it and emphatically expelled the smoke in a relieved gust, as a smoker who was overdue for a cigarette. He had a gold metal watch band. Against the sun-bleached white hairs of his arm it was the only feature resembling the male attractiveness of youth.

Should he speak? It would be unbearable. But it was intriguing. And wasn't he there for *that* sort of thing—to see some of it again. He wasn't sure whether he wanted to see it all again. But wot-the-hell, archy.

"Harrison," his voice came out light, almost camp. He roughed it up. "Harrison."

Harrison Bryant turned around and saw him. Quickly taking the cigarette from his mouth, smiling widely, he came over. "Bernie, for Christ's sake, it's been a long time." He came over with his hand out. They shook hands. The last time we touched, he thought, was when we were eleven and your hands were on my penis and my hands were on yours. Remember?

"Well, bugger me," Harrison said. "Where you been hiding yourself? Christ, you've changed." Harrison's eyes made appraisal.

"I've been overseas," he said. The appraisal sent a fizz of agitation through him. He wished he hadn't spoken. He pulled out a cigarette.

"Have one of mine," Harrison offered.

Never.

"No thanks, Harrison. I've got to like these."

"Fussy—nothing but the best." Harrison grinned aggressively.

"I don't smoke that much," he said. Calm down. Calm *down.*
Harrison moved into the stall opposite him.

"Been overseas?"

"Yes, Europe."

"I was going to work in New Zealand but I don't suppose I'll be
going now. Four kids and another on the way—what you think of
that? Married?"

"No," he carefully ashed his cigarette, calmer now, "but it sounds
as if you've been hard at it." What a coarse expression.

"All my own work—unless the milkman slipped in," Harrison
laughed. He smiled involuntarily at the sheer corniness and pride.

"Where do you work, Harrison?"

"Cut out the 'Harrison' bit—Harry—everyone knows me as
Harry. You'd be the only one who'd remember that's my real
name."

"I like it," he said. Oh shut up.

Harrison laughed nervously. "I'm at the Golden Fleece service
station. A fellow called Simpson runs it—you wouldn't know him,
he's from Melbourne. I do a bit of panel beating and work the
bowsers—you know."

He nodded.

"It's not the best job in the world. I've got ideas about starting
my own panel-beating place or getting a station, but you know."
Harrison smiled a lost smile.

He nodded. "Who'd you marry, Harry, anyone I'd know?"

"Betty Harris—don't think you'd know her—she would a been
a year behind you at school."

He didn't know her.

"You'll have to come up and see us. We got a Housing Commission place up in the new part."

"I'm only up for a day or two."

"Perhaps next time then."

"Yes."

"Anyhow, what you been up to?"

"I teach. At Grammar."

"Posh school."

"Kids are the same anywhere." Except some have richer parents. Which makes all the difference.

"God you've changed. I mean from what you were at school." Harrison laughed, again nervously, in case he had said something wrong, partially realising what he meant, realising what was different.

"We've all changed," he said, defensively.

There was a silence.

"Ever feel like leaving the old town?"

Harrison tried to consider the question. "I was thinking of moving to Goulburn. Wife's mother lives there. But it's not a bad old town."

Another lapse.

Then Harrison asked again: "What do you do for a crust?"

He tried to answer it as a fresh question, rephrasing his answer to avoid embarrassment.

"Teach school."

"Oh yeah—I asked you that." Harrison stubbed out his cigarette uneasily.

"How's Jimmy Hagan?"

"Don't see much of Jimmy. He's on a farm near Captains Flat. He comes back now and then but I don't see him much. At the football sometimes."

"He always wanted to work a farm."

"He's share farming or something."

Harrison went to take out another cigarette but remembered that he'd just finished one. He played with the packet.

"It's hard to realise that we were in infants school together and grew up together," he said, watching Harrison's face.

Harrison laughed and shook his head as if trying to deny it or shake away the embarrassment of his childhood. It was impossible to know if he remembered the sexual game they had shared. He kept shaking his head and laughing. "It's funny how you grow old."

"We're not *that* old yet." Let's not talk about *age*.

"I see your mum and dad about the place. Your dad drinks in the saloon bar down at Cassidy's. That's where I drink. I see him in the saloon bar after work some days."

"Who do you drink with? Any of the boys I'd know?"

"Sonny Buckley—you'd remember him. Lyle Bates? Used to be real fat?" Harrison warmed to safer talk.

He nodded. He remembered them. He remembered them as kids he'd played football with. Who for years seemed to wear a football jersey or football socks whether they were playing or not.

"Why don't you come down and have a drink with us? They'll be down there about now. We all get down there Saturday mornings."

Curiosity tempted him but his discretion grimaced.

"No thanks, Harrison . . . Harry . . . I have things to do."

Harrison didn't repeat the invitation.

Harrison stood up and said that he had to go and to call in if he was up around the Commission area.

Harrison left the milk bar.

He'd left too. His mind had gone back to among the lantana and grape vines grown wild where he and Harrison had crawled and made a hide-out and where one day, on some forgotten pretext, they had taken off their clothes, lain together and fondled each other's penis to erection. This had occurred—how often? Each time had been initiated by some pretext which even at eleven they had needed to justify the innocent, curious, and affectionate reaching out to each other. Then the first ejaculation—Harrison—and the amazement of it. Harrison had called it "spunk" and seemed to know something about it. But there had been fear and boyish bravado and a need to understand it. They had looked in *Pears Cyclopedia*, Arthur Mees' *Children's Encyclopedia*, and the book *Enquire Within Upon Everything*, and dictionaries. They looked for all the taboo words they'd ever heard—penis, prick, cunt, shit, spunk, and masturbate. The dictionary had told them that spunk meant courage. All the books together left them in a mocking darkness. They didn't touch each other after that—as though the signs of manhood had frightened them away from each other into the "proper" sexual distance for men. He'd been frightened too, of losing his courage.

He remembered their young, hairless, vibrant bodies. His penis stirred even now. Oh God, ageing was miserable. And foolish. An unbelievably foolish process.

Football matches came back to him. Rising on cold, frost and mist mornings to travel by bus to football carnivals. The vigour, and the bodies. The closeness of the team. The beautiful smell of the bodies in the dressing room spiced with the smell of liniment. The male heat of the bodies before and after. The dressing room had been an exciting, male place.

He dug and ground the sugar spoon deep into the plastic sugar container on the table, angry about ageing. The anger drifted away leaving the grim, impotent acceptance.

He thought again about Harrison's abashed reaction to him. How obviously different from other men he must appear and how he sometimes forgot this. Perhaps he'd never quite accepted that he was. Perhaps he had pretended that if he wanted he could conceal it. That no one need ever know. But it wasn't like that anymore. And it wasn't that he had changed. He hadn't *changed*. He'd simply unwrapped himself. That was that.

Drinking a banana malted in the Red Rose and thinking of the ghosts of childhood princes—princes who had become toads— was a disturbing game. Exciting oneself by remembering pubescent experiences was saddening. Next thing he'd be panting after twelve-year-olds and that would be *the end*. The End. Grammar School scandal.

He dragged himself out of the stall. The milk bar was agitated now by loud adolescents who moved restlessly between the juke box and the street. "Juke": of African origin, he'd told his class. He tried to buy his brand of cigarettes but couldn't and settled for Craven A.

He strolled along the sunny side and around the post office corner. A former primary school teacher came towards him erect with the same ageless authority he had twenty years ago. Was *he* like that to *his* pupils? Existing in the limbo especially allotted to school teachers. He felt like speaking but it would be meaningless for them both. Young people were always so aware of their own identity but for teachers, they were simply part of a straggling procession. The teacher passed with his shopping bag.

There had been a teacher later in high school, and a seduction. He remembered the playground stories about the teacher which had come first, and which had kindled him. The breathless, fearful desire which he had felt when first alone with the man in his office. With the inevitability of mutual desire he had become the teacher's special boy—first for his messages, then for his special conversations and then for his special pleasure. The conversations between them had quickly become personal with the teacher asking about his dreams and about his father and mother. Then the fondling. They had been sitting together at a desk one afternoon when the rest of the school had gone to sport. He remembered being asked to report to the teacher's office instead of going to sport and he felt again the wild excitement which had trembled through him.

They had sat at the desk reading figures from a sheet with the teacher checking them off. He had known it would happen. The teacher's hand came down on to his leg. Firmly then caressingly. His body seemed to silently hum changing then to a silent, low urgent moan but the only sound was the sound of his voice intoning the figures. Trying to control his breathing which wanted to break into grunting or panting. Up and down the columns of figures. The teacher's hand working up slowly and warmly towards the screamingly rigid penis. Up his leg to the fly and then firmly stroking the penis through the trousers. Then in the fly and down in through the underpants. When the hand reached his penis and gripped it he had wanted either to bury his head on the teacher's shoulder in erotic surrender or to run run run away from the embarrassment and guilt which swirled way down under the desire and excitement—an excitement ten thousand times as intense as anything he had ever felt before, with Harrison in the childish bushes or with Peter in the furtive bed. The tickling and caressing brought out the first thrusting of a new feeling—the trembling ecstasy of male touch and sexual submission.

He did nothing for the teacher. He did not look at him. He had stopped reading, suspended in the intensity of the hand on his penis. Then the teacher coughed and the hand withdrew and the fly was zipped. Why did he stop? The unejaculated penis subsided in cold disappointment. Why did he stop? The reading began again.

His voice took hold of the figures, up and down the pages. Why did he stop? Then the smile and the gathering of the lists when they finished. The gathering of the pencils and the thank you and the teacher's squeeze of his shoulder. Why had he stopped? His legs were unsteady as they had been on rare occasions since when a certain pitch of sexual intensity was reached with strange boys in strange ways in strange flats. Why had he stopped? The brightness of the playground, empty except for the sound of singsong rote learning somewhere from a defaulters' class. He had gone to the toilet and locked himself in a cubicle to cry against the wall from utter frustration. He had been close to rage and couldn't masturbate. He just cried and beat his hand against the terrazzo wall. Why had he stopped?

God, he'd been so attractive then. So golden, so smooth and so sexually hungry. Soft clean blond hair and clean finger nails—one of the few boys who had clean nails—and not only because his mother insisted. His fully-grown eyelashes and a physical movement light and without conceit.

There had been three other times with the teacher, again wordless and never as blindingly intense and again never to ejaculation. Why had he always stopped? The sexual occasions with the teacher were flashes from the grinding school year. His place as special boy for the teacher had ended when he left at the end of that year to go to another school. It ended with a dull shaking of hands and pleasantries with him hating the teacher for having always stopped. Their friendship was cracked. He could not straddle the distance between them because of the inadequacy of youth. If only the teacher had not stopped and had spoken to him, tenderly, and coaxingly, he could have had him and gone on totally for years. He would never have opted for another school or gone to teachers' college. He would have stayed at that school to be with the teacher.

He stopped feeding the fantasy. Still alive after all those years. He was now away from the town's shopping centre and moving towards its outskirts where it was circled by bush. The teacher had obviously been blocked and hung up. Probably scared to death. Ejaculating would have demanded something, perhaps would have advanced it all further than the teacher was prepared to go. He wondered about himself. Would he one day begin to fondle favourite boys in his classes? He blanched at the risk and was relieved to see an ethical qualm, large and strong, standing in the way.

He had reached the streets which were half sealed with tracks at the edges for horse traffic. He then came to the end of the sealed streets where only kerbing and guttering had reached. The beginning of the bush. Houses had marched along the new streets with plumbing, cement footpaths, and kerbing running alongside.

The bush had been a place to go. It was, he remembered, at first a frightening place in which one did not go far. Each foray required a mustering of courage which, because of the gang, had become a forced courage which had taken them further than they wanted into unknown territory. But over the years it was explored and then roved. Familiarity came and the bush offered up its facilities—caves for hideouts, trees for lookouts, creeks to swim in, bamboo for blow pipes, berries to eat, and places to lie quietly concealed. There had been birds to kill although he never had—always firing blind hoping to miss. If the others had known that! But perhaps they all fired to miss.

He crouched on a rock and smoked. He had smoked for the first time in this bush. With Jennifer. What was her other name? Sims? Smoking had given him something like a sexual feeling. It wasn't clear. He remembered the dizziness and the forbidden excitement. She had been the only girl among them. He had kissed Jennifer later, around about puberty. It had been in a dark room and he could not see her. Somehow he had found her hand and then felt her lips against his, moist and moving, like some alive animal. His first kiss. Tinged with nausea.

That had been his childhood—sweet uneasiness. He rocked forward, his legs hunched under his chin.

He became aware of his bracelet which had slid down over the back of his hand. "From Mark." Given before Mark had returned to the States on his wandering from girl to girl and from boy to boy. It was not in memory of Mark that he wore it. Their affair had been brief, passionate, but socially difficult because of possessiveness. The bracelet was a reminder of his sexual identity. His sexual identity bracelet. He put it to his mouth and tasted the cold silver. The cold silver of his youth.

"My youth was nothing but a storm, tenebrous, savage,
Traversed by brilliant suns that our hearts harden,
The thunder and the rain had made such ravage,
That few of the fruits were left in my ruined garden."

He threw up his metaphorical eyebrows. His life didn't warrant poetry.

He glanced back through the thin bush to the Commission houses. He saw a sagging woman in woollen slippers hanging washing on a sagging line. Outside another house a man in overalls lay beneath a car, as though submitting to some sexual machine.

Was that woman Mrs Bryant? She was straightening up, bracing herself against her pregnancy. A child crawled around her feet. He let himself believe it was. Made himself feel a devious and superior sexual connection with the woman. But I was there first, darling, he thought, and I was there when it was beautiful and Harrison was fresh and sweet. She had picked up the child and was dragging the clothes basket towards the house.

He jumped from the rock and began to walk back towards the town.

Children. What about children? Sometimes he wanted them. Teaching them wasn't close enough. Did he want to mother a child? He remembered a strange night when he had gone to bed with Terri and she had wanted a baby. They talked about her and Mervyn and him bringing the baby up together. He'd loved the fantasy. Mervyn would kill him if he found him thinking like that. "Let those thoughts loose, sweet, and God knows where you'll end up—in the clinic at Rozelle—and hospital visiting is such a bore." He smiled. For Mervyn certain thoughts were taboo. He wondered if Mervyn could really control his mind as well as that.

Mervyn had bought him a Siamese cat. "You need a family to look after," Mervyn had said. He'd bought himself an alley cat to prevent the Siamese cat from becoming snobbish and spoiled. He wanted to see Marlon, the Siamese cat. He missed Marlon. He wanted to stroke him and have him give back a purring warmth. God he needed that purring warmth all of a sudden. He preferred Marlon to James Dean. James Dean whined and had no pride. Like all alley cats. Like alley boys, too.

Perhaps he was ready for a Big Affair. With Mervyn? They

hadn't talked *that* way. But perhaps it was getting to be *that* way.

For Christ's sake why was he going in for the introspection bit? Why didn't he just let it all happen—if it was going to happen? Why did he pester himself all the time? Why didn't he leave himself alone—stop picking at his mental nose? It was the damn homecoming, of course. But even at other times he was always picking at himself. As if to see if he would fall to pieces when prodded. Why did he bother? Everything was OK. He was a bloody good teacher. He had Mervyn, he had other friends, he had the garden, and his colonial cedar furniture. And they were always doing things.

Everything was OK. Everything was going fine. He walked up the curved green cement drive to his home. He hoped that his father would have lunched and gone to bowls.

He went inside. His father was still eating. His mother had waited for him.

"What did you do, dear?" his mother asked, putting his lunch in front of him.

"Walked about—up the street—up to the bush."

"See anyone you knew?"

"Only Harrison and a couple of others—from a distance."

"He's married with four children."

"So he told me."

"What did you do today?" asked his father, putting the newspaper aside with effort.

"Bernard has just been telling you," his mother said before he could reply, "if you'd only listen."

"You didn't come into the store—should see the extensions," his father said.

"I went up the street and looked around the new Commission houses," he answered his father. They both knew he wouldn't go near the store.

"The town's growing," his mother said. His father began to read the newspapers sideways.

He ate his lunch.

"Something wrong, Bernard?" his mother asked.

"No, just thinking," he said. "Beautiful salmon."

"You seemed quiet all of a sudden," his mother said.

He would have liked to think that his visit home resolved something or other. But that was Young Thinking—to want to resolve everything simply by doing something dramatic. And really that hadn't been the reason for going home. Perhaps it had confirmed something about himself or his parents or something or something.

Mervyn was at the platform exit. "Oh come let us adore him! Really!"

Mervyn took the bags.

"How were the mater and pater?"

"Oh, you know . . . "

"Well, you've done the Right Thing—now you needn't bother till Christmas."

"I really don't think I could bear to go down again. There's *nothing*. And Mother comes to the city fairly often."

They walked to the taxi rank.

"How are Marlon and James Dean?"

"Marlon's been restless and moody—missed you dreadfully. Kept prowling around looking for you in such a possessive way."

He smiled.

"And James Dean is very happy—hasn't missed a meal. Absolutely without any feelings."

"Alley boy." They laughed at their joke.

They waited for a cab.

"I met my first love again—after fifteen years—nineteen years."

"How devastating. I never think of you having a First Time."

"He's gross—and married with four children. Lives in a *Housing Commission* area."

"Of course."

"He's not camp. I mean, he's never been camp. It was just kids' stuff."

They got into the cab.

Any cabs in the vicinity of St Mary's Cathedral—a Father Henderson for Vaucluse—thank you one-oh-nine—he'll be outside the main entrance. Someone for O'Sullivan Street, Rose Bay . . .

The traffic and buildings of the city gently ingested him. Mervyn laid a hand on his. He let the city take him. Its browns, blacks, and greys dressed with the red-amber-green of traffic lights and the mechanical dance of purple and orange neon.

Two Hanged Women (1934)

HENRY HANDEL RICHARDSON

Henry Handel Richardson is a pseudonym for Ethel Florence Lindesay Robertson. In this brief tale, as in her highly regarded novels, Richardson demonstrates her skill in evoking competing tensions. The central character is pulled in opposing directions, torn between her own inner impulse and the rewards of familial and social approval.

Hand in hand the youthful lovers sauntered along the esplanade. It was a night in midsummer; a wispy moon had set, and the stars glittered. The dark mass of the sea, at flood, lay tranquil, slothfully lapping the shingle.

"Come on, let's make for the usual," said the boy.

But on nearing their favourite seat they found it occupied. In the velvety shade of the overhanging sea-wall, the outlines of two figures were visible.

"Oh, blast!" said the lad. "That's torn it. What now, Baby?"

"Why, let's stop here, Pincher, right close up, till we frighten 'em off."

And very soon loud, smacking kisses, amatory pinches and ticklings, and skittish squeals of pleasure did their work. Silently the intruders rose and moved away.

But the boy stood gaping after them, openmouthed.

"Well, I'm *damned!* If it wasn't just two hanged women!"

Retreating before a salvo of derisive laughter, the elder of the girls said: "We'll go out on the breakwater." She was tall and thin, and walked with a long stride.

Her companion, shorter than she by a bobbed head of straight flaxen hair, was hard put to it to keep pace. As she pegged along she said doubtfully, as if in self-excuse: "Though I really ought to go home. It's getting late. Mother will be angry."

They walked with finger-tips lightly in contact; and at her words she felt what was like an attempt to get free, on the part of the fingers crooked in hers. But she was prepared for this, and held fast, gradually working her own up till she had a good half of the other hand in her grip.

For a moment neither spoke. Then, in a low, muffled voice, came the question: "Was she angry last night, too?"

The little fair girl's reply had an unlooked-for vehemence. "You know she wasn't!" And, mildly despairing: "But you never *will* understand. Oh, what's the good of . . . of anything!"

And on sitting down she let the prisoned hand go, even putting it from her with a kind of push. There it lay, palm upwards, the fingers still curved from her hold, looking like a thing with a separate life of its own; but a life that was ebbing.

On this remote seat, with their backs turned on lovers, lights, the town, the two girls sat and gazed wordlessly at the dark sea, over which great Jupiter was flinging a thin gold line. There was no sound but the lapping, sucking, sighing, of the ripples at the edge of the breakwater, and the occasional screech of an owl in the tall trees on the hillside.

But after a time, having stolen more than one side glance at her companion, the younger seemed to take heart of grace. With a childish toss of the head that set her loose hair swaying, she said, in a tone of meaning emphasis: "I like Fred."

The only answer was a faint, contemptuous shrug.

"I tell you I *like* him!"

"Fred? Rats!"

"No it isn't . . . that's just where you're wrong, Betty. But you think you're so wise. Always."

"I know what I know."

"Or imagine you do! But it doesn't matter. Nothing you can say makes any difference. I like him and always shall. In heaps of ways. He's so big and strong, for one thing: it gives you such a safe sort of feeling to be with him . . . as if nothing could happen while you were. Yes, it's . . . it's . . . well, I can't help it, Betty, there's something *comfy* in having a boy to go about with—like other girls do. One they'd eat their hats to get, too! I can see it in their eyes when we pass; Fred with his great long legs and broad shoulders—I don't nearly come up to them—and his blue eyes with the black lashes, and his shiny black hair. And I like his tweeds, the Harris smell of them, and his dirty old pipe, and the way he shows his teeth—he's got *topping* teeth—when he laughs and says 'ra-*ther*!' And other people, when they see us, look . . . well I don't quite know how to say it, but they look sort of pleased; and they make room for us and let us into the dark corner-seats at the pictures, just as if we'd a right to them. And they never laugh. (Oh, I can't *stick* being laughed at! —and that's the truth.) Yes, it's so comfy, Betty darling . . . such a warm cosy comfy feeling. Oh, *won't* you understand?"

"Gawd! why not make a song of it?" But a moment later, very fiercely: "And who is it's taught you to think all this? Who's hinted it and suggested it till you've come to believe it? . . . believe it's what you really feel."

"She hasn't! Mother's never said a word . . . about Fred."

"Words?—why waste words? . . . when she can do it with a cock of the eye. For your Fred, that!" and the girl called Betty held her fingers aloft and snapped them viciously. "But your mother's a different proposition."

"I think you're simply horrid."

To this there was no reply.

"*Why* have you such a down on her? What's she ever done to you? . . . except not get ratty when I stay out late with Fred. And I don't see how you can expect . . . being what she is . . . and with nobody but me—after all she *is* my mother . . . you can't alter that. I know very well—and you know, too—I'm not *too* putrid-looking. But"—beseechingly—"I'm *nearly* twenty-five now, Betty. And other girls . . . well, she sees them, every one of them, with a boy of their own, even though they're ugly, or fat, or have legs like sausages—they've only got to ogle them a bit—the girls, I mean . . . and there they are. And Fred's a good sort—he is, really! —and he dances well, and doesn't drink, and so . . . so why *shouldn't*

I like him? ... and off my own bat ... without it having to be all Mother's fault, and me nothing but a parrot, and without any will of my own?"

"Why? Because I know her too well, my child! I can read her as you'd never dare to ... even if you could. She's sly, your mother is, so sly there's no coming to grips with her ... one might as well try to fill one's hand with cobwebs. But she's got a hold on you, a stranglehold, that nothing'll loosen. Oh! mothers aren't fair—I mean it's not fair of nature to weigh us down with them and yet expect us to be our own true selves. The handicap's too great. All those months, when the same blood's running through two sets of veins—there's no getting away from that, ever after. Take yours. As I say, does she need to open her mouth? Not she! She's only got to let it hang at the corners, and you reek, you drip with guilt."

Something in these words seemed to sting the younger girl. She hit back. "I know what it is, you're jealous, that's what you are! ... and you've no other way of letting it out. But I tell you this. If ever I marry—yes, *marry!*—it'll be to please myself, and nobody else. Can you imagine me doing it to oblige her?"

Again silence.

"If I only think what it would be like to be fixed up and settled, and able to live in peace, without this eternal dragging two ways ... just as if I was being torn in half. And see Mother smiling and happy again, like she used to be. Between the two of you I'm nothing but a punch-ball. Oh, I'm fed up with it! ... fed up to the neck. As for you.... And yet you can sit there as if you were made of stone! Why don't you *say* something? *Betty!* Why won't you speak?"

But no words came.

"I can *feel* you sneering. And when you sneer I hate you more than any one on earth. If only I'd never seen you!"

"Marry your Fred, and you'll never need to again."

"I will, too! I'll marry him, and have a proper wedding like other girls, with a veil and bridesmaids and bushels of flowers. And I'll live in a house of my own, where I can do as I like, and be left in peace, and there'll be no one to badger and bully me—Fred wouldn't ... ever! Besides, he'll be away all day. And when he came back at night, he'd ... I'd ... I mean I'd—" But here the flying words gave out; there came a stormy breath and a cry of: "Oh, Betty, Betty! . . . I couldn't, no, I couldn't! It's when I think of *that*. . . . Yes, it's quite true! I like him all right, I do indeed, but only as long as he doesn't come too near. If he even sits too close, I have to screw myself up to bear it"—and flinging herself down over her companion's lap, she hid her face. "And if he tries to touch me, Betty, or even takes my arm or puts his round me. . . . And then his face . . . when it looks like it does sometimes . . . all wrong . . . as if it had gone all wrong—oh! then I feel I shall have to scream—out loud. I'm afraid of him . . . when he looks like that. Once . . . when he kissed me . . . I could have died with the horror of it. His breath . . . his breath . . . and his mouth—like fruit pulp—and the black hairs on his wrists . . . and the way he looked—and . . . and everything! No, I can't, I can't . . . nothing will make me . . . I'd rather die twice over. But what am I to do? Mother'll *never* understand. Oh, why has it got to be like this? I want to be happy, like other girls, and to make her happy, too . . . and everything's all wrong. You tell me, Betty darling, you help me, you're older . . . you *know* . . . and you can help me, if you will . . . if you only will!" And locking her arms round her friend she drove her face deeper into the warmth and darkness, as if, from the very fervour of her clasp, she could draw the aid and strength she needed.

Betty had sat silent, unyielding, her sole movement being to loosen her own arms from her sides and point her elbows outwards, to hinder them touching the arms that lay round her. But at this last appeal she melted; and gathering the young girl to her breast, she held her fast.—And so for long she continued to sit, her chin resting lightly on the fair hair, that was silky and downy as an infant's, and gazing with sombre eyes over the stealthily heaving sea.

FROM *For Love Alone* (1944):
Brown Seaweed and Old Fish Nets

—

CHRISTINA STEAD

Christina Stead is interested in both the victims and the perpetrators of economic, social, familial, and sexual exploitation. Her novels explore questions of power and the relationship between power and gender.

The heroine of For Love Alone, *like the author, separates from her family and leaves Australia. After she experiences rejection in a love affair, she goes forward to shape her own destiny according to two sacred values: love and creativity.*

This excerpt, set in Australia, is the first chapter of the novel. It makes clear why Teresa has to leave home.

Naked, except for a white towel rolled into a loincloth, he stood in the doorway, laughing and shouting, a tall man with powerful chest and thick hair of pale burning gold and a skin still pale under many summers' tan. He seemed to thrust back the walls with his muscular arms; thick tufts of red hair stood out from his armpits. The air was full of the stench of brown seaweed and old fish nets. Through the window you could see the water of the bay and the sand specked with flotsam and scalloped with yellow foam, left by the last wave. The man, Andrew Hawkins, though straight and muscular, was covered with flaccid yellow-white flesh and his waist and abdomen were too broad and full. He had a broad throat and chest and from them came a clear tenor voice.

" . . . she was sitting on the ground nursing her black baby, and she herself was black as a hat, with a strong, supple oily skin, finer than white women's skins: her heavy breasts were naked, she was not ashamed of that, but with natural modesty, which is in even the most primitive of women, she covered her legs with a piece of cloth lying on the ground and tittered behind her hand exactly like one of you—" he was saying to the two women sitting at the table. "Then she said something to her husband and he, a thin spindle-shanked fellow, translated for me, grinning from ear to ear: she asked how it was possible for a man to have such beautiful white feet as mine."

He looked down at his long blond feet and the two women looked from their sewing quickly at his feet, as if to confirm the story.

"I have always been admired for my beautiful white skin," said the golden-haired man, reminiscently. "Women love it in a man, it surprises them to see him so much fairer in colour than they are. Especially the darkies," and he looked frankly at Kitty Hawkins, who was a nut-brown brunette with drooping back hair. "But not only the dark ones," he went on softly. He kept on coaxing.

"I have been much loved; I didn't always know it—I was always such an idealist. When girls and, yes, even women older than myself, wanted to come and talk to me, I thought it was a thing of the brain. One poor girl, Paula Brown, wrote to me for years, discussing things. I never dreamed that it was not an interest in speculative thought. I used to tell her all my dreams and longings. I could have married a rich girl. In the Movement there was a quiet, pale girl called Annie Milson. Her father, though I didn't think about it at the time, was Commissioner for Railways and was quite the capitalist. They had properties all around here, dairy-farms down the south coast. I could have been a wealthy man if I had become Milson's son-in-law, and I believe he would have been delighted. He seemed to approve of me. I spent the afternoon at their Lindfield house two or three times—and spent the afternoon talking to Milson! I never suspected the girl liked me. I believe she loved the good-looking, sincere young idealist—but I had no inter-est in earthly things at the time and I never suspected it. Poor Annie! She used to send me books. Yes, I believe I was loved by many women but I was so pure that I had no temptations. 'My mind to me a kingdom was.' I suppose, now, when I look back, that I was a mystery to them, poor girls, such a handsome young man, who didn't dance, didn't take them to the theatre, and worried only about the social organism."

He laughed, his brilliant oval blue eyes, their whites slightly bloodshot, looking gaily at the two girls. He sighed, "I didn't know that I was a handsome lad. I didn't know then what a woman, a married woman, said to me much later, a fine, motherly soul she was, Mrs. Kurzon, but she said it with a sigh, 'Mr. Hawkins, how many women have wanted to put their hands in your wonderful hair?' She said it with a twinkle but she said it with longing too; and then she asked me if she could, laughing all the time and sweetly too, in a womanly sweet way. I let her, and she plunged them in and took them out with a sigh of gratification, 'Oh, Mr. Hawkins, how wonderful it is!' And how many women have told me it was a shame to waste such hair on a man, they would give anything to have it."

One of the girls, the younger one, who was blond, looked up at the marvellous hair of the man.

Andrew Hawkins ran his hand through it, feeling it himself. A thought seemed to strike him; he brought down his hand and looked at the back, then the palm. It was a large, pale, muscular hand, an artisan's hand, hairless, diseased-looking because streaked and spotted with fresh cement. "Not a bad hand either," he said. He had something on the tip of his tongue but couldn't get it out, he went on about his legs instead, "Poor Mrs. Slops said I had legs like a 'dook.' And I have seen 'dooks,' at that, and not half so well-calved, I'll take my affidavit. But do you know, Kit," he said, lowering his voice, and his eyes darkening with modesty or wonder. "You see this hand, my good right hand, do you see it, Kit?"

Kitty laughed in her throat, a troubled, sunny laugh, "I've felt it, too, in my time."

He said mysteriously, lowering his voice again, "Women have kissed this hand." They both turned and looked at him, startled. "Yes, Kit, yes, you disbeliever," he said, turning to the younger girl. "Teresa won't believe me perhaps, for she doesn't want to love me, but women, several women have kissed this hand. Do you know how women kiss men's hands? They take it in both their hands, and kiss it first on the back, and then each finger separately, and they hate to let go." He burst out suddenly into a rough ringing laugh. "You would not believe that has happened—not once, but several times—to your Andrew!"

"Handy Andy," said Teresa, in her soft, unresonant voice. She did not glance up but went on sewing. Each of the girls had before her on the table the wide sleeve of a summer dress; it was a greyish lavender voile sprinkled with pink roses and they were sewing roses made of the material in rows along the sleeves. "Ah, you think you know a lot about love," went on Andrew, coming into the room, and throwing himself full length on the old settee that stood underneath the window that looked upon the beach. "Yes, Trees is always moaning about love, but you don't know, Trees, that love is warmth, heat. The sun is love and love also is fleshly, in this best sense that a beautiful woman gladdens the heart of man and a handsome man brightens the eyes of the ladies. One blessed circle, perpetual emotion." He laughed. "Many women have loved your Andrew, but not you two frozen women." He continued teasing, waiting for an answer,

> "Orpheus with his lute made T'rees
> And the mountain tops that freeze,
> Bow themselves when he did sing:"

"We will never be finished," said Teresa.

"And there are the beans to do, I must do them," said Kitty, throwing the long sleeve on the table. "When they're done, I'll call to you and you put away the sewing. You must have some lunch, the wedding breakfast won't be till late."

"Beauty," mused Andrew, looking at them. "What a strange thing that I didn't have lovely daughters, I who worship beauty so much! Yes, Fate plays strange tricks, especially on her favourites. My dream as a lad was to find a stunning mate, and different from most youths, I dreamed of the time when I would have beautiful little women around me. How proud I was in prospect! But of course," he said confidingly to Teresa, "I knew nothing of a thing more sacred than beauty—human love. My dear Margaret attracted me by her truth-loving face, serious, almost stern—as sea-biscuit! he-ha—but soft, womanly dark eyes, like Kitty's. I don't know where you got your face of a little tramp, Trees, a ragamuffin. If I had had three beautiful bouncing maidens like old Harkness! I saw the three of them coming down an alley in their rose garden last Saturday and I went up and pretended I couldn't see them, I said, 'Where are the Harknesses? Here I see nothing but prize roses!' They burst out laughing and Mina, she has a silvery, rippling laugh, said, 'Oh, Mr. Hawkins, how very nice!' "

"Do you mean that fat one?" asked Teresa, spitefully.

"Ah, jocund, rubious, nods and becks and wreathed smiles," said Andrew, writhing on the settee in ecstasy, a broad smile on his face. "I peered in among the roses and then I pretended to see them and I said, 'I was looking for Mina, Teen and Violet, but all I see are the Three Graces!' "

"You should be ashamed," said Teresa, morosely.

"That just shows you don't understand the world and your Andrew," he retorted comfortably, leaning back and flexing and stretching his legs. "The girls were delighted! They went off into happy peals of golden laughter, like peals of bells. Mrs. Harkness came running up and said, 'What have you been saying to my girls, Mr. Hawkins? I must know the joke too.' We all laughed again. Mrs. Harkness—I wish you could meet her—is a wonderful woman, motherly, but full of womanly charm and grace too. In her forties, plump, round, but not ungraceful, the hearthside Grace. And she too told me how beautiful my hair is. They can't help it, the desire to run their fingers through it is almost irresistible."

"Did she kiss your hand? Mrs. Harkness, I mean," enquired Teresa in a low voice.

Hawkins looked at her sharply, "Don't jest at things that are sacred to me, Teresa. I have suffered much through love and when you come to know human love, instead of self-love—"

"The beans are done," called Kitty. Teresa gathered up her sewing.

"If you ever love! For I verily believe that inward and outward beauty strike one chord."

"You do," said the girl, "do you? Well, I don't. How simple that would be."

"An ugly face is usually the dried crust of a turbid, ugly soul. I personally," he said in a low, vibrant voice, "cannot stand ugliness, Trees. I worship beauty," he said, throwing his limbs about in a frenzy of enthusiasm, "and all my life I have served her, truth and beauty."

Teresa took the worn damask cloth out of the sideboard drawer and set five places.

"I want to be loved in my own home," said Hawkins, contemplating his long legs and speaking in a fine drawn silken murmur. "Sometimes I close my eyes and imagine what this place would be like if it were a Palace of Love! All your ideas of decorating the walls with fifteenth-century designs, peepholes, twisted vines, naked-bottomed fat and indecent infants on the ceiling—that's dry, meaningless, dull work, but if this house were peopled with our love, murmurous with all the undertones, unspoken understanding of united affection—a-ah!" He opened his beautiful blue eyes and looked across at her, "And yet, in a way, you're like my dear Margaret, but without her loving nature. How tender she was! I was her whole life, I and you babies. She knew that I had something precious in my head, like the whale with ambergris—"

"A sick whale has ambergris," said Teresa: "A whale that's half rotting while it swims is the sort they go after, because they hope it has ambergris in its head. And you know how they bring in every soapy thing from the beach, everything that's greasy and pale, for ambergris."

"And she was modest," said the beautiful man, joining his hands and looking down at them. "She had a curious thing she used to say, 'Andrew, how did a mouse like me get a man like you?' What charm there is in a modest woman! If you could learn that, Teresa, you would have charm for men, for they can forgive a lot in a woman who is truly devoted to them. What do we look for in women—understanding! In the rough and tumble of man's world, the law of the jungle is often the only law observed, but in the peace and sanctity of the man's home, he feels the love that is close to angels! A pretty face, a lovely form, cannot give that—or not those alone. No, it is because he knows he is loved. . . . Don't forget, Kitty, to clean my boots," he said, sitting up. "I'm going into town this afternoon."

"On the same boat with us?"

"No, later. And ask Trees if she sewed the buttons on my white shirt. Trees! Buttons—shirt?"

"Well, you could have gone to Malfi's wedding, you're going into town," objected Teresa, bringing in a vase of flowers.

"Ha—I don't approve of that hocus-pocus. You know that, Teresa. Love alone unites adult humans."

"We're not illegitimate," Teresa grinned.

He had risen to his feet and half turned to the window; now he partly turned to her, and she could see the flush on his face and neck. "Teresa," he said gently, "your mother and I were united by a great love, by a passion higher than earthly thoughts, and I should have kept to my principles, and she too was willing to live with me, bound only by the ties of our affection, but—I had already rescued her from the tyranny of that hard old man and we were too young and weak, we could not harden ourselves to hurt her mother's feelings as well."

The young girl went on smiling unpleasantly, "And if you loved someone else?"

The man looked out over the beach and bay for a moment and the girl flushed, thinking she had gone too far. He said, sotto voce, "My girl, since you bring it up, I am in love again, with a young woman, a woman of thirty, a—" His voice dropped. He came towards her, seized her arms and looked into her face without bending. "A wonderful, proud, fine-looking woman, pure in soul. My whole life is wrapping itself around her, so I'm glad you brought it up for you will understand later on—"

She angrily shook her arms free, "Don't touch me, I don't like it."

He sighed and turned his shoulder to her, "This is no way to treat men, men don't like an unbending woman."

"I am unbending."

"You will be sorry for it."

"You ordered us never to kiss or coax or put our arms around you or one another."

"A coaxing woman, a lying, wheedling woman is so abhorrent to men," he said. "I have seen a woman sitting on a man's lap, trying to coax things out of him, isn't that shameful to you? I hope it is. I was firm on that one point and your mother agreed with me. *She* never flattered in hope of gain, she never once lied—never once in our whole married life, Trees. Think of your dear mother if temptation ever comes your way—although you will never be tempted to lie, I know, but the other little things in women, the petty, wretched things, the great flaws in female character—flightiness—" He paused and forced himself to go on with a grimace, "flirtatiousness—though," he continued, looking round at her with a broad smile, "*that* is not likely to be your weakness, nor Kit's. If, I say, you should ever be tempted to tricks like that, thinking to please some man, remember that they detest those tricks and see through them. They know they are traps, mean little chicane to bend them to woman's purpose. I was at Random's the other day. He let his little daughter climb over him and beg him for something he had refused. He gave in. It was a humiliating sight for me, and for the man. I could see her years later, because she is pretty, a warped, dishonest little creature, only thinking of making men do things for her."

"Have you ever seen me coax or kiss?" asked Teresa, indignantly. "Have I ever begged for a single thing?"

"No," he said, "and in a way it's a pity, for you have no attraction for a man as you are now, and it might be better if you knew how to lure men." He smiled at her, "Why can't you be like me, Trees? I am known everywhere for my smile. I have melted the hearts of my enemies with my smile. You know Random Senior, the man who did me that great injury—we used to pass in the street, afterwards, every morning on the way to work. I always smiled and offered him my hand. After a month or so, he couldn't bear it. He used to go round by a back way, to avoid me, he couldn't bear the smile of the honest man. If you would smile more, men would look at you. Men have their burdens. How delightful it is to see a dear little woman, happy and smiling, eager to hear them, delighted to cheer them. No one can say why a woman's bright face and intelligent eye mean so much to a man. Of course, the sexes are made to attract each other," he said with an indulgent laugh, "don't think I'm so innocent as I seem, Teresa, but sex has its delicious aspects. Sex—what a convenient dispensation—yes, sex," he said, changing his tone and coming close to her, ardently, intently, "I am not one to inveigh against sex! You don't know the meaning, the beauty of that word, Teresa, to a loving man. On the other side of the barrier of sex is all the splendour of internal life, a garden full of roses, if you can try to understand my meaning, sweet-scented, fountains playing, the bluebird flying there and nesting there. There are temptations there but the man sure of himself and who knows himself can resist them and direct his steps into the perfumed, sunny, lovely paths of sex. Oh!" he cried, his fine voice breaking, "who can tell these things to another, especially to you, Trees? You are too cold, you have never responded to me, and my soul, yes, I will use that word, had such great need of understanding! I saw right away that Kitty, my dear girl, was a woman's woman, a womanly little girl, pretty, humble, sweet, but in you I saw myself and I determined to lead you out of all the temptations of your sex, for there are many—many of which you are not aware—"

"There is simply nothing of which I am not aware," said the girl.

"You don't know what you are saying," he said tenderly.

Her face became convulsed with anger. "How stupid you are," she cried and rushed out, upstairs, into the breezy part of the house. All the doors were open. Her room at the back of the house, painted Nile green, was an inviting cell, almost bare, neat, cool. She rushed in, flung herself on her bed, and stared upwards at the ceiling, mad with anger. In a short time, however, she cooled down, and thought once more that she would cover the walls, the ceiling, yes, the walls of the corridor, the walls of all the house, with designs. She got up and began to draw fresh designs on a large piece of white paper stretched by drawing pins on her table. She had combined all sorts of strange things in it; patriotic things, the fantastic heads of prize merino rams, with their thick, parting, curly, silky wool and their double-curved corrugated horns, spikes of desert wheat, strange forms of xerophytic plants, pelicans, albatrosses, sea-eagles, passion-flowers, the wild things she most admired. She forgot all about her dress, which she had to wear at the wedding that afternoon, and which was not yet finished. She came downstairs reluctantly when Kitty called her.

Andrew, viewing her solemnly from the end of the table where he unfolded his worn damask serviette over his bulging naked belly, laughed and chanted as he banged his soup-spoon on the table, "Ants in her pants and bats in her belfry." Teresa turned pale, half-rose from the table, looking at Andrew, and cried, "You offend my honour! I would kill anyone who offends my honour." There was an instant of surprise, then a low, long laugh, rolling from one end of the table to the other. Andrew began it, Lance with his hollow laugh, Leo with his merry one, Kitty's cackles joined in. It was far from spiteful, healthy, they had a character there in the simmering Teresa; she never paused for reflection, she rose just the same in defence of her "honour."

"Your honour," said Lance, her elder brother, low and sneering. He was a tall, pale, blond lad, chaste and impure.

"A woman's honour means something else from what you imagine," said her father, laughing secretively.

"A woman can have honour," declared Leo, a dark, rosy boy. He turned serious in honour of his admired sister.

Lance muttered.

"You would not kill, you would not take human life," said the handsome man, the family god, sitting at the head of the table. "Don't say such things, Teresa."

"Honour is more sacred than life," said Teresa sombrely. Andrew said abruptly, "What's the delay? Where's dinner?" Kitty brought in the soup.

No more was said, and they fell to in a gloomy, angry silence. The unappeased young girl, relentless, ferocious, was able to stir them all. They suddenly felt discontented, saw the smallness of their lives and wondered how to strike out into new ways of living. She did not know this: she brooded, considering her enemies under her brows and made plans to escape. She reconsidered the conversation; she had not said the right thing, but exploded into speech in the usual way. Her father meanwhile had been thinking it over. She supped her soup and without looking up, declared to him, "I am formed, on the moral side. You're ignoble. You can't understand me. Henceforth, everything between us is a misunderstanding. You have accepted compromise, you revel in it. Not me. I will never compromise."

Lance and Andrew, from laughing up their sleeves, came out into the open and burst into joyous roars of laughter. Leo considered her seriously, from above his soup-spoon. Kitty looked from one to the other. Teresa sat up, with a stiff face and a stiff tongue, too, and tried to crush them with a glance. She buried her mouth in another spoonful of soup. Several of them threw themselves back against their chairs and laughed loudly; but the laugh was short.

"Eat your soup and don't be a fool," said Andrew.

Teresa flushed, hesitated, but said nothing. Andrew said, "She dares to say her own father is contemptible, her brothers and sister."

Teresa looked ashamed. Hawkins pursued the subject. "Mooning and moaning to herself and it's evident what it's about—no one is good enough for her. She hates everything. I love everything. I love everyone. My one prayer, and I pray, though to no vulgar god, is for love."

"You disgust me," said Teresa, lifting her head and looking at him.

He began to laugh, "Look at her! Pale, haggard, a regular witch. She looks like a beggar. Who would want her! What pride! Pride in rags! Plain Jane on the high horse! When she is an old maid, she'll still be proud, and noble. No one else will count!"

The nineteen-year-old said calmly, "I told you I would kill you if you insult me. I will do it with my bare hands. I am not so cowardly as to strike with anything. I know where to press though —I will kill you, father." With terror, the table had become silent, only Kitty murmured, "Terry! Don't be silly!"

The father turned pale and looked angrily at her.

"You don't believe me," said the girl, "but you should, it's for your own good. Base coward, hitting your children when they're small, insulting them when they're big and saying you're their father. Base coward—to think," she said, suddenly rising, with an exalted expression, staring at him and at them all, "I have to live in the house with such a brutal lot, teasing, torturing, making small. I know what to do—keep your yellow blood, I'll go away, you'll never see me again and you can laugh and titter to your heart's content, look over your shoulders at people, snigger and smirk. Do it, but let me live! I'll go this afternoon and after the wedding, I'll never come back."

The answer to this was a terrifying roar from the father, who knew how to crush these hysterias, and the subdued, frightened girl sank into her place. Presently, she burst into tears, threw herself on the table and shook with sobs. "When we are all suffering so much," she cried through her hair and folded arms, "you torture us."

"Meanwhile," said the beautiful man quietly, "you are letting Kitty do all the work."

She rose and went ashamedly to work.

"Dry your eyes," whispered Kitty hastily, "or you'll look terrible when you go out." "I have suffered too much," said Teresa, "I have suffered too much." But the storm was over.

Meanwhile, Hawkins sat on the stone seat in the wild front garden, whistling. They came down, their hands still red from washing dishes. He saw them running for the boat, burst into laughter, then suddenly, "How wonderful is marriage—the Song of Songs . . . makes the women leap like roes . . . "

The Woman at the Window (1989)

MARIAN ELDRIDGE

This is the title story in Marian Eldridge's second collection of short stories. Eldridge's fiction works by nuance, suggestion, and subtle ironies. The central character in this narrative has a fragile sense of identity, as well as fragile maternal ties. The lucky charms she invents to protect herself from a harsh world ultimately fail her.

Sharon takes out another cigarette and reaches for the lighter. Today, before she catches sight of Mickey again, she is letting herself use the lighter; after that it's matches. It's one of her good luck things. She's standing by the kitchen window but she can't take anything in yet because she's still shaking. Thank God people in the other flats wouldn't have heard, they'd have left for work. When Mickey nags it's not a soft mosquito's whine like little Trace but a piercing shriek, as though she's belting the life out of him when she's never so much as laid a finger!

"*Stop* it, Mickey!" she hisses as the sound goes on echoing in her head. She touches her shin. It's going to come up like one of those purple and green eggfruits where the little devil's heel caught her. She grabbed his arms and pushed them into his jacket, the one he ripped but it's got his name and address pinned on to it, then she dragged him, roaring and flailing, out to the landing and gave him a push towards the stairs. "Get lost, Mickey!"

She jabs out her cigarette in a dirty cup. It's matches now — she can see Mickey's bobbing blonde head. He's fine, he's just fine. Arms spread like wings, he's scattering dozens of magpies as he runs across the grassed area between the flats and the church centre. His sneakers will be soaked again. There's a perfectly good path but he never remembers. Sometimes a man comes on a toy tractor and mows the grass. Squawk park, Sharon calls it, because of all the magpies flapping and clamouring and poking their beaks down one another's throats. Now Mickey's stalking one of the parent birds. Walking just ahead of him, the magpie keeps one eye on him and one on the grass. A young bird flies clumsily towards it, overshooting the spot and landing yards away. You often see them dead on the ring-road. Mickey watches the parent run to feed the squawking baby, then himself continues to run, arms outspread, towards the flats.

The magpies nest in the trees overhanging the flats and some of the residents feed them. It stops them swooping, the woman in the adjacent flat tells Sharon. She corners Sharon one morning on the landing, just as Sharon is about to close her door on Mickey and the woman is coming out of hers, all rugged up against the sharp August morning and clutching a plastic bag full of something soft and oozing. Chopped up rump, she tells Sharon. I feed them every morning on my way to work, she says. Sharon ducks her head; the memory of her voice is as sharp as a beak. They don't like mince, the woman says, even though Sharon's door is three-quarters shut by this time and Sharon is staring over her head at a patch of blue sky through the landing window. I told the butcher, I said That says something about the quality of mincemeat, doesn't it, when the magpies refuse to eat it!

Maybe if they swooped a bit more the ranger would come and shoot a few! Sharon says, or thinks about saying. After that morning she's careful never to open her door at the time the woman will be leaving for work, not even if Mickey's teasing baby Tracey or demanding more Cocopops or screaming till Sharon's head bursts.

I could ring the ranger myself, Sharon thinks, hurrying from the kitchen to the living room where the window looks on to the ring-road. There's a phone box below her, next to the pedestrian crossing. She sees herself going down the landing stairs and around the corner, pushing the phone box door inwards so that it folds up on itself like a trick door and dropping in the coin and then the ranger coming with his gun bang! bang! He's wearing his smart ranger uniform and Mickey's off playing somewhere—standing by the pedestrian crossing actually, with his hand on the button. In the palm of her own hand Sharon feels the button beating like a slow loud heartbeat. *This time, this time, this time.* The baby's still asleep in Sharon's bed—no, Mickey's cot, it would have to be Mickey's cot—and she says I have always admired that uniform would you care for a sherry . . . only she drank the last of it yesterday, the empty bottle is lying in the middle of the living room. Would you care for cocoa?—cocoa because she's run out of tea and coffee, milk too she remembers, Mickey had that on his Weetbix. Sure would! says the ranger. I have always admired—

But, Sharon interrupts herself, how can I make that call, is it still twenty cents or has that box been changed over to thirty? Is it twenty or thirty? And she twists her hands in her nightdress until it tears a bit more at the shoulder.

Mickey is still standing by the crossing. He's swinging his foot at a dead baby magpie squashed on the ring-road. Every time a car rushes past, its feathery wings blow as though it is trying to fly. Traffic is heavy at this time of day. A stream of cars is pouring into the car park. The signal on the crossing changes from red to green, then back to flashing red. As people from the flats hurry across towards the shops and offices of the city centre, Sharon feels a surge of excitement. The drunks on the seat under the elms at the corner have been shopping already. This time the big man is carrying the paper bag. He places it carefully between his feet, opens a bottle, drinks and passes it to the next man. One of them starts to laugh, bending over then flinging back against the seat until the others join in, rocking backwards and forwards and slapping one another's shoulders. The big man grabs the bottle and, putting it to his mouth, holds it high like a trumpet.

Stragglers on the crossing scurry as the light turns red. Mickey isn't with them. He is pushing between the road edge and the low hedge in front of the flats. Sharon can see his bright curly head through gaps where the hedge has died. His hair curls on to his shoulders. It's like Rob's, soft and fair, whereas Tracey's is straight and dark like Peter's. It was Peter who helped her get this flat.

You're in luck, he said. Most people have to wait months. Peter doesn't know about Tracey. He's working in Sydney now.

Sydney, Sharon says, and feels a wave of nostalgia, bitter as morning sickness. Sydney is sand and tanning oil, and your thoughts melting like ice-cream. Sydney is your sisters chatting up that lifesaver with the gold crucifix while you whined Come *on*, Mum'll get mad! Sydney is voices creeping out from broken tiles, Come on Shar, come and have fun!

That's how she met Rob.

It was at a party. There was this guy down from Canberra. He kept looking at Sharon. His eyes felt like hands on all the secret parts of her body. Sharon's friend shouted Who wants a ride on Rob's Harley Davidson? When it was Sharon's turn she heard herself saying Why don't we keep going till we get to Canberra? and that made Rob laugh. You'd like Canberra, he said. Sharon pictured a big white Parliament House surrounded by enormous houses with curving drives and huge green lawns where no one had to fight over whose turn it was in the bathroom. They arranged to meet the next day. It was Rob's last day in Sydney. She rode on the back of the Harley to a quiet beach where Rob had to see some people. Sharon thought she would go mad if Rob didn't keep touching her. She thought Rob's friends looked at her funny; didn't talk much in front of her. Try this, Rob said, passing her a thin, damp cigarette. They lolled around on the sand while the sun roared over them like gigantic surf.

When she returned home her mother, who thought she had gone into town for the day to look for a job, took one look at her and screamed "Don't start telling me a pack of lies, I don't want to hear it!" The next morning, while her parents were still sleeping, she stuffed what clothes she could into her old school haversack, stole her mother's collection of Charles and Di fifty cents and climbed out the bedroom window. She could have walked out the front door but the window seemed right. At Central Station she bought a ticket to Canberra and she hasn't been back home since, not once, nor written, nor telephoned.

"God, this place!" Sharon exclaims, turning her back to the window. There's a new stain on the sofa, and Mickey must have been at the horsehair again; it looks like a little animal trying to hide. Panic washes into Sharon's throat like a scummy tide. There are dirty cups on the TV and the floor and the window ledge; how long is it since she washed up? She seizes the empty sherry bottle; rushes cups, plates, baby's bottles and cutlery into the sink and pours cold water on to them; snatches up all the clothes she can find on the floor, over chairs, under the bed, never mind if they're dirty or not, she doesn't waste time looking—out, out they go, into the laundry basket. If they all go in, she thinks, if they all go in and nothing falls on the floor, *it will mean good luck*. Sometimes she starts off the day like that: if a bird flies past the window . . . if Mickey wakes up before Tracey . . . or it might be the other way round, if Tracey wakes up before Mickey. The last thing, Mickey's bottom sheet that he's wet again, catches over the edge of the basket and hangs there, touching the floor but not falling either. Sharon's hands are shaking. She needs another cigarette. She's using the lighter again; that's allowed now.

She's down to her last cigarette. There are plenty in the shops of course, milk too, cigarettes and milk and the other things she has run out of. The shops are on the other side of the car park and the car park is on the other side of the ring-road and the ring-road is on the other side of the window.

She has to look away quickly.

She looks away to the seat under the elms where the drunks sit all day, even on days as nippy as this. She has a little fantasy that Rob is one of the men on the seat. Any minute now he'll look up and wave and she'll lock the kids in the flat and go down and they'll share the bottle or maybe a joint. It couldn't be any colder under the elms than it was in midwinter in the garage where she lived with him when she first came to Canberra.

Canberra was ace! Rob took her to parties and gigs or they stayed in the garage smoking hash or cuddled inside two sleeping bags zipped together, or they went over to the house where people were always coming and going. She never got to like the people in the house as much as Rob did; they talked to him more than they talked to her, and they'd bang hard on the bathroom door when she was daydreaming under the shower. Also they never cleaned up the kitchen, no one did except herself. Annie, the other girl who lived there, said "I don't know why you do it." But then Annie ate out; she could afford to, she had a job. She was a very bossy sort of girl, *woman* she insisted on, she hated *girl*. Sharon took to going over to the house only when Rob did, even if she was bursting, or she'd hang on till night time and squat behind the fig tree.

At first she thought it was just her body playing a trick. Rob said "Shit! You'd better do something, Shar!" and gave her six brand-new fifty dollar notes but she kept on putting it off, she got scared, she kept hoping her mother would write or just turn up on the doorstep.

And after a while it was too late.

Rob left Canberra soon after that. He said it was what they'd been talking about all winter, him and her zipping north on the Harley. He's back again now; he does the lighting for a new theatre group just up the road at Gilmore House. He stopped her one day when she was taking the two kids for a walk. "Sharon! How's things?" He's even been around once with a huge Mickey Mouse for Mickey, but when Sharon said "What about some regular maintenance, Rob?" he laughed. He said "You must be joking, Shar. I'm on the dole."

It was Annie who put her up to saying that to Rob. Annie's at Gilmore House, too—she's part of a women's video group—and she drops in at the flat sometimes for coffee. She drinks dandelion coffee so she brings her own. When Annie's talking, Sharon nods and says Yes Annie, yes, I should do that. Get your name on the waiting list for a three-bedroom house, Annie tells her. You're eligible, Sharon. When Rob cleared out, Annie persuaded her to move into a group house with Annie and two other women. They brought Sharon cups of herbal tea to stop the retching. They massaged her temples. They showed her articles about the effects of smoking on the developing foetus. They said You'll have no trouble getting family day care, Sharon, that's one of the good things about Canberra. They wanted her to have the baby in the house, with everyone helping. They began to talk about "our baby." One afternoon, while someone was practising on the drum kit in the living room, Sharon got dressed, climbed out her bedroom window and caught a bus into the city. In the city she did two things; she booked herself in at the hospital, and put her name down for a government flat.

The baby Tracey totters into the living room. She is crying, slow tears washing down her face like July rain. She's wearing an old pyjama coat of Mickey's, so shrunken her arms stick out to the elbows. Her napkin and plastic pants have fallen around her knees. Sharon pulls the napkin right off, then, sliding down to the floor, takes Tracey on to her lap and puts her to her breast. Tracey is going on two but if Sharon tries to wean her she cries, not a full-blooded roar like Mickey but *NnnnNnnn* like an insect trapped against glass.

When Mickey was starting to walk Sharon tried to get a job, a cash-paying job so as not to lose her pension. Cleaning, she thought. Annie wrote her a reference. Every Saturday she bought the paper and went through the Sit. Vac. The first lady she cleaned for asked her not to bring Mickey again, "little sticky fingers," so Sharon left him locked in the flat until one of the neighbours said that he cried and Sharon got scared of losing her lease. The second lady worked during the day so there were no worries there about taking Mickey. Sharon had the run of the house, she could dream out the windows, gaze all she wanted to at the pool and the green lawns, the mountains so sharply blue they made her throat wobbly, the fledgeling new Parliament House with its seven cranes bending down to it. Two days after starting work for this lady she received a letter: "Dear Sharon, Here is the money I owe you. I shall not be requiring you again. I wonder my dear if you have ever cleaned a house before? . . . " Sharon cried. She thought Tracey wasn't showing yet but the third lady said "You wouldn't be able to continue for long, would you dear? I'm very sorry but I really want somebody permanent."

"It isn't fair!" exclaims Sharon, putting Tracey aside and jumping to her feet. "It's all right for you!" she declares, staring at someone invisible across the room. Tracey tugs at her nightdress. Sharon snatches her up and thrusts her back at the breast, but the baby twists her head away. "Go down on the floor then, Tracey," Sharon sighs. She can't get over how different girls are from boys, even kids this age; when Mickey's inside he's at her all the time for Weetbix, fizzy drinks, biscuits. "What *is* it? Stop it, Trace. You want more titty? Trace?" She bends to lift her once again, but the child slips out of her grasp and, going into the centre of the room, falls to the floor and cries, *NnnnNnnn. NnnnNnnn.*

Sharon goes into the bedroom and closes the door. Stumbling over Mickey's broken tip-truck she discovers her purse on the floor, so she sits on her bed and empties it into her lap. She puts the five dollar notes on one side of her, the twos on the other; with the coins she makes a little tower that keeps falling over. After a while she peeps into the living room. Tracey has fallen asleep on the floor. Sharon picks her up and puts her into Mickey's unmade cot and pulls the side up. Heaving at it, she feels sick again, and remembers that she hasn't eaten anything since yesterday lunch-time when she finished off Tracey's tin of chicken dinner.

At the back of the refrigerator she finds a slice of bread in its plastic wrap. As she eats it at the kitchen window she watches the magpies in squawk park. The parent birds jab at wriggling things underground, run to the nearest begging baby, run run run on legs like twigs to find more food. The baby birds never stop pestering. Sometimes one of the parents gets really bossy, standing over a young one until it shuts up and pretends dead. Suddenly they all fly up into the trees. Two women and two children are coming along the path. One of the women is much older than the others; she is the mother, Sharon decides. The other woman is younger than herself, a girl really. She is swinging a man's purse by its wrist strap, and she isn't wearing a parka and beanie and scarf like the others, but a coat patterned with great zigzags of colour, red, green, purple, gold.

The mother and the girl in the coat stop to study a map. Visitors to Canberra, Sharon thinks, just as she once was. A tiny bubble of excitement surfaces. The visitors disappear around the corner of the flats and she runs to the living room window to see them reappear by the road. While they are waiting for the green light she tiptoes into the bedroom and pulls on her Indian cotton dress and the thick woollen cardigan that Annie gave her. She stuffs her money into her purse and hurries back to the living room window. There they are; the light has turned green but they are not crossing. *They are waiting for her.*

Mickey is still there between the hedge and the road, jumping on the spot as the cars fly past. Maybe he's said something cheeky to the family because as Sharon watches, the mother pushes past the hedge and speaks to him. He's not listening to her at all, jump jump jump, Sharon can feel those little pounding feet in the back of her head. She'll give him such a belting if he's been swearing again! The mother edges back to the others and speaks to the younger woman, the girl. The two kids giggle. The girl looks up at the flats, shrugs, then, although the light is angry red, turns her back on her mother and stalks across the road. Sharon feels a hot wave of excitement. When the light is green again the others cross too. Now the mother and the girl seem to be having a row. They stand under a pine tree in the car park, the woman pointing back at the flats and waving her arm and the girl staring down at the ground, sulky, Sharon decides, a bad girl, a runaway. Finally the woman and the two kids return to the lights and cross back towards the flats, but whether the girl follows Sharon doesn't wait to see. She didn't want the family to fight. She goes into the kitchen and puts the kettle on. There's a used teabag on the sink. Maybe she can squeeze another cup out of that.

The doorbell rings. That little shit Mickey! She's told him once this morning that there aren't any biscuits. He must have found a chair somewhere to stand on to reach the bell, must have dragged it all the way up the stairs. RRRing! RRRing! If she doesn't answer, if she holds her breath and pretends he's not there, he'll give up and go away again. She hears him ring the bell of the flat next door. The cheek of him! Pity the magpie woman's not home to give him what for.

She lights her last cigarette and goes back to the living room window. The family is still there, all four of them. They're standing by the phone box with their heads together. The mother goes into the box and after a moment comes out. The girl fiddles about in her purse and hands her something, a coin, Sharon supposes, then moves off a short distance, not quite part of the family and not separate either. The mother goes back into the box, leaving the door open. The two kids poke their heads in and listen.

Mickey's down there with them. He's holding on to his doodle and if she's told him not to do that she's told him a dozen times.

Before she has time to think she hurries downstairs and around the corner.

"Get upstairs, Mickey."

The mother is out of the phone box by now, the two kids at her elbows.

"Excuse me," says the mother. "Is this your little boy?"

The girl in the bright coat comes a bit closer at this.

It takes Sharon a few moments to register that the woman is speaking to her. "Yes?" she says, abrupt and questioning at the same time. The girl and the mother exchange glances. The two kids are staring. Sharon pulls Annie's cardigan closer.

"He was standing—jumping—right on the edge of the road," the mother begins, as though she wants someone, the girl, Sharon, to take over.

"Yes?" Sharon repeats.

"The traffic's pretty heavy," the girl tosses in, then stares over everyone's heads as though it's all nothing to do with her.

"And that pretty fair hair," the mother adds eagerly, so that Sharon thinks Bet you wish yours was still the same! "He's so pretty," the mother is saying, "I mean I didn't realise he *was* a boy until I saw his name pinned on his jacket."

"And his address," puts in one of the kids importantly. "That's how we knew . . . "

Sharon says slowly "Well what business is it of mine?"

Their faces crumble with doubt. "But he *is* your little boy?" the girl asks, while the mother echoes "This is your mummy, darling?"

"Of course he is!" Sharon snaps. She adds "He knows about going out on the road. I've told him. He knows."

"But playing right on the edge—!" says the girl, while the mother cries "Such a pretty child! Someone might snatch him away!"

"Then it'll be his own fault, won't it?" retorts Sharon. "If he goes out on the road it'll be his own fault. He knows!" cries Sharon. "I've told him! You get along upstairs, Mickey!"

On the stairs she keeps saying "Hurry up, hurry *up*, Mickey!" She adds "You heard what those two said—if you're not a good boy someone will try to steal you!"

"*They* did!" wails Mickey. "That old lady tried to steal me! She telled the other one she would give me to a policeman. She said Come on, Mickey, you come with me. And the other one said—"

But what the runaway girl said Sharon doesn't hear, because at that moment the door bell rings again. This time, since it can't be Mickey, she opens it at once. On her doorstep, sharp as a mountain peak in his trim blue uniform, stands a policeman.

He says to Sharon, "Good morning, madam. Madam, we have just had a phone call . . . "

Sharon stands at the window. Through a dead patch in the hedge she can see Mickey clearly. As his mouth opens she stuffs her fingers in her ears but she can't shut out the bellow. Her hand is still smarting. As though he can't bear to stand still Mickey jumps up and down, up and down, jump jump jump jump, he jumps out into the road and as a car whizzes by he jumps back against the hedge, out and back, out and back—

This time! shrieks a voice in Sharon's head. *This time, Mickey, this time, this time!*

A Woman with Black Hair
(1985)

———

BEVERLEY FARMER

Farmer looks at varied aspects of female experience in her fiction. "A Woman with Black Hair" can be read on more than one level. A chilling crime story, it is also, from a feminist viewpoint, a parable of power relations between the sexes.

Her front door locks, but not her back door. Like the doors on many houses in her suburb, they are panelled and stained old pine ones, doors solid enough for a fortress: but the back one opens with a push straight into her wooden kitchen. Moonlight coats in icy shapes and shadows the floor and walls which I know to be golden pine, knotted and scuffed, having seen them in sunlight and cloudlight as often as I have needed to; having seen them lamplit too, cut into small gold pictures by the wooden frames of the window, thirty small panes, while I stood unseen on the back veranda. (The lampshades are lacy baskets and sway in draughts, rocking the room as if it were a ship's cabin and the light off waves at sunset or sunrise washed lacily inside it. Trails like smoke wavering their shadows over the ceiling are not smoke, but cobwebs blowing loose.) These autumn nights she has a log fire burning, and another in her front room just beyond. With the lights all off, the embers shine like glass. They fill the house all night with a warm breath of fire.

An old clock over the kitchen fire chimes the hours. One. Two.

259

Off the passage from her front room is a wooden staircase. Her two small daughters sleep upstairs, soundly all night. Beyond the staircase a thick door is left half-open: this is her room. In its white walls the three thin windows are slits of green light by day, their curtains of red velvet drawn apart like lips. There is a fireplace, never used; hardly any furniture. A worn rug, one cane armchair, a desk with a lamp stooped over books and papers (children's essays and poems drawn over in coloured pencil, marked in red ink); old books on dark shelves; a bed with a puffed red quilt where she sleeps. Alone, her hair lying in black ripples on the pillow.

For me a woman has to have black hair.

This one's hair is long and she is richly fleshed, the colour of warm milk with honey. Her eyes are thick-lidded: I have never been sure what colour they are. (She is mostly reading when I can watch her.) They seem now pale, now dark, as if they changed like water. On fine mornings she lies and reads the paper on the cane sofa under her shaggy green grapevine. She is out a lot during the day. She and the children eat dinner by the kitchen fire — her glass of wine glitters and throws red reflections — and then watch television for an hour or two in the front room. After the children go up to bed, she sits on and reads until long past midnight, the lamplight shifting over her. Some evenings visitors come — couples, the children's father — but no one stays the night. And she has a dog: an aged blond labrador, half-blind, that grins and dribbles when it hears me coming and nuzzles for the steak I bring. It has lolloped after me in and around the house, its tail sweeping and its nails clicking on the boards. It spends the night on the back veranda, snoring and farting in its sleep.

The little girls — I think the smaller is five or six, the other not more than two years older — have blond hair tied high in a sheaf, like pampas grass. (The father is also blond.)

Tonight, though the moon is nearly full, it is misted over. I may not even really need the black silk balaclava, stitched in red, that I bought for these visits, though I am wearing it anyway, since it has become part of the ritual. I am stripped to a slit black tracksuit — slit, because it had no fly — from which I unpicked all the labels. I have the knife safe in its sheath, and my regular tracksuit folded in my haversack ready for my morning jog when I leave the house.

Tonight when the clock chimed one she turned all the lights out. When it chimed two I came in, sat by the breathing fire, and waited. There is no hurry. I nibble one by one the small brown grapes I picked, throwing the skins and the wet pips into its flames of glass, making them hiss. Nothing moves in the house.

When the clock chimes three I creep into her room—one curtain is half-open, as it always has been—to stand watching the puddle of dimness that is her pillow; the dark hair over it.

I saw her once out in the sun untangling her wet hair with her fingers. It flowed over her face and over her naked shoulders like heavy dark water over sandstone. The grass around her was all shafts of green light, each leaf of clover held light. There were clambering bees.

There is a creek a couple of streets down the hill from here. I wish I could take her there. It reminds me of a creek I used to fish in when I was a boy. There were round speckled rocks swathed with green-yellow silky weed, like so many wet blond heads combed by the fingers of the water. (My hair was—is still— blond.) I used to wish I could live a water life and leave my human one: I would live in the creek and be speckled, weedy-haired, never coming out except in rain. I lay on the bank in spools and flutters of water light. A maternal ant dragged a seed over my foot; a dragon-fly hung in the blurred air; a small dusty lizard propped, tilted its head to take me in, and hid in the grass under my shadow.

Over the weeks since I found this woman I have given her hints, clues, signs that she has been chosen. First I took her white night-gown—old ivory satin, not white, but paler than her skin—and pulled it on and lay in her bed one day. It smelled of hair and roses. I left it torn at the seams on the sofa under the grapevine that shades her back veranda. I suppose she found it that night and was puzzled, perhaps alarmed, but thought the dog had done it; anyone might think so. Another day I left an ivory rose, edged with red, in a bowl on her kitchen table. She picked it up, surprised, and put it in a glass of water. She accused her daughters of picking it, I could tell from where I was standing by the kitchen window (though of course what she was saying was inaudible), and they shook their heads. Their denials made her angry; the older girl burst into loud sobs. Another frilled rose was waiting on the pillow in the room with the three red-lipped windows. I wonder what she made of that. They looked as if they were crumpled up then dipped in blood.

I drop a hint now: I sit down in the cane armchair, which creaks, and utter a soft sigh. Her breathing stops. She is transfixed. When it starts again, it is almost as slow as it was when she was asleep, but deeper: in spite of her efforts, harsher. Her heart shudders. For long minutes I take care not to let my breathing overlap hers; I keep to her rhythm. She does not dare to stop breathing for a moment to listen, warning whoever is there, if anyone is, that she is awake. And at last—the kitchen clock chimes four—she starts to fall asleep again, having made herself believe what she must believe. There is no one there, the noise was outside, it was a dream, she is only being silly.

I make the chair creak again.

She breathes sharply, softly now, and with a moan as if in her sleep—this is how she hopes to deceive whoever is there, because someone is, someone *is*—she turns slowly over to lie and face the chair. Her eyes are all shadow. Certainly she opens them now, staring until they water, those eyes the colours of water. But I am too deep in the dark for her to see me: too far from the grey glow at the only tall window with its curtains left apart.

This time it takes longer for her to convince herself that there is nothing here to be afraid of. I wait until I hear her breathing slow down. Then, as lightly as the drizzle that is just starting to hiss in the tree by her window, I let her hear me breathing faster.

"Who is it?" she whispers. They all whisper.

"Quiet." I kneel by her head with the grey knife out.

"Please."

"Quiet."

The clock chimes. We both jump like rabbits. One. Two. Three. Four. Five. I hold the knife to her throat and watch her eyes sink and her mouth gape open. Terror makes her face a skull. "Going to keep quiet?" I whisper, and she makes a clicking in her throat and nods a little, as much as she dares to move. "Yes or no?"

She clicks.

"It's sharp. Watch this." I slice off a lock of her black hair and stuff it in my pocket. "Well?"

Click.

"Well?"

"Yesss."

When I hold her head clear of the quilt by her hair and stroke the knife down the side of her throat, black drops swell along the line it makes, like buds on a twig.

"Good. We wouldn't want to wake the girls up, would we?" I say. I let that sink in, let her imagine those two little girls running in moonlit gowns to snap on the light in the doorway. Then I say their names. That really makes her pulse thump in her throat. "They *won't* wake up, will they?"

"No," she whispers.

"Good."

I press my lips on hers. My mouth tastes of the grapes I ate by her still fire, both our mouths slither and taste of the brown sweet grapes. I keep my tight grip of my knife and her hair. She has to stay humble. I am still the master.

"I love you," I say. Her tongue touches mine. "I want you." Terror stiffens and swells in her at that. "Say it," I say.

"I—love you," she whispers. I wait. "I—want you."

Now there is not another minute to wait. I throw the quilt off and lift her nightgown. She moves her heavy thighs and the slit nest above them of curled black hair. There is a hot smell of roses and summer grasses. I lie on top of her. "Put it in," I say, and she slips me in as a child's mouth takes the nipple. "Move," I say. She makes a jerky thrust. "No, no. Make it nice." Her eyes twitch; panting, she rocks and sways under me.

I have to close her labouring mouth with my hand now; in case the knife at her throat slips, I put it by her head on the pillow (its steel not cold, as hot as we are), and it makes a smear where the frilled rose was. Her nightgown tears over her breasts, black strands of her hair scrawl in red over the smooth mounds of them, warm wet breasts that I drink. Is this the nightgown? Yes. Yes. Then we are throbbing and convulsing and our blood beats like waves crashing on waves.

None of these women ever says to me, How is your little grub enjoying itself? Is it in yet? Are you sure? Can it feel anything? Oh, well, that's all right. Mind if I go back to sleep now? No, move, I say, and they move. Move nicely. Now keep still. And they do.

"Now keep still," I say, picking up the knife again. She lies rigid. The clatter of the first train tells me it is time. Day is breaking. Already the grey light in the window is too strong to be still moonlight and the dark tree has started to shrink, though not yet to be green and brown. "I have to go. I'll come again," I say as I get up. She nods. "You want me to. Don't you." She nods, her eyes on the hand with the knife.

I never will. I never do. Once is all I want. At night she will lie awake thinking I will come to her again. Just as she thinks I might cut her throat and not just slit the skin; and so I might. But their death is not part of the ritual. The knife is like a lion-tamer's whip: the threat is enough. Of course if the threat fails, I will have to kill her. She, for that matter, would turn the knife on me if she could. Chance would then make her a killer. Chance, which has made me the man I am, might yet make me a killer: I squat stroking the knife.

"Well, say it," I say.

"Yes."

"You won't call the police." She shakes her head. "Or will you? Of course you will." My smile cracks a glaze of blood and spittle around my mouth. In the grey mass on the pillow I watch her eyes roll, bloodshot, bruised, still colourless. "I want you to wait, though. I know: wait till the bird hits the window." A bird flies at her window every morning. I see her realise that I even know that; I see her thinking, Oh God, what doesn't he know? "That's if you love your little girls." Her eyes writhe. "You do, don't you. Anyone would." Girls with hair like pampas grass. "So you will wait, won't you." She nods. "Well?"

"Yes."

Her coils of dark hair are ropy with her sweat and her red slobber, and so is her torn gown, the torn ivory gown that I put on once, that she never even bothered to mend. A puddle of yellow haloes her on the sheet. She is nothing but a cringing sack of stained skin, this black-haired woman who for weeks has been an idol that I worshipped, my life's centre. The knowledge that I have got of her just sickens me now. Let them get a good look at what their mother really is — what women all are — today when they come running down to breakfast, her little girls in their sunlit gowns.

"You slut," I say, and rip her rags off her. "You foul slut." Just having to gag her, turn her and tie her wrists behind her and then tie her ankles together makes me want to retch aloud. Having to touch her. But I stop myself. Turning her over to face the wall, I pull the quilt up over the nakedness and the stink of her. I wipe my face and hands, drop the knife and the balaclava into my haversack, and get dressed quickly.

The dark rooms smell of ash. Light glows in their panes, red glass in their fireplaces. The heavy door closes with a jolt. I break off a bunch of brown grapes with the gloss of the rain still on them. The dog snuffles. Blinking one eye, it bats its sleepy tail once or twice on the veranda.

I have made a study of how to lose myself in these hushed suburban mornings. (The drizzle stopped long ago. Now a loose mist is rising in tufts, and the rolled clouds are bright-rimmed.) I am as much at home in her suburb as I am in her house, or in my own for that matter, though I will never go near the house or the suburb, or the woman, again. (I will find other women in other houses and suburbs when the time comes. Move, I will say, and they will move. Move nicely. They will. Keep still. Then they will keep still.) And when the sirens whoop out, as of course they will soon, I will be out of the way. I will wash myself clean.

I am a solitary jogger over yellow leaves on the echoing footpaths. No one sees me. I cram the grapes in my haversack for later.

I know that soon after sunrise every morning a small brown bird dashes itself like brown bunched grapes, like clodded earth, at the bare window of her room, the one with its red curtains agape. Again and again it launches itself from a twig that is still shaking when the bird has fallen into the long dry grass and is panting there unseen, gathering its strength for another dash. (The garden slopes away under her room: no one can stand and look in at her window.) It thuds in a brown flurry on to its own image shaken in the glass. It startled me, in the garden the first morning. I think of her half-waking, those other mornings, thinking, It's the bird, as the brown mass thudded and fell and fluttered up to clutch at the twig again: thinking, Only the bird, and turning over slowly into her safe sleep.

But she is awake this morning. She is awake thinking, Oh God, the bird, when will the bird? Twisting to free her hands and turn over: Please, the bird. Her shoulders and her breasts and throat are all ravelled with red lace. Her hair falling over them is like dark water.

Blood and Water (1987)

—

TIM WINTON

"Blood and Water" is the story of a birth and a relationship. It is part of a strong collection, Minimum of Two, *in which most of the stories concern the same young family: Jerra, Rachel, and Sam.*

Since it was the day of Preparation, in order to prevent the bodies from remaining on the cross on the sabbath (for that sabbath was a high day), the Jews asked Pilate that their legs might be broken, and that they might be taken away. So the soldiers came and broke the legs of the first, and of the other who had been crucified with him; but when they came to Jesus and saw that he was already dead, they did not break his legs. But one of the soldiers pierced his side with a spear, and at once there came out blood and water.

John 19:31–34

Rachel laughed and there was water down her leg.

'It's coming,' she said.

Jerra leapt up and switched the TV off. For a moment they stood there and regarded the trails on her thighs. A car accelerated up the hill and passed with a hiss outside. Rain fell; the gutters were thick with it. They heard it chug in the downpipes.

'This is gonna be the happiest night of my life,' he said. He put on a record. Suddenly the house was full.

The midwife came, felt Rachel's abdomen, and commandeered their bed. Fires purred in the stove and the fireplace. The street was quiet. They played Haydn on the stereo and held hands during Rachel's contractions. They heard the midwife's snores. Her name was Annie. She was a tall, athletic woman who always wore her hair tied back in a scarf. She believed in God and healing and the goodness of people's bodies. Rachel and Jerra thought she was a little weird, but they had come to love her these past months. She was gentle. She warmed her hands. Her smile was reassuring. In the light of the fire, Rachel's flesh looked polished. Jerra rubbed her back and whispered in her ear. She breathed across her contractions.

'It's fine,' she said. 'I can do it. Nice here. Look at the fire.'

The rushes came on like advancing weather. Jerra saw her knotting up till her flesh became armour and she hissed and they counted and Annie came out to sit by the fire.

'Having a baby?'

Rachel laughed. In the lull, Jerra sponged the sweat from her. She rested her head on his chest and closed her eyes. Her long braid fell across his thigh. He saw Annie by the fire. She too had her eyes closed and she was moving her lips. Praying, he thought; she's bloody praying. He remembered the prayer his mother had sung him at bedtime when he was a child, before it all got too embarrassing.

> Gentle Jesus, meek and mild
> Look upon a little child
> Pity his simplicity
> Suffer him to come to Thee . . .

Maybe I'll even sing it to this little critter, he thought; just out of nostalgia—what the hell.

At two o'clock the contractions took Rachel with such force that pauses between became moments of irony rather than serious relief. Jerra rubbed oil on her lips. He massaged the small of her back. He felt the vibrations in her flesh. He tried, he stayed close, he felt it in his skin, but he couldn't know it for himself; he couldn't know what it was like.

Annie gloved up for an internal.

'Having babies'd be fine,' Rachel panted, 'if it wasn't for other people's hands up you.' She winced, writhed a little.

'You're not dilating,' Annie said. 'You're so angry in there I can't feel it right. We've got twins, people, or a breech. How you feel?'

'Better when you. Get. Your. Hand. Out. Ah. I got plenty left.'

'Better call the doc. We might have to go to hozzie.'

'I need a crap.'

'Get the commode, Jerra.'

He heard his footsteps on the plastic-draped floor. It was like walking on water.

Jerra drove and the women sat in the back. Though he knew the way, he needed to be told. Annie shouted directions over his shoulder and comforted Rachel at the same time. He saw their moving shadows in the mirror. The hospital loomed. He had forgotten a jumper. He wished he hadn't worn overalls. They'll think we're hippies, he thought.

'Don't cry,' murmured Annie to Rachel. 'You got plenty left.'

They waited outside the emergency entrance. It was a private hospital. They had saved for insurance in case this should happen.

In the lift they propped Rachel up during contractions. At the desk they asked her to fill out a form. Jerra tried to be calm.

'I can only be an observer now,' Annie said. 'But the doc'll be here soon. Let's hold tight.'

Nurses and orderlies crowded round, strapping things on, tucking, adjusting. Someone cheerful inserted an intravenous drip.

'Try it at home, eh?'

'Be tough,' Annie whispered.

Jerra saw Rachel on her back on the bed. She breathed slow and deep in a trough.

'Let's just get this little fella out and go home,' she murmured.

It was five in the morning. At six their doctor came. He was a small man, a conservative dresser. He seemed to like people to think he was a conservative man as well, though it was just a front. Rachel liked him. She said he was old-style, that he didn't play God. She called him Doc.

'Four centimetres,' he said, wiping his glasses. 'Like trying to drive a bus through a gas-pipe.'

Jerra felt hyperventilated. He wished the big clock across the room could be covered somehow. He saw blisters of sweat bursting on Rachel's face.

'We're getting two heartbeats here,' someone said. The room seemed full of people.

'Can't we get a scan?' Jerra asked. 'We don't really know what we've got here.'

Someone mumbled something. Rachel let out a tiny yelp of pain.

'Time for an epidural,' someone said.

'I got plenty left,' said Rachel.

'Can't we get an ultra-sound?' Jerra asked.

A masked face tutted. 'All that technology. Dear, dear.'

'That's why we're here,' Jerra said quietly through his teeth. 'It's not for the warm feeling it gives us.'

'What do *you* think, Rachel?' the doc asked.

'Can't you send them all out?'

'It's their hospital.'

'I didn't want drugs.'

'Neither did I. But you're tired. You've worked hard enough for two babies already.'

Her face went white-hard. Jerra breathed through the contraction with her. He kept his face close to hers. They had trained for this and it worked. She beat the pain.

'I'll think about it,' she said in the short lull.

'I've got to get back for morning surgery. They'll call me about the scan. Be yourself.'

It went on all morning. Rachel whooped and hissed and panted and turned to ice only to melt and begin again. Breathing with her, Jerra was almost delirious. His head was gorged with oxygen. The clock was cruel with him. Rachel got older and older.

At nine someone wheeled a trolley in and inserted an epidural into Rachel's spine. Jerra watched it happen as though he was absent from himself. 'We don't want drugs if it can be avoided,' he said to the white smock. 'We want to be reasonable—'

'This is a hospital,' the smock said.

. . .

At ten he paced the room alone. Annie was asleep down the hall on the floor of the fathers' room. Rachel had been wheeled out to the ultra-sound room and they'd stopped him going. I'm weak, he thought. I'm piss-weak. He paced like somebody on television and it didn't seem funny. He was almost jogging. He felt ill. He paced. He knew he'd die if he stopped. Outside, through the frosted glass, a day was happening; it was going on without him.

By the door of the delivery room he saw Rachel's candlewick gown hanging from a peg, and below, her sheepskin boots. He picked up the boots and squeezed them; he held the gown to his face, and in that moment it seemed possible that they might not bring her back. He stood out in the corridor. A nurse smiled at him. He felt something logging up behind his eyes. He ran to the toilet down the hall. On the toilet it felt as though his blood was running out of him. He was afraid.

He woke with his ear against the white wall. Sleep. He had been asleep. A few minutes? A moment?

The flush of the cistern sounded like a mob in a stadium. Out in the hall, a thread of that old tune stuck to him. *Gentle Jesus, meek and mild . . .*

The delivery room was still empty. He paced in a wide arc from one corner to the other. His head ached. He began to jog. Fifteen hours. He wondered what he had been like fifteen hours ago.

Twenty minutes later a white crew wheeled Rachel in. They shepherded Jerra into a corner while they renewed her spinal block. Annie came in looking sick. He wanted to speak to her but he couldn't decide what to say. Instead he elbowed his way to the bed.

'Just one,' somebody said. 'Breech.'

'Will it fit?' he asked.

'Has to, now. Too late for a C-section.'

'You okay?' he whispered to Rachel.

She nodded. Her lips were dry. Her eyes had retreated. He found a flannel and squeezed some droplets onto her mouth. It was suddenly conceivable to him that she might die, that she was *able* to die. He lurched.

'Get him a chair.'

He heard Annie whisper in his ear from behind. 'They've brought in a gynie. Be brave.'

'Doctor O'Donelly will be down soon,' someone said, plugging in something.

'The Knife,' Annie muttered. 'Isn't there anyone else?'

'You don't work here anymore, Annie.'

'I remember. But these people are paying for this. They're consumers. They have rights. Did the patient request or assent to the epidural? The IV? To be lying flat on her back?'

'I didn't consent to any fucking thing,' Rachel hissed. 'They're gonna do what they want.'

'Annie, I'm warning you,' a smock said.

'I want to squat,' Rachel breathed.

'You've got no legs.'

Jerra got down close to her. 'C'mon. We have to beat these fuckers. Let's breathe, c'mon, don't lose it, let's breathe.' He stayed close to her. He could not imagine what must be happening inside her; it was another universe beyond that hard-white flesh.

Shifts changed. Annie sat by Rachel, crooning and stroking, and he went to call his parents. They must know something's up, he thought. His mother wept. He wanted to throw up.

Breathing. Breathing. Walls bent. He was in a bellows. *Gentle Jesus, meek and mild, stop me going fucking wild . . .*

Eat, they told him.

Pant, they told him.

Die, they told him.

They told him.

The gumbooted gynaecologist strolled in at one after the pushing had begun.

'Okay, let's get this job underway. She doing all right?'

'She's fine,' Rachel croaked. 'And. We been. Going. Eight. Een. Hours. Mis. Ter. Ummmmh.'

'Isn't she terrific?'

Jerra knew that all the hatred he had ever felt before was merely ill-will and mild dislike.

'Ten centimetres.'

Trolleys clattered. A ticking box appeared behind Rachel's head and someone connected it to the IV.

'I don't want syndemetrine.'

'You're tired, lovie.'

'And you're not me.'

Annie gave Jerra a defeated look. He whispered. 'Beat him, Rache.' He saw she couldn't go much longer. When she pushed, her veins rode up through her flesh.

There was a crowning of sorts. The perineum strained. Rachel's anus dilated like a rose opening. At each contraction something showed like a tongue at the mouth of her vagina. It was flesh. Then he saw black. Meconium.

'That's shit,' he said. 'It's in distress.'

'Are you a midwife?' someone asked.

'Testicles,' he said. 'God, it's a boy before it's a baby.'

At each contraction the raw, swollen testicles came out a little further, only to be strangled in the lull by the closing gap.

'I love you,' he said in her ear.

Someone sniffed. A crowd of smocks and masks. O'Donelly moved in. Somewhere Jerra saw the white face of their own doctor. He saw the scissors opening her up. He saw them cut her from vagina to anus. There was blood. There were great silver clamps pendulous from Rachel's flesh. Almost from within hers there was another little pair of buttocks.

'Push, Mrs Nilsam!'

'Legs up round his ears,' Annie said in his ear.

'Heartbeat faint now, Doctor.'

'Okay, let's get him out.'

Rachel reared as hands went up inside her. Jerra saw blood and shit on a forearm. Rachel let out a cry and unleashed a foot from its stirrup. She kicked. A smock took the heel in the chest. She tried again, but hands took the foot and pinned it.

Now there were legs within legs.

'Jerra? Jerra?'

'Beat 'em, Rache. Beat their arses off. At least you can shit and bleed on 'em.'

'No heartbeat.'

They were wrenching now, and twisting out the little arms and applying forceps to the aftercoming head.

'Jerra?'

'Oh, fuck me.'

A little puce head slipped out, followed by a rush of blood and water. Jerra saw it splash onto the gynaecologist's white boots. Across Rachel's chest the little body lay tethered for a moment while smocks and masks pressed hard up against Rachel's wound. He saw a needle sink in. Someone cut the cord. Blood, grey smears of vernix. The child's eyes were open. Jerra felt them upon him. From the little gaping mouth, pink froth issued. They snatched him up.

'Should have been a bloody caesar,' someone muttered.

Rachel groaned to get her breath while they sewed her.

Jerra saw the child hollow-chested on the trolley where the smocks sucked him out. He heard the deadly sound of it and he saw the gloved hands on shiny little valves. With its blacksmeared hair, their baby's head looked like the dark side of the moon.

That's a dead baby, thought Jerra. That's it. She can't see it. How will I say it?

. . . *suffer him to come to Thee* . . .

A chest flutter.

Oh, Jesus Christ, he thought. Gentle Jesus, don't play with me. Let him be dead but don't crucify me.

The chest filled.

Oh, don't fuck around with me!

A hand moved. Five fingers.

Oh dear God.

Other hands were gentle with it. There was grace in the plying of his limbs. A horrible ache rose from low in Jerra's spine. He knew it was love.

'Is he all right?' Rachel croaked. She licked her lips. 'Jerra?'

'They've got him.'

The paediatrician looked up. A little cough entered the room. Then another.

'He's crying,' Rachel said. 'I can't see him.'

They brought him over, wrapped in a blanket. In one nostril there was a clear plastic tube.

'On oxygen,' someone said.

Jerra hugged himself. 'Is he okay?'

'He'll need some help.'

Jerra felt those eyes on him. Blood and water bubbled out of the infant's mouth.

'Son of God,' Annie said.

'Grab that side of the trolley, Mr Nilsam. Let's get this boy down to I.C.U.'

As he ran out with the smocks, Jerra saw that the room was empty of white figures and only Rachel and Annie were left behind. They were holding each other.

Corridors, doors, potted palms. Past them, Jerra ran. People blurred by but he saw those black eyes on him and he wondered who he was a day ago.

The little boy held his hand and bleated up fluid as the paediatrician inserted a tube into the raw-cut navel. Jerra's eyes stung with tears.

'What's his chances? No bullshit. Please don't lie to me.'

The paediatrician looked up from his task. Only his eyes were visible, but he seemed to Jerra to be more than a technician. 'Not bad, I'd say. Then again, I don't know. His lungs're full of garbage, I'd guess. Kidneys and liver won't be too good. Have to wait. Hips might be busted. I haven't checked. He'll have a headache, that's for sure. All that time without oxygen. He's strong though.'

'Like his mother.'

The baby seemed to fill with colour before his eyes. He went a mottled yellow and pink. Jerra wanted to touch the little feet, but he contented himself with the firm grip the miniature hand had on him. So it's a reflex, he thought; what do I care.

'Will he have brain damage, you reckon?'

The man shrugged. 'I'm not God.'

He was sitting by the humidicrib when they wheeled Rachel in an hour later.

'I'm stoned,' she said.

'Pethedine,' said Annie. They'd been crying, he could tell.

'Can I hold him?'

'No,' a nurse said.

A person with a clipboard came in. 'Mrs Nilsam, you're in room 6.'

'Is that a single room?' Jerra asked.

'No. I'm afraid—'

'You see, the thing is I'll need to stay with my—'

'I'm sorry, you—'

'Look, for one, we're entitled under all that bloody insurance we paid, and two, because my wife's just had—'

'Mr Nilsam, I—'

'Okay, I'll sleep in the corridor. I'm about to be hysterical.'

'I'll see what I can do.'

'He's alive,' Rachel said.

'Call him Samuel,' said Annie. 'I reckon you should.'

'Sam.'

'Sure,' said Jerra, shaking as though a fit had come upon him. 'He's alive, isn't he?'

They lay in the dark and tried to sleep. Jerra thought of the dead fireplaces at home. He thought of the empty little house. He turned on his folding cot and felt the huge load rise up in him and he began to weep. His body muscled up against the sobs. He tried to be quiet. Tears tracked into his hair and he tasted salt and it was as strong in his mouth as blood. Jerra Nilsam cried. He wept and did not stop and he thought his eyes would bleed, and when he found a pause in himself, he heard the big bed above him clanking. He got up and turned on a dim light. Rachel lay with a pillow between her teeth. Her eyes were breaking with tears.

'I feel so defiled,' she said.

He turned out the light and held her. She filled his arms.

In the middle of the night he crept out of the room and down the long corridor to the intensive care unit. The nurse looked at his matted hair and his bare feet. In the reflection in the glass window he saw there were bloodstains on his overalls. He went in to the lone perspex box marked *Samuel Nilsam* and he sat down beside it. A heart monitor bleeped. It was a mournsome sound.

His son lay spreadeagled on his front with his head in an oxygen cube. His blood-caked body was bound by tubes and wires. Beneath him, his huge swollen testicles. He had black hair. He did look strong, sleeping there, sucking on a dummy; he looked strong enough to be alive.

When the charge nurse turned her back, Jerra opened the little portal at the side of the humidicrib and carefully reached in. He touched the bright pink buttocks. He ran a hand down the closest thigh and felt the textures of hair and dried blood. There was warmth there.

Footsteps.

He looked up. The nurse regarded him with indignation. Her mouth was tight. She put her hands on her hips.

Jerra Nilsam looked down and gripped an arm. His joined fingers were a bracelet on his son's wrist. He felt blood. Yes, that was blood there, and he looked up at the nurse in defiance.

'Go to hell,' he said. 'This one's mine.'

NOTES

1. James Anthony Froude, *Oceana or England and Her Colonies* (New York: Scribner's, 1886), 104.

2. Ibid., 94.

3. Captain Watkin Tench, *A Narrative of the Expedition to Botany Bay* (1789), quoted in G. A. Wilkes, *The Stockyard and the Croquet Lawn: Literary Evidence for Australian Cultural Development* (London: Edwin Arnold, 1981), 153–154.

4. James Atkinson, *An Account of the State of Agriculture and Grazing in NSW* (1826), quoted in Wilkes, *Stockyard*, 6–7.

5. C. Manning Clark, *A History of Australia*, 6 vols. (Parkville, Victoria, Australia: Melbourne University Press, 1962), 1:128. Clark's history reads as if it were fiction, but is minutely researched, thought provoking and thorough. My introduction draws heavily on his compelling account of Australian history.

6. Ibid., 133–135.

7. Ibid., 237–238.

8. Ibid., 113–116, 155–158, 162–168.

9. C. Manning Clark, *A Short History of Australia* (New York: New American Library of World Literature, 1963), 117–118.

10. C. Manning Clark, *A History of Australia*, C. Carlton (Victoria, Australia: Melbourne University Press, 1973), 3:103, 127.

11. Ibid., 127.

12. Ibid., 359.

13. Clark, *Short History*, 117–118. See also Russel Ward, *The Australian Legend* (Melbourne, Australia: Oxford University Press, 1958), chap. 6.

14. *Australian National Dictionary: Australian Words and Their Ori-*

gins, ed. W. S. Ramson (Melbourne, Australia: Oxford University Press, 1988), 112–114.

15. The idea of the bush is an important part of Russel Ward's classic study of what he calls the "Australian legend" or national mystique. Ward argues that bush workers had a tremendous influence on the shaping of a distinctively Australian outlook and self-image. Many critics have since assailed his view and/or modified it, but it persists as one delightfully articulated approach to Australian letters and culture.

16. Clark, *History of Australia* (1962), 1:3–11.

17. Richard Broome, *Aboriginal Australians: Black Response to White Dominance, 1788–1950* (Sydney, Australia: Allen & Unwin, 1982), 26–27.

18. Ibid., 92.

19. Donald Horne, *Ideas for a Nation* (Sydney, Australia: Pan Books, 1989), 89.

20. Adam Shoemaker, *Black Words, White Page: Aboriginal Literature, 1929–1988* (St. Lucia, Australia: University of Queensland Press, 1989), 21.

21. *Australian National Dictionary*, 162.

22. Shoemaker, *Black Words*, 19, 30, 32, 33.

23. A. A. Phillips wrote an influential collection of essays on Australian literature: *The Australian Tradition: Studies in a Colonial Culture* (Melbourne, Australia: Chesire, 1958). One essay, "The Cultural Cringe," brought this phrase into popular use. Phillips argues that there is a central democratic nationalistic tradition of Australian letters and disputes any need for Australian culture to "cringe" before literary standards imposed from elsewhere.

24. See Lawson's preamble to his first work, a collection, *Short Stories in Prose and Verse*, published by his mother, Louisa Lawson, in 1894. Lawson's *Complete Works*, edited by Leonard Cronin, was published by Landsdowne in 1984.

25. For a brief summary of similarities and differences in Australian and American history and politics see Dennis Phillips, *Ambivalent Allies: Myth and Reality in the Australian-American Relationship* (Ringwood, Victoria, Australia: Penguin Books, 1988), chap. 1.

26. Clark, *Short History*, 192.

27. Ibid., 193.

28. The film *Gallipoli*, made in Australia in 1981, was written by Australian dramatist David Williamson and directed by Peter Weir.

29. John Fiske, *The Myths of Oz: Reading Australian Popular Culture* (Boston: Allen & Unwin, 1987), 138–139.

30. Stuart Macintyre, *The Oxford History of Australia* (Melbourne, Australia: Oxford University Press, 1986), 4:327.

31. Ibid., 335.

32. Robin Gerstner, "War Literature, 1890–1980," in *New Literary History of Australia*, ed. Laurie Hergenhan (Ringwood, Victoria, Australia: Penguin Books, 1988), 347.

33. Dennis Phillips, 72.

34. Dennis Phillips, 75.

35. Dennis Phillips, 86.

36. *Australian National Dictionary*, 390.

37. See Anne Summers, *Dammed Whores and God's Police: The Colonization of Women in Australia* (Ringwood, Victoria, Australia: Penguin Books, 1975), 268–271.

38. *Australian National Dictionary*, 43.

39. Fiske, *Myths of Oz*, 118.

40. For example, see Elizabeth Perkins's comments on Catherine Spence, "Colonial Transformations: Writing and the Dilemma of Colonization," in *New Literary History of Australia*, 146.

41. John Barnes, ed., *The Penguin Henry Lawson* (Ringwood, Victoria, Australia: Penguin Books, 1986), 15.

ABOUT THE AUTHORS

THEA ASTLEY (1925–   )

In recent years, Thea Astley, a writer of novels and short stories, has been getting the acclaim and readership she has long deserved. Born in Brisbane, Queensland, in 1925, she attended the University of Queensland and was a high school teacher before she joined the faculty of Macquarie University. She retired in 1980 from the position of Fellow in Australian Literature.

Her first novel, *Girl with a Monkey*, was published in 1958. Astley is a witty, incisive observer of people and places, particularly of her native Queensland. Her subjects are varied. *The Slow Natives* (1965), for example, probes the difficult lives of the suburban Leversons and their disaffected fourteen-year-old son. The unexpected is the rule in *A Boatload of Home Folk* (1968), in which a tourist cruise turns out to be anything but a vacation. In the political fable *Beachmasters* (1988), Astley tells the story of revolution on a small island in the Pacific. In all her work, she exposes selfishness, exploitation, and brutality, using wry humor as a weapon.

Her short story collection *Hunting the Wild Pineapple* (1979) is particularly strong. *Reaching Tin River* (1990), a look at contemporary mores and the current battle between the sexes, is a deliciously witty novel, filled with Astley's high-quality Australian scene painting and sharp insights into human nature. Astley's latest work, *Vanishing Points*, was published in 1992.

BARBARA BAYNTON (1862–1929)

Barbara Baynton's early years have been shrouded in secrecy. It seems that she did not want her modest origins revealed and so told different versions of her life.

As far as the facts are known, she was the seventh child of a struggling family. Her father was John Lawrence, a carpenter. She worked as a governess and married her employer's son, Alexander Frater. They had three children and lived on his farm until he left with another woman.

Baynton then went to Sydney with her children. There, on the day after she got her divorce from Frater, she married Dr. Thomas Baynton. He was a retired surgeon, a man of culture and means, twice her age. He encouraged her to write and to develop her skill as a collector of antiques. She published her first story in the *Bulletin* (1896). *Bush Studies* (1902), a collection of stories and her major work, was published in London. She wrote one novel, *Human Toll* (1907). After the death of her second husband, she was married again briefly to an eccentric English baron, Lord Headley.

PETER CAREY (1943–   )

Peter Carey was born in Bacchus Marsh, Victoria. He was educated at Monash University, where he studied science. Before becoming a novelist, he worked in advertising firms in Melbourne and London. He also owned and ran his own agency. Carey's short stories have appeared in many journals and in the collections *The Fat Man in History* (1974) and *War Crimes* (1979). The film *Bliss* was based on his 1981 novel of that name. Other works include the inventive, very Australian *Illywhacker* (1985), *Oscar and Lucinda* (1988), and *The Tax Collector* (1991). He is married to the theater director Alison Summers.

MARCUS CLARKE (1846–1881)

Marcus Clarke was a Melbourne journalist during a time of vigorous cultural growth in Australia. He wrote short stories, sketches, and novels, but his fame rests on *His Natural Life* (1874), a popular success in its time and honored in Australian literature since its first publication in monthly installments. It is now available in two editions: a shorter version, with a new ending, and the original.

Born in 1846 in London, Clarke was reared by his father, a lawyer; his mother died when he was very young. His father's sudden death and the discovery that there was very little money in the family estate left Clarke a teenage orphan with limited opportunity in England. Australia was the alternative for him, as for so many others, and in 1863 he journeyed there to be with his uncle, a judge. The young writer tried banking and ranch work, wrote for newspapers, and contributed to and edited magazines, but he did not earn enough money to live as a "gentleman." He married, was the father of six children, and accepted a position as secretary to the trustees of the public library of Victoria to augment his income. He died of pleurisy, harried by debts, at the age of thirty-five.

MARIAN ELDRIDGE (1936–   )

Marian Eldridge was born in Melbourne in 1936, the daughter of farmers. In 1957 she earned her B.A. from the University of Melbourne. She married the forest geneticist Kenneth George Eldridge in 1958 and has four children. She has taught English and history in secondary schools, as well as adult education courses at the university level.

Eldridge currently writes full time and is a regular reviewer for the *Canberra Times*. Individual stories have appeared in a number of anthologies. Her collections include *Walking the Dog and Other Stories* (1984) and *The Woman at the Window* (1989). In 1992 she published her first novel, *Springfield*.

ALBERT B. FACEY (1894–1982)

A. B. Facey was an amateur writer who, using a plain style and the material of his own life, made a stunning success in 1981 with his autobiography, *A Fortunate Life*. The publishing history of this book is interesting: Facey's two daughters brought the manuscript to Fremantle Arts Centre Press, a small, regional house that hoped to increase publishing opportunities for Western Australian writers. The daughters requested that Fremantle print just a hundred copies for members of the family. But the press saw wider potential and worked with the author. The book was a best-seller and was bought by Penguin, soon becoming Penguin's best-selling Australian work. This autobiography not only brought great acclaim to its author but was a financial boon for Fremantle as well. Settings, including the wheat fields of Western Australia, and events, such as the fighting at Gallipoli, evoked tremendous reader response.

BEVERLEY FARMER (1941–   )

Beverley Farmer was born in Melbourne and educated at Melbourne University. She has taught and worked in restaurants to support herself.

Farmer, whose ex-husband is Greek, spent considerable time with Greek immigrants in Australia before moving to Greece for several years. The context for some of her best fiction is the crosscultural encounter that she knows so well. She portrays Australian attempts at accommodation to Greek society in her fresh and original collections *Milk* (1983) and *Home Time* (1985). Her novel, *Alone*, was published in 1984. It is a poetic work about a young woman's obsessional love for another woman and about the temptations of suicide. In 1990, she published *A Body of Water*, a collection of stories and entries from her journal. Her most recent work is a novel, *The Seal Woman* (1992).

HELEN GARNER (1942–   )

Helen Garner's first novel, *Monkey Grip* (1977), won the 1978 National Book Council Award. In 1982, a movie based on the book was released. *Monkey Grip* is a compelling story of obsessive love and drug addiction.

Born in Geelong, Victoria, the eldest of six children, Garner graduated with honors in English and French literature from Melbourne University. She was a secondary school teacher and journalist before becoming a novelist. Her first marriage ended in divorce. She has one child, a daughter, and is now married to a Frenchman.

Garner's short stories and novels generally treat domestic and personal relationships, with a focus on the experiences of women. Among her published works are *The Children's Bach* (1984), *Postcards from Surfers* (1984), and *Cosmo Cosmolino* (1992).

COLIN JOHNSON (1938–   )

Born in Narrogin, Western Australia, Colin Johnson is part-Aboriginal and a member of the Bibbulmun people. He spent his childhood in a Catholic orphanage, where he received some of his education. Johnson worked in the Victorian public service until 1959, when he wrote the play *The Delinks*, which won a contest sponsored by the journal *Westerly*. He then wrote a novel, *Wild Cat Falling* (1965), the first to be published by an Aboriginal. It was runner-up for the 1968 Llewellyn Rhys Memorial Prize.

After its publication, Johnson left Australia to travel in the United States, South America, Britain, and Southeast Asia. He was a Buddhist monk for seven years and is a member of the Maha Bodhi Society of India. When he returned to Australia, he became part of the Aboriginal Research Unit at Monash University in Melbourne. Of particular interest are his novels *Long Live Sandawarra* (1979) and *Dr. Wooreddy's Prescription for Enduring the Ending of the World* (1983). Johnson is also a poet and has published *The Song Circle of Jacky* and *Selected Poems* (1986). Recently, he changed his name to Murdrooroo Narogin, which indicates his tribal affiliation.

ELIZABETH JOLLEY (1923–   )

Elizabeth Jolley's name is associated with the wheat fields of Australia. When she moved from England to Perth, Western Australia, in 1959 with her librarian husband and their three children, the city was not a likely place for forging a literary career. Yet by the late 1980s, Jolley had established herself there as a well-published author, internationally known for her novels and short stories.

Jolley was born in Birmingham, England, of Austrian-English parents. She first studied nursing and wrote fiction for twenty years before being published. She now teaches part time and also works in her orchard.

Jolley's work is difficult to characterize because she is no respecter of easy categories. An experimental writer, she blends irony, comedy, and pathos. She examines all kinds of women in her work—the lonely, the eccentric, and especially lesbians. Among her best-known titles are *Miss Peabody's Inheritance* (1983), *Mr. Scobie's Riddle* (1983), *The Sugar Mother* (1988), *My Father's Moon* (1989), and *Cabin Fever* (1990). *Central Mischief*, a collection of her articles, speeches, and essays, was published in 1992.

HENRY LAWSON (1867–1922)

Henry Lawson is Australia's greatest writer of bush lore. He recognized the imaginative potential of a way of life familiar to his contemporary Australian readers and captured it in his work. His reward was the admiration and the reverence of a people. Lawson was the golden boy of that often-called golden age of Australian letters—the 1890s. His work spoke to his contemporaries of what they knew to be distinctly Australian. He gave them a literary image of themselves, and they embraced it and him.

To the reader unfamiliar with Australian bush life, Lawson's writing offers access to a distinctive, appealing, historically based fictional world, extraordinary in its expression of universal human needs and emotion. Although he wrote poetry that was popular in his time, his enduring works were short stories, particularly those he wrote between 1892 and 1902. Most of his great stories can be found in two collections: *While the Billy Boils* (1896) and *Joe Wilson and His Mates* (1901).

Lawson's mother, Louisa Lawson, was a writer, feminist, and editor of a radical women's magazine, *The Dawn* (1888–1905). His father was a Norwegian seaman who had left home in search of gold. Lawson grew up on a small farm in the Mudgee district, New South Wales, where he attended local schools. He had no formal higher education. His childhood was marred by deafness, poverty, and the hostility between his parents, who later separated. Lawson's own marriage also failed, and alcoholism damaged his health and the quality of his writing in the last twenty years of his life.

DAVID MALOUF (1934–   )

David Malouf is of Lebanese extraction. In the 1880s, his father's parents migrated to Australia. His mother's family came from London just before World War I. Malouf was born in Brisbane, Queensland. His early life is re-created in an autobiographical memoir, *12 Edmondstone Street* (1985). He attended Brisbane Grammar School and the University of Queensland, where he also taught. He left Australia for ten years, traveled, and taught school in England. He was teaching at the University of Sydney when he decided to dedicate himself to writing full time. Although he has since moved to a small village in Tuscany, Italy, he returns frequently to Australia.

Now recognized as one of Australia's most significant contemporary novelists, Malouf was first known as a poet with several prize-winning collections to his credit. In 1975, he published his first novel, *Johnno*, which is partly set in Brisbane. A story of youth, it is taught in many Australian secondary schools. He won the New South Wales Premier's Literary Award for fiction in 1979 for *An Imaginary Life* (1978). In 1990 he published *The Great World*, a novel that deals with the experience of war. In addition to a number of novels, he has written for the stage and created the libretto for the operatic version of Patrick White's *Voss*.

OLGA MASTERS (1919–1983)

Olga Masters, a writer whose work has many fond readers, was brought up in a poor family on the southern coast of New South Wales. Because she was the second of eight children, she endured heavy homemaking responsibilities. Her adult years as a mother of seven and part-time journalist provided material for her fiction. Her first book, a collection of stories entitled *The Home Girls* (1982), was a success and launched her career. Subsequently, she published *Loving Daughters* (1984), *A Long Time Dying* (1985), *Amy's Children* (1987), and *The Rose Fancier* (1988), a partly unfinished collection completed from drafts after her death.

FRANK MOORHOUSE (1935–   )

A masterful short story writer, Frank Moorhouse was born in Nowra on the southern coast of New South Wales. He was a journalist for many years, working in Sydney and on smaller papers. Many pieces of his early fiction were published in literary journals and men's magazines. Mainstream magazines were uncomfortable with his frank treatment of sex. Moorhouse is associated with the Balmain writers—a loosely linked grouping of intellectuals, radicals, and academics active during the late 1960s.

The technique of discontinuous narrative, which Moorhouse did not invent but has used with great success, is associated with his work. Characters, localities, and groups reappear in different, discrete stories, provoking tensions and connections among them. This lends his work the flavor of novels. A strong stylist with notable wit, Moorhouse writes stories that chronicle social change in Australia, particularly during the sixties and seventies. He has edited anthologies and written screenplays. Among his eight collections of short stories are *The Everlasting Secret Family* (1980), *The American's Baby* (1972), and *Forty-Seventeen* (1988).

SALLY MORGAN (1951–   )

An artist and a writer, Sally Morgan has paintings in the Australian National Gallery at Canberra, among other collections. Her first book, *My Place* (1987), an autobiography, was a best-seller published by Fremantle Arts Centre Press.

Born in Perth, Western Australia, Morgan has a B.A. in psychology from the University of Western Australia. She is married and has three children. Her creative interest in tracing Aboriginal roots and Aboriginal family history, often lost or deliberately suppressed, shapes both *My Place*, her own family history, and *The Story of Jack McPhee* (1989).

KATHARINE SUSANNAH PRICHARD (1883–1969)

Daughter of a newspaper editor whose life was marked by financial struggle, Katharine Prichard started out as a governess unable to afford schooling at a university. She educated herself by reading widely and through her work as a journalist in Melbourne and overseas. In 1915 she won a writing contest and shortly thereafter became part of a circle of Australian intellectuals, some of whom were to be her colleagues in founding the Communist party of Australia. She wrote political pamphlets and was an active political organizer while she was writing prize-winning short fiction and novels such as *Working Bullocks* (1926) and *Coonardoo* (1929). She continued to write novels and short stories through the 1960s but was increasingly isolated intellectually as Australian society became strongly anti-communist.

Her works are a blend of realism, lyricism, politics, and romance. Her short stories, recently published by her son in a selected edition (*Tribute* [1988], edited by Ric Throssell), are rich in Australian life and lore.

HENRY HANDEL RICHARDSON (1870–1946)

Henry Handel Richardson is a pseudonym for Ethel Florence Lindesay Richardson, born in Melbourne, who left Australia when she was seventeen. Her father was an Irish doctor and her mother emigrated from England to Australia at the age of fourteen with her parents. Richardson's first aspirations were to be a pianist, and she studied music in Leipzig. In 1895, she married the Scot J. G. Robertson, who became the first professor of German language and literature at the University of London. When her husband died in 1933, Richardson lived with her housekeeper/companion in Sussex, England, until her death.

Her novels reflect much of her life. *Maurice Guest* (1908) and *The Young Cosima* (1939) came out of her experiences as a music student in Europe. *The Getting of Wisdom* (1910) is largely autobiographical, re-creating her student years at the Presbyterian Ladies College in Melbourne.

Her masterpiece, the novel that secures her a place as one of the leading women writers in Australian letters, is the trilogy *The Fortunes of Richard Mahony* (1917–1929). Starting in 1912, she wrote it over a period of twenty years. The principal character is based on her father, and the movement of the characters from place to place reflects the realities of her parents' lives. Historians of Australian literature cite rich European influences on her work, which, in turn, broadened the scope of Australian writing.

STEELE RUDD (ARTHUR HOEY DAVIS) (1868–1935)

Rudd's father was a blacksmith who farmed land at Emu Creek, Queensland. The author left school at twelve years of age to work at shearing sheep until 1885, when he moved to Brisbane. Until 1904 he held various positions in the Justice Department and contributed sketches to the local newspapers using the pseudonym Steele (in honor of Richard Steele, the eighteenth-century English essayist) Rudd (short for Rudder—his early skits were about rowing). The popularity of his work enabled him to found his own magazine and to buy a farm. He published plays and about twenty-four works of fiction. His best work is found in the collections *On Our Selection* (1899) and *Our New Selection* (1903).

CHRISTINA STEAD (1902–1983)

Christina Stead was born in a Sydney suburb in 1902. Her father, David Stead, was a well-published naturalist. Her mother died in 1904 and three years later her father remarried. Eventually, there were six children in the Stead household; Christina, being the oldest, assumed many of the household responsibilities. Her family life is of literary significance since she drew from it for her master work, *The Man Who Loved Children* (1940).

At Sydney High School and Sydney Teachers' College, she wrote for and edited school magazines. After college course work in education, she taught school briefly. For five years she worked at secretarial jobs and took business courses at night in order to finance a trip to London in 1928, where she met William Blake, an American writer and economist, who brought her fiction to the attention of her first publisher. Christina Stead lived with Blake in Europe until 1937, when they moved to the United States. During nine years in the U.S., she worked as a script writer, college teacher, and literary reviewer.

In 1946 Stead and Blake traveled to Europe, settling near London in 1953. After living together for twenty-four years, they were married. Blake had been unable to get a divorce from his first wife until then. Blake died in 1968, and Stead returned to Australia in 1974.

Stead's major novels are *The Man Who Loved Children* (1940), *For Love Alone* (1944), and *Dark Places of the Heart* (1966), although critics do not necessarily agree on the relative standing of several of her thirteen novels. The last, *I'm Dying Laughing*, was edited and prepared for publication in 1986 by her literary executor. There are two collections, *The Salzburg Tales* (1934), an unusual and original group of stories largely set in Europe, and *Ocean of Story, The Uncollected Stories of Christina Stead* (1985), posthumously published.

Feminist readers are responsible for the current revival of interest in Stead's work, but she did not see herself as a feminist. She was, however, interested in uncovering exploitation of any kind, and the restrictive nature of women's lives during Stead's time is well documented in her fiction.

RANDOLPH STOW (1935–   )

By the age of twenty-two, Randolph Stow had published two novels and a collection of poems. He was born in Geraldton, Western Australia, to a family with early roots in the country. His father was a lawyer, and his mother came from a pioneering background.

After Guildford Grammar School and the University of Western Australia, where he majored in French and English, he had a variety of travel and work experiences, some of which are reflected in his novels. In New Guinea, for instance, he was involved in anthropology for the government. He also worked at a mission for Aborigines and was a tutor at the University of Adelaide. In 1979 Stow won the Patrick White Award.

Stow's fiction is lyrical and carefully structured. *To the Islands* (1958), revised in 1981, draws on his experiences with Aborigines. *Visitants* (1979) builds on insights gained in New Guinea. *The*

Merry-Go-Round in the Sea (1965), which he wrote while in New Mexico, is a fictionalized memoir of childhood in Western Australia. *Tourmaline* (1963) is also set in Western Australia. *The Girl Green as Elderflower* (1980) and *The Suburbs of Hell* (1984) draw heavily on England, where he has lived since 1960. He has also published music theater works, poetry, and a children's book— *Midnite: The Story of a Wild Colonial Boy* (1967), in which a cockatoo and a cat are the mates of a guiltless bushranger living in the bush.

PRICE WARUNG (WILLIAM ASTLEY) (1855–1911)

Price Warung is the pen name of William Astley. Astley emigrated to Melbourne from Liverpool, England, with his parents in 1859. He was a working journalist in several cities and became editor in 1893 of the *Australian Workman* in Sydney. A radical socialist, he was active for labor in various political groups. In his later years he was in poor health, weakened by the effects of drug addiction.

Astley had a brief stunning period of success when he wrote about ninety stories of convict life published in the Australian newspaper *Bulletin* between 1890 and 1892. Many volumes of his stories have been published, including *Tales of the Convict System* (1892) and *Half-Crown Bog and Tales of the Riverine* (1898).

ARCHIE WELLER (1957–   )

Archie Weller's work recreates the modern black Australian experience. Most of his characters are poor, both the Aborigines and the whites with whom they come in contact. Weller's *The Day of the Dog* (1981), a novel of growing up, offers penetrating insights into the hopelessness and brutality of life in the Aboriginal subculture. Weller's story collection, *Going Home* (1986), deals with similar themes. It was the first collection of short stories published by an

Aboriginal writer. In 1987 Weller co-edited an anthology of Aboriginal writing, *Us Fellas*. Weller is an Aboriginal of the Bibulman people, born in Subiaco, a suburb of Perth, Western Australia.

PATRICK WHITE (1912–1990)

Patrick White changed the face of Australian literature. His deliberate effort to create a new fictional Australia in novels rich in symbol, language, and vision opened paths for younger writers and brought attention to his country's letters. He was the first Australian author to win the Nobel Prize for Literature (1973).

Although he was born in London, he was of Australian background. His family owned pastoral land in the Upper Hunter Valley of New South Wales. He spent his childhood in Sydney, attending school at Tudor House, Moss Vale, New South Wales, until he was sent back to England for schooling. He went on to King's College, Cambridge, to study modern languages.

For two years before entering King's College, he worked as a jackeroo in Monaro and Walgett (a jackeroo is employed on a sheep or cattle station to gain the skills and experience required to be a station owner or manager). After graduation in 1935, he spent time in London writing plays. During the war he was a Royal Australian Air Force (RAAF) Intelligence Officer, serving in the Middle East, Africa, and Greece. After the war, White decided to return to Australia with his lifetime companion, Manoly Lascaris. He cultivated an orchard, raised goats and dogs on a farm named Dogwoods, at Castle Hill outside of Sydney. In his later years, he became involved in social and political issues.

White's fiction is the most significant body of work by any single Australian writer. With *The Aunt's Story* (1948), White's important work begins. *The Tree of Man* (1955), *Voss* (1957), *The Solid Mandala* (1966), *The Vivisector* (1970), and *The Eye of the Storm* (1973) are central, although the rank and status of individual novels in his canon are matters of critical controversy.

A Fringe of Leaves (1976) is a particularly accessible novel that draws together several strands of Australian history. Using an actual shipwreck, that of the *Stirling Castle* in 1836 just off the coast of Queensland, White re-creates some of his heroine's experiences from the true events that happened to Eliza Fraser, wife of the ship's captain. She survived the wreck, lived with Aborigines, and after much difficulty, was reunited with white civilization.

White published his last work, *Three Easy Pieces*, in 1987. He died in 1990.

TIM WINTON (1960–   )

Tim Winton has had amazing success for so young a writer. Born in 1960, he wrote his first novel, *An Open Swimmer*, when he was twenty. He is from Western Australia and lives on the coast in a small town north of Perth. The coastal area is an important setting for his work, which includes the novels *Shallows* (1984), *That Eye, the Sky* (1987), *In the Winter Dark* (1988), and *Cloudstreet* (1991), and the short stories collections *Scission* (1985) and *Minimum of Two* (1988). Winton often writes about adolescents, young men, and young families. A graduate of the Western Australian Institute of Technology, he is married and has two sons.

SUGGESTED READINGS

[Excluding titles already represented in this collection]

THE IDEA OF THE BUSH

Voss (1957)	Patrick White
Tourmaline (1963)	Randolph Stow
An Imaginary Life (1978)	David Malouf

IMAGES OF AUSTRALIA

The Fortunes of Richard Mahony (1930)	Henry Handel Richardson
Capricornia (1938)	Xavier Herbert
The Battlers (1941)	Kylie Tennant
My Brother Jack (1964)	George Johnston
Bring Larks and Heroes (1967)	Thomas Keneally
The Chant of Jimmy Blacksmith (1972)	Thomas Keneally
A Fringe of Leaves (1976)	Patrick White
The Visitants (1979)	Randolph Stow
Illywhacker (1985)	Patrick Carey

RELATIONSHIPS

My Brilliant Career (1901)	Miles Franklin
The Man Who Loved Children (1940)	Christina Stead
Tirra Lirra by the River (1963)	Jessica Anderson
Dark Places of the Heart (1966)	Christina Stead
Loving Daughters (1984)	Olga Masters
Lilian's Story (1985)	Kate Grenville
Reaching Tin River (1991)	Thea Astley
Cloudstreet (1991)	Tim Winton

GLOSSARY

Balaclava—Headgear originally made of wool.

Battler—One who battles, who works doggedly, who struggles for a livelihood, who displays courage in so doing. Usually refers to someone who has few natural advantages. Used also for unemployed itinerants.

Beaks—Slang for magistrates or justices of the peace.

Beagle, The—The ship of the naturalist Charles Darwin, who visited Sydney in 1836.

Bell-bird—Australian species known for its bell-like call.

Billy—Cylindrical container usually made of tin, aluminum, or enamel used to boil water over an open fire; an odd-shaped teakettle.

Blackguarding—Talking about or addressing someone in abusive terms.

Black Mary—An Aboriginal woman.

Blethering—Grumbling.

Bloke—A person in authority or of superior status.

Bowls—A game similar to Bocce.

Bowsers—Gas pumps.

Bullock—Castrated bull or steer, ox.

Bull's eye—A large hard mint-flavored candy.

Bully beef—Corned beef.

Bush fire—Fire that often spreads over long distances and causes great damage.

Bushranger—One who engages in armed robbery escaping into or living in the bush as an outlaw.

Butcher bird—A shrike. A bird with a shrill voice, hooked beak, gray, black, and white feathers, and long tail.

"C"—A C rating for a convict indicated a superior educational background.

Cockatoo—A crested parrot, large and noisy.

Cockies—Originally small farmers, now used for larger landowners or those with rural interests.

Combo—A white man who lives with an Aboriginal woman, often within an Aboriginal community.

Cooboo—An Aboriginal baby.

Coolgardie safe—A water-cooled receptacle for keeping food refrigerated.

Corroboree—An Aboriginal dance ceremony with song and music.

Damper—Unleavened bread baked in the ashes of an outdoor fire.

Digger—A miner on the Australian gold fields.

Digger's shack—Miner's shack.

Dingo—A native dog, often tawny yellow, thought to have been introduced by the Aborigines.

Dook—Duke.

Draper—A dealer in cloth and textiles.

Drover—Driver of large numbers of sheep, cattle, or horses over long distances.

Fair trimmer—Outstanding in some respect.

Fig—Square stick of tobacco.

Fire-stick—A smoldering stick used to light a fire, often carried by Aborigines.

Gin—Aboriginal wife or woman.

Gina-gina—Dress worn by an Aboriginal woman.

Golliwog doll—A black-faced doll.

Gum tree—Of the genus *Eucalyptus*, the most numerous tree of Australian forests.

Haversack—Strong bag to carry provisions, worn on the back or shoulder.

Humpy—Temporary, makeshift Aboriginal shelter, built of primitive materials.

Jarrah—Western Australian tree that yields hard, durable, reddish-brown wood.

Koo—An Aboriginal cry.

Kurrajong—Several plants and trees known for their useful fiber; used to make nets, for example.

Lamb's fry—Lamb's liver.

Larrikin—Hooligan, street gang member, young, urban tough.

Lolly—Candy, especially hard candy.

Lorry—Truck.

Lucerne—Alfalfa.

Lyre-bird—Two species of ground-dwelling birds noted for their ability to mimic. Male has a lyre-shaped tail.

Mate—Equal partner in an enterprise, chum.

Matilda—A swag or bag, the bundle containing the swagman's worldly goods, carried over his shoulder.

Moleskin—Strong cotton cloth used for trousers of rural workers and miners.

Mopoke—A nocturnal bird; the name sounds like the call.

Moreton Bay Fig—A large fig tree with small fruit.

Mulba—An Aborigine raised in the Pilbarra area of Western Australia.

Mulga bush—Shrub or tree with grey-green foliage and brown- and yellow-tinted timber.

Muster time—The gathering together of livestock in one place.

Nammery—A gift or compensation for services.

Num—Ghost, term for a white man.

Nyoongah—An aborigine.

Paddock—Enclosed land fenced off or marked by natural boundaries; a small field near a stable or a large area on a sheep or cattle station.

Paddymelon—A wallaby, one of the smaller marsupials.

Petrol—Refined petroleum, gas for cars.

Pram—Baby carriage.

Publican—Owner or licensee of a pub.

Ria Warrawah—The spirit of evil often associated with the ocean.

Ringbarking—Killing a tree by cutting a ring of bark around the trunk or preparing land for clearing in this way.

Roo—Shortened form of kangaroo.

Rover—A position in Australian football, one of a group of three players who do not have fixed positions but follow the play.

Sawney—A simpleton, a fool.

Screw—Salary or wage.

Scrub—Usually brush wood or stunted forest.

Selection—A small-to medium-size rural property.

Shanty—Small cabin or hut; cabin serving as a pub in a rural area.

Shearer—Itinerant worker who is employed seasonally to shear sheep.

Shingle—Loose, round pebbles on a beach.

Shire officers—Elected town council or governing body.

Slewed—Swung around, turned, twisted.

Southerly—Wind blowing from the south.

Squatter—One who occupied a tract of Crown land and used it for livestock grazing; modern usage: a large-scale rancher.

Station—A large sheep or mixed farming ranch.

Stockman—One who takes care of livestock, a herdsman.

Stringy bark—Variety of eucalyptus (gum tree) with a long-fibered, thick, rough-to-the-touch bark.

Stubbies—Short, squat beer bottles and their contents.

Sulky—A light, horse-drawn vehicle used for transport.

Swagman—One who carries a swag (a blanket-wrapped roll filled with possessions) on his back or across his shoulders; an itinerant worker, especially one in search of a job; a tramp.

Tailers—A marine fish found in coastal waters that tastes like mackerel.

Tench—Penitentiary.

Ticket of leave—Document that allowed a convict freedom within certain limits; a ticket-of-leave man could reside and work in a specified location until his prison sentence was over.

Tray—The flat open part of a truck on which goods are carried.

Trifle—Dessert; a sponge cake soaked in wine or spirits with jelly and/or fruit, topped by cream or custard.

Tyre—Tire.

Uloo—Camp.

Up country—Inland country away from heavily populated areas.

Van demonian history—Tasmanian history.

Van Diemen's Land—Early name of Tasmania.

Victoria Cross—A decoration awarded to members of the commonwealth armed services for an act of bravery.

Wadgula—A white person.

Wallaby—Small species of kangaroo.

Warder—Prison guard.

Whip bird—Small, olive-green bird that makes a sound like the cracking of a whip.

Wiah—Aboriginal expression used to attract attention to something.

Willy-wagtail—Black and white bird of the fantail family.

303

ABOUT THE AUTHOR

Phyllis Fahrie Edelson is a Professor and Chair of the Department of English and Communications at Pace University in White Plains, New York. She is a founding member of the American Association for Australian Literary Studies and book review editor of *Antipodes*, the first American journal of Australian Studies.